D1564174

# Hive
# Records

a novel by
**Frank M. Young**

RedwingBlackbird

First RWBB printing, April 2021          10  9  8  7  6  5  4  3  2  1

*This novel is dedicated to Tiger Moody, who challenged me to write something outside what came easiest to me; I hope this book is worthy of his esteem.*

*Kudos to my longtime friend Kelly Shane, who read drafts of the manuscript and helped me understand what was and wasn't working. He also helped me get over some fears I had about certain characters and my right to write about them.*

*Special thanks to Emily Siskin for her friendship, good vibes and encouragement. Here's to our day trips; long may they live.*

# *1*

***Downhill, on the highway,*** cars swooshed and rumbled. Uphill, rain spattered into mud and pelted the leaves in the trees overhead. The tin roof of Cecil's shack drummed. It was a good time to go to sleep, but Cecil had to leave for work. He stood at the door of his home and sighed. This was a miserable night to walk three miles. Least it wasn't hot, but it was wet.

He wished he had a second pair of shoes. That way, he could work with dry feet. He would be on his feet til dawn. Mr. Howard had a rush job: 500 copies of the new Rusty Gordon record. It was selling big in Detroit, Houston and Chicago. Juke operators and deejays wanted it all up the coast. The way things were going, he could soon afford another pair of shoes. He needed better pants too. There was a hole in the crotch that only showed when he sat, but it would only get worse.

Cecil had a cat who stuck around, an orange tabby he named Coaxial. Cecil saw that word in passing, and it stuck with him. Words got his attention and he didn't forget them. It was a strange name for a cat, but Coaxial was a great friend. He always had a look on his face like he was glad to see Cecil. He had his own way to show that he was hungry. Coaxial purred and made chewing moves with his mouth. It would steal anyone's heart, and it always got results. Cecil had a bit of ham, some black-eyed peas and buttermilk. Coaxial got a meal from that. He tucked into the ham and purred. "You gonna be here on your own tonight." Cecil bent down to the cat and patted him. "You stay in out the rain."

The cat looked up at him, acknowledged him with a blink and returned to his feast. Coaxial was good to have around. Anyone who thought a cat was dumb was dead wrong. *Wish I could get someone to take care of me, give me food and tell me I was something special,* Cecil thought. *Might be a song in that somewhere.* He pictured Rusty Gordon singing it and laughed. That wasn't Rusty's style at all.

Rusty Gordon was hot, and Hive Records had him on a three-year contract. It was good for him, good for Mr. Howard and good for Cecil, because he'd had a song on every one of Rusty's records. The new hit was one he wrote a couple of months back sitting here in this shack. Cecil fooled around with the piano and the guitar, fooled around with words and music, and liked to read. When he was at the library he spotted a book called *The Decline and Fall of the Roman Empire.* Cecil's tastes ran to mysteries, historical stories and some non-fiction. The heft of the book scared him off, but he liked that title.

It took him an hour to come up with "Decline and Fall," which he knew was a natural for Rusty. *Some people say I will decline and fall/but what do they know, them so-called know it alls?* The gist of the song was that Rusty was going to live big and outlast all the nay-sayers. *Man, my future ain't nothing but bright/got a different lady every day of the night.* Cecil liked that line. "Every day of the night" sounded funny. It made you smile. And it made Rusty Gordon laugh out loud. That's what sold him on the song.

Mr. Howard liked it too. It wasn't much of a tune, but it didn't need one. The lyric sold the song. Rusty's band played it solid. He had a man on baritone sax could blow like a hurricane. Mr. Howard asked him to take two choruses in the middle. Everybody, including Miss Tinkle, the secretary, hunched around a microphone and clapped their hands while Earl the sax man blew. Cecil caught Mr. Howard's eye and got a smile. *This is gonna go big*, that expression said. *Good job, Cecil.*

Mr. Howard wasn't like other white men. Cecil's experience had been that white men were one of two things. Too nice or too mean. Both kinds made him feel like a moron, in different ways.

***Cecil started to make up songs in the Army.*** He lived in terror from the day the draft card showed up in the mail. He had never left the state of Mississippi. The farthest he'd traveled was from Tupelo to Gulfport with his mother and father. They had some legal business there. Cecil had never seen such commotion, and he didn't care for it. Tupelo was more his speed. He hoped they would send him somewhere close.

They shipped him to Fort Benning in Georgia for basic training. And right away he got on the bad side of Sergeant Rutland. He kept to himself, and didn't speak unless spoken to. Then he answered with "sir" like he always did with white men. Politeness didn't cut the mustard with Sergeant Rutland. He took a dislike to Cecil the moment he gave the new fish the run-down on army life.

Every bad name you could call a man, black, white or polka-dotted, Sergeant Rutland had thrown at him. Fat-Ass, Rufus, Blackie, Jungle Bunny, Fuck-Nuts. And Cecil stood there in the hot sun, at attention, and took it. He couldn't show anything on his face. A reaction made Rutland light up.

To keep from panicking, and from going AWOL, Cecil made up songs about Sergeant Rutland. He could tune him out that way. At first he didn't write them down. They were something to keep him from imploding. Long as he didn't crack a smile, as he played them in his head, he was okay. After a while, he shared one of them with the other black soldiers. They guffawed at his words. One of them was caught singing it by Rutland, and got his ass kicked, but he never spilled about where he learned it.

 Cecil never went to Korea. "Your fat ass ain't worth the bullets," Rutland told him. He spent two years putting together pieces of tanks and guns. He never saw the whole things, except in newsreels at the movie show. They let all the enlisted men use the same theater. A couple of Alabama crackers might get mouthy, but they were all talk. Cecil kept the frozen face he used on Rutledge and just watched the picture. When the white boys laughed, he let himself laugh. They loved the Three Stooges. Cecil liked them for a different reason. It was a pleasure to see three white men make such fools of themselves.

They promoted Cecil to fuses. That was better because he worked on his own. No Rutland to yell in his ear. The white people were afraid of the fuses. Fuses can't do nothing til you put them in a bomb. Any fool knows that. Or should have known.

Fuse detail was when he first wrote down his songs. Real songs, not digs at Sergeant Rutledge. Cecil learned to read music as a kid and could get the music set on paper, which was the important part. The words could always change, but you had to have a good tune. That's what he thought from his first serious song.

When Cecil was let out of the service, he had 30 or 40 songs he thought were as good as anything he heard on the radio, or on the jukes. He came back to Tupelo to find his mother had died. She had been hit by a truck on the highway one night. She had no identification and was in an unmarked grave in the colored cemetery.

Cecil was never close to his father, who was more interested in straying than staying and might have still been alive; he was too mean to die. His mother worked hard all her life and saw to it that her boy got a proper education. Cecil graduated from high school, spoke well and had a larger vocabulary than most of the white people he encountered. He hid his intellect in silence and submission. If anyone was able to get through his wall, they found a well-read, philosophical person with a PhD in Advanced Irony.

Most of the time Cecil felt he'd never find another human being around whom he could just be himself. Other black folks seemed suspicious of him. He didn't use slang and kept to himself. He was respectful and polite to his elders but didn't have a clue how to relate to anyone his own age. He was still a virgin—not that he'd had any opportunity to experiment. Women, aside from his mother, and women like her, mystified him. And other males were so competitive. What seemed most important was who had the sharpest clothes, the biggest bankroll and the best luck with the ladies.

Cecil was poor but inherited real estate. The shack they lived in was on land his mother and father had bought. They had no intentions of working the land. His father insisted they live in their own house. Cecil wasn't sure if his father built it himself, but that was his mother's story. If so, he was no craftsman. The structure was on its way to becoming a rhomboid. Cecil figured it had about two more years until it fell apart. So he had two years to find something better for himself.

Everyone treated Cecil about the same, black or white. They understood that he was different; they either derided or patronized that difference. "My, you're well spoken," white woman at the A&P remarked, on the rare occasion that the situation called on him to say anything beyond yes'm no ma'am. All white men found him a threat, Cecil figured. They could see he was smarter than them, but powerless to do much with his intelligence. Their unspoken job was to keep him cut down to size—to insult, belittle and otherwise defuse him.

Cecil scouted around for a decent job, but none were there for him in Tupelo. He asked the editor of the local newspaper if they could use a colored reporter. The editor, a progressive man by Tupelo standards, replied: "Come back in 10 years and we'll see." Cecil didn't have that luxury. He got a job bagging groceries at an A&P downtown. He worked six days a week, 8 to 6 with 15 minutes for lunch. The pay wasn't much, but Cecil didn't need much.

Mr. Grass, his manager, was another Rutland—not as nasty; no one could match that man for sheer meanness. But he made Cecil the butt of his jokes and blamed every mishap on him. This made Cecil nervous and caused him to foul up. No matter how composed and sure of himself he felt that measure of confidence vanish when Mr. Grass started in on him. He was a big man with red hair and a double chin. He looked like a big baby with a toupee. When he laughed, his double chin jiggled in a sickening way.

Cecil took almost three years of Mr. Grass and his wisecracks. One afternoon Mr. Grass crossed the street in front of the store, coming back from his lunch, and was knocked dead by a truck. When Cecil heard the news, he laughed out loud. That got him fired on the spot.

And that was how he got on with Mr. Howard. He had no idea there was a record company downtown, but the name painted on the glass, in red and yellow, caught his eye. *Hive Records—Recording Service—Custom Recordings for Any Occasion.* And taped over the word *Occasion* was a hand-written sign: *Assistant needed. Inquire inside.*

Cecil inquired, and met Hank Howard. In the three years Cecil had been eating Mr. Green's insults, Hank Howard, done with his hitch in the service, had turned an accounting business into a record company. By the summer of '53, he'd had a couple of national hits on his own, and several regional successes. He leased record masters to bigger labels in Chicago and New York.

"What I'm looking for is a fella who likes music and is willing to learn the business along with me, Cyril."

"Cecil, Mr. Howard. Cecil."

Mr. Howard laughed at his own mistake. "Cecil! Well, I'm Hank. If we're gonna work together, we gotta be friends." Cecil nodded a cautious agreement. "Here's our little studio."

Mr. Howard held the door open. You'd never have guessed it was in there. Big enough to fit 12 people without crowding them. They had egg cartons nailed on the walls. Amidst a scramble of music stands and folding chairs was a drum kit and an upright piano that had the back stripped off.

Cecil pointed to the piano. "Oh, yeah. It records better that way. Sounds good and clear."

Cecil nodded and played a C major chord in two octaves. "She's tuned up."

"Do you play?"

"Yes, M… Hank. In fact, I write songs. Jump tunes with funny lyrics. Least I think they're funny."

Mr. Howard's eyes widened. "You had anything published? Or recorded?"

Cecil chuckled at the idea. "Not so far."

"You wouldn't feel like singin' me one right now, would ya?" Cecil wasn't sure how to answer. "'Cause I'm looking for good material. I've got some of the best artists around, and they all need new stuff. You might have some hits sittin' there! What do you say, Cecil?"

"Well…" Cecil sat down at the piano. He was nervous, but not Mr. Grass nervous. Here was a total stranger, treating him like a human being, and enthusiastic about him. At some length, Cecil hammered and sang his way through three songs he could remember. Mr. Howard pardoned himself and went into a smaller room in the back. Through a tinted window, he saw Mr. Howard talk to a blond-haired scarecrow with a big Adam's apple. He came back and asked to hear them again. Cecil was more confident in his voice and playing, and the scarecrow behind the glass recorded him.

"Terrific! Terrific! Okay, Chuck! Roll 'em!"

To his great shock, Cecil heard his voice and playing over loudspeakers.

12

He felt like hiding, but there was nowhere to run—and no reason. Mr. Howard was all smiles, like he'd found a hundred-dollar bill on the street.

"Cecil, I think you've got real talent. This is exactly the kind of material I've been looking for. I don't know where you came from, but I'm glad you're here." He invited Cecil into his office and talked turkey with him about the music business. Mr. Howard talked a mile a minute, and when he offered Cecil a steady job as his assistant, it took a moment for it to sink in.

Mr. Howard tried Cecil's songs out on Rusty Gordon and Grover Epps, a ballad singer he hoped to build up. Between them they took all three, and Cecil recorded demonstration versions of all his other songs. Some of those never went anywhere, but enough of them made good that right before Christmas 1953 Cecil was offered a third of the company. It amounted of 33.3% of a concern that was in debt and edging towards bankruptcy. Cecil's presence was valuable to Mr. Howard—as a songwriter, an assistant in the shared grunt-work of running a record label and as a liaison in the recording studio. Mr. Howard understood that a white man's presence, no matter how sympathetic, put a damper on a black man's enthusiasm and expressiveness.

Cecil knew what sounded right, so Mr. Howard could hang back in the recording booth with Chuck Honeycutt, and give the musicians breathing room. If a performance really excited him, he'd come out and praise it in-between takes. Cecil saw that Mr. Howard had a real ear for the music, and that his suggestions were worth trying out. His main concern was getting a record that people wanted to hear enough to pump their pocket change into the juke-box or buy the record and take it home.

The biggest thing Mr. Howard watched out for was the brass and reeds taking too many choruses. That could run a record too long. A real hit record needed to sit about two and half minutes. He and Cecil worked out a system. They let the sidemen blow all they wanted on the first take or two. Then Cecil would say, "We'll save that for when we go into modern jazz. Now let's cut one for the juke boxes!" That meant one, maybe two instrumental breaks and a tempo that kept the song inside the 2:30 window.

If a performance was on fire, Mr. Howard might let it edge past three minutes. With Cecil as his ears on the studio floor, he could watch the second and minute hands on the studio clock. Mr. Howard had a pocket flashlight and he'd give it three blasts when the 2:30 mark was coming up. Cecil would then give the rhythm section an index finger in a circular motion. That meant to bring it home and let it rest.

The musicians went home with acetate records of their longer takes. The band learned the shorter take and took it on the road. Mr. Howard saved all the takes. He had a safe deposit box at the bank to store the tapes. He'd had mold and mildew ruin recordings, and he'd heard about the fire at Trumpet Records, over in Jackson, and how Lillian McMurtry, the owner, had lost all her master tapes. It sounded like a big pain in the ass. It was worth the $7.50 a month to have those tapes in the bank vault.

The moment that Cecil became a bona fide co-owner of Hive Records was noted in the music industry magazine *Cash Box*, but no one in Tupelo knew about it. Cecil felt his heart beat faster as he read the item in the magazine's "Rhythm & Blues Ramblings" column:

*Sepia cleffer Cecil Madison, scribe of a dozen r&b comers for Hive, Cross and Dash diskeries, joins Henry Howard and Charles Honeycutt in joint ownership of the Mississippi waxery. With current chart stands from Rusty Gordon, Grover Epps and The Four Fellers, Hive is abuzz with sepia hit potential and just needs one national breakout to do a Goliath in the crowd of r&b indies…*

"The people of this town aren't ready for that," Mr. Howard said. "Maybe someday they'll be ready. 'Til then, we'll beat 'em at their own game," That was one of his pet sayings. It went for dee jays, distributors, the tax people, anybody that had his hand out for a piece of the action.

That was how come Cecil had to walk three miles in the rain tonight. Mr. Howard got sick of a company called Applied Plastics out of Dothan, Alabama. They pressed more copies of records than they sent to Mr. Howard. They sold the extras to distributors and got themselves some easy money. Turned out it was cheaper to make the records yourself. That way, if you made 2,000 copies of a record, nobody else was going to muscle in on it. There were already enough open palms.

They still had to send the masters to Nashville, to have the stampers made of each song. How they turned a reel of recording tape into one of those heavy metal plates was beyond Cecil's technical savvy. All he knew and had to know was that you laid down the label, face down, and made sure you had the right one. Mr. Howard had a system. The A side was the top one. He wrote A and B in grease pencil on the backs of the labels. He and Cecil. A job printer down the street ran them off.

You got the labels set into their spindle. They you laid a "biscuit" of black plastic between them. You worked the press like a waffle iron. The black stuff was the batter. You pressed the lever down hard. The stamper heated up, made the plastic soft and pressed the grooves into it. The heat stuck the labels in place. You trimmed off the extra around the edges with a wooden stick. If you were lucky, you had a lady, usually Miss Tinkle, to put them into sleeves. The sleeves had the slogan of Hive Records. "It's Buzzin', Cousin!" A cartoon of a winking bee with a trumpet was on the right top. The hive he flew out of, and the Hive Records name, was on the bottom.

The label had a gold and beige design with the hive and bees flitting around it. Mr. Howard said it was to promote Tupelo, which was known for its excellent honey. "And, hell, when we get goin' we can beat any bees in the woods."

When Hive had a new record, Miss Tinkle—her real name was Bell; Tinkle was a nickname she didn't know about—would walk the label info over to Mr. Jessup. He had a big pile of pre-printed sheets with the label image. He'd set type and bang them out. He had a machine that cut the labels in perfect circles. They'd be ready on the same day, wrapped in newspaper and tied with string. Sometimes he put the print too close to the spindle hole and the top of the title was cut off.

The record pressing room, or plant, as Mr. Howard called it, was in the back room, past the recording studio, bathroom and closet. Mr. Howard had an office to the left of the pressing plant. Miss Tinkle's desk was in the lobby right outside Hank's office.

Chuck Honeycutt was Hive's recording engineer. Cecil wasn't sure where he stood with Chuck. He was polite, but with some frost. Cecil felt that Chuck tolerated him; Mr. Howard was a friend.

◊◊◊

The rain wouldn't quit. Cecil shrugged into a plastic raincoat and stuffed his shoes with newspaper. That helped. It didn't matter much. It was hot and humid in that pressing plant. The smell from the warm plastic gave Cecil headaches, but he put up with it. There weren't many jobs a black man could get where he got treated like Mr. Howard treated him. And he paid him every week. Sometimes it wasn't much, but it was always enough to keep him going.

The shack was his. Aside from the electric bill and the gas bill he didn't have expenses. When he had a song getting airplay and good sales, Mr. Howard gave him royalty payments. Cecil guessed they called it royalty because it made you feel like a king when you got it. One time he got four hundred dollars. Cecil made that last all summer. It felt good to have money in your pocket.

Most of it he buried until he needed it. There was a couple hundred dollars in canning jars under the porch.

"Bye," Cecil said to Coaxial. The cat, curled up on the unmade bed, opened one eye, yawned and scrunched into a ball. "You got you the right idea."

Cecil's shack had no lock, but only a fool would venture up that slick clay hill on a night like this. Cecil scaled the liquid path down to the highway. He hated walking the highway at night. It had no shoulder and it twisted into one long blind curve. People drove like madmen at night. Add some rain to the story and you were in for some sad news.

Cecil had a short cut that shaved two miles off the trip to town. You had to know it was there. He had a couple of bad curves to get past first. The air was still and quiet. All he heard was the downpour of the rain and birdsongs in the night. Underneath that was the frog chorus. *Cheap, cheap, cheap,* they sang. Or was it *sheet, sheet, sheet*?

A truck came up behind him. He had time enough to climb up off the highway. The truck roared by and sprayed water in its wake. The water just missed Cecil. *Always something to be thankful for,* he thought. *This world is a hard world, but sometimes it's a fair world. Sometimes…*

Cecil spotted his turn-off. The mile marker caught his eye. He crawled up the embankment into the woods. He followed a well-worn trail. People had used this shortcut for years. It went in a diagonal through the woods, around a pond and let out behind a meat processing plant. You had to put up with the stench of that place for a while, but it beat risking your life on that highway. Cecil was good at holding his breath. He could hold it for four minutes if he had to.

While he walked, Cecil thought over a couple of song ideas. This walk was a good time to think. Nothing else to do, except to watch your step and know where you're headed. He had one phrase that stuck with him. He'd seen the word *ignoramus* in the paper. *Ignoramus…* he rhymed *famous* with it. That made him laugh. And then the phrase came to him: *he's a famous ignoramus.* Now, he could do something with that idea.

It sounded like a song that Louis Jordan would do. Cecil remembered the jaunty sound of Jordan's records and rolled the words around… *he's a famous ignoramus…just an educated fool.* Yes! That was good. He'd remember that line, because his grandfather said that about a lot of people, word for word.

A low-hanging tree branch touched Cecil's forehead and he ducked. He was close to the pond. Sometimes there were snakes, so every step had to be a careful choice. He couldn't come up with the next line, but he knew the rhyming word had to be *school*. Cecil thought through the alphabet. *Cool, duel, ghoul, jewel, pool, rule, spool, tool, yule*. Those were all possibilities. But *school* went with *educated*, so that had to be the rhyme.

*Da da da-da, da da da-da…that he never learned in school. That he* didn't *learn in school.* That was better. *Ne-ver learned. Di-dn't learn.* Yeah, it had to be *didn't learn.* It sang better.

Cecil almost walked into the pond. When he was on a song, the world around him got fuzzy. He surprised some creature who slipped into the water with a splash. *Fool/school.* He could hang onto that. That damn da da da-da; that wasn't nothing yet, but it would be.

The pond was more of a lake. It took 10 minutes to walk its perimeter. The smell of the processing plant stung him. He walked onto the worn-down path behind the plant. Cecil held his breath. Thousand and one, thousand and two. Cecil liked to pretend that he was underwater and had to hold his breath 'til he reached the surface. The meat packing place hissed and grumbled and stunk like hell. *That must be the smell of hell,* Cecil thought. And there's another good line, but Mr. Howard wouldn't go for the word *hell* in a song.

At a thousand one hundred and seventy-two, Cecil was past the plant. He exhaled and coughed. He took in a deep breath. A little of that stink hung on, but the smell of night and rain was stronger. Mr. Howard always brought a case of cold Co-colas when they pressed records. They'd go through the whole thing, and they sweated the liquid out; it never had a chance to turn into pee. "This is better than a sauna," Mr. Howard always said. Cecil was never in a sauna, but he knew it was hot.

◊◊◊

He came to the alley behind Hive Records. Mr. Howard's Desoto still clicked and sighed. He had just gotten in. The back door was open. Waves of heat rolled out. "Hank?"

"Mister Madison!" Hank Howard was stripped down to his T-shirt. The underarms were dark with sweat. They shook hands. "Why can't these dang records be hits in the winter? Whew!" He had the press warming up. "You start in on them labels. A an' B 'em."

This was the hottest part of the job. They couldn't run the fan because the labels would go everywhere. Cecil got shed of his raincoat and eased off his shoes. Nobody cared if you went barefoot in here. The concrete felt cool on his toes. That helped.

Cecil opened the supply cabinet—as high as the ceiling and with more space than they could ever use. He got a red china marker from a box.

He sat at the table and checked the stacks of labels. Mr. Howard never had them wrong. "Decline and Fall" was on the left side, and "My Regrets," a ballad Rusty Gordon's guitar man wrote, was the B-side. Both sides of a record made the same amount of money. If one side went big, both songwriters made out. Cecil never mentioned it, but "My Regrets" was a take-off on a song by Dinah Washington. Same chord changes, same tempo, and some of the same words. The guy came up with a different melody, but it wasn't like "Decline and Fall." That maybe didn't have the best melody in the world, but it was his, and didn't come from something else. That was a point of pride with Cecil.

He wrote A, A, A, A in china marker and tried to crack that third line of the lyric. *Da da da-da, da da da-da…* Nothing came. Sometimes it was that way. A song could come spewing out faster than your hand could write, or you gave birth to it one word at a time. Patience was the key. And it always came easier if he had a piano to use. That made the notes more solid. That was when a song wrote itself. Cecil wished he had a piano.

At home, he had a pawn-shop guitar and a long piece of cardboard where he'd drawn out the keys of a piano. That was some help. Not the same as the touch of the keys—that give they had under the fingertips, and the resonance of a chord. Someday he'd manage to get a piano.

B, B, B, B… "Done," Cecil shouted over the hiss and hum of the equipment.

"Let's smoosh 'em!" Mr. Howard mopped his forehead. His hair was stringy from the steam. He was tidy during the day. But there wasn't nothing tidy about making records. Cecil burped from his third Co-cola. The gas came out his nose. It hurt but it also felt good. He licked his lips and tasted sweat.

There was no getting around the slog of this process. You had to load one set of labels and one biscuit at a time. Once he got going, Cecil could set a rhythm and stick to it. His left arm got tired from pressing down on the lever. An area under his wrist always hurt and the skin chafed from the heat. But there was excitement every time he saw *C. Madison* in parenthesis under the song's title—and above "Rusty Gordon and His Jesters" on the label. Most people could care less who *C. Madison* was—they liked the song enough to buy the record or pay to hear it on the juke. Every time that happened, *C. Madison* got something. Five jukebox plays made up one penny in royalties. Every record sold earned two pennies. Chicken feed, but it added up.

As Cecil pressed, Hank produced warm biscuits. These were made of unsold flop records and new pellets of vinyl. Past failure and future success blended in these blobs. Hank brought them over 20 at a time on a large baking pan.

Place, place, place; press, trim, release, remove. Sweat, hurt, burn, wheeze, sigh. If Miss Tinkle had been there, the removal and sleeving would be her job. She was quick. Cecil could press 80 records an hour with Miss Tinkle. She wasn't comfortable around Cecil. She never said anything, but he could tell. Mr. Howard never let her be alone in the plant with him. If he had to take a call, it was always "Take a breather, Cec."

Not that Cecil was ever a threat to Miss Tinkle—or anyone but himself. It was part of the unwritten laws of the world he lived in. Laws that turned in on themselves; laws that didn't matter sometimes and were life-or-death when you least expected it. A man Cecil's color had to toe that line and hope the laws didn't twist against him. Miss Tinkle could say something to a friend and that friend could say something to a cop, and that would tear everything up. It was best without Miss Tinkle. 60 records an hour wasn't bad, long as Mr. Howard didn't drop too many. They always allowed for breakage. By the end of the night, the floor crunched with busted vinyl. Record labels stuck to the bottom of his feet. It was funny to see *C. Madison* on his instep.

There were other problems. Bubbles in the plastic, blobs under the labels or anything that would mess up the record surface. Every 50th record was test played on a portable phonograph. That took five minutes away; you had to hear both sides. If you could stand to hear the same record five, 10, 20 times in a night, you knew you had a good record. That's what made a hit. People would hear it over and over on the radio, on the jukes, and they'd have to have a copy. It was a kind of hypnosis.

*Hypnosis.* Now there's a song idea. What goes with hypnosis? *Supposes. Exposes.* Probably a lot of words. But I still got *da da da-da* on my mind, Cecil thought.

Dawn came through a cloudy haze. The rain slowed to a stop about four, when Cecil and Mr. Howard test-played the seventh record. It was a little off-center. This worried Cecil, but now Mr. Howard. "Hell, once that thing gets a couple plays, no one will notice the difference."

"Long as you're okay with it."

"Jukebox plays ruin a record, Cecil. After two days it's just noise for people to drink to. Ain't no music left on the record."

Cecil shrugged and sleeved the record. He kept count of the records he had pressed with tick marks on a piece of newspaper. One X meant five records. Once he got 25, the row of four Xs got a slash across it. Four of those and Cecil began a new row. He had just made the 350th record that was good. He ignored the ones that were bad. The ones he could pick clean would be melted down. He tried to be thrifty, but Mr. Howard walked all over the rejects. And him always complaining about expenses. He ruined enough plastic to make a bunch of new records. As the owner of one third of Hive Records, Cecil took exception to waste.

He had a box under the table where he tossed the ones worth salvaging. That was the last part of the job. After the good ones were in their sleeves and boxed up to get shipped, Cecil took the bad ones and got them ready for the melting pot. They had to be soaked so the labels would peel off. But that was a long time from now.

How many Cokes had he drunk? He sweated them out his pores, but the kick of them made his head hurt. The sides of his head; it felt like he had a horseshoe stuck in there. It made pressure on his temples. He forgot it as he got lost in the work, but when he stopped it came back to him.

Sounds of traffic came in through the back door. White people going to work, going to school, getting them some money or smarts so they could make more money. Mr. Howard heard it too. He stuck his thumb towards the back door. "There go the working stiffs. Can you imagine, Cec? Going to a job sellin' shoes or something?" He looked concerned. "How you holdin' up there?"

"Good enough. We ain't got far to go." Cecil was bone tired. If he could, he would lay down under the press and sleep on the dirty floor. If he was lucky, Mr. Howard would give him a ride home. He went home to have breakfast with his family. It was about the only time he ever saw them. Talk about a man who didn't sleep. Mr. Howard would stay up for three, four days straight. He had him these pills in a little tin box. Took those with coffee or Coke. They made him a little crazy in the eyes, but he got his work done.

Place, place, place; press, trim, release, remove. Sweat, hurt, burn, wheeze, sigh.

Then Cecil's tick marks added up to 500. "We done," he yelled to Mr. Howard.

Across the room, Mr. Howard was on the phone. He didn't hear. Cecil stood up and walked outside. The air felt heavy and wet. Like you were walking right into a sponge. Some of the clouds looked like swirls of ink in water. It could rain again any time.

The tiredness hit Cecil hard. He leaned against the doorframe. He stretched his shoulders and back, cricked his nick one way, then another. Heard a snap and then he felt better.

"We finished?"

"Mm hm."

"Miss Tinkle can tape them up. The freight man won't be here 'til 11." Now came the stand-off. Mr. Howard knew Cecil wanted a ride home. Cecil knew he had to wait for Mr. Howard to offer him a ride. He didn't want to look desperate. But he sure as hell didn't want to walk home.

The phone rang and Mr. Howard started his work day. When Miss Tinkle showed up, Mr. Howard would leave to have breakfast at home. Then he'd get a shower, shave and change his clothes. Back to the office, where he stayed 'til midnight, with recording sessions, auditions, and phone calls. Telling Miss Tinkle letters. And pulling his box of pills out; taking them with coffee.

While Mr. Howard was going on and on with some record people up north, Rusty Gordon dropped by. "You up late, brother?"

"*You* up late, brother?"

"Nah, man. I got my beauty rest. We goin' hit the road. My new record gettin' big out there." Cecil smiled; it was a faint compliment. "You got somethin' new for me?"

"Workin' on it. Got one might turn into somethin'."

Rusty grinned. "Well, don't you give it to no one else. Don't let Snake Eyes take it." He widened his eyes in imitation of Wesley Aker, who had a couple of records out on Hive as Snake Eyes and His Serpents. He had eyes like a cartoon character; they bulged out his sockets. He was more blues than Rusty. Rusty was citified rhythm and blues; up-tempo and brassy. Snake Eyes was backwoods: sly and low-down. It was the difference between a clown and a confidence man. The con man would get you to like him despite who he was. The clown wanted your love right there on the spot.

Cecil wondered what it was like to be like Rusty. He always dressed sharp and looked like a magazine picture. Bright, clean and colorful. His skin tended towards red-brown and he wore orange and yellow clothes. He played up his nickname.

Cecil felt bad in his sweaty shirtsleeves and dirty old pants. He was still barefoot. He hoped his shoes were dry by now. He couldn't bear the idea of walking home with squishy shoes. But he still had to sweep up the dead records and soak them for the melter.

"*Mis*-ter *Gor*-don!" Mr. Howard came in, shook Rusty's hand and patted him on the shoulder. "You got the best of us. We been here all night pressing your record."

"Yeah. I was gone ask you could I get 100 records. We goin' on the road an' I like to stop in at the stations, talk our record up. An' I *got* to have some for friends."

Cecil sneered to himself. *Friends* meant lady-friends, a new one every night. *Man has more ladies than I got fingers and toes.* It occurred to Cecil that he had just thought up a good line. That could work up into something. He wrote the words down on the edge of the newspaper and saved it in his pocket. Then he put on his shoes. They were still a little damp, but not bad.

The gist of it all hadn't hit Cecil yet. On his mind was getting home and sleeping. Old Coaxial would be happy to see him. They'd have themselves some breakfast then rest a while. As Cecil focused on this notion, Rusty helped himself to 100 of the fresh records. He left, and Mr. Howard broke the bad news to his partner. "Cec, ol' buddy, I'm afraid you gotta bat out another hundred. We got two hours. Can you do it?"

"Why'd you give him those records?"

"He goes out and works the deejays. He helps our records to sell. I *have* to give him something to sell." Cecil said nothing. He felt anger come on like a sore throat. "Hey, Cec. It's a pain now, but it'll mean you get more royalty later. It's what-you-call. An investment."

"All right." The stamper was still hot and they had just enough biscuits left. There wouldn't be time to test these. And this meant that soon as Miss Tinkle came in, she'd come help him. She'd try to be nice. Make small talk like she didn't have anything better to say. And all he could do was nod and say "mm-hm."

Place, place, place; press, trim, release, remove. Sweat, hurt, burn, wheeze, sigh. It was going to be a long time before he got to sleep. And from the look of it, he was going to have to walk home.

◊◊◊

Hank Howard liked to give his artists a big show when they came by. He wanted them to feel that they were on a hot label, that Hive was going places and getting notice. He never let them into his office, where bills past due littered his desk and spilled onto the carpet, alongside empty amber prescription bottles and cardboard coffee containers.

Hive was breaking even, dogpaddling, and the market showed signs of improvement. Most black stations played their records, and a few white pop deejays spun the releases that were close enough to pop. Sid Williams and The Four Fellers had a smooth sound, right up there with The Mills Brothers, but with more jive, more energy. They'd had one record creep up the pop chart in '53. It got to #17, which took every ounce of push, nerve and time Howard could muster. The song was a beauty—"The Chapel Bells," a slow, dreamy ballad that was originally a country song he cut on one of his artists. Sid heard it and liked it. He churched it up a little, and that cat could sing like a canary. His Fellers had a great ear for harmony. Hank kidded them about being jazz, and some of their chords were out there. They explained one of them as "the flatted fifth," and it sounded like something you'd hear in the middle of the night, when the freight trains rattled and rolled through town.

"Decline and Fall" had some pop spins. Nothing on the national charts yet, but it was played in Philadelphia, Detroit, Kansas City and Oakland. It was building. Those 100 records would do Hive more good on the road than in the shops. Glad-handing and back-patting won deejays over. They worked hard and they had the power to make or break your record.

*Broken records*, Hank thought. He heard the crunch of dead wax under Cecil's feet. *Poor guy. Working so hard. He's the best guy in this firm. And one hell of a songwriter. He is gonna come out to something.*

Cecil and Miss Tinkle were on the home stretch. Miss Tinkle looked tense next to Cecil. He had no small talk. The man was lost in his work. Miss Tinkle loved to talk. She was the perfect receptionist. She held off Vincent Cross for an hour last year. Just about saved Hank's butt. That was when the Cross brothers took Moanin' Jones away from him. Hank stopped himself. Those thoughts could get bitter fast. Too far down that road could ruin his mood for the day.

He had other thoughts about Miss Tinkle. She was one hot little number. Hank had come close to putting a move on her—at a Christmas party, when everyone was pretty smashed except for Hank. The diet pills he took kept him like a hummingbird. He pretended to be drunk and made a pass that was too subtle for her.

For something he hadn't done, per se, Hank went home in a fog of guilt. He didn't sleep well, in part from the pills and in part out of fear that she would quit her job. Hive Records would fall to pieces without her on the front lines. If she noticed the pass, she never acknowledged it, and the only thing she showed up with, the next morning, was a hangover.

Hank glanced at his watch. 10:40. It was way too late for breakfast. Carl and Kitty were already in school. *I ought to go home. Check in and take my lumps.* His wife Elizabeth was not keen on this record business, and with two kids on board, the pressure felt like five tons. If she could only see that Hive was bound to get a break. It was so close to bubbling over. All it needed was one big artist. Someone who could push the whole shooting match into the pop charts, and appeal to the whites, the blacks, the Chinese—everybody. Music has the power to do that, Hank knew. *It bridges over everything I hate about this country. A song that's good and real can get to anyone. And once they realize that it's the black artists that can do this the best…*

Cecil sighed. He was dead on his feet. "We're done." He had to say it twice to get Hank's attention.

He snapped out of his speech-to-self. "Wonderful! I knew you could do it. I really appreciate it, Cec. I know I ask a lot of you."

"Well, you were in there pitchin' too." Cecil wiped the lens of his glasses. He looked a wreck. Hank needed a clean shirt and a shower, but he was still presentable. Cecil resembled someone who crawled out of a mine after a cave-in.

Miss Tinkle was fresh and neat, with her frozen smile and worried eyes. She sleeved the last records and put them in the square boxes. Ten boxes of 50 discs each. She wadded up newspaper or used wads of excelsior to protect the records. It was cheaper to ship them that way and safer for the records. One box gets lost or damaged—that's nothing. Lose the whole deal and you're in a hell of a fix. Miss Tinkle had a big FRAGILE ink stamper and she smacked the boxes with that purple word.

Hank and Cecil hefted the boxes outside. The freight driver came up the alley, signed off on the shipment and threw them in his truck. Hank liked to remind them to gentle those records. They said UNBREAKABLE on the label, which was a total fib.

"Lord." Cecil looked up at the sky. He saw two layers of clouds. The thick yellow-tan ones covered up the sun. Dark swirls like ink suspended in water floated closer. Those looked in the mood to burst.

Hank opened his wallet. He had a 20 and three ones. *The guy worked so hard; he deserves something.* Hank debated, thought so hard he forgot to breathe. He caught his breath and pulled the 20 out. He folded it in thirds and put it in his shirt pocket. Then he walked into the pressing room. "Ah, Cecil…"

Cecil turned to him, silent, his face lined with exhaustion.

"Don't worry about sweeping up. I'll get Carl to do it later. Ah, Cec… it looks like I've got to stick around here all day. I know I usually run you home, but…" He handed over the 20. "Why don't you get a taxi home? Looks like it's gonna rain."

Cecil unfolded the bill and saw the big forehead of Andrew Jackson. "This come out of my royalties?"

"This is on the house, Cec. A token of my esteem."

Cecil nodded. He couldn't say *thanks*; it seemed awkward. He had to say something. "I 'preciate it, Hank."

"Aw, I wish I could do more. We're in this together—"

"It's Mr. Cross for you, sir," Miss Tinkle interrupted.

"Which Mr. Cross?"

"The angry one, sir."

Hank sighed. "They're *all* angry. Okay. Come by tomorrow night, Cec. I'm recording Snake Eyes and his boys."

Cecil nodded. He went for his shoes. They were almost dry. He needed new shoes and new pants—new everything. If he could come up with a big song or two, he'd be able to get those things.

*Now Mr. Howard, there goes a man who acts like he the boss.* Cecil regarded his scuffed gray shoes and frayed trouser cuffs. *Me, I'm lucky to be a slob with a job.*

He walked down the alley, hungry and fried. But a phrase kept at him. *A slob with a job. A slob with a job…*

***The First Colored Church of Christ*** was a half mile away, on the other side of town. Cecil played piano there if the regular person, Miss Oleatha, couldn't do it. He walked that way, head down, as words and music came to him. He had it all by the time he climbed the church steps. He couldn't wait to get it written down.

There was an old upright piano in the basement. They used it to rehearse the choir on Wednesday nights. He knew he could play it and not attract attention. He found a couple of shirt cardboards on the floor and a pencil on top of the piano. He played the melody in the key of C. That had no black keys except for the blue notes.

Cecil recalled his time at the grocery store. He still woke up at night smarting from something Mr. Grass had said to him or about him. He couldn't dance on the man's grave—he didn't know where it was—but he could write a song about it. The words he scrawled down were from personal experience:

*I go to work down at the grocery store*

*And ev'ry morning when I blow through that door*

*They keep me going 'til I'm dead on my feet;*

*They never let me take a seat…*

*I'm just a slob with a job, sweeping up the place*

*A slob with a job, sweat runnin' down my face;*

*A slob with a job for thirty bucks a week—*

*I barely make enough to sleep and eat…*

Perhaps because he was in a church, the melody sounded more like a gospel song. He knew the gospel chord changes and he threw them all in. The words made him laugh. He turned over the cardboard and started on the second verse…

*The ladies look at me like I'm a clown*

*My boss ain't happy 'less he's putting me down*

*Sometimes I'd like to tell him where he could go,*

*But man, I really need the dough…*

He knew the last verse had to have a happy ending. If you could get a little story going in a song, people loved that. He thought about it and came up with this:

*Someday I'll be the boss and run my own place*

*And then I guarantee I'll laugh in their face*

*When I drive by in my new Cadillac*

*With my pockets loaded full of jack…won't be no slob with a job…*

The song needed a middle part, and he had enough space on the second cardboard to get it down:

*Stocking the shelves and sweeping the walk;*

*No time for coffee breaks or making small talk.*

*It never stops 'til I'm plumb out of breath—*

*That boss of mine like to work me to death…*

Cecil knew this was good. It was a hit. He took the time to write down the notes on music paper. He found a sheet behind the piano. He could get it down good enough to save it. He never got the rhythms perfect, but it was close enough for him to remember it. The singers always fussed with the melody anyway. But this was a big one. He knew Mr. Howard would like it. This was worth a whole new wardrobe.

Cecil bought a quart of milk and a couple of hamburgers. He felt so good he walked home. As he walked, he ate and drank and hummed his new melody. He saved a little bit of hamburger and milk for Coaxial. He still had 18 dollars cash in his pocket. He could live on that for a month if he was careful. And maybe he didn't have to be so careful anymore.

***Hank Howard drove his 1952 DeSoto*** up the driveway. These long summer evenings fooled him. It felt like it was 6:30, maybe 7. But he feared it was later. He looked at his watch. 6:56.

Their house was two years old, and part of Silverbell Glen, a subdivision on the way out of town. The area had once been deep woods. All the trees and vines and underbrush were bulldozed, burned and carted away. New sod was laid, neat asphalt streets pressed, and 48 houses built from three blueprints. The houses came in four colors and the Howards' home was "peach." It looked like skin. Hank wondered if a house could get sun burned.

Hank heard television laughter from the Briers across the street and a snatch of the McGuire Sisters doing "Goodnight, Sweetheart Goodnight" as Jim Calkins toodled by in his Buick. They exchanged waves. Hank thought about that song. It was a hit in pop, rhythm and blues and country. That was the ideal. Sweep across all the markets. *I don't want no McGuire Sisters, but I sure do want a record like that.*

Sheets flapped in the wind. Hank caught them out of the corner of his eye. The drying carousel was a big selling point for the house. It creaked at night and sometimes it kept him up. He oiled it but it kept creaking. He heard it now.

Applause from the Briers' TV spurred Hank out of the DeSoto. *I feel like I'm going to the principal.* He closed the car door quiet and walked past the shaggy lawn. *Got to get that mowed.* Hank stood before the door, sighed, prepared himself. *What's the worst that could happen?*

Liz and the kids were still at the table. He felt relief. "Hiya, everybody! What's to eat?"

"Meat loaf!" Carl and Kitty shouted in near unison.

Hank dropped his briefcase on the couch and circled the dinner table. First came the young 'uns. "Hiya, slugger; hiya, Kitty." He leaned in to kiss his wife. She smiled, but there was an edge to that smile. He knew how sharp and fine that edge could get.

Hank's plate was ready. He didn't care if it was cold; he was starved. "Boy, what a day. So much goin' on!"

"We missed you last night." Liz paused for a sip of coffee. "And this morning."

"Where were you, Pop?" Carl asked.

"We was worried," Kitty said. She had ketchup on her chin from the meat loaf.

"Folks, I apologize. Daddy's tryin' to run his own company, and sometimes there's just so much work I can't see straight. See?" Hank crossed his eyes. That was a sure-fire laugh getter for the kids.

"Do it again, daddy!" Kitty was in hysterics. Hank gave her a quick goofy face, to her delight.

"Honest, my dears, I hate to do this to you. But I'm home tonight. And I'll be here for breakfast in the morning! We've got a recording session in the evening, but I can swing it to come home for supper."

"I'm so glad you can," Liz said.

While Hank digested that, Carl bragged about hitting a home run and said he was going to be in the science fair. "I'm gonna do a volcano, Pop!"

"Wassa ball-*cay*-no?" Kitty asked. A pea bounced off her plate and under the table.

Carl told Kitty was a volcano was. Hank tried to tune out his son's rambling lecture. He turned to Liz. "I really am sorry, hon. I know I should have called. But we had to press 600 records. We've got a big hit building up and sometimes I just have to give things a push."

"I don't mind that you're busy, honey. I know you're trying hard…" She took in a piece of meat loaf. "But you're not on your own. You have us. And we miss you when you're not here."

"I promise I'll call you if I'm gonna be held up. I mean it."

"I wish I could believe that, Hank." She stirred her coffee and sipped.

"You take everything so personal. I don't mean it that way."

"It feels like we're just something you… remember all of the sudden. Not what you have on your mind."

"Aw, honey, that hurts." He ate. The diet pills had worn off and he needed to eat, to relax, to let himself sleep. The tension in the room buzzed in his head. He wanted a drink. But food came first. "So how was your day?" Hank smiled to show he meant it.

"Busy. We had the plumber back to do the sink. That was 11 dollars. I gave him a check."

"How'd he do?"

"He got the drip. He says it ought to be permanent."

"The drip?"

Liz rolled her eyes. She smiled and it felt like a smile. "And I had a meeting with Carl's teacher after school. She says he needs some help paying attention. Don't you, Carl?"

"Huh?" Carl looked startled.

"Miss Keeler says he has a great imagination, but it's hard for him to finish anything. To stay on track. Unless it's something he really likes. Then you can't tear him away."

"That sounds like someone I know." Hank pointed his fork at himself. "Well, that just means he's gonna hafta try a little harder. Right?"

"Yessir."

"You got any homework tonight?"

"Spellin'."

"Well, let's you an' me get together on it. You're pretty good at spelling."

"Yessir."

"Probably better at it than me. Maybe you can teach me something."

Carl beamed. There was blackberry pie for dessert, and Carl scarfed his

32

slice down. "C'n I be 'scused?"

"Yes. Let's take a look at that spelling." Hank touched Liz's hand. "I really am sorry. I'm going to try to turn over a new leaf. You know I mean well."

"Yes." Kitty's job was to take the dinner dishes from the table to the sink. She got serious about this task, and it tickled her parents. Liz touched Hank's hand. It was like she understood. She got that everything Hank did was for this. The roof over their head. Their kids. Their future. You couldn't put all that in words. Only a touch gave that information.

Spelling homework took half an hour. For the assignment, the parent read off a list of 25 medium-tough words from a mimeographed sheet sealed inside a manila envelope. Carl had not seen the list, and the parent was asked to put a check-mark on successful words and to note what went wrong in the others.

Carl corrected his father on a couple of I before E mistakes; Hank pointed out an extra R in *scarecrow*. They kidded their way through the homework, and it went well. Miss Keeler was not a kidder. Merriment and spontaneity died in her orbit. That was why Carl's attention wandered. If you got Carl to laugh, he was all yours. Miss Sheffield, Carl's first-grade teacher, was onto that wavelength. She understood human nature. Hank knew that and worked with it every day. Some people you had to get excited; some you had to calm down. Some people wanted to be helpful; others you had to rescue like a cat up a tree. You had to size people up and see what opened their doors.

"I bet you're about the best speller in school, bud."

"Hey, do the face, Pop. Do the face." Hank crossed his eyes and wiggled his ears. Carl's laughter was a warm reward.

They were done in time to see Red Skelton, which everyone liked. Carl and Kitty wanted to stay up and see Danny Thomas, but 9:00 was their bedtime on school nights. They griped, but Hank and Liz herded them into their pajamas, got them to brush their teeth and say their prayers. Carl could read for half an hour. He was reading *Treasure Island*. He lasted about 10 minutes. One the last things Hank did at night was to move the book away from Carl's face, mark the page he was on, and set it on his end table.

The kids were in bed. Now Hank could take off his shoes, relax on the sofa and unwind. A couple of bourbons helped. He only let himself have two a night. His old man had a booze problem and he read that could carry over. Liz didn't drink, save for white wine when they went to Giglio's for ravioli. They hadn't done that for a while. That was for when the bank account was a little fatter.

Liz switched to Postum after dinner. She couldn't stand to sit in silence, so the radio or TV was always on when she was up. She sat in her chair, on the other side of the TV set. Hank always had so much he wanted to say, but the words didn't come easy. He sipped his bourbon. The cool liquid burned his throat at first swallow but settled down to a warm smooth glow in his stomach. He exhaled and let the steam of the day out.

Whoever spoke first held the floor. He wanted to lead the discussion tonight. He indexed his thoughts. *I can't talk about work; it isn't interesting to her. I can't tell her we're doing good because we're not. Carl! We can talk about his school stuff.*

"Carl is on the ball in there with his spelling."

"What's that?"

"Carl. That's one smart kid. He's a great speller."

"Takes after his daddy."

"I wish Miss Keeler was—well, *warmer*. Kinder. She's got a pretty hard shell."

"She was a missionary. Did you know that?"

"Nuh uh."

"She and her husband. They went all through Africa bringing the Lord's word to the natives there."

"I guess that'd make anyone crabby. The heat, and all that."

"I ran into the Kimballs today."

"Uh huh?" *Oh, crap. Here it comes.*

"Bob said they'd hire you tomorrow at the savings and loan. If you wanted the job."

"Did he?"

"They need a good comptroller there. Their old one's retiring."

"Aw, hon, we've talked about this…"

"*I've* talked about this. You just…you humor me. Like I'll just forget about it. Hank, we need something we can count on. It hurt to write that check today. I didn't know if it would bounce." She paused for emphasis. "We have 37 dollars in our checking account. As of today."

"Ooh. I thought it was more like 87."

"Hank, Bob talked turkey with me. He knows your company is having trouble. He said they'll give you 75 dollars a week. And in six months, you'd get a raise. We could make that work. If you want to run your music company on the side, do it on weekends, that's fine."

"But we're getting close—"

"You always say that. That's always your excuse."

"I made 350 dollars in March. Just one month. We had two hit records on the charts."

"Yes, and I'm grateful for that." Liz leaned forward—a sign that the sermon was about to hit its stride. "I know this is your dream. Owning your own business, putting out records. But when does it pay off? When does it really bring in enough money? You have to pay the rent on the building. You have Miss Bell's salary. That black boy."

"Cecil's not a boy. He's 25. And Miss Bell…I don't really need her, but she makes a good impression. She answers the phone and keeps things organized. I guess I do need her."

"If you worked for Southeastern, you wouldn't have those worries. Can't you see? You could just go to work, do your job, and come home with money in the bank every week. We could save out of that—when you got a raise we could be all right."

Hank sulked into his bourbon. *Damn her, she's right. She always is. From a practical point of view. But…* "I don't know if I can sit at a desk all day," Hank said out loud, before he realized it. "I get so fidgety. I've got to be doing something. Something that makes sense to me."

"Doesn't your security make sense to you? Don't I make sense to you? And them?" She gestured towards the back of the house, where Kitty and Carl slept.

Hank buried his brow in his hand. He sighed. "Can we make a deal? Will you hear me out for just a second?" He looked hard at Liz. She nodded. "I feel it in my bones that in six more months, Hive Records will be on top. I can't tell you how; I can't tell you why. I just feel it in here." He tapped his chest. "And if I'm wrong—and I might be, I don't know—if I'm wrong, six months from now… I'll close the place. I'll give it up. Do you want me to sign something?"

"You're shouting."

"I'm sorry. It's just…can you give me six more months? Bear with me that long. And if I'm wrong about it, I'll burn the place down. I'll—I'll get a shovel and bury it. Would that please you?"

"Hank, I just want you to be successful. No matter what you do. That's all I could ask for. That's the only way you'll ever be happy. Or me."

"Six more months?"

"Daddy, you're too *loud*," Kitty shouted from her room.

"Sorry, kiddo." He swallowed the cold liquor and fixed his eyes on Virginia's. "Six months. What do you say?"

"All right. And I hope you're right. All I want is for you to make it. And you're bound to make it somewhere."

Hank realized he had won. She had heard him. He wanted to tell her about why this was so important to him. Why music was the thing that made him get up in the morning. And the thing that kept him from going to sleep at night sometimes. How music had something that could bring everyone together, if they'd just listen. And if he could find one person who could get everyone's attention. In some significant way. Whether they loved that person or hated them—that person had the potential to change the world.

He knew that when he talked about that, little of it made sense. He felt himself being a bit crazy, like a tent preacher. He didn't want to come off that way. It was better to let the records he put out say that message. They had it already, but they needed to say it louder and stronger, if that was possible.

Into his last drink, Hank nodded off twice. He got himself off the couch and showered. It felt good and relaxing to scrub off all the sweat and worry of the day. He would sleep—he knew it. Eight hours in the sack and then it was off to the races.

***Cecil took the day off.*** He read a little, napped a bit, and spent a long time staring through the trees down to the highway. Coaxial took a nap beside him, then woke and groomed himself. He was good company. You knew where you stood with him.

Cecil thought about going to the movies. He wasn't sure what shows were on. With his luck, all there would be was a Doris Day movie with too much singing. Nothing there he could hang onto. And there was always a black person tending to the white people—making their meals, setting out their clothes, cleaning their houses.

Cecil liked crime movies and some Westerns. He didn't like the Westerns where the white men killed Indians, like they were paper cups in a dispenser. Or that business at the fair with the tin ducks in a row. You paid a dime and you got five shots. Just about all movies had something wrong with them. They were reminders of who owned and ran the world. Cecil left the theater shaken and anxious. Once a year he might feel entertained. The odds were against him.

He thought about his new song. He was going to show up at Snake Eye's session and get him to record it. It was a natural for Snake Eyes. He did sarcastic songs about what a joke the world was. His records were usually hard blues. This might be too light for him, but Cecil would do his best to be persuasive. Once Mr. Howard—Hank—once he heard the song, he would be all for it. Maybe they couldn't cut it on Snake Eyes, but he'd have *somebody* to sing it.

Hank was looking for *somebody*. Anyone who showed up and said they could sing or play got a free audition. No catches. Hank and Chuck Honeycutt set up the studio every morning. The tape recorder had a fresh reel and a live microphone waited for any voice that came into that room. Good, bad or mediocre, they got their shot. If they were good, Hank asked them did they write songs. If they did, how many did they have? If they had four good ones, sometimes he'd set up a session right then—call some boys he knew who were good in the studio, have the singer run through his songs and get them on tape.

That was how Snake Eyes got on Hive. He was a filling station attendant. Walked by on his lunch hour and saw Hank's sign. He got into the studio and laid out a song called "Mister Moron," about how his boss thought he was smart but was dumber than a doornail. The way his sense of humor worked, you had to think about it for a minute; then you laughed. Snake Eyes had a real dead pan. He could tell you the most outrageous fib and you'd be sold on it until you started to think. Hank got Cecil to play piano behind him, just chords, and called in a high schooler, some white kid who played drums. He was all right. He'd been listening to the race records and soaking some of that up.

Sometimes Hank's judgment was a puzzle. This little bitty white woman with big orange hair came in and said she could sing good as Kitty Wells. Maggie Woodburn was loud, but she had a gift for missing the note. If you had an ear for music, it got hurt by her singing. He put out three records on her. One got a C+ review in *Cash Box*; that was it. She had been a waitress and she went right back to it. They finally melted down all her unsold records. That kept Cecil busy for two weeks straight.

Whoever that *somebody* was, Hank Howard hadn't found them yet. He didn't know where they were, or what they did. He didn't run an ad in the paper. Didn't advertise on the radio, even though he was good buddies with Whit Lawson, who everybody knew as "Dixie Doodle" on the air. Dixie played all of Hank's records. That was how Hank found out that white kids liked rhythm and blues. They needed something to sink their teeth into. Patti Page and big bands didn't cut it. They were being given someone else's idea of music and it didn't work for them.

Cecil's watch said 4:35. Not enough time to see a show, even if they had something good on. He planned to be there at the studio at 7, when everyone drifted in. Recording time was usually 8 on evening sessions. That gave Cecil an hour to convince Snake Eyes. The thought made his stomach knot up. He was raised to not be pushy or make demands of others' time and attention. It had gotten him so far, saved him from some real trouble. But to get your song heard, you had to step in and make some noise. You were selling a product. It did everyone good if a song took off. It gave the artist more popularity, it made money for them, for the record company and for the songwriter. Nobody lost out on that proposition. It took a lot of work to get a song to that point. Work and good luck. No one could predict what people will go crazy for. They can try, but the damndest things take hold of people.

Cecil had some pork chops and greens. This meant that Coaxial had pork chops and greens. Another amusing trait of that cat was to growl when he ate something extra tasty. As he ate, his growl, punctuated and distorted, was the stuff of great comedy. And he tucked into the greens. Cecil enjoyed having his meals with Coaxial. Life felt less lonely, less limited with him around.

◊◊◊

Hank intended to get supper at home, but the Cross Brothers kept him on the phone too late. They wanted some new sides from a local bluesman who called himself The Lonesome Shadow. His real name was M. M. Butts, and anyone that laughed would soon regret it. Lonesome was 6' 4" and built like a freight train. His electric guitar looked tiny in his hands, but that cat could wail. He did the hard blues, all about thievin' women, whiskey, gamblin' and feelin' so low you could die.

Lonesome only did his own songs. He didn't care for anyone else's. Hank tried a couple of Cecil's out on him. Lonesome shook his head. "That's candy, man. That for kids." The Shadow's records were big in Chicago, Detroit and Baltimore, and the Cross boys couldn't get enough of them. They went so far as to set up a makeshift studio two miles away. They set up shop in an abandoned gas station. Their equipment was terrible and the acoustics worse. They gave up after three weeks. The point of it all was that they tried to get Lonesome away from Hank. They wanted him in Chicago, under their supervision. Lonesome lived alone and had a small dairy farm. Sometimes he worked in a lumber mill. Hank couldn't get much out of him; he'd tried. Lonesome was not one for small talk.

But his records sold, and they were a lifeline for Hive Records. Hank had never put Lonesome out on Hive; he was afraid to do it. But it was standard business for Cross Records. The rougher, tougher and gutsier the music was, the more they wanted it. In his last session, The Shadow brought in "Lectric Chair." It was about a man who killed his best friend with an ax after he found him in bed with his wife. The judge sentenced him to die in the electric chair, and the record ended with him dying with a shriek.

Lonesome did three takes of "Lectric Chair," each more intense, and the last take was frightening. That night, Hank sweated in bed, the minor-key melody circling in his head. It was like hearing a nightmare with your eyes wide

39

open. It went to #1 on the national race records charts.

"Lectric Chair" was too big a record for Hive. Hank would have had to hock everything he owned just to keep up with the demand for the records. He couldn't trust other pressing plants. They'd run off 1000 copies on their own and cut into legit sales. Hank had no control over that, and by the time he got a lawsuit going, the trail was cold. All it meant was another enemy, which he didn't need. He was swimming with the sharks, and he knew it.

The record had sold like dope for six months, and when Hank got the royalty statement for Hive's cut of the pie, his heart dropped. 702 dollars and change. That record sold half a million—though maybe a third of those were bootlegs. Under separate cover was Lonesome's royalty statement. Hank didn't open it; he was afraid to. But he was sure it was under par.

Talking with the Cross brothers did nothing but strain him. His blood pressure boiled, his head hurt, his eyes burned with sweat. He couldn't tell them what he really thought of them—he needed them too much. They needed Lonesome; they wanted him for their own. It all came down to that, and Hank wasn't ready to let go. The Shadow was a real artist. His records challenged you, shook you down to your core. The sound of his voice, like sandpaper on tarpaper, and the force of his guitar…Hank was not a religious man, but he heard the gospel in The Shadow's voice and songs. He wasn't for everyone. Hank could not imagine The Shadow making it with white teenagers. He was what they'd been told, all their lives, was their worst nightmare. He was important. The whole world would see. What he did meant something.

"Y'all done for the night?" Miss Bell poked her head in Hank's office.

"Thank God. Those bastards. Sorry, Miss Bell. I got a headache."

"There's aspirin in your drawer."

Hank grinned. "I forgot. See you in the morning."

"Bye." In her broad Tennessee accent, it sounded like *bah*. Hank watched her walk off. *She's a hot little number*, he thought. A flush of guilt went through him. Lives and careers had gone down the shitter with thoughts like that, especially from a married man—a family man. That's all he needed: a good scandal.

Still, Miss Bell was a hot little number. That he could not deny. Those thoughts, that desire, came more frequently to him. It troubled him, because he knew himself. Given the slightest invitation, he would succumb to temptation.

His heavy head cancelled out any possible lust. Hank slugged down four aspirins with cold black coffee. It was 6:20. He had time for one more grueling phone call.

This one wasn't with some record company, or some shyster, but with Virginia. Another apology, another empty promise to try and be better. Another awkward silence when he had plenty to say but no way to say it. Then, if he lived through that, he could cop two hot dogs and a bag of boiled peanuts from old Jolly, down the street. That and some fresh coffee would keep him going til midnight. By then, he'd have a new record—maybe two—on old Snake Eyes.

◊◊◊

Cecil didn't have any best clothes. They all had problems. But he picked out his least bad shirt, trousers and suit coat, spit-polished his shoes, and he looked miserable but presentable. Everybody else would be way better dressed than him. He tried to act like it didn't matter. He was too busy with his work to bother getting all dolled up.

He put all his papers in an artist's portfolio, zipped it up and gave Coaxial a chin scratch. The cat yawned and head-butted him. "You good people, man. Keep an eye on the place." Coaxial responded with a happy meow—more like a chirp.

Evening forced the sun down on the horizon. Blaring orange light stabbed Cecil's eyes, magnified in power through his glasses. He squinted and found his way down the hill to the highway. He turned his back to the sun and felt better.

He walked against oncoming traffic. That side of the road had more shoulder, and while it was still light he could walk it without fear. Without normal fear. Some yobbo could decide to take his bad day out on him—scare him by driving right at him, knocking him down in the ditch or saying something cruel to which there was no reply. Cecil was always prepared for trouble. If it didn't come, he felt better about the world.

It didn't come. He walked peaceable to his short-cut, made his diagonal through the woods and played his pretend game as he trotted past the slaughter house and its smell. He didn't have a watch, but from the light outside he guessed it was 7 or close to 7. With luck, he'd get Mr. Howard all to himself for a few minutes. Lay this new song on him. Cecil felt nervous singing in front of anyone else. Mr. Howard always wanted to hear his songs. Cecil was welcome to sing, not some fool to tolerate.

◊◊◊

Hank regretted his second hot dog after he finished it. He already had gas from the raw onion. He let a long rattling fart out and had to evacuate his office. His throat felt dry from the black coffee. He needed some water. He took a long drink at the water cooler; four paper cups followed by a gargle.

Everyone at the session would be smoking. That would hide his gas. *A co-cola would help*, he thought. He laid awake with heartburn too many nights. It wasn't fast living, but it felt like it could kill him. He moved too much to be fat, but he didn't take real good care of himself. He didn't smoke, but he lived in a world of it. Musicians were like chimneys. You couldn't get away from it; you had to learn to accept it.

He did a final check of the studio. All the equipment was on and warmed up. Chuck Honeycutt sat in the booth. Hank had the air conditioning on as cold as it would go. To record, he had to shut it off. Otherwise, an out-of-tune buzz came through on the tape. It threw some singers off. It was better to sweat it out through the takes.

Chuck motioned to Hank. He made the come here move with a crooked finger. Hank went into the booth. "Mister Honeycutt."

"How's about you say somethin' into mic number two? Wanna make sure it's working right."

"Can do." Hank crossed the room to mic #2, the vocal microphone. Before he could open his mouth, a loud, keen fart escaped him. It went on and on and got louder. He saw Chuck shake with laughter. "How's that?" he shouted into the mic. Chuck gave him a thumbs up.

Chuck had the mic too low. He adjusted it to Snake Eyes' height— one inch less than The Shadow—and cinched it in place. Cecil surprised him; when Hank turned around, he was just *there*. "Mister Madison!" He put out his hands and Cecil took it. They shook. "You're looking good."

"I, uh, Hank…I got one for Snake Eyes. I think he'd do real good on it…"

"I'd love to hear it. But first, could you do me a favor and go get us some cold cokes? Jolly's got 'em in six packs. I've got a little indigestion. Then

I'd love to hear what you got." He gave Cecil a five. "Thanks, buddy."

Cecil went to Jolly's, a place they'd call a delicatessen up east. Jolly was an old blind man, a veteran of the first World War. He couldn't see what color you were, and he didn't care.

Jolly was busy with an order when Cecil entered. He made for the coolers in the back of the store and pulled out a wire container of six 10-ounce Cokes. They were two for three dollars, so he got another. He knew the drill. Hank had gas whenever he was excited or worried, and recording was both of those at once.

"What we have here?" Jolly felt the cold, wet glass and metal. "12 bottles of Coke. King size."

"Yes sir."

"What you got?"

"A five."

"I gotta take your word for it." He gave Cecil back three half dollars and other change. "I thank you," Jolly said. "Bring back the empties."

"Yes sir."

Cecil hurried up the street. He needed five minutes alone with Mister Howard. He wanted him to hear this song. It just had to be a hit.

*Aw, shit*, he thought. He saw Snake Eyes, a head taller than anyone else, standing in front of the office. Hank shot the breeze with him and his boys. They laughed and smoked. They were dressed to the nines. All the latest styles, slick and sharp. Cecil felt ashamed of himself. He was just the good colored boy who pressed the records and got the musicians co-colas…

He flashed back to the army camp. Everyone staring at him. He couldn't run through those tires. He tripped and his glasses went flying. Would that make Sarge mad! You couldn't hate someone for not seeing well, but in the army they could. Cecil was…he didn't let himself think of that phrase. It had three words that started with the letter S. He was called that for two years and change, and he sometimes called himself that when he got frustrated. *Come on, boy. Walk proud. You are nobody's sad sack of shit. You got a song to sell.*

"There he is!" Hank shouted. "I got us all some cokes. And I understand Cecil has a song for you."

43

"'Lo," Cecil muttered. He felt embarrassed and small.

"Cecilio," Snake Eyes said. He put an extra O on everyone's name. "Gimme one o' those." He uncapped the coke with something on his key chain. He leaned his head back and took a swig. "This need somethin' special." He pulled a silver flask from his back pocket and poured some dark liquid into the bottle. He took a sip. "Aaahhh. That's more like it."

Everyone laughed. "You got a song for *me*? Not for Rust Bucket?"

Cecil shrugged. "I don't know if you even like it…"

"Well, hell, I got to *hear* it first! Lay it on me, man."

Cecil stammered. "Ah…ah… at the piano…"

"Well, all reet. To the piano for Cecilio." The guys in his band started to come in, but Snake Eyes paused them. "I don't wanna give him worries. Gimme a minute."

"But man, we gots to hear it if we'na do it," Earl the sax man said.

"If it's good, we sure gonna do it. But *I* got to hear it *first*!" He grabbed another bottle from the wire carrier and pushed it into Earl's chest. "What you want…is a Coke!" All the cats laughed at the way he said it—with a snide nasal sound that mimicked a white man. Hank laughed loudest of all.

Cecil felt his heart in his throat. *It's okay*, he told himself. *I know this is good. I know it's good…*He sat at the piano and unzipped his folio. The crude sheet music fluttered to the floor. Hank handed it to him and Cecil set it with the lyrics on the piano's music desk. He cleared his throat and found it dry. "Hey man, can you slip me one of them Cokes?"

Hank uncapped it and Cecil took a big draw. It burned going down. That felt good.

"What you call this song?" Snake Eyes said with a smile.

"Um, I call it 'A Slob with a Job.'"

Snake Eyes laughed. "I like it already. Lay it on me, brother."

Cecil felt like he was on the ceiling and watching himself strike the keys. He started to sing, shaky at first. The first verse was hard. He had to sell himself on singing it out loud. On the chorus, Snake Eyes started to tap the rhythm on the top of the piano. Cecil felt better. He looked up at Hank, who was all smiles.

They laughed at every line and Snake Eyes sang along with the second chorus. Cecil noticed that, but was too focused on getting through the song to see the others drift in. He repeated the third verse and heard a snare drum, felt the thud of a stand-up bass and, on the chorus, had the answering phrases sung in two-part harmony. Earl uncased his sax and blew solid gold. Cecil felt bold and good and sure of himself.

He repeated the third verse, and everyone joined in. Snake Eyes was just right for the lyrics. He invested them with a sardonic feeling and Cecil could tell he dug the song. The band came up with a good ending and the drummer hit the last bang on a cymbal. Then everyone clapped and whistled. Cecil was sure they were kidding him—that this was a trick. Like when they got him to sing at the service talent show, just so they could heckle him. He looked up; all eyes were on him. They all registered approval and joy. Cecil's fear faded.

"Gentlemen, I think we have a hit here," Hank said. "You run 'em through it again and warm 'em up. Chuck can get his levels and we'll be good to roll."

Snake Eyes sat next to Cecil on the piano stool. "Let's take it from the bridge, man. I think we got the chorus." The bridge had some circle-of-fifth chord changes—kind of a vaudeville sound—and Snake Eyes had to find his way into that. They ran it three times, and Earl joined in the last time.

"Those are good blowin' chords," he said. "We could do that for a break. What key we doin' this in?"

"B flat?" Snake Eyes turned to Cecil. "Can you take 'er down a peg?"

Cecil felt nervous, but he knew enough about the chords to transpose them down a whole step. When Earl blew on the bridge, in the new key, it sounded like a hit record. This would get played on juke boxes. People would sing this song to themselves when it played on the radio. People would buy this record.

"Cecilio, why don't you sit in with us. Ride this one out..." Cecil looked up at Snake Eyes and knew he meant it.

"Naw man, I ain't no professional."

"You sound fine to me. 'Sides, Willie bound to drown you out." Willie was on drums, and he played them like a battering ram. He was better on the slow numbers, but Snake Eyes didn't do those much.

Cecil looked around the studio. He felt guilty, like he was impersonating a real musician. Before he could sink inside his shell, the sax man ran an introduction riff past him. It was four bars and had a swinging sound. Cecil smiled and played the chords. Earl the sax man wailed, and the bass man played a descending line. Willie joined in with a solid backbeat. "Yeah!" he shouted.

"Gentlemen, how about it? You got one?"

"We got one." Snake Eyes patted Cecil's shoulder. "Cecilio, count us offio."

"Rolling!" Hank shouted from the booth.

Cecil got to "three" and the sax riff kicked in. Willie locked into a loping rhythm and the bass man caught it quick. They did the opening bit twice because it felt so good. Cecil nodded to Snake Eyes. He stepped up to the mic and half-sung, half-spoke, in his signature style:

*I go to work down at the grocery store…and ev'ry morning when I blow through that door…*

◊◊◊

They did three takes of "A Slob with a Job." One was too long to release. Earl kept blowing and everyone caught a ride. "We could put that one out as an instrumental," Hank said from the other side of the room. "Once more, gents, and keep it tight."

The third take was the keeper. Snake Eyes was solid in the zone. He tossed off Cecil's lines with a flippancy that touched on anger and betrayal. Snake Eyes knew what those words were about. They were about eating shit and asking for seconds. Most singers would have played up the anger, but Snake Eyes turned it inside out, especially on the third verse, which he punctuated with a satisfied chuckle after the words "I'd like to tell him…"

Cecil's piano playing got better with each take. He felt confident and pushed past his usual wooden performance. He pounded triplets with his left hand and echoed Earl's riff with his right. He joined in singing on the phrases that countered the lead singer's lines. How Willie and Junior the bass man could sing and play at the same time was wild. Cecil filled in the third harmony part by ear. Some notes were raw, but that added to the good feeling of the

46

song.

The third take came in at two minutes and forty-four seconds. "Perfect," Hank said. He walked into the center of the studio. "That's a hit, my friends. Now let's get the other side. What you got?"

Snake Eyes and Earl, the saxophonist, had worked up a duet about two old friends arguing over a girl who clearly wasn't worth the fuss. It was three chords and gave Earl room to blow. They did it in E, which was a tough key for the piano, but Cecil stayed put and pounded the chords. He came up with a piano figure, noodling in the rehearsal, that Snake Eyes liked enough to keep on the recording. "She Is—She Ain't" was a B-side for sure; an amiable goof that people might play by accident. "Slob with a Job" had something solid—from Snake Eyes' knowing vocal to the solid harmony singing on the chorus to Willie's battery at the end, punctuated by a low honk from Earl.

They were done by 10. They could have kept going, but Hank felt like he was in enough hot water. *Quit while we're ahead,* he said to himself. Earl and Junior wanted to do some instrumentals, and Hank talked with them for a few minutes. What they had in mind sounded more like modern jazz than jukebox stuff. He invited them to come in with Willie and see what they could cook up.

Before the band cats left, Hank made sure he had their current address. He always sent his artists two copies of each record. They made it; the record would be blank without them. That also let them know the record was out.

"Hi, Cecil." Chuck Honeycutt's nice, kind voice startled him. Cec was still in his head, still swimming that disbelief that he had got his song cut and played on the session. "Man, you sure can write 'em. That's one funny song."

"I'm, ah, I'm glad you liked it."

"I'll bet you got a hit there. I hope so." Chuck said goodnight to Hank and whistled Earl's riff as he walked off. It *was* catchy. Maybe before long a lot more people would whistle it, sing it, buy the record…

"You like a ride, Cec?"

"I-I-I would. Thank you."

"Congratulations, my friend. We've got a hot one here. I can't wait to get this out." In the morning, Hank would send the master tape to Nashville where a real studio would go through the steps to make the stampers. That would take two weeks unless Hank could afford a rush job. When the box showed up, Cecil and Hank would do an all-nighter to get promotional copies pressed. Miss Tinkle would pack up the boxes and Cecil's song would be out in the world. After that, anything could happen.

"Hank, I got to ask a favor. I hope you don't mind."

"Mind? I owe you, my friend. You brought in a real winner tonight!"

Cecil gestured to his shoes. "I can't hardly walk in these no more. Hurts my feet." He turned one shoe up to show the stub of a heel and the oval pattern of wear on the ball of the shoe.

"Oh, Lord. My feet hurt just lookin' at that, Cec. What size do you take?"

"I could do with a 10, 10 ½…"

Hank looked at his watch. "You come by tomorrow and I'll drop what I'm doin'. We'll get you a good pair of shoes. You deserve it. And I'll give you a lift home right now. You can throw them old things out."

"I 'preciate it."

"It's an advance on your royalties. And you're gonna get 'em on this song. I will eat my shirt if it doesn't get to #1."

◊◊◊

On the ride home, Hank chattered about anything that came to mind. That meant he was excited. He might not close his eyes tonight. He'd been taking those little white pills and washing them down with coffee and Coke.

First thing in the morning, he'd be on the phone, cutting a deal, pushing a record that wasn't even made yet. He'd get Chuck to run off some acetates for Dixie and other DJs who were Hive-friendly. Dixie would be playing "A Slob with a Job" tomorrow afternoon. He'd take to it—he loved funny songs.

Cecil knew Hank was talking a blue streak—about weather, baseball, movies, his children, his wife, his belief in the company. Cecil caught the pauses and dropped in an "uh huh" or a chuckle. But his own mind talked about this new song, and how this record could be the one that changed his life. He'd have a new pair of shoes tomorrow and hear his song played on the radio by a white man who would whoop it up and have white kids calling in to hear it again.

*I might not close **my** eyes tonight*, Cecil thought. But he felt tired—the good kind of exhaustion from a big event. In the quiet of his shack, with Coaxial passed out beside him, he'd sleep like a bag of rocks. That's what his momma called it. She said his daddy slept like a bag of rocks. She had to splash cold water on him to get him up.

Cecil tried to recall his father's face. He got a general picture, but it looked the way things did when he didn't have his glasses on. The outlines fuzzed and the features ran together. He would recognize him if he saw him, but it would take a minute. He might be dead or in jail. It wasn't likely Cecil would ever find out. He had to let that go. Just as he had to let his mother go. He went to that graveyard a couple of times. He walked those rows of dead bodies. Some had a little tin cross or a brick to mark them for somebody's sake. Cecil considered those rows and felt like he was dying.

What hurt most was that no one thought to tell him. If he was a white serviceman, he'd have gotten a telegram and some time off to tend to her funeral. But he wasn't, and she was just bones in the ground, never to be seen or remembered again. Cecil wasn't ready for her to be gone. Sometimes the thought of her passing gave him a deep grief.

He couldn't cry. If he really felt bad, the corners of his eyes would get a little wet and his nose would run. That was it. He saw people who cried like a fire hose. He wondered what that felt like. To get that out of your system and off your chest. He knew when something was sad, but it stopped on its way up to his eyes and never got past his throat. If he ever started crying, lord knows if he'd be able to stop. It was better to dam up those tears. Shore 'em up and keep 'em down.

Cecil fell asleep without knowing it. He slept with his clothes and his ratty old shoes on. Coaxial got after him for some breakfast—chirping and purring in his ear. Cecil woke with a start. The sun was out. He sat up with a heavy head. He guessed it to be at least 10:00. On automatic pilot, he got to the kitchen and dumped a can of Kozy Kitten cat food onto a saucer. The cat loved it. The smell turned Cecil's stomach, but Coaxial's chomp and growl assured him it was a feline feast.

He remembered about the new shoes. And that got him thinking about the money in the mason jars under the porch. He could spend some of that money on shoes. But it would mean a lot to Mr. Howard to buy him a pair. Like he was providing for Cecil, giving them as a tribute. It was a kind gesture, and he might as well accept it.

He found one of the jars and brought it inside. He had 116 dollars rolled up inside, all ones and fives. He took out 20 and put the jar on the shelf above the sink. He made sure it was behind other things and couldn't be seen. There was no reason for anyone to come up here—or even know there was a shack on this hill. There was no hunting here, no lake or park or anything that would make a stranger curious. Just trees and dirt and overgrowth. It suited his needs.

Cecil gave himself what his mother called a sparrow bath at the kitchen sink. He took off his clothes and scrubbed himself down with a wet washrag and soap. The cat stared at him and then groomed himself. "We both on the same wave length," Cecil said. He washed off the grime and sweat and felt clean enough. It was too much trouble to run the bathtub. He saved that for when he could soak in the hot water and relax. It took an hour to fill up the tub. He wanted those shoes.

He dressed and put on those nasty, worn old shoes for the last time. He'd had them for nearly two years and worn them every day. They were headed for a garbage can. He couldn't count the miles they'd put in. He thought about getting some new trousers and a new shirt. If he was a success he should look the part. He hesitated and then got another 20 from the mason jar. The black clothing store would give him a break; he wouldn't ask for it, but they'd always knock a few dollars off.

"Maybe all of this going in the trash," he said out loud. He looked for the cat and spotted him on the wrinkled bed. Coaxial was asleep on his back, sprawled in a display of comfort. Cecil smiled and headed out.

***Hank Howard had not slept.*** He never could after a good recording session. He was sure this song about the slob with a job was going places. That was a hit record, and he debated with himself. Should he lease it to Cross? Should he put it out on Hive? Was it too big for Hive? How could he make Hive big enough for the kind of hits he daydreamed about having?

He felt jittery and hot under the sheets. Virginia slept like a bag of rocks next to him. The house was quiet. He could hear if one of the kids stirred in their bed or mumbled in their sleep. His mind raced and he felt his heart beating like a drum.

*I gotta calm down. Gotta get ahold of myself. A man's gotta rest.*

He tried a trick he'd learned in the service. He listened for a consistent sound and focused on it. The chirping of the frogs and crickets outside never seemed to stop. He closed his eyes and put his arm over his forehead and listened. The crickets were like the rhythm section, right on the beat and constant. The frogs were like a vocal harmony group, with different voices and parts. They were distracting because they didn't stick to a set thing. A low-voiced frog did one long note when he felt like it. The high-voiced frogs sang on, off and around the beat. They were like jazz musicians improvising. And the rest of the frogs droned along, mostly in sync with the crickets. They would sometimes skip a beat, like they stumbled over it.

*Everything comes down to music, man. That is the one true language. It speaks to everybody. Only a deaf man can't recognize its tongue. Even then, they can feel the vibration of it.*

This thought brought Hank joy and kept him up through the dawn, when Virginia's alarm went off. Kitty heard that and she padded into the bedroom. "Mornig, Momma."

"Morning," Virginia said. She sounded weary.

"'Mornig'?" Hank sat up. "That's a new one." Kitty beamed. Hank was surprised how alert and good he felt. He stayed in bed as Liz fed the children and thought, thought, thought. He had ideas on how to market his records, how to build up his artists—and how to get them into the white pop market. He recalled a jumble of ideas in the light of day. They were such good ideas that they were bound to come back to him. He'd write them down then.

He had four cups of coffee and a bowl of Wheaties and drove Carl and Kitty to their school. Then he went to work. He was the first one there. Miss Bell came in at 9:30. Chuck showed up at 9:45.

As Hank unlocked the door, the phone was ringing. "Dangit!" His key was bent a bit and there was something wrong with the lock. He had to lift the door up by the handle and move it towards and doorframe with one hand and turn the key with the other. It took several tries as the damn phone jingled. "If it's important, they'll call back," he said to himself.

He dialed Chuck's number and got him out of bed. "We got a hit song, buddy! Come on down and cut me some acetates. We can get that on Dixie's show soon as you have one ready." Chuck agreed to get dressed and show up. Hank cradled the phone and the office felt too quiet. He turned on the radio and the voice of Kitty Wells came on. It was still early enough for the hillbilly programs to be on. Kitty Wells made him think of Maggie Woodburn. What a dumb move. His enthusiasm could get the best of him. He'd get so damned excited and lose his smarts. He had to remind himself to cool it down, think about it before he did it. He had good instincts, but those alone weren't enough. You had to have savvy behind those instincts, or you were flying blind.

Thinking about Maggie Woodburn made Hank tired—heavy tired and dead-feeling. He took out his little white pills and shook four of them into his palm. He swallowed them without water. They would kick in and take that dead feeling away. Then he could get anything done.

They kicked in. He felt full of color and decision and drive. He had to hear that hit song again. He knew it was a big song last night. He had heard it with an open mind and applied his knowledge about the market, plus his instinct about the feeling. Every good song had a feeling that anyone could relate to, if they let themselves take it in.

Hank bolted into the studio and whacked his elbow on a music stand. It hurt, but it didn't register. He navigated the drum kit and the folding chairs and opened the booth door. He popped on the lights and surveyed the engineer's board. Chuck had last night's tape boxes lined up, ready for army inspection. He labeled the boxes with artist name, song title and the takes of each song, with the best one circled in red.

Hank warmed up the reel-to-reel set, threaded the tape and made sure to hit only PLAY, not RECORD. He saw that the tape was smooth and clean as it moved along.

He turned the studio speakers up full blast and soaked up the raw, pure sounds. Heard the sax man blow his head off on the long version; heard Cecil's piano playing—timid on this first take, then more assured on the second and third. Snake Eyes painted a picture in the way he sang and spoke the words of Cecil's song. And those words. Cecil had suffered! Hank could feel that down to his bones. Cecil had known misery and worry a thousand times worse than any white man. Hank tried to imagine that much worry. He was in hock up to his chin, with a record company mostly in the red, no line of credit, everything cash on the barrelhead, but that was nothing. At least he could do those things! How would a guy like Cecil—smart and reserved and sensitive—get to where he had gotten? Not by the color of his skin. *There but for pigment,* Hank thought. *It's a damn shame.*

His rumination turned to glee as the final version of "Slob with a Job" started up. Those men were tight as a drum. Listen to that sax! And those drum fills leading into the chorus! Cecil's piano sounded free and sprightly. And lay on top of that Snake Eyes with his sly put-on of a voice…this was real! This was electrifying! And it was funny as hell! "Funny as hell!" Hank shouted out loud. The words of the song and the way Snake Eyes got them cold… he put on those words like a Sunday suit of clothes.

Hank didn't realize he was singing out loud as the final chorus started. Singing and clapping his hands, lost in the sound and the feeling. The song ended and he heard applause. It took him off cloud nine. Chuck had that look—that *Hank's gone nuts* expression. It made Hank laugh. "Mis-ter *Honeycutt*! I was just making sure we had us a hit!"

"What's the verdict?"

"We have us a **hit**!" Hank banged his knuckle on a cymbal to emphasize his excitement. He became aware of the pain in his knuckles as the metallic tang decayed in his ears. "Make us up six—no, ten. Ten of that third take. Let's get this ball rolling!"

Miss Tinkle was at work. The morning mail had come. While she fielded phone calls, she opened Hank's correspondence and bills, sorted them into piles and sipped at her coffee. *She's a force of nature,* Hank thought.

"Any checks in there?"

Miss Tinkle jumped. "Law, you scared me, Mr. Howard!"

"My apologies. Anything good?"

There was. Cross Records had coughed up a year's worth of royalties and sent an advance for another Lonesome Shadow session. Folded over the check, which exceeded $1,000, was a handwritten note on Vincent Cross' stationary: *Call me when you receive this. Would like to discuss a long-playing record for this artist. Would like new tracks for a single as well.*

A box contained six copies of The Shadow's record "'Lectric Chair." Three would go to Shadow along with the cash payout of his royalties. The other three Hank would file away just in case.

These long-playing records were a coming thing. *Cash Box* had articles every issue about how retailers and labels were making way for these 12-inch discs. They could hold over a half hour of music and were less prone to damage or breakage.

Filling up a long-player wouldn't be hard. He had eight titles on The Shadow, plus an out-take that was held back due to its length. It went for over six minutes. That would fit on an LP. Why, it'd make a great closing track. It was a tour de force for Shadow's harmonica work. He took four choruses with that blues harp taped to a microphone. It got a nasty, distorted sound that could peel paint off the walls. What a finale!

That took care of two more tracks' space. Two new songs and they'd have an album. Hank wasn't sure if the black music audience would buy an LP. Like country, it was a singles market. Far as he knew, you couldn't play a 12-inch record on the jukes. It was a gamble, but all that Hank needed was the Shadow to do a session. They could try out songs that wouldn't be so commercial. Not that The Shadow was commercial. He was The Shadow; he was a force of nature—

"Miss Bell, remind me in half an hour to call Cross Records. No matter what I'm doing."

She nodded and went back to her sorting. Hank walked through the studio to the booth in back. Chuck had the Scully machine on. It was really a two-man job, but there wasn't elbow room by the record cutter. The machine put Hank in debt to purchase, but it had paid for itself as a mobile recording device. Chuck and Hank had recorded hours of after-dinner testimonials, wedding and funeral services and political speeches. The trick with those was not to fall asleep at the wheel. Some people could drone on and on and never get to the point.

Chuck looked perturbed. "I am sorry to get you here so early, buddy, but once we get this on Dixie's program, he will play it like mad and they'll hear that signal from here to Texas up to Maine. And people will want to buy this record!"

"You could get me a coffee from Jolly's," Chuck replied.

Hank patted him on the shoulder. "Coming right up, pardner. And what would you think about a record album? One of those 12-inch affairs?"

"I would not wanna think about that this mornin'."

"Okay." Hank shook his head in amusement. He patted his coat pocket; the wallet was there. He walked past Miss Tinkle's desk—he must remember never to call her that!—and said "Be right back." And he walked smack into Cecil Madison. "Oh no! You okay, Cec?"

Cecil nodded. His glasses were askew, but no harm was done. "I came for the shoes."

"The shoes."

"The new pair of shoes. From last night."

Hank had to shuffle through his memories. "Oh! Oh yeah! C'mon with me to Jolly's. I got to get Chuck his coffee. We're gettin' set to cut an acetate of your song. For Dixie's show."

"I though it turned out pretty good."

"Pretty good? Brother, it's a stone-cold hit! I can feel it in my bones. Snake Eyes did a terrific performance. And whoever wrote that song, why he was pretty good, too. He shows promise."

That got a grin out of Cecil. Hank laughed. "Say, I might have a job for you. You heard The Shadow? Lonesome Shadow?"

"Mm hm." Cecil's one encounter with The Shadow was uncomfortable. The man outsized him by 100 pounds. His presence made Cecil feel the way his father did when he was a kid. Looming and moody and silent.

"And you know about these new long-playing records? Albums, they call 'em. Twelve inches, 12 songs."

"I've seen 'em. Gansser's has 'em."

"I don't think Gansser's is gonna carry this one. Cross Records wants an album on The Shadow. We need two songs. Do you think you could write a blues? A real low-down blues song?"

They entered Jolly's. Daytimes he had Clara, a little wrinkled chain-smoking sparrow behind the counter and register. "Two coffees, Clara." He turned to Cecil. "How 'bout for you?"

"I could drink a coffee."

"Three, dear." She poured hot coffee from the tureen into three cardboard tubes. Hank gave her a half dollar and she put the coffees in a cardboard tray. Cecil felt obliged to carry the coffees. He was getting coffee, shoes and another song out of it.

"I could write that song."

"Huh?"

"For The Shadow. I could come up with a song."

"It doesn't have to be real commercial. You can take it anywhere you please. Just keep it clean!"

"My songs are always clean."

"I wasn't sayin' they weren't. That was a joke."

"Oh." They walked in silence.

*I must be having an off day,* Hank thought. *I don't feel bad. Sometimes the wavelengths ain't right. You're broadcasting, but the signal ain't workin'…*

Hank held the door for Cecil. "Coffee comin' through," he said in his most personable voice. "Let's run this back to Chuck. He's needin' it today."

Chuck had his back to the door. Hank could see that through the tinted window. He had headphones on, and he leaned over the record lathe, sweeping off the curlicues the cutting needle left behind. He couldn't see how far through the record Chuck was. "Let's wait. Genius at work."

That wasn't a joke. Chuck understood electronics and how all these devices worked together to get the sounds onto tape and record. He could take the tape deck apart and put it right back together. Hank could change a lightbulb and open a tin can and that was about it. His strength was his ear and his instinct. That made them valuable to each other. And Cecil...well, Cecil gave the whole affair balance. If Cecil didn't like something, then Hank knew his own thinking was off. If he liked something, it was a sure-fire bet that the market would support it. *We're like a see-saw*, Hank thought.

He took a sip of hot coffee, flavored with the acidic note of cardboard. It was too hot, and hurt his tongue, but he swallowed. It felt good doing down, like good news when you really needed to hear it.

Chuck took off his headphones and lifted the needle from the record surface. He brushed the shiny brown surface with a soft flat paintbrush. Hank tapped on the window. "Coffee!"

"Thank God!" Chuck took off the top and sipped. "How many of these do we need?"

"Half a dozen. I want to mail 'em to some of the jocks who like our stuff. They'll get the ball rollin'. We'll need two for Dixie. So—eight."

"You wanna hear the record?"

"You bet." Chuck gentled the disc off the lathe and onto the studio turntable. As the introduction bopped along, Chuck came out to join his partners. Cecil was fascinated. He noted that they put a little reverb on Snake Eyes' vocal, but the band sounded dry. That little touch helped Snake Eyes' laconic voice stand out above the piano, sax, guitar and bass. When Snake Eyes hit a hard consonant, at the end of a phrase, you could hear the echo. It really gave it impact.

Cecil remembered how it sounded as they performed the song. You heard everything all over the room in person, and some of it was swallowed up, dampened or dulled. On this record, everything was in balance, crisp and clear. It all grooved together. It was an idealized version of that moment, captured for as long as the records would be played and heard.

"Wow!" Hank shouted at the end. "Double wow! Chuck, that sounds like a million bucks! Dixie is gonna *need* two copies of this one. He'll wear the first one out by tonight!" Chuck, happy now, retreated to the booth to make another acetate. "Cecil, would you mind running the records over to Dixie? Just tell the receptionist you're from Hive Records. Tell Dixie you've got a natural born hit—and he's the first jockey to play it!"

"And then my shoes?"

Hank smacked his own forehead. "The shoes! By God, we're gonna get you those shoes. I have a big phone call, and then we'll get some lunch…and your shoes!"

Cecil nodded. Nothing ever happened in an orderly way with Hank. He eeled his way through life. That was just his style. Cecil liked to have things happen straightforward. No sideways moves, no curve balls. *We're all different*, he thought.

◊◊◊

Half an hour later, Cecil entered the lobby of WELO. He felt ashamed of his shabby clothes and remembered the 40 dollars in his pocket. He would take care of that next thing. There was no reason for a grown man to go around looking like he did.

The receptionist was made up like a circus clown and had a curvy mound of auburn hair. "I'm, uh. I'm here from Hive Records. For Mr. Hank Howard. He said to tell Mr. Dixie that I had a natural-born hit record for him." He showed the acetate discs in their green paper sleeves.

"He's doin' his mornin' show, but you can go on back there. Just wait 'til he stops tawkin'." Cecil nodded and pushed a little wooden gate aside. He didn't need directions. He heard Dixie Doodle's rapid-fire patter, punched up with shrieks, whoops and mad laughs. He talked a new record by The Midnighters on the air. Through a window, Cecil waited to catch his attention. Dixie looked up, sweaty and frozen, like a deer in the headlights.

Cecil held up the records and smiled.

"You got some'n for me, son?"

"Yes'r. I'm from Hive Records, and Mr. Howard sent me right over. This is the new record by Snake Eyes. Hank says it's a…"

"'…a natchel-bawn hit!'" Dixie cackled. "They all are, hear him tawk about it. What's the song?"

"Huh?"

"The name of the song, son?"

"Oh. It's 'A Slob with a Job.'"

Dixie laughed. "A slob with a *whut?*"

"A job. Y'know, like work… an occupation!"

"Damn if that ain't a *funny* title. That's right clever! Who thought *that* one up?"

"Um…I did, sir."

Dixie did a double take. "My goodness! You got a few minutes? I wanna do somethin' special here!"

The Midnighters record finished and Dixie took the mike. "'Work with Me, Annie!' Brothers an' sisters, I could use me a helpin' o' *that* kyna work!" He guffawed. "Nice work 'f you c'n git it! Right now, hold y'all's horses, 'cos we got somethin' special for y'all right here, right now! You gonna be the fu'st people in all the world t' hear a brand-new record from our buddies over to Hive Records. An' I got the man what wrote the song right here in the studio!" He motioned for Cecil to step over the threshold into the studio. "This young feller's name is…" Dixie held the mike up to Cecil's face.

"Uh…Cecil? Cecil Madison?"

"Well, Cecil, y'all come on in heah an' sit down an' visit with us! So you a songwriter, huh, Cecil?"

"Yess'r."

"Is this your first song?"

"No s'r, I have a couple of 'em out there. Y-you know 'Decline and Fall?'"

Dixie cackled. "*Do* I? Do we know that *record?* Why, that was our number one record for three weeks runnin'! It's a big hit all over the country. An' you wrote it!"

"Yess'r, wrote it myself."

"Y'know, mos' people might think the singers, why, they must make their songs up on the spot. But that ain't the case at all, is it?"

Cecil laughed. "No s'r. Like me, they have to sit down and think 'em out. Sometimes you get the words goin' and a tune'll come to you. Or you got a good tune and you have to work to fit the right words to it. It's a lot more thinkin'… and walkin' around, you know. Just rollin' the words over an' over in your head. It's like solvin' a puzzle. You got to get everything in the right place."

"Now, 'Decline an' Fall' was what you might call a *humorous* song. What's th' word? Eye-*ronic*. Would you say that's about right?"

"Yess'r. That'd describe it."

"So how about this new one? What's it called again?"

Cecil cleared his throat. "It's called 'A Slob with a Job.' It's about a guy who doesn't like his job. But maybe someday he'll do better for hisself."

"Well, let us have a lissen. 'Case you're just tunin' in, kids, we got ourselves a bran' new record. This ain't even released yet!"

"No s'r. This is a special for your show."

Dixie howled with glee. "I got mahse'f a dad-burn *exclusive*! This is, uh…" He struggled to read Chuck's hasty handwriting. "Snake Eyes. He's a character, folks. An' here he is with his new song, 'A Slob with a Job.'"

Dixie dropped the needle on the acetate and switched off his microphone. The full force of Snake Eyes' combo rocked the broadcast chamber. Right away, Dixie snapped his fingers and stomped his feet and clapped in time to the song. It was like he was absorbing it rather than hearing it. During the sax break, Dixie popped on the mike to shout, "Blow man *blow*!" He let out a yell like a couple of cats in a fight. He was lost in the performance. Here was a white man who loved what he heard. He got it. Cecil felt a sense of hope as the record reached its climax.

"Ho-lee *cow*! What a *record*! You wanna hear that again? You give ol' Dixie a call at WELO. I'm tellin' you we got us a big fat *hit* here! So, Cecil. How you come up this song? What, uh, what inspired you?"

"Well, everybody's had them a job they didn't like. But they had to put up with it. They needed the money. An' I had a job just like that, back a few years, an' I was thinkin' about it an' the words came out faster than I could write 'em down."

"Well, sir, I may be just a slob with a job, but it's my job to tell you that this is gonna be *big*! Big, big, *big*!"

"Thank you, Mr, Dixie. I'm glad you like it."

"*Like* it? Why, I *love* it! And you gonna *love* these words from a whole buncha sponsors whose stuff you oughta go out an' buy. Take 'er away, Ernie!"

Dixie silenced his mike. In another studio, an announcer read off spiels about a drive-in restaurant and a used car lot.

Dixie took a fifth of whiskey from under his desk, uncorked it and took a swig. "That'll do 'er." He turned to Cecil with watery, bloodshot eyes. Cecil felt fright and his muscles tensed. Then Dixie smiled. "Son, I wanna shake your hand." They shook. "'N I wanna tell you...you are in the right bidness. You bring me anything you come up with an' I'll play it."

The receptionist tapped on the glass. Cecil stood up and opened the door. "I...I was just leavin'..."

"Dixie, we've gotten 20 calls. That record you just played. A swab with a mob? They all wanted to hear it again."

Dixie clapped his hands and cackled at the receptionist. "'A swab with a mob!' You kill me, Gracie."

Cecil smiled. "We, uh, brought you two copies. Just in case."

"You tell ol' Hank he better get this one out on the double. He can sell these by the truckload!"

◊◊◊

Cecil felt the muggy heat of mid-day. He daubed the sweat off the back of his neck with an old rag from his pocket. He realized he felt good. Happy. He almost never felt this way. Life had trained him to wait for the other shoe to drop. It took him a minute to realize how good the world seemed and how happy he was. There was a lot wrong with the world, but a moment like that made everything look better and brighter.

As he turned the corner to the street where Hive did its business, he heard his song blasting out of a car radio. It was a blue Plymouth parked by a fire hydrant. Inside, two white high-school kids sat and listened. One of the boys looked like a peacock, with his yellow hair piled high on his head and gaudy clothers. Cecil couldn't help but stare, and the boy returned his gaze. "What *you* lookin' at, *nigger?*"

Cecil showed no reaction as the boys whooped and laughed.

The world went back to how it always was. That high was gone. It never lasted more than a few minutes.

Cecil felt like a Christmas ornament fallen to the floor. Shards of glass.

He stood still under the shade of a store awning. His heart pounded. He held his breath to try and slow it down. He felt a burning in his chest and his heart got down to normal. As he waited, he thought. Why was it that people couldn't get along, and just accept one another? Why did one set of people always have to call themselves better than everyone else? Wouldn't it be better for everyone to just get along and let each other be? Why can't mankind make that decision and stick to it?

*It isn't that simple*, he told himself. *Else, we'd already by doing it.* If there was an answer, it was somewhere up in the stars, hidden where mankind couldn't get their filthy hands on it. *I'd like to feel like this was my world. Not a place where I took up space. Where I was tolerated.* That was an ugly word, *tolerance*. It meant that someone bore up a burden to allow another person in their presence. It was a bother, not a pleasure. It only meant *to put up with*, not to *accept*. And that was as good as things were likely to get.

By the time he got back to the office, his anger and disgust had leveled off. He had to remind himself: *I was just on the radio, not an hour ago. Where they're getting requests for my song. My song and Snake Eyes' way of singing it. But without my song he wouldn't have nothing. Nothing.*

Hank had heard the interview and he was over the moon. "Cecil! What a surprise! And what a great send off for your song! Dixie's played it five times already. Your message is getting sent all over the airwaves. Who knows how many people have heard it by now?"

"Can I still get my shoes?"

"Shoes. Oh, Lord. It's been such a busy day. But yes. *Shoes.* We will go right now and—"

"Victor Cross is on the line, Mr. Howard." Miss Bell held up the phone.

"See what I *mean*? Just one damn thing after another. But it's all good." Hank smiled, but he could see Cecil was out of patience. "How much you think you'd need for some good shoes. And I mean *good* ones. Ones that won't hurt your feet or fall apart in a month."

"Twenty dollars oughta do it."

"Mr. Howard. He's on long distance." And Miss Bell whispered: "He sounds real crabby."

Hank hesitated, and then felt for his wallet. A promise was a promise.

He had to live up to his word. A 20 went into Cecil's open palm. "Come back an' show 'em off after you've got 'em. And I should have some good news for you about this album business." Hank smiled and retreated to his office. "Victor! Good to hear from you…yes, yes I got them…thank you so much…"

Cecil felt let down, like he remembered from his childhood. His father made empty promises that he forgot or reneged on. Cecil was supposed to get a bicycle for his ninth birthday. Instead, he went with his mother to the county jail. She used all the bicycle money to get his father out of the can. Nothing more was said about the bike.

Hank wasn't like that. His heart was in the right place, but he was spread too thin. He had more to pay attention to than he could handle. It would have meant a lot for Mr. Howard to go with him and pay for the shoes with his own hands. But the bottom line was a new pair of shoes, and this picture of big-headed Andrew Jackson fulfilled that promise.

Cecil went into Gannser's Department Store. It was owned and run by an old Jewish man who only saw the color of money. The men's clothing department was in the bottom floor. Cecil rode the narrow moving stairs. The smell of wool and leather hung in the warm air.

He dodged white ladies and kids and made a quick selection. He knew the shoes he wanted. They were $17.95 plus tax. They were made for laborers and were stitched and nailed together with the idea that hard use wouldn't mess them up. They had a simple, clean look and wouldn't get wet on the insides. The heels had a solid grip to them. Cecil took an 11 wide, and the salesman seemed surprised that he didn't want to try them on. "Why not walk around with 'em? Get the feel of 'em?"

"I know the feel of 'em. Thank you."

The cashiers were upstairs. Before Cecil rode up, he walked past the record department. They had a display of those long-playing albums. They had a spinning metal rack for them. Cecil picked up a few and perused the colorful covers. There was Ella Fitzgerald, Frank Sinatra, Dave Brubeck, Chet Atkins, and other big names.

One cover caught his eyes. It was called *Shorty Rogers Counts the Count*. It had bright, modern graphics like a Mr. Magoo cartoon. It held a dozen songs, like Mr. Howard said. This was the future of music. He looked the other records over. No blues and no hillbilly; just jazz and popular tunes. They weren't taking big chances yet. But someone would—maybe Mr. Howard would be the first.

Cecil paid for his shoes, said hello to Mr. Gannser, who called him Hugo, and sat on a bus bench outside. There, he took off his old shoes. Those battered, worn-down, gray things that had once been bright and new. He put his new shoes on and stood up. His feet felt good. It gave him a warm feeling to not hurt when he walked. "Thank you," he said to his old shoes before he dropped them in a trash can.

Then he walked 10 blocks to Savoy Sepia Styles, where Rusty and Snake Eyes and all those hot-shots got their threads. A friend of Cecil's from school was the manager. He got 20% off his purchase. 33 dollars and change got him a crisp white dress shirt, gabardine slacks with a stylish pleat and a suit coat that was a darker shade of the pants' grey-brown-blue. He changed out of his old clothes in the men's dressing room and chucked them in a large metal trash bin.

He studied his new look in a store mirror. The clothes fit well and made him look more important. He'd heard that saying *clothes make the man*, and never thought it meant much. In these new duds he felt more important and confident. It felt like he had cast off something of his old self when those old rags went in the trash. Cecil would make sure he kept himself up. He would hang these up and brush them and take good care of them. And he'd buy more clothes, so he'd never wear one pair of pants down to the shine or have to wear a shirt with a hole in the sleeve.

That was the way of the sad Cecil who went around looking like a hobo. That Cecil let the world walk all over him. This Cecil Madison would look out for himself and test the world around him and let them know he meant business. He was a successful songwriter now, part of a growing business that was sure to take off and give him a better place in the world.

◊◊◊

While Cecil changed his image, and shed some of his old self, Hank Howard negotiated with Victor Cross, a stern and humorless Polish man. Victor hated small talk. It pained him to say more than was needed. A discussion with Victor had many silences, and Hank had learned to respect them. Victor took his time to think about things. His decisions were cast in stone.

Hank cut to the chase. He had nine masters in the can for Lonesome Shadow. One of them was the length of two regular songs, so it counted as two. That left two new songs to record. He had his best songwriter working on a number for The Shadow, maybe two. He'd get Shadow into the studio as soon as possible.

The album would sell, with four hit singles on it. 66.667% proven material and 33.333% new music. Hank wanted to make a joke about how right that was, since these new records played at 33 1/3 RPM. With anyone else, he would've made it. With Victor Cross, he stressed that the bulk of the album was recorded. And getting two new tracks would be easily done.

Now came the hardball. Since this was a new format, it called for new lease fees for each of the album's tracks. The tracks would have to be re-mastered for the long-play version. The booming, bottom-heavy sound of the 45 and 78 RPM masters would make the tonearms jump off the LP. Hank would have Mister Honeycutt redo the masters and have lacquers made.

Hank grabbed the sum of $3000.00 out of the air. He spoke it over the phone. There was silence. More than usual for Victor. *I've gone too far*, he thought. *You big idiot—*

"Fine." Silence.

*Shoulda asked for more*, Hank thought.

"Are there any other conditions?"

Hank had none but made one up. "Yes. The two new tracks cannot be issued as singles. Not in any format on 45 or 78 speeds. They will be exclusive to this long-play album."

*Now I'm gilding the lily...*

"Agreed. And you will have Mr. Butts record a new single for us at this session. *Those* tracks are not to appear on the long-play album." Cross mimicked Hank's way of saying *long-play album*, with the o in *long* drawn out.

"We have ourselves a deal, sir. I'll have my attorney draw up a contract and I'll get word to Mr. Butts."

"We will need a photograph of him for the cover. You might consider having that done at the session."

"Say, that's a good idea. Show him in the studio, with his guitar and the microphone and all."

"That is what is needed." Victor hung up after that. Goodbyes were not his métier. But a deal was set, and Hank didn't feel torn into several pieces. He

65

exhaled and let himself relax. He felt like he could close his eyes and drift away there in his office chair…

"Huey Griggs on the phone for you, Mr. Howard." Miss Bell opened Hank's office door. She knew he didn't want to take another call, but Huey was an old friend. You didn't say no to an old buddy. "*Mis*-ter *Griggs*! How are you?"

Skinny Griggs made the 98 lb. weakling in the comic books look fat. He worried himself to skin and bones. He ran his own record company. Uranus Records caught the overflow of the blues and hillbilly talent Hive couldn't (or wouldn't) use. His studio was in his garage, and his records sounded like amateur hour. He'd gotten a freak country hit—#2 on the national charts—with a high, lonesome-voiced kid called Lefty Willis who worked at a sawmill. "Moonbeams" came out of nowhere and, in its rise up the charts, fought off four competing versions. Georgia Gibbs covered it for the pop market and Varetta Dillard did a sepia version. Lefty raked in terrific royalties and Columbia Records snatched him up. Lefty hadn't signed a contract with Uranus, so he was free to walk. Columbia put out two singles, didn't promote them, and within a year Lefty was back at the sawmill, his head still swimming from the blows fate delivered.

Skinny? He'd gotten screwed, as all independent labels do, by bootleggers and DJ bribes, but he'd still cleared several thousand bucks on the record. He put that money into new equipment for his facilities. His records now sounded like better crap.

"Hank, I hope I ain't botherin' you, 'cos I know you're a busy man an' all…"

"I always have time for you."

"Well, or'narily I wouldn't bother you, 'cos of you bein' so busy an' all, but I got this young feller in here the other night…he was somethin' different."

"How so?"

"This white kid with yeller hair. Handsome fellow. Couldn't be 20. Well, he sings the blues like you never heard." Skinny chuckled. "It's like another voice is comin' outta his mouth. It don't sync up, but this kid's got somethin'. I couldn't do nothin' with it. I'm too small potatoes. But, boy, if you'd let him audition, man, I bet you could get some action on him. He's…it ain't hillbilly, it ain't blues…it ain't even pop. Hell, you'd hafta make up a new name

66

for it!"

"Hmm!" This sounded different. Enough to make Hank curious. "You didn't happen to do any takes on him, did you?"

"Yess'r, I did. He was wantin' to hear what does his voice sound like on a record. I thought of you 'cos one of the songs he sung was that 'Decline an' Fall.' Man, it's somethin' diff'rent!"

"Can I drop over and take a listen? You busy right now?"

"You come on over. I'm curious what you might think of 'im. Name's Cottner." Skinny reached for a note he'd scribbled down. "*Cam* Cottner. I guess that's short for somethin'.'"

"I'll drop by in just a bit. I got one thing to take care of here, an' then…"

Skinny signed off. *This could be anything*, Hank thought. *Probably a big bunch of nothing. Some kid who thinks he's tough.* But Hank had heard all the stories about people who'd passed on a talent that became huge and rued the day thereafter. Half an hour would tell him yea or nay.

◊◊◊

Cecil bought the *Daily Journal* on his way back to Hive headquarters. He hadn't been keeping up with the world, and it seemed important. He read as he walked. Eisenhower was still president, and the Communists were still making trouble in their part of the world. Nothing jumped out at him as being a big deal.

At the bottom of page four was a small item about two black high school students who had been found dead hanging from an old oak tree. They had made the mistake of going where they weren't meant to go. There were no suspects and no arrest in the works. The article skirted the horror of the story; it was neutral. This was—or should be—important news. Something like this wasn't supposed to happen to people anymore. This was 1954. The world was supposed to be smarter and bigger and more accepting. Except that it wasn't.

*This could be me*, Cecil thought. *This could still be any of us. One wrong move. In the wrong place at the wrong time.* The idea chilled Cecil. It was part of the ugly side of life that Cecil and people like him were supposed to not think about. They were supposed to do their work and raise their families and walk extra careful so they didn't find themselves out in some field in the middle of the night. It was a thought you had to block out or you'd never get out of bed in the morning.

Maybe the *Daily Journal* didn't want to worry its black readers. They knew it was news, and that they had to report it, but they buried it so you had to be looking to see it. It was one column of type on the bottom of the page, in-between an ad for Holsum Bread and an *everything-must-go* announcement from a furniture store. It was no more important to them.

Cecil folded the paper and tucked it under his armpit. Better not to dwell on it like this.

◊◊◊

"Holy cow!" Hank exclaimed. Cecil's new attire stopped him in his tracks.

Cecil had forgotten about his new clothes. Then it came to him. He smiled. "You like it?"

"Wow, Cec! What a difference!"

"I was lookin' like something the cat dragged in. It was time to spruce up a little."

"Wow! Hey, I got just the thing to complete your new look. Hang on!" Hank rummaged in his office and emerged bearing a silk necktie. It was a burnt orange-green shade that agreed with the coat and pants. "That looks just right! I never had any jacket that went with that color. On you, it looks good!"

Cecil accepted the gift. This was meaningful. He knotted the tie and buttoned his collar. "What you think?"

"Suave, Mister Madison. Suave. Say, I'm takin' a run out to Skinny Griggs. This might interest you."

Cecil shrugged. Why not? "Let's go."

On the way, Hank kept remarking on Cecil's wardrobe. Cecil thought he seemed pleased and impressed. Maybe *too* pleased and *too* impressed. But it had an effect on him.

They stopped for Cokes along the way. Hank tried to describe what Skinny had told him. "So it's some white guy who thinks he's black?"

"I guess so."

"Sounds ridiculous to me."

"Maybe. But what if it's good? What if this kid could build a bridge?"

"He's an engineer or something?"

"No, no. I'm talking about…a *bridge*."

*Here comes the sermon*, Cecil thought. Hank had delivered this speech many times. Cecil agreed with him. But he had to let him speak his piece.

"It's the only thing that can build a bridge. Music can do that. It's the universal language. Everyone gets it. Unless they're deaf. And then they can still feel the vibrations of it. So, it gets to everyone in some way. And what I wanna do is to help build that bridge. Because once that bridge is built, everyone is gonna see. Everyone is gonna realize that down deep, we're all the same. We're different in some ways. But we're all the same under our skin. We all gotta eat, have water, sleep at night. And music can bring that message home. And it can make us all proud that we come from different places."

Hank stopped to finish his Coke. "Hell, Cecil, I thought about becomin' a minister when I was your age. I really felt like I had the calling. But I got impatient. You know, in anything like that, they lay out all these damn hoops you got to jump through. And you got to jump through 'em in the right order, or you don't get anywhere. I couldn't take that. I guess I had to make my own hoops. You get what I'm sayin'?"

Cecil nodded. He started to speak, but he was too slow.

"So, this is my ministry. I am spreading the gospel of the word of Negro music. I am showing that it's for everyone who has an ear to listen. And a heart to feel. I am preaching the gospel of sheer…music. And how it gets into all of us. From the time we're born. From the first song we hear. It's inside us, Cecil. It's deep inside us. It's…it's a river that flows right through us all."

"I agree."

They had driven past Fernwood, the street they needed. Hank did a U-turn in someone's driveway and backtracked. Griggs' studio took up all his garage space. His 1948 Dodge sat in the front yard. Skinny had the garage door open. Anyone who drove by might think he was puttering in his shop.

Uranus Records had no sign—nothing to ID it as a business. Skinny cleaned the recording heads on his tape deck. It was newer than the one Hank had at Hive. He felt envious, but he knew Skinny would give up and have a fire sale. "Mis-ter Griggs. It is I!"

Skinny startled and banged his head on part of the garage door. "You got a way of sneakin' up on someone."

"I've brought my business partner Cecil with me. He composed that song you told me about."

Skinny assessed him and nodded to himself. *That'll do.* "Well, wait 'til you hear this kid sing it. He's diff'rent all right. Where'd I put that reel…"

Hank could have driven his car around the block five times while Skinny sifted through tape boxes. He felt sweat trickle down the middle of his back and pool in his underwear. Sweat sparkled on Cecil's forehead.

"Here we go. Yawl come on in here. I gotta close the hatch."

Hank and Cecil ducked under the garage door and huddled. Skinny yanked the door down. It didn't quite close. "Good enough. Awrighty. Tell me what ya thinka this."

He started the tape. An acoustic guitar strummed a few chords. Skinny spoke: "Now, you step up t' here. An' let's…" An echoey scrape and scoot sounded as the microphone stand was positioned. "Just sang right inta there. That center. The little circle."

A younger voice spoke: "Would y'mind, sir, lookin' away after you get 'er rollin'?" He laughed. "I'm kyna shy."

"We're rollin'."

The boy cleared his voice and strummed a slow, sultry rhythm with an E chord. . *Some people may say I will decline and fall…but what do they know, them doggone know it alls?* The kid took it at half the tempo of the Rusty Gordon version, but it felt more low-down. He had a way of breaking up phrases with a gulp and a sort of stutter. The voice had a buttery Southern smoothness, but at the bottom was a rasp like a junior edition of The Shadow.

But none of the Hive artists ever delivered such a torch song. The pace was torrid. That voice made anything it sang…well, *sexual.* Sensual; suggestive.

"He sure plays with the lyrics," Cecil noted. "And he's playin' those triplets like it's a church song."

"You're right." Hank studied the performance. It should have been ridiculous. This kid couldn't be shaving yet and he sounded so damn worldly. There was none of this in Rusty's record. He played everything light and jolly, and if there was any raunch, he delivered it with a wink, to let you know it was just for play. With this kid, it was for keeps, every tortured, elongated syllable of it.

He ended the song with a falsetto whoop and a bang of his guitar, which had gotten out of tune during the performance.

"Well, that's diff'rent," Hank said, almost in sync with Skinny's voice on the tape. The three laughed. "Man. Put that on pause for a second." Skinny stopped the tape. Hank groped for the right words. "I…I have never… heard *anything* like this in all my life. I don't know what to think." Hank paused. "But I have to say I like it. There's something there." Hank looked at Cecil. "That's your song. How'd he do with it?"

Cecil shook his head. "It's…different. Real different. It didn't feel like my song anymore." Cecil paused. "He made the tune better. I will say that."

Skinny grinned. He vibrated like a chihuahua dog. "You'll never guess what he did next." Skinny started the tape up. The kid mumbled an introduction: "This is one we usta, uh, usta sang in church, back when I would go to church." With the same intensity of feeling, he began "If You See My Savior," a spiritual song by Thomas Dorsey.

The way he sang it, it could have been about his woman. As he sang about crossing the swelling tide and taking a message to the other side, he had his audience spellbound. Just a voice and a guitar, which he banged more than he strummed. His voice took on more of the rasp; he was deep in the song. There was nothing anyone could do but stand and listen.

"Good gracious!" Hank exclaimed. "I have never heard *anything* to compare to that."

"He skipped about half the chords," Cecil noted.

"But it doesn't matter! It doesn't matter. And I'll tell you why. Because it's got that message! That message comes through like a freight train. Man alive! Did you watch him when he was singin'?"

"A little." Skinny grinned. "He was…it was like them Pentecostals. He couldn't keep still. I was 'fraid he was gonna knock all my equipment over."

The tape ran on, and the kid began "I'd Cry Like a Baby," which Hank recognized as a Dean Martin song. He felt Dean Martin was just another junk-peddler doing vapid pop music, but this version had…well, *conviction* was the phrase. It was lighter than the other two songs, and it had a swing, but the kid sang it like he meant it. You believed he'd weep like a weeping willow. It was crazy, but it worked.

The tape ended, and Skinny rewound it. "All's he wanted was to get 'em on a record. He said one was for his momma, one was for a friend an' one was for his girl." Skinny shook his head. "Now me, I got no idea what to do with this kid. Or if he even wants to go into records for real. But I thought you might could do somethin' with him. At least get him in, put him with a band, an' see what happened."

"Can I borrow that tape, Skinny? I'd like to study it some more."

"Go 'head. I made a copy for ya. I figgered you'd take to it."

Skinny had the boy's name, Cam Cottner, and a phone number. "Jus' tell 'im Skinny said you should call. An' if anything comes of it, well...remember your buddy showed him to you."

"I'll remember." Hank removed the rewound reel from the tape machine and shook Skinny's hand. They chatted for a couple more minutes. Hank mentioned he might be going into long-play records; Skinny said he had a couple of numbers on the Tupelo Twins, a pair of teenage girls who sang lovey-dovey country stuff. Cecil stood in the shade, grateful for the trees that shielded him from the sun but stuck until the talk wound down.

Darker clouds roiled above them. The breeze got that *it's-gonna-rain* smell. And then it came down in sheets. With the rain came a flash of lightning, shadowed by a thunderclap. "Lawd, that was close! I better shut things down here."

"C'mon Cec!" Hank ran for the car and Cecil followed. Both were wet; Cecil's glasses were crooked and fogged over. "Well, what the hell do you think about that?"

Cecil looked at Hank; he wasn't sure what *that* was.

"The kid. That Cottler boy, the way he sang."

"It's different. I don't know if it's good or bad, but it's different."

The rain slowed traffic. As they crawled, another lightning/thunder combo hit close by. "They say there's a moment in every man's life where he comes across something big. He might not recognize it right there at the moment, but later, he'll look back and say to himself, 'why in the high holy hell

didn't I jump on that?' Right now I wonder if this is that moment for me."
Hank paused in his speech. The windshield wipers whined in the silence. "Cecil, what do you think about God? Is he real? Are you convinced there's a God?"

"I…I guess so. No reason not to think so."

"I've been on the fence about it. But right now, I'm startin' to think that maybe there is someone…some thing…out there. We call it 'God' just to put a handle on it. Like how they call it 'Allah' in the Islam faith and 'Buddah' in the… the…"

"The Buddhist faith."

"Yes." Hank swerved onto the shoulder of the road. "Cecil. I know this is gonna sound nuts, but…I want you to join me in prayer. I've heard so much about the power of prayer. I wanna see if it works." Hank put out his hand. Cecil understood that they were to join hands in prayer. With suspicion, he clasped Hank's hand.

Hank cleared his throat. "Heavenly Father…whoever you are, whatever you are…I hope you don't mind me askin' you a favor. I've just heard somethin' that's got me buffaloed. Is this something I should pursue? Is this anything that's gonna make a difference? I feel…well, I feel like this young man might have somethin' I've been lookin' for…he might be the bridge you've heard me talk about. You're prob'ly tired of hearin' about it by now, but it's true.

"I wanna know right now…is this my future? Give me a sign. Tell me yes or no: should I get ahold of this kid? I thank you for your time. Amen."

"Amen," Cecil mumbled. He felt foolish and he was sure Hank felt foolish. They sat in silence, as if that little pixie from *Peter Pan* was going to show up with her sparkles and grant them a wish.

A bolt of lightning hit a power line. The strike shattered the ceramic transformer and the pole splintered almost down the middle. The wires pinged as they broke, one by one. A jagged half of the pole fell right into oncoming traffic. A couple of cars just dodged it, but it smashed the cab of a moving truck. Horns lowed and brakes screeched across wet pavement. The passengers in the truck weren't hurt, but their cargo was smashed flat. Cars began to circle around the wreck. A highway patrol car stopped, and an officer got out. He directed traffic; the patrol car's driver talked with the moving van's ex-passengers.

"I believe there's your message," Cecil said.

"What…what does it say?"

Cecil paused. "It says…proceed with caution."

Hank sat in silence, as if he was stunned. He nodded his head so slowly Cecil wasn't sure if it was moving. Hank cleared his throat and spoke:

"That I shall do."

They waited for their chance to merge into the moving traffic. It took a while, and not one word passed between them in that time.

# 2

**Cam (short for Camren,** as it was mis-spelled on his birth certificate) Cottner admired his reflection. He had reddish hair and paid some queer nigger hairdresser to make it blonde. He'd had a whole childhood of being called Carrot Top and soon as he learned about hair dye he put an end to that.

That nigger was hot to get into his pants, but no way in hell would he even think about that. Cam led him on, but it was just for laughs. That boy made such a fool out of himself it was funnier than any show.

Cam had to admit that boy was good at his job. He inspected the roots of his hair, which he had Brylcreemed into an upswept pile atop his head. You couldn't tell this hair wasn't blond. He didn't mind a little orange coming through, but red hair was for dumb hillbillies. And Cam was no hillbilly. His family was, but he had willed himself into something different. His momma let him do as he pleased. Her elevator didn't go up to the penthouse. She was sweet and kind but dumb as a hammer. His old man worked at a department store doing shipping. At night, he sat in his chair, listened to the radio and read his Western story magazine. If you saw them side by side you'd doubt how they could be related and you'd be right.

Cam's momma was a looker in her youth and older relatives said the boy took after her. He had her eyes—the way they were before her accident. Back then, they were quick, and they had a twinkle. She looked like she had a secret she couldn't wait to tell. He had her nose, which turned up a little, and her bone structure. He weighed 115 pounds dripping wet at stood at five feet seven inches. In high school they called him "Sprite" until he knocked some teeth out.

Cam hated to think about the old days. He'd suffered through them and that was enough. Every so often, he'd see one of the fools from his school days. They were saddled down with kids and wives and all that depressing adult crap. For a moment, he felt a flash of sadness. He looked at himself in the mirror and made the feeling go away.

It was a good day, and he had something important to do. Today the new records came in at Blues City, the nigger record store. Cam was about the only white boy to set foot in that place. The first time he went in there, he was scared to death. The guy behind the counter looked shocked. Once Cam made it clear he was wild about the music, and knew the artists, they settled down. Jimmy Lee, the guy who ran the place, always set aside new records he thought Cam might like. It was Jimmy Lee made him think that some niggers were okay. Some of them were smart and civilized and knew what they were doing. It was the same for white people. You had some real idiots most of the time and a few sharp ones.

Cam watched his tongue around Jimmy Lee and said "black" or "negro" when he referred to the music. They'd had some good conversations, but it never went beyond that. He wasn't about to have Jimmy Lee to the house for supper. That wasn't done in Tupelo. It was fine for a nigger to set the table and serve you supper, but they ate at their table in the kitchen after the white folks were finished.

Cam didn't think niggers were that bad. After all, they made some fine music and the best ones had real style. He was raised to call them niggers, and the habit stuck. They lived in their world and he lived in his. Their paths never crossed except by servitude or accident. That was how it had always been—and it had been worse in the past. Compared to how they treated niggers 50 years ago, they were on Easy Street now. They had their own homes, their own businesses and they served their own kind. And then they did the work no white man wanted to do. They cut the grass, painted the houses and fixed flat tires. And they did it right because there was no room for mistakes.

Since he got his diploma, Cam's life was one long day off. He tried a couple of jobs—one as a delivery boy for a drug store, the other as a truck driver for a furniture store. He was fired from both. The drug store showed him the door after four days; the furniture company tolerated him for almost a month. Cam's momma just shrugged her shoulders. His old man talked about getting him on at the department store, but he was so bombed on beer at night they never had that conversation.

Left with open days and nights, Cam caroused, drank, played music and lived dangerously. Some nights he felt so randy he'd fuck anything with two legs. He'd been with men and women, in various combinations, and all parties concerned felt honored to be in his orbit. Cam had charisma. You knew he was trouble but you wanted to be around him. He made life more colorful, funny and thrilling. And when he brought his guitar along and would sing, his voice wrapped around everyone. He was a rudimentary guitarist. He could churn out chords, and he'd memorized plenty of them. Latin rhythms still confounded him, but he could play pop, blues or country without a hitch.

He went to church every Sunday with momma just to sing. He could care less about the sermon, or the hypocrites in the congregation. Some of them he'd encountered in his night activities. He'd nod or wink their way; he knew it bothered them. He had no intention of exposing them; it was too much fun to see them sweat it out. It was all a game, to be played by those young and beautiful enough to enjoy its benefits, and to be paid for by those too old to cut the mustard.

All else was forgotten when the congregation raised their voices in song. Cam's was the finest voice in the church, and as he sang, those close to him stopped their voices to listen. It made him feel like something to sing those songs. He knew there had to be a God and a Jesus, and that in those moments, they looked upon him and thought he was all right. It had to make up for the many things they watched with chagrin and disappointment. But hell, he was only human, right? And ain't no person pure of heart or perfect. Long as you tried to do something, you were bound to be okay.

He made the recordings for Christmas presents. He saw a flier tacked to a phone pole. He smelled the creosote as he read Skinny's typed message:

## CAN YOU SING? HEAR YOUR VOICE ON A RECORD?

**For a low fee, you can have a genuine record of you or a loved one singing, speaking or reciting a speech. Call the number for an appointment.**

Cam thought about it for several days. He was curious to hear how he sounded. People liked to hear him sing; they always gave him compliments. Maybe he had something special and could get on real records.

"That's Skinny, from Your Anus Records. He a small timer," Jimmy Lee said. "You be better off goin' to mister Hank at that Hive Records. He does Rusty Gordon an' the Shadow."

"No shit! They live around here?"

"Rusty come in here all the time when he home. I'll introduce y'all. We got a new one in on Otis Blackwell. 'My Josephine.' I bet you'd like it."

Cam trusted Jimmy Lee's advice. He also got the new Ray Charles and Clovers singles and one by The "5" Royales with a title he liked—"The Devil with The Rest." He was going to go home and listen to his new discs, but instead he got on the #4 bus and found Skinny's house. It was near the Black and White Produce Store. He didn't expect a house, but it was. Painted on the garage door, in small red letters, was URANUS RECORDS.

He found Skinny in. "I saw your flier, sir. About making records."

"Oh! Yeah!" Skinny had been soldering and unplugged the solder. Its tip smoked in a dainty wisp. "What you innerested in doin', son?"

Cam smiled. "I sing a little an' play some gittar, an' people say I'm pretty good. I wanna know what I really sound like."

"Y'cain't tell when you're singin'," Skinny agreed. "An' some people got a tin ear. Y'know, some of the biggest guys in the bidness can't sing in tune. You know Webb Pierce?"

"Yes, sir."

"He tends to sing flat. But he's a good singer. He can put over a song. An' that's what people like."

"That's right, sir."

It cost $2.50 a pop to record a song. Skinny took down his name and they set a date for Friday, three days away. "Booked up 'til then," Skinny lied. He had no bookings, but he'd been advised to act like he was up to his neck in work. That made people think you were prosperous, and they trusted you more.

For the next three days, Cam practiced—in his room, in the back yard, in a parking garage that had a great natural reverb. He picked songs that he knew by heart: a hymn for his momma, a Dean Martin song for a girl he was trying to nail, a Rusty Gordon tune for Jimmy Lee and a fourth one, in case he was going good. It was "Funny (But I Still Love You)," a Ray Charles record he liked. Imagine that—being a blind nigger! How bad can your luck get? But Ray was one hell of a singer and his records were the best.

He only did three songs that Friday. He had a hangover, and it gave him a headache to sing too loud. He felt bashful in Skinny's garage studio—it felt like he might turn the wrong way and knock over the recorder. He had no problem singing in front of a group of people, like at church, or in the parking lot of the Tupelo Hideaway. One person made him feel panicky. He asked Skinny to not watch him while he sang, and the guy was nice enough to agree.

He decided to do "Decline and Fall" first, because it got a good reaction. The words seemed to suit him. As he sang, he felt that he was doing the song differently. It was like he felt it more. He had to prove something with his singing. He had to convince himself he sounded good.

When he finished, Skinny stopped the tape recorder. "That was something, son! You wawna hear it back?"

"Naw, sir, I wanna keep goin'. I feel warmed up."

Next, he did one of his favorite church songs the way he sang it on Sundays. He wasn't sure he had all the chord changes right, but he had the feeling for the song and he sang it hard, almost like it was a blues song.

Skinny offered him a Coke; Cam needed it. It felt good on his throat. He thought the Dean Martin song would be an easy one. He liked Dean Martin. He was as far from the blues as you could get, but the man could sing. You liked the way he sang. Cam hoped that he would come across that way—likable.

He had shoplifted the sheet music for "I'd Cry Like a Baby" and learned the right chords. Some of them were hard to finger. Those *dim* chords—what in hell did that mean? All he knew was they were hard to get your hand to learn. He skipped some of those *dims* as he sang in what he hoped was the jaunty way Dean Martin had.

"I think that's good for now, sir." Cam felt sweat under his arms and down his back.

Skinny rewound the tape. "Let's give 'er a lissen." Cam bit his lower lip while Skinny laced the tape through the playback heads and onto the takeup reel. He felt his heart beat hard. He wanted to run, but he made himself stay put. Then he heard Skinny's voice: "…get us some levels here. Say somethin'."

79

Cam heard his voice—shy and mumbly. He hemmed, hawed and cleared his throat. "Awright. I'm ready." Cam launched into the song without guitar. He always sung the first few words solo, and then banged on his guitar when the moment felt right.

Cam surprised himself. He sounded good. He listened hard, his heart thrumming in his ears. He wanted to find fault in his singing, but he couldn't. He wasn't much on the guitar, but that was for other people to take care of. The singing was the important thing, and Cam delivered the goods. He looked over at Skinny, who was all smiles. He shook his head; he'd never heard a white boy sing like this.

The church song was Cam's favorite. He wasn't sure what he believed about heaven and hell and God and Satan, but when he sang those songs, something came through he couldn't name. Maybe a kind of wonder. He sang that song like he believed every word.

Jimmy Lee razzed him for liking Dean Martin, but hell, the guy sang with personality. Like he was talking to you. He had something the other pop guys didn't. Like Frankie Laine. Cam couldn't stand him. And the rest of those smooth guys you could have. Dean could sing rhythm and blues if he wanted to. He was close to that feeling. And Jenny Gully would flip for the record. He was sure he could parlay this into a good fuck.

"Son, you got somethin' there," Skinny said as he rewound the tape. "I might could play these for someone I know. I think you could get onto records if you had a mind to."

Cam shrugged. "Yes, sir, if you think so."

"I can't do anything myself. I got too much tied up in equipment. I gotta get all this paid off." He gestured to the recorder and mixer and a lot of other equipment. "You come back t'morra 'bout noon and I'll have your records done for ya."

Cam got out his wallet. He gave Skinny a 10. "I ain't got no change," Skinny said.

"Just keep the rest. You done me a big favor today, sir."

This was the only recording income Skinny had seen in three weeks. "Thank you, buddy. I'll see you t'morra."

The records paid off. Momma loved the hymn, Jimmy Lee looked amazed at Cam's take on "Decline and Fall," and Jenny surrendered her panties without a fight. Cam thought he might make a couple more records; no telling what doors those might open for him.

His self-evaluation in the mirror ended when Momma swung open his door. "Honey, you got a telephone call."

"Momma, I ast you and ast you—knock before you come in!"

Momma looked a bit hurt. "You put on a shirt, honey." She shuffled down the hall to her perch in the kitchen. Cam heard the voices of a couple of the neighborhood hens. They killed the days with idle gossip and whatever the hell passed the time. He shrugged into a shirt and tried to make it down the hall without being spotted by the hens.

"There he is!" a fat hen with glasses croaked. "You come on in here, Carmen!"

"I got a call, ma'am." The phone was tethered to a crude alcove in the wall. The cord didn't quite reach a comfortable height to stand and talk. He pulled up a hassock and sat. "Hello."

"Is this…" Paper crinkled on the other end. "Cam…Cottler?"

"Yes, sir. My last name's Cottner."

"Oh! So it is. My name's Hank Howard. I run a record concern, Hive Records. You might have heard of us."

"Yes, sir! I have a lot of 'em. They're terrific, sir."

"Well, that's kind of you to say. We try to get a real authentic sound here. What I'm callin' about…a fellow named Griggs played me a tape of some things you recorded. I think you've got a real different sound. I don't know what to call it. I'd like to hear more of it."

Cam searched for an answer but his tongue was numb. He muttered a non-word.

"I'd be obliged if you could bring your gittar down here and we can see what you sound like in a real recording set-up. Would you be willing to do that?"

"Yes, sir. I would. When—"

Hank cupped the mouthpiece. He asked some woman something. She replied. She had one of those nasal country voices. "I could see you tomorrow at 2. Nothing formal. Just…I was impressed by what I heard and I think you have real potential."

"2:00."

"Tomorrow. If that will suit you."

"Yes, sir, that suits me fine. Mr. Howard, is that right?"

"Just call me Hank. Well, we're set, then. I'll see you tomorrow, then."

Cam cradled the phone. He felt light-headed and stunned and a little afraid. He sat on the hassock and got his bearings. Hell, of course they'd be calling him. Because he was good. He would impress the hell out of this Hank guy. Of course, he would.

Momma called Cam into the kitchen so the hens could coo and fuss over him. Mrs. Bickford, the plump hen with crooked glasses, cackled first. "You're sure looking grown up, Carmen. I remember when you were in diapers!" The others laughed.

"Yes'm, that was a while back." He shuffled his feet.

"What are your plans for the future, hon?" Miss Welsh, a skinny, shriveled old biddy rasped.

"I can't say right at the moment, ma'am. But there could be something big coming up. I might have some news for y'all soon!"

As the hens clucked and cooed, Cam excused himself. He needed to see if Skip and Clue were busy. Skip worked at the post office; he'd try him first. Clue was about as likely to hold a job as Cam. But he might have him a new gig.

*Cecil stayed away from the Hive offices* for two days. He didn't leave his shack except to take a walk and think. He had a song in his head. Nothing he'd written was like it. It wasn't funny or even sardonic. It was based on that newspaper article about the two black boys. They had their whole lives ahead of them. They'd be starting their last year of high school. And that was all cut off—dead as they were. The *Daily Journal* printed one small follow-up story. It said the police and sheriff could find no evidence as to the culprits. Those with information on the incident were advised to contact the cops. The article ended with a mention of the boys' funeral service, which had been paid for by members of a Baptist church.

Who was the man who hanged the boys? Why did he do it? Was there anything in it for him? Did he have a score to settle with them? And what could they have done to move him to kill them? Cecil burned with these questions. He knew there weren't answers; there couldn't be.

Coaxial noticed Cecil was upset and inquired, with miaows and rubbings against Cecil's legs. "You must be hungry."

If the cat was, this was his cue to do the chewing routine. He didn't. He stared up at his person with concern. He reached one paw up to touch Cecil's knee. Cecil got it and picked Coaxial up. "It's all right, bud. I'm just thinking. Doing me some thinking." He scratched the cat's chin to reassure him. That got him purring; he looked up pleased at Cecil.

They sat in Cecil's reading chair. Coaxial curled up on his lap, yawned and settled in for a nap. Soon he snored—an amusing razzberry sound that calmed Cecil a bit. *I could take a lesson from him*, he thought.

And then the words came to him. He had a shirt cardboard and a #2 pencil to the side of the chair. He reached them and wrote down the words of what felt like the song's chorus:

*Hangman, hangman by the big oak tree*

*Shadow man whose face I cannot see*

*Is the shade of my skin going to mean the end of me?*

Cecil almost scratched the words out. But he stopped himself. These were words anyone like him could understand. It was something his people hated to think but thought. One wrong move, like the one these two boys made, and everything could be over. Those who did the deed were anonymous. They were protected. Nothing could be said or done against them. *I wish the world was better than this*, Cecil thought. *You think it is and then you see something in the paper. It reminds you that this isn't as good a world. Not for me…*

That gave Cecil the idea of what to do with the verses. Tell the story of reading that article in the paper. Tell what happened. And say that it can't be a better world until mankind can get past this hatred. There can be a better world, but not until the hangmen are gone.

The song was for The Lonesome Shadow, so it had to be a blues. Cecil wondered if it would be too much to put it in a minor key. This was another song that didn't need a great melody. He might just give the words to The Shadow and let him set the tune. It was the message, the story that mattered.

He had all the words in half an hour. He related the news story with no names or details—just that two young lives were snuffed out by a stranger. That was it. There was no remorse, no justice. It was just something that happened. Cecil didn't point a finger or call anyone names. That was too easy, and it didn't solve anything. He ended the song on what he meant as a hopeful note:

*What kind of world, what a world this could be*

*If there wasn't no hangman and they cut down that old oak tree?*

*If your fellow man would rather give you a hand*

*And we all really could be free.*

Cecil felt emptied out when he wrote the last words. He set the cardboard aside. It was a rule of his. After you finished, you put it down and take your mind off it. Look at it in an hour, two hours. If it still looks good, you've got it. If not, you figure out how to fix it.

He sat in that chair as dusk crept through the house. He didn't think or speak. He stared out the open door into the trees and the woods. Coaxial snored and shifted. Cecil stroked the cat's back and felt the vibration of his purr.

84

It took Hank Howard five hours to track down The Lonesome Shadow. He wasn't working his land and his shack was silent. The muddy, rusty Ford truck wasn't there. The Shadow's closest neighbors knew Hank from previous searches. Hank worked through his checklist. If he wasn't working his property, he was in his house. If he wasn't in his house, he was at the colored folks' general store. If he wasn't at the store, he was at the creek, fishing. If he wasn't fishing, he might be down to Green Street, playing music with his friends. They had a spot across from the Dixie Belle Theater where they could draw a crowd on an afternoon.

The Shadow wasn't at any of those spots. He was helping a neighbor right an overturned tractor. Two old women in the house across the way pointed the farm out for Hank. He felt self-conscious as he drove up towards the other farm. It was five acres of corn and soybeans.

Hank spotted the red of the tractor. The Shadow's large, raw-boned frame appeared behind the tractor as it moved. He heard the sound of splintering wood, followed by some first-class swearing. Then the tractor righted itself. It almost tipped over the other way, but the farmer leaned against it and it centered. Hank heard The Shadow's hearty laughter and headed in its direction.

Hank was never sure what to call the man. He knew "Mr. Butts" wouldn't do; neither did "Mr. Shadow" sound right. He felt the same towards his wife's relatives. Different people from different worlds that he didn't quite fit into. But he had to make his spot.

The Shadow saw him as he wiped his brow on his dirty checkered shirt sleeve. "Well, looka here!"

"Boy howdy! How'd you get that thing upright?"

Shadow rasped a chuckle. "Couldn't not do it."

"I come bearing money and good news! Which would you like first?"

"You pretty honest with the money, so gimme the news up front."

Hank explained about the general idea of long-playing record albums, that Cross Records was launching a rhythm and blues series and that they wanted Lonesome Shadow to be their first 12-incher. It was guaranteed good sales and more money for Shadow. After that, Hank gave him two copies of his latest Cross single and $500 in cash—in 10s and 20s, as Shadow preferred. Hank counted it out into Shadow's huge palm. "Mm hm," Shadow said every time the pile got one bill larger. "I can 'bout afford to retire," he said when the last was counted. He laughed; that invited Hank to laugh.

Shadow's colleague was impressed with the transaction. "I might be in the wrong line of work," he said to himself. He walked a slow line to his barn.

"Well, sometimes I wonder that myself. Now, we're needing four more songs to make the album, and a new single. I'd sure appreciate it if you and I could set a time to get some new numbers done."

"I got three I been workin' up. Don't know about any more…"

"Well, worse comes to worse, we can always do one of the old songs. Like 'Motherless Children.' Or 'Down in the Valley.'"

Shadow shook his head. "I don't do nobody else's songs."

"We'll figure something out. The important thing is to get you some time in the studio. I'm excited to hear your new songs."

Shadow nodded in appreciation. He fell silent. Hank wasn't sure what to do. It seemed wise to do nothing. He listened to the sounds of the field; distant machinery, crows cawing, wind whipping the cornfield behind him. There wasn't the empty feeling he got when he took stock of things at home, or even at the office.

"Thursday," Shadow said. "I ain't got nothin' goin' on Thursday."

"Thursday is fine. Day or night?"

"Night. Everything sounds better at night." They settled on a 7:30 session time and shook hands. Hank felt small in Shadow's grip, and glad that he was the conduit to this man and his music. *I wish I could handle an artist like him,* Hank thought. *I'm a small-timer. If I had a number one hit, I don't know what I'd do.*

◊◊◊

Cam caught Skip on his lunch hour. It was strange to see him wearing a tie and a dress shirt. The guy was a damn good guitarist, but he hung onto this job. Sorting a bunch of letters all day; what a waste of time!

"I know Hank Howard. Done a couple of sessions for him. For that gal singer with the tin ear…Woodwork? Oh. Woodburn. Lord God." He wrinkled his face as if someone had let off a long greasy fart.

"He wants to see could I make a record for his company. I'd sure feel better if I had you an' Clue there. We could just run down the songs we know good. I think we stand a chance."

Skip shrugged. "He gonna pay us something?"

"Ida know. I guess so. It's a test to see how would we sound on a record."

"What time?"

"Mr. Howard said to just show up. It's up to you."

Skip finished his salami sandwich and licked his thumb. Some Durkee's sauce had dribbled on it. "I might could get the day off. I got one comin' to me."

"Oh, man. I know we'll do it up right."

"You run down Clue. Make sure he can do it."

Cam felt excited, like a kid. Skip was about the only person who took him seriously as a singer. They sounded good together. Skip didn't sing, but his guitar filled in all right spaces. Cam felt better when Skip backed him up. And with Clue thudding along on his bass fiddle, they kept good time. Clue had a way of speeding up the tempo.

Clue was asleep on his front porch when Cam showed up. He'd had a big lunch and his intention was to mow the lawn. His mother was always harping about how he didn't do anything to earn his keep. It was so warm and the shade on the porch felt so nice. He propped his long legs against the trellis and fell into a coma.

"Hey," Cam shouted. "Wake up!"

Clue startled and sat up. "Shit, man, I like to have a heart attack." He stood up. He was 6'4" and thin as a board. "I got to get that lawn mowed."

Cam followed him to the backyard shed. "This is big news, man. You an' me an' Skip? We might get on records."

Clue banged his forehead on the shed door. "Crap!" He pulled out the lawn mower. The blades were a little rusty. "Now, what was that?"

Cam ran down the story as Clue gave the lawn a trim. "If Skip's in, man, I'm in. We gettin' money for this?"

"Ida know. We might. It's what-you-call—an audition. To see how we sound."

It took half the front yard for Clue to commit. Cam had a way of pulling you into his ideas. He got so excited and alive and it was contagious. "What'll we do?"

"You know. The stuff we run down when we're playin'. Songs we know."

"None o' that Dean Martin crap. I can't stand that son of a bitch."

"We can do 'Money Honey.' We go to town on that one. And 'Wine Spo-Dee-O-Dee.' He might wanna hear some hillbilly songs too."

"Let's do 'Heart Trouble.' Skip sounds good on that one."

"Hell, I'll sing the want ads if it gets us a record deal."

Clue did a half-assed job of mowing the lawn. It would shut his mother up. Cam helped rake the clipped grass out to the gutter. "You missed a couple of spots," Cam noticed.

"Shit." Clue ran the mower over the forgotten areas and finished the task. He'd get the back yard tomorrow. Or the day after.

"Skip's gonna call you about Tuesday. Mr. Howard said to just show up, but I prefer to call first. Let him know we're comin'."

Clue shrugged. "Suits me."

◊◊◊

"Tomorrow's parent-teacher night," Liz said. Carl was a nightmare of tomato sauce as he tried to eat spaghetti. Kitty poked at hers, doubtful of it.

"What's wrong, honey?" Hank said.

Kitty glowered. "These are worms, Daddy. I don't eat worms."

"Honey, that's spaghetti. It's good. See?" Hank stuck a forkful in his mouth and chewed. He bugged out his eyes and smiled. It got Kitty to laugh.

"Daddy, you're crazy."

"Tomorrow's parent-teacher night," Liz repeated. "Carl is going to be in something special."

"Like what?"

"You'll have to come and see. But it'll be a big deal, won't it, Carl?"

Carl beamed in-between pasta and sauce.

"Well, how about that? Good goin', buddy! Spell spaghetti for me."

Carl frowned. "I can eat it better 'n I can spell it."

"Try it. I bet you can do it."

"S…p…a…g…e…t…t…i?"

"Not bad, bud. You left out one letter. 'Spag-*het*-ti.'"

"Oh! H! After the g."

"I bet no one else in your class can spell that one. That's a hard one."

Liz interrupted. "It would mean a lot to me if you could come."

"What time is it?"

"It's from 5 to 7."

"I got an audition. Some kid who's pretty good. I can make sure we wrap that up in time." Hank got out a small loose-leaf notebook and wrote the time and event in it. "It's in the book, hon."

"I still think it's worms," Kitty said. "But they're good worms."

After spaghetti there was Jello with whipped cream—another layer of color on Carl's canvas. Kitty dropped hers and cried for 10 minutes. The whine of her voice got on Hank's nerves. *How can such a little thing make such a nasty noise?*

"All done!" Carl dropped his spoon in the parfait glass. "J-e-l-l-o!"

"You're wearin' about half of it, bud. Let's get you cleaned up."

"I got science homework, Daddy."

"Well, we'll tuck into that after we get you mopped up."

Tag-team parenting proved a success. Kitty had her cry and got some of her mother's Jello. *Kukla, Fran and Ollie* were on TV at seven. Liz got a kick out of the show and Kitty loved Ollie. Liz heard Hank and Carl going over science questions in the children's room. Hank was a good father—patient and kind. He listened and always had something positive to say. In the rare event that Hank had to punish his children, he never raised a hand or his voice. *He has a way with people,* she thought. *I wish he and I had that. More of that.*

The news came on and Kitty went for her coloring book. Her face was a caricature of concentration. She tried so hard to color inside the lines. She used a green crayon on Ollie. Liz stared at the TV without taking it in. She heard Carl's voice, high and piping, and the lower tones of Hank's as they muddled through whatever the homework was. *They're so comfortable. They get along.* She had rapport with her children; they knew she was the one to turn to if they skinned a knee or wanted a peanut butter sandwich. She took pride in their triumphs, comforted them in their sadness and wanted nothing in the world but their health and happiness. But there was a distance between them. Hank didn't have that distance. Was it the role of a mother to be the caretaker, a comforter but not a chum?

She spent the most time with Carl and Kitty. The nights Hank was home for supper, and not at his office, not an apologetic voice on the phone, filled with the best intentions…they were rare. And maybe that was it. Hank was a novelty. She was their everyday reality. People took their everyday reality for granted. They could count on it being there.

The news was long over when Hank's voice startled her. "Well, we're about experts on the life cycle of plants!" He sat next to her on the couch and slid his right arm around her shoulder. "He's a bright young man. He's gonna get somewhere. He's… he's *innerested* in things. He wants to know, you know, what makes things tick."

"He is." She relaxed into his arm. "How did things go today?"

"I went out to see one of my artists. Gave him his royalties and got him to do a recording session. You know, you should come down and see a session sometime. It's a lot of fun. I lose track of time—it's like the clock stops. I wish it could…"

"I'd just make them nervous. Those colored people. I wouldn't want to do that to them."

Hank lit up. "All you got to do is get to know 'em. See them as people, not 'colored people.' They go through all the same things you and I do. They have it harder than us. And I'm sorry about that. There ain't a thing I can do about that, on a big scale. But I can give them a chance to get their music out on record. Why, a couple of the boys have quit their old jobs. Music is their living. They had the talent; they just needed…you know, a—a…a conduit.

Someone to move them into a place where they could succeed. And that's really—that's what I do, Bets. I help people succeed."

*Everyone but yourself*, she thought. And then she regretted the thought, but she felt the burn of resentment. Right now, they were getting by. Every cent of money that went in and out had to be budgeted. If she didn't do that, it wouldn't get done. Money just fell out of Hank's pockets. He didn't think about the practical side of life. If he did, they'd be doing better…

"…this young feller can sing anything. And he's white. He gets the real Negro feeling in his voice." She tuned back into the present. Hank had fixed a drink. Booze excited him.

"I'm sorry, hon. My mind was wandering."

"Aw, I'm just goin' on about all my business. I'd like to hear about you. How was your day?"

Betsy, confronted with the question, felt a loss for words. "I…I run the kids to school in the morning. Then I look at my budget and I go to the store. Sometimes I have dinner all planned, and sometimes I make it up while I'm there. I…I get home, and I put things up. I pick up after you and the kids. You all leave things everywhere. I've found socks in the damndest places, Hank."

Hank's face creased with pain and grief. "Have I given you a good life, Bets? I worry all the time that I haven't. And that matters to me. I want you to not have to worry about so much."

"You make me sound like a pet. Like a cat or something."

"That isn't what I mean. You're taking it the wrong way. I…" He sipped his bourbon. "When we got hitched I took those words to heart. They weren't just words we were supposed to say. I'm the first to admit I have fallen short. Bets, I haven't given you…not yet. But I will. The day's gonna come…you're gonna look back on this time and realize that we're *there*." He tapped the coffee table for emphasis. "We used to be here…and someday we'll be *there*. Does that make any sense?"

"I think so. I don't mean to complain, Hank. But…"

"I haven't forgotten my promise. If my company isn't doing better in five months, I'll—I'll sell it. I'll get a regular job. But I don't think that's gonna happen. I have faith in myself. Bets, I—I feel like I'm on the verge. I ain't there yet, but I'm not gonna be *here* for long. You an' I, we're both gonna be *there*."

He repeated his tap. "An' none of it matters unless you're there, front an' center. You an' our kids."

Hank glanced at the TV. "Hey, Sid Caesar's on!" He settled back, his sermon delivered, and cackled at the show's skits. Despite herself, Betsy laughed along with him. Hank had a way of making you like him, even when you didn't want to.

*Cecil awoke Tuesday morning* with a feeling of pride. For the first time, he had gotten something down on paper that felt truthful. It wasn't just to get a laugh out of someone, or to make fun of something.

He spooned out some kippered herrings for Coaxial. The cat caught a whiff of the fish and had a fit. Cecil smiled at the sheer pleasure on his buddy's face. He spooned instant coffee into a cup and heated a saucepan of water on the stove.

A wave of shock cut through him. *What if Hank doesn't like the lyrics? What if they're too blunt for him?* This could be…he didn't want to give himself a swelled head, but this could be an important song. Like "Strange Fruit." And then Cecil worried that Hank would think it was a copy of "Strange Fruit." Perhaps it was. Cecil tried to run through the words of "Strange Fruit." That song was like a code. It didn't come right out and say what his lyrics said. It was the best a black person could do before the war. He remembered hearing Billie Holiday's voice singing those words on the radio. He had a clear memory of standing by the front window and feeling upset—not understanding the words but feeling their pain.

*I could reach a lot of people with this song. If Hank likes it and* he *likes it…* Cecil thought about the man who might record the song. *He might have seen something like that happen in his life. He might be the man to send this message out in the world, to people who would understand it and…*

Cecil put some condensed milk into his instant coffee. It mitigated the bitter taste. And as he convinced himself that he was right to put down those words on paper, a lyric he'd forgotten about started to come to him.

As Coaxial groomed in the morning sun, pleased beyond description, Cecil scrawled words down on the back of a manila envelope:

*I'm a famous ignoramus, with the wisdom of a fool…*

93

*All the knowledge they teach in college never made a man be cool…*

Finally! He had gotten past that rhyme problem. Whatever the words had been before, these were better.

Okay, that would be the chorus. Got a little story there. Why is he famous?

*I graduated from the school of love with a bachelor's degree*

*And that's the way it's going to stay; I always will be free…*

The words came to him in clumps, faster than he could write them down. The tune could just be a jump blues—something simple with a bouncy beat. This would be a natural for Rusty. The singer is kind of making fun of himself, and that was right up Rusty's alley.

*On every station 'cross the nation I'm the number one request…*

*And that's the way it's going to stay—I'm better than the rest!*

That second line could be stronger, but the first was good. Cecil could improve it once the whole thing was down on paper. He moved ahead to the middle part, which was his favorite when he wrote a song.

*The ladies scream; they kiss my pictures in the magazines…*

*And when I sing of love, they know exactly what I mean.*

That would do. Rusty often riffed on the words and sang whatever came into his head. Cecil wrote a concluding verse and a coda and called it good. He shaved in a basin over the kitchen sink with his father's straight razor. That man terrified him as a kid, waving that thing around, slashing the air right next to his ear. Cecil's shrieks, as his hands went up to his face to be sure it was still there, made the old man howl with laughter. Sometimes that would be enough to wear him out. He'd drop in his tracks and sleep for half a day.

Cecil wielded the razor with great care and precision. He almost never cut himself. He didn't have a mirror, but he didn't need one. He knew the contours of his face.

He donned his new clothes, polished his shoes with a rag and put the new lyrics into his satchel. It was hot and bright out. He'd have to get a hat. That would complete his new look.

A bus came down below on the highway on the half hour. It took colored people. Cecil rode into downtown. He sat at the back. It was an unspoken rule. He liked the back seat anyway. He could eavesdrop on conversations. Sometimes he'd get a good turn of phrase from what someone said. Book writers—novelists—did that, so why not a songwriter?

He walked the six blocks from the bus depot to Hive Records with excitement and dread. *I'm laying it on the line*, he thought. *Sink or swim*. He felt sweat glide down the small of his back. The air was thick and dead. Clouds held in the humidity; he could see the sun, a dim disc fighting to get through.

"Hello, Miz Bell," Cecil said as he entered the front office.

Miss Tinkle looked up, shocked them relaxed. "You here for the aw-di-tion?"

This was news to Cecil. "I… I suppose so. Is M…Hank in?" Miss Tinkle jerked a thumb back to Hank's sanctum. Cecil hesitated until he heard laughter, then poked his head in. Hank acknowledged him with a raised index finger. "I think we'll all be surprised by the sales on this thing. We will take the market by surprise…say, one of my partners just walked in. Cecil Madison. He's written a slew of hits for us. He might have something for The Shadow today."

A hornet buzz responded. "Yeah, I get you. But time's…the clock's ticking. And if The Shadow likes the song…" Hank cupped the phone. "What's it called?"

"'Hangman,'" Cecil replied with embarrassment.

"'Hangman Blues.' How's that for a title?" The buzz replied in a lighter tone. "Well, of course, it's all up to our artist. He only records what he likes… we got a guy from the paper coming over. Gonna get some candid shots of Shadow in the studio. He's got a real good eye. You want color or…" *Buzz, buzz*. "Black and white's fine. That's what we'll get. I tell ya, the picture of that man holdin' his guitar…singin' his heart out…that's gonna sell like hotcakes." A longer buzz ended with laughter. "Well, I'm glad you feel thataway, Vincent. That's how we all feel about The Shadow. He's a real artist."

The call ended and Hank fanned his face with a manila folder. "Man, that guy is loud! How you doin'?"

Cecil nodded. "I'm fine. I…I got the song for The Shadow…a-and another might be good for Rusty…like to run 'em down for you, if you got a minute."

95

"For you, Mister Madison, I've always got time." They walked across the small lobby into the studio. It was empty and the lights were off. Cecil fumbled with his lyric sheets, adjusted the piano bench, and hit an E minor chord. "This one, it's a little different…"

"I'm always lookin' for different. Let 'er rip."

Cecil steeled himself and began. It was a blues in E minor and followed the classic 12-bar structure. Cecil vamped until he got up the nerve to sing the opening lines:

*Hangman, hangman by the big oak tree*

*Shadow man whose face I cannot see*

*Is the shade of my skin going to mean the end of me?*

In his nervousness, he played the A major chord instead of A minor. It made a big difference. He glanced at Hank. His eyes were wide open. He leaned on a folding chair, rapt. Cecil felt better; most white people would have shown him the door after those first lines.

He got to the last verse and felt emotion surge up his throat as he sang:

*What kind of world, what a world this could be*

*If there wasn't no hangman and they cut down that old oak tree?*

*If your fellow man would rather give you a hand*

*And we all could really be free.*

He improvised a coda and let the last chord fade away. This was the moment of truth.

Hank nodded his head as if to say *no*, but the look in his eyes told Cecil he was at a loss for words. He cleared his throat. "Cecil…wow. That is dynamite! Boy! That is a powerful…that's what I'm looking for. A song that tells it like it is. Man, if The Shadow doesn't like it, I'll cut it on you and put it out. I don't care what people might think. Someone's gonna raise a fuss. But the hell with 'em."

Cecil grinned with relief. He felt his heart thud in his chest.

"You keep that one under cover 'til Thursday. I'm gonna get Shadow to do this if I can. Man, is this gonna sell records! Cross might have to put this out as a single. If they've got the guts. 'Cause it takes guts to put that out into the world. I'm proud of you, Cecil. You tell the truth. You're not afraid."

"Actually," Cecil said, "I'm shaking in my seat. But I'm glad you under-stand. W-what I'm tryin' to say with this. I saw an article in the paper about a…a lynching took place last week. It made me realize a lot of things about how the world is…how it still is…"

"Let's hear the other one."

"N-now, this is just silly stuff. I don't study Rusty Gordon doing a se-rious song." Cecil launched into a bouncy, shuffling G major chord and sang "Famous Ignoramus," such as it was. He caught Hank grinning and tapping the folding chair with his palm. As he sang it, he winced at lines that needed work, but felt that it was fine for what it was.

"Ha ha! You keep writin' funny songs, brother! You've got a knack for it. Boy, I really got to put out a record on you."

"Aw, I couldn't…"

Miss Tinkle peeked in. "Mister Howard…I got these boys out in the lobby. They're here for their aw-dition."

Hank lit up. "Oh, yeah! You remember that fellow we heard on Skin-ny's tape? I'm gonna see how he sounds in a real studio. 'Scuse me a minute."

Hank turned on his emcee personality and greeted the three white boys. Cecil recognized the short one. He'd broken his good mood from that blue car. He acted like a peacock, strutting and proud. He was like an ofay version of Rusty, from the look of him. An older guy held a guitar case; a tall, hippy kid struggled with an upright bass fiddle. They chit-chatted; Hank's way to put them at ease and get their nerves settled.

"…Cecil Madison. He's one third of this company, and he's written some hit songs you might know. 'Decline and Fall…'"

The peacock looked like Miss Tinkle—shocked and excited at the sight of Cecil. "Well, this is somethin' new. A nigger runnin' a company!"

"Hush," Skip, the guitarist said. "That's just rude!"

"Hell, I didn't mean nothin' by it. It just slipped out my mouth."

"Well." Hank had to think what to say. "Well, let's get y'all set up. Take your time. Get comfy. When you're ready, we'll do a test. See how y'all sound in here." Hank went back to the control booth. Chuck was in there.

*He must live there*, Cecil thought. Then he realized the peacock was staring at him. "I…I thought you did a fine job with my song."

"Jew really write that?"

"Yes, I did." Cecil produced the handwritten lyrics, which were stained with coffee and booze from the recording session. The peacock looked it over and laughed. "Damn. I ain't never met no songwriter before. An' def'nit'ly no n—"

"Jeez, Cam, you gonna wreck it for us?" the beanpole said.

"I don't mean nothin'. I just speak my mind. If that's okay with y'all…"

"Shut it," the guitarist growled. "You only open your mouth to sing. Or I walk out."

Cam, the peacock, looked shocked. "I didn't do nothin'. This ole feller here, he didn't take no offense to what I said. Did you?"

"I take the fifth," Cecil replied.

Cam laughed. "Hell—now there's an idea." He produced a bottle of bourbon and took a swig. "Aw yeah. That'll get *me* warmed up!" He offered the bottle to the beanpole and the guitarist. They passed.

"Mr. Howard?" the guitarist said. "Mr. Howard?"

Hank emerged from the control booth. "You all ready to go?"

"I got an echo-plex for my guitar. Okay 'f I use it?"

"Sure! I've been meanin' to buy one for the studio." The guitarist turned on the studio amplifier. It hummed and made a loud buzz as he plugged the cord from his guitar into the thing. He clicked on a small device and strummed a couple of chords. The guitar had a powerful reverberation. He adjusted the dials on the thing and got a warmer, thicker sound from it.

"You tuned up, Clue?" The beanpole shrugged. The guitarist played the low string on his instrument. The beanpole thudded his bottom string; it was off. Cecil played the E note on the keyboard, then the chord. "Shew! I'm off. Give 'er another coupla bangs there, friend…"

Cecil repeated the E note until the musicians were satisfied. As they tuned, Chuck came over and adjusted microphones. He took more time with the bass fiddle. The beanpole played a boogie-woogie line; the guitar man joined in. He played in the Chet Atkins style, with a bass line, melody line and chords all at once. They had talent; it didn't sound formal and wooden like white folks usually did. There was feeling. They were making something up in the key of D, and Cecil joined in, playing chords and adding some fancy ones so they'd know he knew what he was doing. The piano added depth to the sound. The peacock smiled and shouted, "Well, awright! We goin' to town now!"

Chuck gave them the high sign from the booth door. Hank approached the musicians. "Well, gee, Cecil, you're soundin' pretty good with these boys. How about it, fellers? Can Cecil sit in?"

Shrugs and murmurs of assent answered the question. "Well, let's just have you play some songs you do all the time. Show me what y'got."

"Well, we got the songwriter here," the peacock said. "Let's do his song. We know that one good."

"What key's good for you?" Cecil asked.

"It sounds good in A," beanpole answered.

"Shit man, that's a little high… hell, let's try it. Y'all rollin'?"

"Yep," Chuck's voice fuzzed over the intercom.

"Gimme the A," the peacock said. Cecil sounded the chord. A capella, the peacock lit into the lyrics:

*Some people say I will decline and fall…*

*but what do they know, them mean ol' know-it-alls?*

The peacock had his way with the song. This wasn't a clown's boast; it was a voice of experience, full of swagger and suggestion. The peacock sounded like he lived by the words of Cecil's song. Cecil's playing became bolder as he responded to this interpretation. The guitarist took a solo, blazing away on his six strings as Cecil hammered the chords in sync with the bass fiddle. In the solo's most fervent spot, the peacock yelped with delight. He had the microphone stand in his left hand and swung it back and forth as he sang. Spittle flew from his mouth; his brow creased and dark circles of sweat bloomed under his arms.

The peacock had a slowed-down coda for the song. Cecil dropped out for a moment, then caught the drift and helped bring the song home. The last notes and chords died in the air. Then Hank burst into the studio. "Holy cow! My goodness! How long you boys been playin' like that?"

"Aw, a coupla years," the peacock replied. "We never done much with it, but play a dance or two…"

"Whatta you think, Cecil?"

"It's different. It's not country music. Got a blues feeling to it. I wouldn't know what to call it."

"Well, why don't you fellers do another couple for us? How's about a slow number?"

After discussion, they chose "Midnight," a blues ballad that had given Red Foley a hit a few years back. "It's a blues in E," the guitarist told Cecil.

The peacock made a torch song of it, with a touch of Ray Charles to his treatment. Cecil did his best imitation of Ray and hammered the chords slow and sad. The beanpole joined in on harmony with the second verse. The kid could sing too. Cecil hadn't heard "Midnight" before, but he felt sure whatever version they'd learned it from didn't sound a thing like this.

Hank was over the moon. "I haven't had much luck with white artists, but I think y'all have got somethin' special here. Cecil, play me that song you just wrote. The funny one."

"But that's for Rusty…"

"Humor me, buddy. Show 'em the song."

All eyes upon him, Cecil pulled out the lyric sheet to "Famous Ignoramus." "Now, this isn't finished…I intend to clear up the lyrics…"

"Aw, just sing it, Cec."

Cecil sang it. The lyric got chuckles throughout, and one horselaugh from the peacock. Cecil smiled; these white boys were tuned in to what he was saying. At the end, the peacock clapped. "Damn, man, that's my song. Let me do it. Please."

"But it's for Rusty…"

"Naw, man, that's *me*. That's who I am. You been keepin' tabs on me?" The three laughed.

"Cecil's about the best lyric writer in town." Hank looked at Cecil with pleading eyes. "I'm sure he wouldn't mind you givin' it a go…"

Cecil shrugged. "I wanna change one line that's a little weak."

"Hey man, run the whole thing down again for me." The peacock stood behind Cecil at the piano. In the process, they fixed the line of convenience that had bothered Cecil:

*On every station 'cross the nation I'm the number one request...*

*And every girl I give a whirl is better than the rest!*

Cecil's life was alien to that boast; it was what Cam Cottner expected. Cecil got the internal rhyme, but the sentiment was right out of the boy's loud mouth.

He took another pull on his bottle and cleared his throat. He spat a gob on the floor. "Well, hell, we got this one down! Let's make it!"

"Take us in, Cecil," the guitarist said. He smiled; Cecil could tell he liked his style.

Cecil did a locked octave hammering of the opening chords. He stopped on the first beat of the third measure. The guitarist took the cue and drove the three beats home. The guitarist looked at the peacock and nodded. With a rasp in the back of his throat, the peacock sang:

*I'm a famous ignoramus, with the wisdom of a fool...*

*All the knowledge y'get in college never made you half as cool...*

Cecil was used to his lyrics getting changed in the studio. It was part of the process, and he accepted that intuition was maybe more important than sticking to the words. The peacock ranted, railed and proclaimed that he was a happy, horny idiot—the idol of millions, without a lick of sense and tickled about it. This is a hit song, Cecil thought. *A big one.* With joy in his heart, he hammered the ending home. The guitarist played a complex chord with a bit of dissonance and they were done.

The four shared a moment of silence. They knew they had done something new, different and that it was better than anyone could have expected. But the verdict came from the control booth. The intercom clicked on with a startling buzz. "Gentlemen," Hank's voice cried, *"that* is a record! That is a *record!"*

He crossed the studio floor in a few long strides. "This is...I don't know what to call it. This is somethin' the world ain't heard...and they're gonna shit bricks when they get an earful!"

"We call it cat music," the peacock said. "You know, 'cause only cool cats dig it."

Hank laughed and clapped his hands. Cecil couldn't tell who was ahead in the sweat contest. Hank and the kid were drenched. He glanced over to the guitarist, who hadn't shown any outward sign of the miracle they'd just pulled off. The bass player had a wall-to-wall grin. For a guy named Clue, he didn't have one.

"I would like to make you all Hive Records artists. Exclusive. My secretary will draw up an artist contract. But we need a name for you boys… something that'll look good on a record. Miss Bell…" Hank zoomed into the lobby. He talked and waved his hands. Miss Tinkle nodded. She knew the drill.

The kid took another sip. "Hell, what we gonna call us?"

The beanpole spoke. "Howzabout 'Cam an' The Cats?'"

"That's good," the guitarist said.

"'Cam an' The *Cool* Cats,'" the peacock countered.

"'Cam and The Cats' is the best. They can get that in bigger type on the label." The trio looked at Cecil and they knew he was right.

Hank returned with a pile of forms. "This is just a standard one-year artist contract. If we're all happy 'bout how things are goin' next year, you can sign a renewal. If not, you can walk an' no hard feelings." Hank distributed the contracts to the trio. "Oh. One thing. You gotta be a consenting adult to sign this."

"A what?" the peacock said.

"Free, white an' 21," the beanpole joked. Then he glanced at Cecil. "No offense."

"None taken."

"It's just a sayin'."

"I'm 19 'bout to turn 20," the peacock said. He handed the papers back. "What do I do?"

"I'll need to meet with your parents. Explain the situation, have them sign these for you. It's their say. But I'll give 'em on helluva sales pitch."

"Gimme a ride home an' we can do 'em now. My ole man's prolly home. An' my momma would sign anything you put under her nose."

Hank looked at the clock. It was almost 5. Where did the time go? The parent-teacher meeting was at…crap. 7? He hated to call her; that was a sign that he had forgotten. Then it came back to him: 5 to 7. Crap. He felt torn in two. He didn't want this young man to get away from him. This was…well, it was history in the making. He hated to let Carl and Bets down. But maybe this would go fast, and he could show up by 6. It was a boiler-plate thing—an agreement to a reasonable royalty rate per record sold, with a cash bonus every time a record exceeded 10,000 sales. It was a guarantee of money—with the promise of more if things went well. And Hank felt, in his gut, that this kid was going to shoot the moon.

"Well, son, I'd like to, but I've got a meeting. At my boy's school. I'm s'pose to be there now…"

Cam shrugged. "You c'n come by tomorrow. But you know…things could happen. I could go tell that guy with the garage that I got an offer from you."

"Him? He couldn't give you bus fare home, son. I can get you—all of you—" he gestured to everyone in the studio "money soon's the record starts to hit. An' this is gonna hit."

"Your call," Cam said. His friendly expression cooled. His eyes looked beady.

"Don't be a fool," the guitarist said to Cam. "You gotta gum up every-thing?"

Hank Howard suffered a crisis of conscience. It was the hardest deci-sion he'd made since he started this business. He'd warded off his wife's distrust and impatience with the belief that he was going to succeed. And right here was a young man who represented that belief. Hell, it wouldn't bother Carl if he was late. Liz he could talk down. She'd give him the Frigidaire routine for a few days, but she'd thaw.

"Let's go. C'mon." Hank headed for the door. Cam shrugged, a smile on his face and warmth to his eyes. He waved goodbye to his bandmates—and Cecil—and trailed Hank out the door.

The house was small, untidy and warm. An ancient fan roared in the living-room window. "Momma?" Cam called from the other side of the screen door. A casserole smell wafted out. "Momma!"

Clinks and clanks came from the kitchen. "Oops," a feminine voice said. "Oh, well. Who's there?"

"It's Cam. I got a man here t'see you."

A foggy-looking, pale woman with flabby upper arms came to the door. "To see me?" She looked toward the kitchen. "I got dinner in the oven…"

"We're comin' in." Cam opened the screen door and let Hank in, then let the door slam hard in the frame. Hank saw someone's head jolt in an easy chair.

"Do you have to always slam that damn door?" the person in the chair grumbled.

"It don't close right." Cam smiled. "Uh. Mr. Howard, this is my ole man."

"What's he sellin'." Hank headed for the chair, but stopped when the man didn't move.

"He ain't sellin', he's buyin'! This is the big time, Pops!"

That got Jackson Bigger out of his grey-green-brown easy chair. He had none of Cam's petite features. He reminded Hank of a movie actor. Fella in *From Here to Eternity*. Borgnine! Like a skinny Ernest Borgnine. He was burly and wore an old brown-green leather jacket that was worn white at all the stress points. He looked askance at Hank in his neat taupe suit and wiped his palm on his shirt before shaking hands. "Mr. Haard. You wawna bah some'n? Whadda we got's worth bah-in'?"

"I'm here about Cam."

"Hell, you c'n have 'im." Mr. Cottner laughed—a low laugh that became a phlegmy cough.

Hank waited out the cough and continued. "Mr. Cottner, your son has got talent as a singer. And I believe he will sell records. Why, I have a gut feeling he'll be on the hit parade. I wanna sign him to my record company. Hive Records. Right here in Tupelo."

"What's in it fer us? Is there a catch 'er sumth'n?"

"No sir. Just a standard one-year contract, with an option to renew for another two years. Your boy ain't 21 yet, so I need your consent." Hank produced the contract from his coat pocket. "It's a basic contract. No hocus pocus."

"Have Edda look at it." Mr. Cottner returned to his newspaper and cigar.

"Momma? *Momma!*" Cam stood his ground. "Get in here!"

"Oh, lord." A clatter of metal, glass and aluminum foil came from the kitchen. "Oh, well," her voice said. She joined them in the living room, dazed and sweaty from the kitchen heat. "Well, what can I do for you, mister?"

Hank repeated his pitch and showed her the contract. "Now, you can go through it and read all the fine print, but it's gonna bore you silly. I'll do right by your boy, Mrs. Cottner. He's got talent and the world needs to hear it."

She wiped her hands on her apron and accepted the paper. "I was never good at readin'. Gives me a headache." She looked at Cam. "Honey, is this what you want? Is this good for you?"

"Yes'm. I wouldn't be doin' it, wasn't good for me."

"Now, what is this for?"

Fifteen minutes later, it had been explained three times and to Mrs. Cottner's satisfaction. Hank showed her where to sign. She made a wobbly, diagonal signature with Hank's fountain pen. "Oh…what day is it?"

"September 14th, Mrs. Cottner. But I can fill that in." He collected pen and paper from the baffled woman. "I need both your signatures for this contract to be legal. Mr. Cottner, could I trouble you for a moment?"

"Hell with it. Leave it here an' I'll get around to it."

"Pops. Sign the damn paper like the man wants." Hank saw Cam's eyes get steely and hard.

"You don't talk to me thataway."

"Sign the damn paper. Now."

"Why?"

Cam's face reddened. "'Cos it's what I damn want you to do! I'm gonna make us some money. Earn me a honest livin'. You got trouble with that?"

Mr. Cottner sighed. "Gimme the paper."

Hank felt shock. He still wouldn't talk to his father that way, no matter how mad he felt. Maybe things were different with this generation. Would Carl turn out this way?

Despite these thoughts, Hank got Jackson Bigger's signature on the line. It was done. Cam Cottner was now a Hive Records artist. As Hank tucked the contract in his coat pocket, a clock chimed. It was 6:15.

"Won't you be stayin' for supper, Mr. …was it Howard?"

"I'd like to, ma'am, but my own family's waitin' for me. I've got two kids who need their daddy to come home."

"You'll have to bring them over sometimes. I'd like to meet 'em. I can make cookies."

"Why, that'd be…I'll ask my wife about it. Well, thank you…thank you all. I hate to run, but…" He glanced at Cam. "Why don't you come by tomorrow an' we'll listen back to the tracks. See which ones to put out."

He shook Cam's hand and pulled on the screen door. It didn't give. "Push it," Cam said.

"Oh, right. Good evenin,' folks."

Hank's joy clashed with anxiety. *Time has just gotten out of hand today. Bets is furious with me,* he thought. *She can't understand how important all this is. For all our futures…*

He sped to Lawhon Elementary School on Lake Street, as his panic spiked. He was sure this would be the last straw. Liz wasn't happy in this marriage. It was plain as day. He had been a disappointment. But he had such good news, something of such promise and potential…she couldn't walk out on him now. The kids. They needed a loving home. He would plead with her, beg her to stay. Promise her he'd change…

He found a parking spot. The lot was crowded; things were in full swing. He heard music and laughter as he strode through the doors and into the gymnasium. It looked like they were doing a talent show. Three girls sang

"In the Chapel in the Moonlight." *Sang* was a polite word, but they were cute as the dickens and they charmed their audience. Hank waited until they finished. During the applause, he found Liz and sat beside her. "Oh, lord, what a day. I am sorry I'm late. I signed a new artist today."

Liz smiled and squeezed his hand. "You're here. Where our kids can *see* you're here."

Relieved, Hank pointed a thumb at the stage. "A talent show?"

Liz nodded. "A surprise they've put together for us. They're just...delightful. It gives you hope."

"That's wonderful..." A big-haired female teacher introduced the next act. "We have lovely Miss Kitty Howard, who's going to tell us a poem about a kitty. Let's give her a big hand, folks!"

Hank looked at shock and surprise towards Liz, who nodded and smiled. "She's been working on this for weeks." They watched Kitty drift onto stage, looking away from the room. She turned around as the teacher lowered the microphone for her. "The owl anna pussycat. The owl anna pussycat went to the sea in a beautiful s-sea-green boat..."

She maimed the words, left out some lines, got stanzas mixed up, but she made it to the end. "They danced by the light of the moon. Thank you." She curtsied to applause.

"Hurray, Kitty!" Hank shouted. "Man, she's good!" He stood up so his daughter could see him. He waved; she saw him and waved back.

"Carl's in this, too. I don't know when, but they took him backstage. He's all dressed up."

They watched as a blackboard and three chairs were arranged on-stage. A man in horn-rims pulled the mike up to his level. "Y'know, game shows are all the rage on television." The audience chuckled. "Here at Lawhon, we believe in keeping up with the times. So, here's *our* game show—'Spell the Beans!'" More applause. "Our three contestants have gotten the highest marks in spelling this term. Well, tonight we're going to see who's the spelling champ of ol' Lawhon. Is everyone ready?" He looked stage left. "Ladies and gentlemen, let's give a big welcome for our contestants..."

Two boys and a girl marched onstage. Carl, in his bowtie and tweed jacket, was in the middle. Sam waved both arms overhead to get his son's attention. Carl spotted him and beamed. He waved back.

"Now, contestants, the kid gloves are off tonight. We've got some real toughies to test your spelling skills. Are you ready?" The three nodded and sat in their chairs. "On our left is Grover Felton, from 4B. In the middle is Carl Howard, from 3A. And last, but not least, is Violet Draut from 5A. Now, I'm going to fish a word out of the bowl here, and my assistant, Miss Dawson, will write it on the blackboard, where our contestants can't see it. They'll have 30 seconds to correctly spell each word. Every correct word gets 10 points. And, just like in baseball, three strikes and you're out. The first contestant to reach 50 is the winner. Now where in the *world* is that bowl?"

The audience chuckled at his mock-exasperation; the bowl was right in front of him on a lectern. He spotted it and reached in. He showed the slip of paper to Miss Dawson, who nodded and began the word with her chalk. "Conspicuous. Contestant Felton, can you spell the word *conspicuous?*"

Contestant Felton missed the second U. Carl caught the error and delivered the goods. The applause delighted him. "That's my boy!" Hank shouted from the audience. Other parents laughed.

Contestant Draut succeeded with *inconceivable* and was tied with Carl. Felton, up next, muffed *phenomenal,* which Carl got. Contestant Draut aced *incapacitated* and was still tied with Carl.

Felton lost again with *meretricious* and left the stage. "Better luck next time, contestant. He tried his best, so let's give him a big hand, folks." The applause left him less crestfallen.

Carl got *furlough* without hesitation; he and Hank had discussed the *ough* business in homework sessions. The audience gasped as Violet fumbled on *colloquy.* Carl got it; Violet ended the word with *ie* and Carl picked up the *y.*

"This is it, folks! This next round will determine who's the best speller in all of Lawhon Elementary! I'll need some extra-hard words, please…" A short, stout woman walked out and gave the emcee an envelope. He opened it and feigned astonishment. "Oh, my goodness. Why, I don't know if I can even pronounce this one!"

He showed the word to Miss Dawson, who did her best to feign a state of shock. "I can't even *write* this one!" she cried. Everyone, contestants included, laughed. He cleared his throat. "Well, here goes. Contestant Draut, you get the first crack at what could be our final word. And that word is…*hemorrhage.* You have 15 seconds."

"H…e…m…o…r…r…a…g…e. Hemorrhage." She smiled but it was clear that she'd lost the game.

"I'm so sorry. And that is a tough one. I don't imagine many folks sitting in the audience could make it through such a hard word. You win second place, Violet. And now, let's see if Mister Howard can crack this tough word. *Hemorrhage,* Mister Howard."

Carl's face scrunched in concentration. He remembered what his daddy had said about the silent H in some words. "H…e…m…o…r…r…h?"

"Way to go, buddy!" Hank shouted.

"A…g…e!" Carl continued. He spelled it again and was surprised by the hand he got. He won a blue ribbon and a book about rocket ships. He held both up and beamed. Violet got a watercolor set and a red ribbon. She seemed okay with it.

"Well, folks, we couldn't hope to top that, so we'd like to wish you all a good night and thank you all for coming out. Your children are what makes Lawhon the best school in town. I want everyone to stand up and give these kiddos a real Lawhon welcome!"

The parents got to their feet. Hank whistled through his teeth and clapped. The children shuffled onstage and were feted with whistles, handclaps and hurrahs.

"I'm so proud of our kids! What a surprise! Wow!" Hank felt so worked up he could burst. He wasn't in the doghouse; his children were wonderful; he'd signed a new recording artist. Life rarely delivered three good things in a row. Maybe this was a sign. Things were finally going in the right direction…

They went home and got the kids to bed. Carl had fallen asleep in the car and sleepwalked inside. Kitty wanted to work on her coloring book, but she nodded off fast and Hank carried her to bed. He turned off the lights in the kids' rooms. They were dead to the world.

"Boy, it hasn't been this quiet in the house since…" He sat beside Liz on the sofa. She had the TV on; the Pepsodent program was almost over. The reception was poor; they heard Bob Hope's voice but saw pulsing stripes and wrinkles.

"I wish you could have been there the whole time, hon. Miss Pinsky says Carl is a natural straight A student. Were your ears burning?"

"Yes, but maybe for another reason."

"His teacher commented that Carl must have an excellent tutor. I told her he does." She squeezed his hand. Hank knew, in that moment, that he was not behind the eight-ball.

"I'm so proud of him. Both of 'em. Kitty doin' that poem. She was concentrating so hard to remember it."

"She did a real fine job."

"Today, Bets…today I signed a new artist—a trio. I've got a big feeling about 'em. I think this is the bunch. They're white kids—well, one of 'em has to be in his 30s—but they get a black sound. They get the feeling of the music. They're not trying to sound black…it's like they absorbed it and can just squeeze it out, like a sponge."

None of this made much sense to Liz. She was resigned to the preacher routine. Hank had to have his say and then he'd wind down. She trained her attention on the TV set. *Make Room for Daddy* was about to start. *I have my own Danny Thomas right here*, she thought. Hank liked the program, too, and he relaxed and laughed along with his wife.

*Danger* came on next, but Hank was done for the day. He got to sleep without incident and slept hard. For the first time in many months, he relaxed and he felt at home.

*In the morning, Hank had breakfast* with his family, and dropped Carl and Kitty off at school. He couldn't wait to get to work and get the day rolling. He was onto something big and he wanted to get all the wheels in motion. *I sure hope those takes sound as good today as they did yesterday.* He got stuck at a railroad crossing and had a spike of anxiety. A freight train moved at 10 miles and hour. He stopped counting cars at 100 and they kept going. The damn thing stopped a few times. Once it backed up. When the caboose showed, Hank realized he'd not been breathing. He gasped a lungful of air and lightened his grip on the steering wheel.

Big week. New artist, and The Shadow coming in. *Man, Cecil's song would be great for his new single. Shame to waste it on a long-playing record. That song is dynamite. Hot ginger and dynamite.* He'd never have the nerve to put that song out on Hive. Not in Tupelo. That would get his place of business burned down. But in Chicago, they could do wonders with it. And it would reach all the black folks who lived in the city. The people who had left the South because of how it was. Who were making real lives for themselves up north. Cross Records could put that "Hangman" song into the big time. They had the money, the distribution and an in with all the right people. Even if the jocks wouldn't play it—if it got banned from the air, just think what that could do for the record! That's free publicity, buddy, worth its weight in gold…

Hank realized he'd driven a mile further than the office. He U-turned and wound around the alley into his parking spot. He walked in the back door and surprised Miss Bell. "Aw, shoot!" She pulled a page out of her electric typewriter. Hank's entrance had caused her to type excess zeros on a line of an invoice.

Hank stopped in his tracks. He remembered that he'd had a dream about Miss Bell. He struggled to pull the incidents of the dream from his thoughts; smears and blurs came to him, nothing more.

"You okay, Hank?"

"Oh. Oh, yes. Just thinking... sorry 'bout that. Any fires need puttin' out around here?"

"I'm tryin' to get these invoices out to distributors. You know, S&P owes us for an entire year. This is the fourth invoice I've done. They don't answer; nothin'."

Hank sighed. He hated to dun people for money past due. It never ended well, even though he was in the right. "Gimme their number an' I'll call 'em. What's the past due?"

"$788.08."

"Gee, we could use that. 'Specially now." S&P were in Muncie, Indiana and had been Hive's Midwest distributor since '52. There wasn't a big market for black music in that neck of the woods—it was polka and hillbilly country—but they had been good about getting records in shops and to jukebox distributors. "Can I see that invoice, please?"

A glance told Hank they hadn't paid a cent since March 1953—and they'd accepted product up to August of this year. "Until further notice, S&P are cut off from our records. I'm gonna get on the horn. Here goes half the day."

It took long distance 11 minutes to connect the call. In that time, Hank rehearsed what he intended to say: *Now, Norm, I expect delays in payment, but it's been...* he had to figure. *It's been 18 months since we got one red cent from you. And we've been sending you records. Look, if you're having troubles, just let me know. Drop me a line. I unders—*

"Your call's ready," Miss Tinkle's voice fuzzed on Hank's desk intercom.

Hank grabbed the receiver. "Hello? Is this Norm?"

A woman's nasal voice answered. "This is Delaware County Taxidermists Association."

"But this is the number for S&P Music Distributors..."

"They gone out of business. Closed up shop in May."

"They're closed?"

"Yes, sir."

"Could I please speak to someone in your shipping department?"

112

"Our what?"

"Shipping department."

"We don't have none. We're a certification board for taxidermy, sir."

"Well, let me ask…have you been getting boxes from a company called Hive Records, out of Tupelo?"

"I'll check." The woman cupped the phone and asked an associate. "We did, sir, but we refused delivery on them. They tried several times. The parcels should have been sent back to you."

"What? We never got anything back!"

"Once the parcel is in transit, it's out of our hands, sir. I'm sorry if you've lost anything."

There was no point in talking to Muncie any longer. Hank excused himself and hung up. *Well, something was bound to put a dent in my good mood. Crap. Eight hundred bucks down the drain! That hurts.* Hank got a grip on himself and took two of his diet pills. They put pep in his step and got him over rough spots. He took them with black coffee and felt their effect. His heart beat faster and a little heavier, then regulated.

He leaned out of his office and waited for Miss Bell to finish her task. That dream bothered him. He looked at her and felt something he wished he didn't feel. It stirred within him like something in a cage. It wanted a way out.

Hank cleared his throat and took stock of himself. "Miss Bell…"

"N'hmm?"

"Don't bother with S&P anymore. They're out of business."

"Oh, no! I'm sorry, Mr. Howard. That's a lot of money."

Hank sighed. "It happens in this business. Remind me to call all our distributors and make sure they're still around. In fact…where's that list? I'm going to check a couple."

From Midland Music Distribution, he learned the story behind S&P's demise. Norm Saafield, the S in S&P, had been embezzling from the firm. Marcus Paulson, the P, confronted him. Harsh words were spoken, and Norm clouted Paulson with a paper weight. He was now serving a life sentence in Pendleton Correctional Facility. It had been a big story in *Cash Box* last July.

Everybody knew about it.

Hank sat at his desk. He felt a little mad, a little sad and realized there wasn't a damn thing he could do about it. He could declare the loss on his income tax in '55. It was his own damn fault for not keeping up with the business. Maybe he could give Cecil the job of reading the trades and taking notes. That would be a regular job and he'd be perfect for it. He had an analytical mind. *Much better at these things than me,* Hank thought.

"Mr. Howard, it's that boy from yesterday..." Miss Tinkle brought Hank's inner monologue to a stop. He looked up and Cam Cottner waited, his arms folded at his waist. He wore a bright red coat with a bright blue shirt. *Cat clothes,* Hank thought. Like the black musicians wore.

Hank shot to his feet and exited his office, his hand extended. "Mister Cottner! I'm glad to see you!"

"Aw, jus' call me Cam. I ain't no mister yet."

"Miss Bell, is Chuck here?"

"He come in an hour ago. I don't know what he does back there."

"Lemme go in an' get him to cue up the tapes. Can I get you a Co-co-la?"

"Yes, sir. I'd 'preciate that."

As Hank walked through the recording studio towards the booth, the excitement came back to him. He saw Chuck fussing with wires and tubes. "Mister Honeycutt! Our new artist is here and we wanted to review yesterday's tapes."

"Cottner?"

"Yep."

"I'll cue 'em up. Y'all wanna get comfortable. It'll take a minute."

Hank motioned for Cam to enter. "Have a seat. We're gonna listen to 'em all right now. I'm pretty sure we've got a releasable record. We just have to pick two sides. I always prefer to have the artist help with that. After all, the record's goin' out with your name on it."

Cam started to speak; Hank cut him off. "You know, most record companies, they just put out a couple of songs. They don't put a whit of thought behind it. But if you plan it out in advance, you have an advantage over—"

"You sure do like to talk, Mr. Howard!"

The remark caught Hank off-guard. Before he could decide if it was an insult, the tape was running. "—bout it, fellers? Can Cecil sit in?"

They listened to "Decline and Fall." It was a solid performance. Hank had his doubts about putting that one out, because Rusty's record of it was still hot. But it was a good version; worth keeping.

"Midnight" was a stronger performance. "I can see this as the flip side, Cam. Never put a ballad on the plug side."

"Man, we sound so good! Where's that backwash comin' from?"

Hank realized Cam meant the reverb to the vocal. Chuck was a whiz at getting that effect. "It's all Chuck's doin' back there. That an' acoustical tiles. They bounce out the sound, you see."

"I have to agree with you, Mr. Howard. 'Midnight' could be the flip side."

Once "Famous Ignoramus" came on, Hank knew it was a hit. He'd had that feeling during the session, but with almost a day's distance, he had a stronger sense that he was right. Everything was fine—the song, Cam's performance, the was the guitar locked in with Cecil's piano and the tall kid's steady thumping bass fiddle. It felt good—funny, sexy and loose.

"This is our plug side," Hank said. "Don't you think?"

"I like it too. But Mr. Howard, it needs somethin' else. I wish we had a drummer."

Hank looked at him, eager to hear more. "Well, sir, all the nig…all the black guys have drums on their records. It really gives 'em a kick. The record stands out on a juke. Them drum beats cut right through the other racket."

"We could do an overdub. The union kinda frowns on it, but it can't hurt. Hell, I can get Chili Burse in here today. He's with Snake Eyes' group."

"Really?" Cam was excited at the thought. "If it won't hurt nothin' to try…"

"I'll have Chuck record the drum part separate. If we don't like it, we won't use it." Hank waved over his head and Chuck stopped the tape. He and

Chuck had a discussion in the booth. While he waited, Cam approached the studio drum kit. He tinged a cymbal with a fingernail, then played a few notes on the piano. He knew nothing about music aside from singing and rudimentary guitar strumming. The idea that you could sit down at this thing and get music out of it...it was some kind of fuckin' miracle.

"Chili will come in at 1 and lay down a drum part. If you wanna stick around, that's fine."

"Hell, yeah. I mean, yes sir, I'd like that."

"Call me Hank. We're gonna be workin' together on a first-name basis."

"Thank you, Hank. I 'preciate that."

"But there's one thing. I don't like to hear that word in here."

"What word?"

"What you call black people sometimes."

"Nigger?"

Hank winced. "Black folks don't like that word. It's a mean word. I don't say it, an' I expect my artists to say 'black' or 'negro.' Not that word. I want you to learn yourself not to say it."

"Hell, everyone says 'nigger' in Tupelo. I been sayin' it all my life."

"But not in this building! Do you *hear* me? Not *here*." Hank stamped one foot on the floor.

Cam laughed. "I won't say it. I'll try real hard not to."

◊◊◊

Charles "Chili" Burse, who won his nickname from his love of the Mexican dish, showed up just before 1. Hank met him in the lobby. "I 'preciate your comin' in. I've got somethin' easy for ya. We got a new artist an' I think we've got a record. But the main fellow thinks it could use some of that ol' Chili magic. He's in the studio."

Chili looked askance at Cam. "Oh. He hangs around the music store. That kid's got a mouth on 'im."

"Hell, I know you," Cam said. "From Blues City! I didn't know you was a musician."

"I didn't know *you* was a musician." Chili stood at a distance from Cam.

"Y'all know each other?"

"Tupelo ain't a big place." Chili regarded this white kid with disdain. He'd seen a few like him: ready to take anything they could, and with nothing to give back. *And the hell of it is, most of these boys don't like our people. They just like our music.*

"...think he's got a lot of potential. He and his boys love your kind of music and they try to get some of that flavor into their performances. I'll have Chuck play the recording for you first. Give you a sense of..."

"I can get it." Chili sat behind the drum kit and waited.

"Famous Ignoramus" started up. In four bars, Chili had the rhythm. "Child's play," he said with a smile.

"You know, I wanna try somethin'. Gimme a minute." Hank had a brief check-in with Chuck.

"Where you get them threads, son?"

"Savoy, man. The only place to go."

"You like them kyna clothes?"

"Man, ya can't look sharp in the crap they have at Gansser's. That's for squares." Cam drew a box shape in the air.

"Okay. I'm gonna have the playback comin' over the speakers kinda low. I wanna get it on tape along with your drumming. Just to see what it sounds like."

Chili shrugged. "Let 'er roll, man."

The tape played at less than half the volume. Chili didn't come in until the fifth measure. He played with the rhythm section and added a backbone to their work. Nothing showy or fancy. He allowed himself a few flourishes and a clattering roll as the guitar took its solo. The original recording stopped on a dime, and so did Chili.

"Let's hear that back, Chuck." They heard the backwards *zwibble* of rewound tape, then both played in sync. Chuck recorded Chili's performance

117

with a touch of reverb. That affected the playback of the original take; it added a faint, fuzzy echo of the voices and instruments.

"Ain't heard nothin' like that before," Chili said.

Hank cackled with glee. "It sounds like it's comin' from Mars!" He turned to Cam. "What's your take on it?"

"I don't know. Sounds kind of phony." He turned to Chili. "Not you, man. You sound great. But…"

"Hang onto that one, Hank. You don't mind another take, Chili?"

"Long as I get paid."

Hank got headphones. With Chuck's help, they were plugged into the right place, so Chili could hear the original take with no bleed-through.

"Rollin'," Chuck shouted from the booth. Chili kicked in on the fifth bar and played an identical performance. His attack on the drums was crisp. It had a bounce. Hank could follow the song through Chili's percussion.

Playback revealed an added kick to the song. The drums didn't overpower the original rhythm section. Chuck and Hank fiddled with the knobs until the drums seemed part of the performance. They had a touch of reverb— just enough to give them an edge.

"Damn, man, that sounds good," Cam said with a smile.

"That's a hit record!" Hank shouted from the booth.

"It don't sound bad," Chili said.

They added light percussion to "Midnight." Chili played with brushes, mostly on the snare, with some cymbal accents. He'd played this slow tempo blues a million times and knew where to go.

Chuck mixed the percussion a little higher on "Midnight." It sounded like it belonged there.

"Gentlemen, that's it! We've got ourselves a record." He gave Chili 50 dollars. It was above union scale, but Hank felt it was a good investment.

"Say, uh, Chili." Cam looked serious. "I'd sure like it if you could record with us again."

"Hank got my number. I'm around, 'cept when I ain't." He tipped his hat and left the studio.

◊◊◊

Hank asked Miss Tinkle to hold his calls. He asked Cam to come back to-morrow. He and Chuck worked all afternoon on a master for both sides of the record. They edged the drums a little higher in the mix on "Ignoramus." It had a beat that made you waggle your foot and tap your hand against whatever was available. And Hank couldn't think of any record on the charts that sounded like it. Maybe on the rhythm and blues charts; but for country and pop it was something new.

"This is different," he said, several times as they mastered the two songs.

They were done by 3:30. Hank got an idea. "Chuck, can you get me a couple of acetates of the top side? I wanna get these to Dixie."

"You think he'll play 'em?"

"Only one way to find out. I'll walk 'em over myself."

Hank found Cecil in the studio. "There you are. What's happening?"

"We've got the kid's record ready to go. And tonight's session with The Shadow." Hank slapped his own forehead. "The photog! I gotta call him now! Gimme a minute."

Hank dialed the paper and got Jerome Keating, the camera man. "Jerry, I just wanted to remind you about tonight's recording session...black and white...yeah, I know, but they don't want to put it out in color...huh. Might not be a bad idea...sure...that's fine...oh? Well, the more the merrier... best for y'all to get set up before 7:30. It might be easier for the guys to walk in and not feel shy...yeah, we've got room in there. I think you'll get some great shots. And we want to get him singing and playing. You know, at the mike...tiles on the wall...cords and chairs and such...exactly. Yeah...I'll be here."

"Man, everything's happening today! But it's good! It's good."

"Anything I can help out with?"

"The big thing is to sell Shadow on your song. Play it with confidence. Put your heart into every word. I think he will read the message loud and clear. I'm hopin' he gets here early. There's gonna be a camera man here, and a col-umnist from the paper. They figure to get a Sunday feature out of this session. But put them out of your mind. Just set The Shadow down and feed him that song."

"Okay. I can do that."

"Cecil, I'm hoping Cross will make 'Hangman' The Shadow's next single. Just think what that could do for the song! What a message—and it could get spread all over the country…"

Cecil was in no mood for a sermon. He cut in: "The kid's record. You were about to tell me some news."

Hank told him. Cecil liked the idea of adding the drum part. "I'd like to hear it. See how it came out."

"Sure, sure. Soon as Chuck gets a couple of dubs run off for me. I'm takin' 'em to Dixie; see if he'll play 'em tonight."

Cecil grinned at the thought. "Things sure do happen fast 'round here!"

"This is a big, big day for Hive Records—for our company. We are making musical history. Why, it—"

"Hank, I got 'em for ya. I cut 'em hot." Chuck came out of the booth—a sign that this was important. He blew a couple of curlicues from the records and sleeved them. CAM AND THE CATS—FAMOUS IGNORAMUS was written across the labels.

"Oh! Say, could you play the mix-down of both sides for Cecil here? I wanna get these on the air. See how they go over." Before Chuck could answer, Hank was gone with the records.

As Hank beat feet toward WELO, Cecil absorbed the beefed-up sound of "Famous Ignoramus" and "Midnight." Chili improved both sides, and his percussion sounded like it had been recorded right there—not dropped in a day later. "This is the damndest thing," he said to himself. "It's new. It's different."

"That it is," Chuck said.

"Who knows? Maybe it'll go big."

"And maybe we got another Maggie Woodburn."

Cecil laughed. "Only one of her."

They laughed at the thought. "Could you tune in WELO? Might as well hear what happens…"

"Yeah!" Chuck played the broadcast over the studio P.A. "Hoo-wee! That was Amos Milburn doin' 'I Done Done It!' An' he sho' done it awright, fokes! Hey ya, Hank! We got us a local celebrity in the stew-joe, fokes. It's Hank Howard. He's the cool cat who makes alla them hot Hive platters y'all dig! We-hell, come an' sit a spell and let us know…what's buzzin'?"

"Howdy, Dixie…howdy, WELO listeners. I'm here to give y'all the premiere of a brand-new Hive record release by a different kinda group. They're called Cam and The Cats, and they're—"

"They're goin' right on the turntable! 'Famous Ignoramus!' Why, that's me! Well, folks, we'll talk with Hank after we spin this here 'Ignoramus.' How new is this, Hank?"

"We recorded it yesterday. Just mixed it an' I thought…"

"You thought right, cousin! Here goes!"

Dixie dropped the needle. Cecil's piano chords pounded; Skip's guitar answered and Cam's voice, drenched in reverb, came in, full of swagger and attitude. Chili's drums, hard-hitting and crisp, sealed the deal. Hank's heart did backflips. He watched Dixie. The deejay's eyes bugged out; his jaw relaxed. The newness hit him. It took him 30 seconds to get his composure; he was hooked. He'd never heard the like of this record. The beat got to him; he sat on the edge of his office chair. Hank couldn't tell if he was still breathing. Dixie's gaze was far away; as if he weren't seeing, only hearing.

With Skip's final guitar chord ringing in the air, Dixie howled—a wild whoop that startled Hank. "Wow wow wow! Folks, what a record what a re-cord—what a record! Have you ever? Have y'all ever heard the like o' that in all your natch'l-bawn lives? Pass the smellin' salts, Matilda! Ol' Dixie 'bout to faint, that record is so doggone good!"

"I'm glad you—"

"Hank, how you come to cut us such a…folks, would you like to hear that one again? I wanna hear it again! I'm unna play it!" He did. He cut his microphone so he could talk to Hank. "This is…I don't know what to call it. That kid is white. Idn't he?"

"Yep."

"You can hardly tell it. He sings like Rusty Gordon. Same kyna feelin'. In-credible! But tell me one thing."

"Of course."

"This ain't country. Ain't rhythm an' blues. It ain't pop. What you call this?"

"Cat music. That's what they told me."

Dixie hooted. "Cat music! That's it!" He went live as the record came to its close. "We got us somethin' new here on the Dixie Doodle show...cat music! Brothers an' sisters, can you dig it? Cat music! Now, y'all get on them teller-phones an' call ol' Dixie. What do y'all think about cat music? An' Hank Howard, what is cat music?"

"Well...I guess it's a meeting of black and white music. Blues and country. It's the place where they come together. It's our attempt at somethin' new. I feel that young people have been wanting something better in popular music. Something with real drive and feeling. Something that speaks their language..."

"So who's this Cam character? An' who are The Cats?"

"Cam Cottner is a young man from Tupelo. He's been a devoted fan of rhythm and blues for years. He's studied it, gotten the feel for it, and he can sing it. On guitar is a fellow named Skip Mosely. He's been around for awhile. And the kid on bass fiddle...doggone, I forgot his name. He's a tall drink of water!"

"Seems t' me I hear pie-anna an' some tub thumpin' on that thing, too."

"The piano is by Cecil Madison. He's a very good songwriter—one of the best in the rhythm and blues field, I think. We were lucky to get Chili Burse, from Snake Eyes' band, to sit in with The Cats." Hank decided against telling WELO's listeners it was an overdub, since someone from the musician's union might be listening.

"Cecil Madison...why, we had him on the show couple-three weeks ago. He's quite a talented feller!"

"I agree. We're lucky to have him on board."

"Does Cecil write alla The Cats' songs?"

"I think he's going to. We've just got two songs recorded."

"Well, y'all better get yourselfs back in the studio an' make us some

122

more—'cause Dixie likes...*loves* this here 'Ignoramus!' You know, I better play it again!"

Hank excused himself. He eased the studio door shut and walked up the hallway to the reception area. Two operators took calls. "I'll send him your request...WELO...yes, ma'am, I'll ask him to play it again...WELO...I'll tell him..."

Hank stared at the stack of notes the women scrawled down. This was all for "Famous Ignoramus." It took him a moment for the realization to sink in. They had a hit on their hands!

On his way back to the office, Hank prioritized what had to be done: *make a master lacquer for the folks in Nashville...how many sets of stampers can I afford to get made? We'll have to press promo copies and get 'em out...get 'em in the hands of jocks...get it reviewed in Cash Box and Billboard...labels...get the copy down to the printer...what am I forgetting here?*

He was greeted by Cecil, Chuck and Miss Tinkle. They beamed and congratulated Hank. The gravity of the situation kept him from really hearing their kind words. "Cec, Chuck, let's have us a pow-wow." Miss Tinkle followed, ready with notepad and pencil.

They gathered in Hank's office. Hank got a flash of some war movie, where the commander outlined the plans for a battle. "We have ourselves a possible hit record. Now, we won't know until we get it out in the world. And there's a lot of work and money...Lord knows how I'm gonna pay for all this. The cupboard is pretty bare, fellows."

Hank assigned Chuck the mastering duties. "Cut it hot, like those acetates. Did it sound good on the air?"

"Sounded fine," Chuck said. "Loud and clear."

"I thought it was good," Cecil added.

"All right. That's your number one priority. Get the masters ready and we'll get some stampers made. If this record goes like I think it will, it'll be more than we can handle. We'll press enough promos to get word out. But we're gonna have to go with a pressing plant—if this goes over.

"Cecil, I'd like you to fill out the label information and take it over to Gorman's. Tell him we need 2,000 labels as soon as possible. 'Midnight' is Acuff-Rose Music...yours...we'll have to do a copyright form on it, but let's put it as Beehive Music for now. You know what to do. I'll call the folks in Nashville and see if they can give me a line of credit. I've always paid them on time…Miss Bell, get me Nashville Lathe and Die on the phone."

He looked up at his co-owners. "Everything clear?" They nodded. "Time is money, gentlemen. Let's—" The intercom buzzed. Nashville Lathe & Die was on the line. Hank took two of the little white pills, downed them with cold coffee and took the call.

◊◊◊

Nashville Lathe and Die was willing to cooperate. Hive was given 60 days to pay for the new stampers. Hank had four sets made—two for Applied Plastics, the devil that he knew, and one for Monarch in Los Angeles. The fourth he had shipped air mail express to the Hive office. He and Cecil would keep busy banging out deejay copies, and getting this credit extension gave Hive some extra money for postage. The bulk rate helped as well.

Cecil drafted up the label copy. The printer gave them a form with an enlarged blank version of the label. Cecil typed the pertinent info into the proper spots. On the right-hand area below the logo, where the category went, Cecil typed Cat Music. Since he was able, he put his full name as composer of the A-side. None of this "C. Madison" if he could help it.

He scanned the pages for typos, saw none, and ran the papers to Gorman's Offset Printing. "Mr. Howard needs these yesterday," Cecil joked. Old Gorman had a sense of humor and he snorted at the joke.

He squinted as he proofed the copy. "'Cat Music?' What'd you do, get 'em out of the alley?"

"It's something new. A cross between blues and country."

"Huh. Looks like Hank's puttin' all his eggs in one basket."

"It's a good basket, Mr. Gorman."

"With 2,000 labels, it better be! Rush, yet…" Cecil watched Gorman take the papers to his typesetter. They had a discussion. Gorman returned.

"Day after tomorrow. Soonest I can do it."

"Well, that'll have to do. Thank you, Mr. Gorman."

Gorman glanced at the sheet. "'Cat music.' Is dog music next?"

***The pieces fell into place.*** Chuck had masters of both sides ready for Nashville. They were ready to be shipped by express the next morning. Nashville estimated the stampers would be in Hank's hands in one week. The labels would be printed, cut and ready by then.

"What a day! And it ain't over yet..." Hank looked at his watch. "Cec, we got an hour 'til the session. You and I better get somethin' in our stomachs."

There weren't any restaurants in downtown Tupelo that would serve black people. They had to settle for bologna sandwiches and potato chips from the corner market. Hank prayed he wouldn't get heartburn.

After they ate, Hank had Cecil run through "Hangman." "I think if you sing it just right, Shadow will like it. Don't be timid about it. It took guts to write this song. Sing it the way you wrote it."

Cecil sat at the piano and smoothed out the lyric sheet. He wished he'd had time to type it up. His handwriting made sense to him, but was chicken scratches to anyone else unless he wrote with great care.

Cecil vamped the opening E minor chord and got himself in the mood. He tried to summon the shock and sadness he felt when he read that newspaper story. His thoughts reviewed the insults, threats and shortcomings he had experienced in his life to date.

He sang "Hangman" as he could never hope to do again—and Hank had Chuck record that performance. He hit the RECORD button just in time. The first seconds of the piano were cut off, but the performance was preserved.

Cecil felt spent, changed, blank as he finished the song. He sat in silence as the piano's chords decayed in the room.

"Terrific! Terrific! I got that on tape, Cecil. If that doesn't sell the song, man, nothing can!"

Cecil felt a sudden shock, as if he'd been violated. Then he realized he was off the hook. Shadow could hear the song without being judge and jury to Cecil as he performed it. Shock became relief; he felt his body relax. His mind became clearer, more acute.

◊◊◊

The Lonesome Shadow showed up, guitar case in one hand, a flour sack of clattering harmonicas in the other, a few minutes shy of 7. His sidemen were often late, and this gave him time to warm up. Cecil waited in the studio while Hank and The Shadow talked business in Hank's office.

The camera man and columnist from the paper appeared at 7:05. Cecil waved them into the studio. "Are you The Lonesome Shadow?" A crinkle-eyed, gray-templed man in a bow tie extended his hand.

"No, sir. I'm Cecil Madison. I'm a songwriter and I'm helping to supervise this recording session."

The photographer, laden with equipment, unloaded his tools. He checked the light levels in the room. "With fast film, this oughta work." He assembled a photo light, in an aluminum cone, and pointed it up at the corner of the ceiling. It bounced light back into the room. "Say, pal, could you stand there...I just wanna be sure..."

Cecil stood where The Shadow would soon sing and play. "Yeah. That's got a good backlight. Very good. Thank you."

The Shadow's bassist and drummer entered the building. Miss Tinkle pointed them into the studio. The musicians were taken aback by the cameras and lights. "It's okay," Cecil said to them. "We're taking some photographs for the record company."

"And for the paper," the cameraman said. "We're going to do a story about this place and the music."

"Well," the bassist said. "Never seed my name in the paper."

"'Cept in the police report," the drummer quipped.

"Gentlemen!" Hank entered the room. "Glad to see you all. This is going to be a special recording session. We're hoping to get enough tracks to complete a long-playing record album. It might be the first of its kind for the blues market."

The columnist quizzed Hank on the record business as he scribbled on a notepad. The Shadow came through the door and eyed the room. "Looks like we're having a to-do in here!"

"Gentlemen of the press, this is The Lonesome Shadow, Cross Records artist, here for tonight's session."

"Pleased to meet you. How should I address you when I'm writing about you?"

"Just call me 'The Shadow.' I prefer not to use my birth name."

"Gee, kind of like Superman," the cameraman joked. Everyone laughed.

"Well, Shadow, before we get going, I'd like you to hear a song. I know you do your own material, but I believe this song is worthy of your time. Can I play it for you?"

"I never knew you to sing."

"It isn't me. I had the composer record it for you. Chuck, if you'll..." Hank made a spinning motion with his index finger.

The piano chords filled the room. They vamped for eight bars and then Cecil's voice came in:

*Hangman, hangman, by the big oak tree;*

*Shadow man whose face I cannot see...*

*Is the color of my skin going to mean the end of me?*

Cecil was no less nervous than if he were at the piano. Everyone in the room listened in silence. Cecil felt his heart drum in his ears. He couldn't hear the words clearly.

He focused again as the song reached its finale:

*...if your fellow man would rather give you a hand*

*and we all could really be free.*

The song concluded and cold sweat trickled down Cecil's back. No one seemed able to speak. Cecil looked at Hank; Hank nodded once.

The Shadow cleared his throat. The deep sound was a jolt. "I appreciate that song. What it's trying to say. I think we could do that up right." Cecil felt himself relax. He realized he hadn't been breathing. "I got my songs I wanna do, but we can make time for that one. Where'd you get that song, Mr. Howard?"

"Right here." He gestured to Cecil. "Cecil Madison wrote it."

"I seen you around, son."

"I've been around. Thank you for..." Cecil couldn't get words together. "Thank you."

"I'd like to get some background on you, Mister Madison...do you have a moment?"

Cecil looked up at the newspaper writer. He was pale and tired-looking with dark circles under his eyes. He chewed gum and his shirt collar was damp with sweat. "Yes, sir. Let's go into the lobby. They're just getting set up, warmed up. Hank doesn't need me so far."

"Cec, could you copy out your lyrics and the chords for The Shadow?"

"Of course." He retrieved the shirt cardboard from the piano and went into the lobby area. He sat at a typewriter, found carbon paper, and sandwiched it between two sheets of stationary. "Sorry to do this while we talk, but 'round here, everything happens at once."

"That's fine. I'll keep my questions simple."

"Shoot." Cecil typed the first line of the lyric.

"I'm sure you're aware that your song is a...controversial number, Mister Madison."

"Yes, sir, I don't doubt that it is. I don't expect everyone to like it."

"Now, you've written several songs for local blues artists. How did you get started in this field?"

Cecil told a sanitized story of his life, with the resentments, disappointments and upsets left out; he started writing songs while in the service, and brought them to Mr. Howard, who liked them and hired him on as an assistant. He didn't mention that he was 33.3% of Hive Records. As he spoke, he made a mistake and had to back up and XXX out the wrong words.

"Now, back to this song we just heard. Where did this idea come from?"

"From an article in your paper. It's probably something most people skipped over. It wasn't on the front page. You might not want to talk about it."

128

"I'd like the real story. Our readers can handle it."

Cecil stopped typing. He told the reporter, in brief, blunt words, about reading the article on the lynching, how it made him feel, and how it saddened him that such things were still a part of American life. "Like it says at the end, I hope that we can all see eye to eye, as real human beings. We're all a part of the world. We all fit into it somewhere. I was taught that the idea of America was a place where anybody had a chance. I'd like it to really be that way. 'With liberty and justice for all,' like they say in the pledge of allegiance. That might seem naïve to some people. But I don't think it's a lot to ask."

"What are your plans for the future? What's next?"

Cecil pondered the question. "I intend to keep writing songs and helping run this business. If the public is willing, Mr. Howard, Mister Honeycutt and I will make a success out of Hive Records. It's a gamble, but, you know, anything in life worth doing has that element."

The newsman nodded. He clicked his pen and put his notepad away. "Thank you, Mister Madison."

The howling of Shadow's harmonica, and the ratatat of drums, called their attention to the studio. "Again," Hank called to the booth.

"Welcome to a recording session at Hive Records," Cecil said. He held the door for the newsman. Cecil stayed on the other side to finish the lyric sheet. He spotted two other errors he'd made while talking, and scrolled up to correct them.

The piercing sound of the harmonica, amplified with reverb, cut in on his concentration, but he finished his task. He left double spaces between the lines as he pecked the keys. When done, he unreeled the pages and wrote the chords where they were supposed to go. E minor was one of the easiest chords to play on any instrument. If that wasn't The Shadow's key, he was free to change it.

Cecil couldn't make out the lyrics of the song being recorded, but it was uptempo and The Shadow laughed as part of the chorus. It was a cutting laugh—not one he'd ever want to receive.

The take ended and Cecil entered the studio. "That sounded good," he said to Hank.

"We need to do that one over," The Shadow said.

"You think so? 'Cause we certainly can."

"I think so. It needs some bottom. Say, brother, you can play that box?"

It took Cecil a few seconds to realize The Shadow was talking to him, and asking him to play the piano.

"I get by on it."

"Well, get by, son, get by!" Everyone laughed and the photographer got some good shots of The Shadow smiling, with his teaspoon guitar hanging from his chest.

"Song's got a bounce to it," Cecil said. "You all doing it in A?"

"You got the ear, son. Bounce along with us."

"Ready, Chuck? 'Goodbye Letter' take two."

Cecil watched The Shadow for a cue. The song began with just The Shadow's voice. He held a giant index finger in the air and brought it down as he hit a shrill chord on the harmonica. Cecil banged an E7 chord along with the drummer and bassist, and then hammered some sixteenth notes while the drummer did a fill.

The song was a standard 12-bar blues about a trifling woman who was going to party The Shadow out of house and home. He'd had enough, and he packed his bag and left behind a kiss-off letter, "nailed to my old front door." She'd need to find another daddy "'cos I won't be back no more."

Cecil got an inspiration to play a discord as The Shadow laughed. It added bite to the moments. The blues was easy to play, but hard to feel. Anyone could play these three chords over and over. Cecil understood the feeling that pinned it all together. The song wasn't subtle; its point was pounded home musically and lyrically. Cecil banged along with feeling; tried to put some anger behind those simple chords. He played a ninth chord at the end to give it more oomph.

"That's good," The Shadow said. "Put that one out." He turned to Cecil. "Be good to have you keep at that box. You willing?"

"I am." Cecil wondered if he'd get a session fee. Anything was possible tonight.

The Shadow got through the five songs he'd brought to the session. It was late. Cecil couldn't see the clock in the studio but he guessed it to be 11, maybe midnight. He was tired, but he'd played good. He took a four-bar solo on a mid-tempo song on impulse. It seemed to be wanting some piano, and he played it.

"Well, my friend, we've gotten the tracks for your first album, and we've got one side of a single. We need one more song in the can..."

It was a leading question, asked as only Hank could finagle it. The answer was obvious, but it needed The Shadow's accord.

The Shadow stood, expressionless, staring at nothing. Then he turned his head Cecil's way and nodded. "We got your song to do. Run it down for us. I got to get the feel."

There was no way out of this. Cecil realized it. He got the shirt cardboard and cleared his throat. He vamped an E minor chord and added a sixth to it, then a ninth, and sang:

*Hangman, hangman, by the big oak tree;*

*Shadow man whose face I cannot see...*

The bassist found his notes and played a walking figure; the drummer worked his brushes and the effect was like a death march. The Shadow looked through his sack of harmonicas and found the right one. He made some wails that completed the picture. The effect was desolate, relentless, like a pursuing figure in a nightmare.

Hank gave the signal to Chuck to roll the tapes; he wanted to preserve this moment for posterity. He felt a swelling pride for Cecil. *I'd shit myself fore I'd ever do what he's doing. He's got guts.*

"We got it, son. You just play like you been playin'. I believe I got the feelin'. Let's get a take. Roll that thing."

The tape kept rolling, and The Shadow nailed "Hangman" in one take. He sang it like he'd lived it, with fear, horror and contempt in his voice. He spat the words out, and when he played the harp, it was a condemnation of the world that wouldn't welcome him as a fellow citizen.

Hank glanced over to the newsmen. They stood breathless like statues. The finger pointed at them, or people they knew; it told the truth no one in their world wanted to hear.

The song's last notes lingered and decayed in the air. "I believe that does it," The Shadow said.

"Boy, does it ever!" The newsman shoveled fresh sticks of gum in his mouth. "Mr. Howard, I may need to call you tomorrow for some additional background. It could be a few weeks before I can get this story approved. If the *Journal* won't run it, I'll sell it to the wire service."

"Call anytime. Thank you, gentlemen. Thanks to everyone here. This was a great session. Big things are gonna come from what we did in here tonight!"

The Shadow and his sidemen packed their gear. As the bassist struggled his instrument out the door, The Shadow paused. He put his hand on Cecil's shoulder. "You done good tonight. Be proud of yourself."

"Yes, sir, I am."

The Shadow smiled and slung his guitar over his shoulder. His harmonicas clacked together in their burlap sack.

Cecil and Hank sat in the studio. "I'm too tired to move," Hank said.

"I hear you."

"The Shadow's right, Cec. You done good." He reached out his hand and Cecil shook it.

Chuck Honeycutt emerged from his room, haggard and sweaty. "Man, if we put out that last song, they'd be comin' after us!"

"That's why it's going to Chicago. Well, get some rest. We'll get those tapes worked up tomorrow. I'll call Victor and let him know the session went well."

Chuck lit a cigarette and left the building.

"This is the calm before the storm," Hank said. "Big things are gonna happen here, Cec. I know I've said that before, but this time I can feel it. Right down to my toes..."

"I agree with you. And it's kinda late for a sermon, don't you think?"

Hank stopped, looked startled and then laughed. "You know me too well. Le'me get you home, buddy."

◊◊◊

The next two days were a blur. While Hank awaited the proofs of the photo session for The Shadow, he and Chuck created the masters for the six songs from that productive session. Hank knew Victor Cross would muddy the sound. Chuck brightened the high end to make up for the murk Cross would bring to the mix.

The reporter called Hank to get the background of Hive, and got more quotes than he could use for a dozen articles. Cecil heard him pontificate in his office and chuckled.

Hank got the contact sheets of the photoshoot and picked three likely images for an album cover. His favorite captured The Shadow singing with his mouth open. His right hand was a blur as it strummed his guitar. To his right, the bass player looked stage left with a smile. Behind them, the drummer concentrated on his work. Cecil and his piano were on the far left. The right side of Cecil's face and shoulder were in the shot.

Jerome Keating printed the three images at album cover size, 12 inches square, and put vellum overlays on each piece. He had layers of heavy corrugated cardboard to help them arrive intact. With Miss Tinkle's help, Hank and Cecil got the goods packed; Hank walked them to the post office and sent them special delivery.

After that, he called Victor Cross and relayed the news. "Victor, we have a terrific side for The Shadow's next single. This song will make the headlines!"

"Is it dirty?"

Hank laughed. "Nope! Just...truthful. I wouldn't dare put it out on my label. But I think you can handle it."

"You haven't sent me any crap yet. But if this is too hot to handle..."

"Hell; hold the line. I'll be right back." Chuck was cleaning tape heads in the booth. The fumes from the cleaner were strong. "You're gonna kill yourself, buddy! Listen. I've got Cross on the horn. Can you cue up 'Hangman' for him? The Shadow's version?"

Chuck coughed. "Sure."

133

"Play it loud over the studio speakers."

Hank picked up the phone in the studio. "Victor! You still there?"

"What is this?"

"I want you to hear the song. See for yourself."

"But I—"

"Just listen." Hank waved and held the receiver up near the speaker. The tape began. Dark chords on the piano, followed by a searchlight burst from The Shadow's harmonica. Then the slow grinding rhythm kicked in. The Shadow's voice, bolstered with reverb, told its hard tale with stark words. It ended with a wish for mankind to be decent to one another. The record closed with a final blat from The Shadow's harp and a couple of cymbal rolls, with the final chord cut off sharp in unison—an unplanned ending that to Hank's ears couldn't be bettered.

Hank returned the phone to his ear. "Well?"

"Mr. Howard, I am a businessman. I am in business to make money. And that is a song that will make money. A lot of money. It might get some innocent people killed in the process, but *tak to już jest*; that's the way it goes."

Hank wasn't sure what to say in response. He mentioned the terrific photographs, and that Victor was sure to like them and the long-playing album was sure to be a money-making smash.

*Tack toe you-gee yest,* Hank thought. *Gotta remember that one!* He signed off and exhaled in relief. Phone conversations with Cross caused him to hold his breath. His heart beat fast as he got oxygen into his lungs. Then he went out the front door and stood on the street. He heard the high keen of the crickets and walked down to the corner.

Across the street, catacorner, the woods began to transition into first place. Businesses became less frequent; a gas station down a block; a hamburger joint with a neon sign across from that. Hank let his mind clear out. He focused on the crickets and started into the cluster of scrub woods. Above, the sky was milky yellow-gray with cloud cover. Above all that the sun shone down, but only its heat was felt. *A good rain; that's what we need*, he thought. He breathed deep of the muggy afternoon air. It smelled of woods and ivy and damp. It was what he'd known all his life.

He ended his commune with nature and went back up the street. In his brief absence, the record labels for the next Hive single had arrived. Cecil and Miss Tinkle inspected them. Gorman was a stickler; he did good work. The printing was centered, in clear-set type. Gorman used that round, moony typeface; Future something. It looked clean and modern.

With nothing better to do, he and Cecil A and B'd the labels and put them on spindles, face down, for whenever the stampers showed up. He hoped they'd be delivered by Monday morning. "Give you a ride home?" he asked Cecil. "I'm gonna get home in time for dinner tonight."

Hank got home in time for dinner.

***The stampers came on Saturday—at 8:30 AM,*** and to Hank's house. Because no one was at the Hive facility to sign for them, the carrier dropped them at the Howard residence.

Hank was still in his pajamas, trying to emerge from the murk of sleep, second cup of coffee before him. He'd gotten up an hour before and let Bets and the kids sleep in. Fat lot of good that did!

"Got a box from Nashville. Says you gotta sign for it." A bland chubby man held out papers on a clipboard.

"Hold on, buddy. I wanna load that in my trunk."

The noise woke everyone. "What's wrong, Daddy?" Kitty mumbled.

"Did fire trucks come?" Carl asked.

"Naw, naw, just something for work. Y'all get on back to bed."

"How can I sleep?" Kitty looked up at him. "You got me all woked up!"

Liz stirred as Hank entered their bedroom. "What on earth..."

"It's nothing. I need my keys." He fumbled on the dresser for them and knocked them under the dresser. They were just out of reach. "Dammit!" he sighed. He thought to move the dresser, but it had all of Liz's perfumes and other lady things, all in fragile glass bottles. "Kitty, dear, can you help your ol' pop out?"

Kitty peeked in. "Is it worth a quarter, Daddy?"

"Gougers. We got gougers for children! Yes. Just fish out Daddy's keys from under the dresser."

Kitty looked wary. "But what if there's espiders down there? I'm scared

136

of espiders."

"There ain't no spiders, sweetie. If there are, I'll give you a dollar. Howz'bout that?"

"Well…" Finance won out and she pushed her hand into the dark space. "Where are they, Daddy? Oh! I got 'em!" She withdrew her hand with the dust-covered keys. "No espiders." She looked disappointed.

"I'll give you 50 cents. How's that?"

"Okay," she said, suddenly chipper.

He slid a half dollar from the top of the dresser and traded her. "Benjamin Fanklin!" she cried.

Hank unlocked the trunk and removed beach toys and cans of paint. He tossed those on the lawn and turned to meet the delivery van. Mr. Bland handed him the crate. It was lighter than Hank anticipated. He almost dropped the box; he caught it and got it into the trunk. He signed for the crate and waved the van goodbye.

Neighbors peered out their front door and peeked out their kitchen windows. "It's okay." Hank waved and smiled. "Special delivery. We're fine."

"What was that all about?" Liz held a cup of coffee.

"That my future. Sittin' in the trunk. It's my next record, and it's gonna go through the roof. I know I've said that before, but this time…I can just feel it." Anxiety spiked in his heart. "We'd better get movin'! I've got promotional copies to send out… we can get 'em ready to go out first thing Monday morning."

"But the kids…" Liz stopped herself. She knew this routine. And maybe this wasn't Hank chasing his tail. He had been working hard, and it was possible he was right. Vague plans to take the children to Tombigbee Lake. There was enough there to exhaust Carl and Kitty and give their parents a quiet evening together.

Hank called Miss Tinkle and alerted her to the delivery. She agreed to come in and help. Hank wished Cecil had a phone…and he remembered the plans for today. It had been proposed four nights earlier, agreed upon and promptly forgotten by him.

He dashed to Liz. "Honey, tomorrow we'll go to Tombigbee. It's supposed to be warm and sunny." He motioned to the window. "Kind of overcast today. It wouldn't be much fun for 'em like this."

"You remembered." She said it without inflection; it wasn't a statement of contempt or surprise.

"Yes, I remembered. Don't you know I think about these things? I dwell on 'em. Hey, maybe you can take the kids to the show. Carl's been wantin' so see that movie about the robot."

"Well..."

"Hey kidlets! Big announcement!" Carl and Kitty crept into the living room. Were they in trouble? "We're gonna go swimming tomorrow. I've got to take care of something big today. But your momma is gonna take you to the movies today! How's that sound?"

It sounded good to them. He kissed his wife and then rushed through a shower. No need to shave or wear a tie. This was really a work day. He wore his yardwork clothes: a grey sweatshirt and old blue slacks. They smelled of grass and gasoline, but they'd do.

"No idea when we'll be done. I'll call you and check in." Hank dashed out the front door and just avoided a collision with the mailman. *Just like Blondie and Dagwood*, he thought.

◊◊◊

Cecil had been up awhile when he heard the crackle of car tires coming up the hill. Its wheels spun against wet clay. The engine died. "Cecil!" It was Hank Howard.

Coaxial meowed and plopped on the floor to investigate. Cecil pulled on his shoes. He had boxer shorts and a T-shirt on. "Hank."

The underbrush spasmed and Hank emerged. "Hey, buddy. Big doings. We got the stampers! We got records to make!"

"I, uh, I'm not..."

"Get some clothes on! I'm gonna back down to the road." The wheels zazzed against wet clay then got traction.

"Murnau?" Coaxial asked, his tail a question mark.

"It's fine, buddy. I gotta go work. You keep an eye on the place." The

138

cat rubbed against Cecil and got his chin scritched. Cecil climbed into trousers and grabbed a shirt. He knew better than to wear good clothes for the job ahead.

"This is a big day!" Hank radiated excitement. Cecil rolled his eyes before Hank could see his face. He climbed in the car. "Yes, sir, big doings!"

"We've done this before, you know. It's a new record."

"Yeah, but it's your song, buddy! It's gonna go big. This is the one gonna make us."

"You say that about every record." Cecil paused for effect. "Said that about Margie Woodburn."

"Well..." Hank sighed. "I was wrong about hcr. But don't think that didn't teach me a lesson. Oh, no. This is a whole 'nother shootin' match. We're onto somethin' different with this one."

"Let's get 'em pressed and see." Cecil felt determined to be the devil's advocate.

"Well, then, I guess that's what let's do," Hank said, in imitation of his partner's reserved tone of voice. His mimickry made Cecil laugh, despite himself. *Might as well laugh,* he thought.

◊◊◊

Seven hours and 15 minutes later, they had 300 copies of "A Famous Ignoramus" by Cam and His Cats pressed and in sleeves. Miss Tinkle helped sleeve the discs and applied a rubber stamped red star to each A-side label. That was a signal to jocks that this was the side they should bother with. Better not to give Acuff-Rose all the royalties from airplay. Having a familiar B-side would help less adventurous DJs warm to the record, but "Famous Ignoramus" was the side that would break, if there was anything to this crazy thing.

Hearing both sides several times confirmed Hank's faith in the disc. It was loud, bright and attention-getting. The kid could really sing. *I better get him some copies*, Hank thought. *Five or 10 oughta hold him for now.*

Miss Bell folded a mimeographed note that went with the record. It read:

## TO ALL YOU GREAT DEEJAYS OUT THERE:

Every new record comes out with promises that it's the greatest thing since sliced bread. Most of them aren't. THIS ONE IS!

If you're looking for something NEW... DIFFERENT...SHOW-STOPPING...you have found it in A FAMOUS IGNORAMUS by our new artists, CAM AND THE CATS.

We're taking a big chance on this one...but we believe it's the best record we've ever released--and we want to give YOU first crack at it!

Give it a listen. If you think it's got that "special something" to punch up your program, PLAY THE DICKENS OUT OF IT!

We think it's terrific...but what matters most is what YOU think of it!

## A FAMOUS IGNORAMUS--ANOTHER HIVE RECORDS SMASH!

There hadn't been time to do an artist biography. Once this record took off, they'd have to get some photographs and a sheet on the singer. His life story, how he became interested in music...boilerplate stuff.

Hank called home at 5:30. The kids had gone to see *Tobor the Great*. Carl loved it; Kitty said it was silly. But there had been two Woody Woodpecker cartoons, so she was happy. Both kids were excited about tomorrow's lake trip. And meat loaf would be out of the oven at 6:15 if he wanted to have dinner with his wife and family.

"You know I do. I got one errand—real quick—and I'll be home."

Miss Bell had sealed the last manila envelope. A mountain of mail-outs were stacked into bundles. Hank would run these to the post office first thing on Monday.

"Terrific! Well, Monday things will be hopping around here. Miss Bell, call a cab for Cecil. My partner ain't gonna walk home tonight."

He handed Cecil a five dollar bill. "Sorry, Cec, but I've got to get home. Thank you. Rest up, and I'll see you on Monday." Hank left before anyone could speak. Cecil and Miss Bell looked at each other; they didn't know how to feel about it.

Cecil was too frazzled to feel anything. He hated riding in a taxi, but no way was he going to hike that three miles. He called Mid-City Cab, the company that would let black people ride without any fuss. He had leftovers in the icebox; all he needed to do was be home.

◊◊◊

Cam Cottner was getting ready for a night out when Hank showed up. "Got something for your boy," Hank said to Cam's momma.

"Mr. Howard!" Cam emerged from the back hall in a pink shirt and black slacks.

"You're all spiffed up."

Cam laughed. "Got my cat clothes on."

"I wanted you to have the first copies of your record." He handed his new artist 10 copies of Hive Record #248. "Congratulations!"

"Holy shit!" Cam said. He pulled one record out of its sleeve. He held the disc up to the light and saw the twinkling play on its surface. "God damn!"

"You watch that mouth," Jackson said from his chair.

"This mouth gonna make us all rich, Pops!"

"Hot damn! Thank you, Mr. Howard!" Cam started for his room. Then he stopped. "I really 'pre-shate it."

"We should get a biography of you and Skip and what's his name..."

"Clue. I'll come down Monday an' give you all that."

Hank bid the Cottners goodnight before Momma could invite him into supper. He had to break bread with his own brood.

◊◊◊

Liz kept dinner warm for him, and he was ravenous. Those diet pills made him forget to eat, and kept him driving, driving. He had seconds of meat loaf and green bean casserole. Carl and Kitty gave him a report on *Tobor, The Great* and enthused about tomorrow's fun at the lake.

"You gonna go swimmin', daddy?" Kitty asked.

"I reckon I'm gonna find a nice, shady tree an' take a nap."

"Aw, you can sleep at night..."

"Sometimes Daddy needs a little extra. He's had a busy week!"

Hank nodded off several times during Jackie Gleason. Liz dragged him into bed before 9. She stayed up reading an hour or so. Hank's example made her drowsy. The house was dead quiet by 10:30.

◊◊◊

Across town, Hive Records' newest artist celebrated his record debut with a night of drinking. He and Clue could get into a roadhouse owned by Clue's cousin's stepbrother. Clue hated going out with Cam; it always ended with something that embarrassed him to death. Once you added X amount of booze to Cam, the worst happened.

Clue's cousin's stepbrother called the cops around 1:30 AM. The problem started after midnight. Cam was almost incoherent. He didn't have the constitution for booze. "All I want. All I want, man. Wanna hear my record. My fuckin' record. Wanna hear it onna jukebox."

"I can't get into that thing. I don't got no key. The whole shootin' match 'longs to Tupelo 'musement Comp'ny."

"Well, you call 'em. You tell 'em they got the key. They better get their asses out here. 'Cause I wanna hear it onna jukebox."

Clue hated to step in, but he always did. "Cam. Cam. Look at me." He grabbed Cam's shoulders. His eyes were glassed over and red with veins. When he got like this, Cam didn't see you. His eyes looked at you, but not *at* you. He stank of booze and cigarette smoke, like everyone else in this shithole.

"You. Listen. Asshole." Clue shouted in Cam's ear.

Cam belched. "Fuck it. Wanna hear it onna jukebox." Then he coughed, gagged and threw up six dollars' worth of whiskey, two dollars in beer and the remnants of his momma's tuna fish casserole all over the bar front.

Clue's cousin's stepbrother did not take this outpouring well. "You drag this pieca shit home. He ain't comin' back in here, neither."

"Shit, Claude, I'm sorry as hell."

"Asshole shouldn't be drinkin'. He can't take it."

"I know. It makes him crazy."

Clue's cousin's stepbrother snorted. "He's crazy as hail without it. He's bad news."

"Gimme a rag, man. I'll get this wiped up."

"You gonna keep cleanin' up after him?" Clue's cousin's stepbrother gave him the *you-stupid-shit* look. It made Clue feel defensive.

Before Clue could put words together—or get the contents of Cam's stomach mopped off the bar—Cam had rallied, picked up a barstool and broken the glass front of the jukebox. He grabbed at the sideways turntable; tried to pry the record playing off its orbit.

"'Ass it. That bastard's goin' to jail. He's gonna pay for that." Clue's cousin's stepbrother had the highway patrol out to the roadhouse in five minutes. Clue spent that time trying to clean up the puke, which had dripped off the bar and gave the whole area a sour, sickening smell. He tried to corral Cam and get him out of the place before the law showed up.

Clue failed in both departments. The highway patrol had them both in the back seat of their cruiser. Clue attempted to reason with the officers: "I tried to get him to go home, officer. Honest. I ain't had nothing but one beer. I don't like drinkin'."

"You ain't the one going to drunk tank, kid. But we need you to tell us what happened. Mister Doakes wants to press charges."

Clue sighed. He looked at Cam. Fucker was dead to the world. His breath smelled of puke and he had spatters of it all over his shirt front. And he'd lost the records. He'd made a big show of them when they came in. Held them up in the air, said that he was the biggest thing on records, and soon they'd be playing his songs all the time. Saying that Dixie Doodle was already playing the record. All the damn time. Hey, give us a shot, Clyde...

The hell of it was that they hadn't even gotten to play one of them. Clue tried to keep a copy, but Cam wanted to bring them all. He gave them to anyone who'd listen. He was the kind of guy who had to prove how good he was. He had to rub it in people's faces. It wasn't something people wanted to have told to them. They wanted to have it take them by surprise.

Like the couple of times they'd all played together. With Skip there, they sounded like something. People clapped after each song, and came up to them afterward and asked, did they have a record? Cam could be a charming guy in those circumstances. Skip made sure he was sober when they played together. He had a big collection of Cam's half-finished fifths of whiskey.

Cam had the idea that you had to drink to be any good. He might have gotten that idea from those black guys. They drank all the time. They had their reasons. With Cam, it was just to look good—to be one of the cool cats.

The car stopped at a police precinct station. Clue came back to the present day as the car shook and sighed. Cam belched in his stupor. "Help him out of the car, son."

"Can I be responsible for him? I don't want to wake up his father. He's mean already. They hate each other, mister. Honest, it would only make more trouble..."

"Are you his parent or relative? Is he your ward?"

"No sir, but—"

"No can do, son. That's the rules."

Clue slid Cam out of the back seat. They hadn't cuffed him; he dropped in his tracks after he broke the jukebox. That act took all the life out of him. For a few seconds, Clue though he was dead.

He was dead weight. He hardly weighed anything, but he was all lifeless resistance. He and one of the officers dragged Cam into the station house.

◊◊◊

Hank Howard was the third person Clue called. His mother bawled him out for waking her up. Skip didn't pick up his phone. Clue remembered Mr. Howard's name and his number was in the phone book.

The shrill of the phone woke Liz instantly; the children moaned and stirred by the third ring. She caught it on the fifth ring. Carl and Kitty were out of bed, wide-eyed and full of questions.

"Who? I don't...he is? Well, doesn't he have someone..."

"Who died?" Hank croaked, half-asleep. She could hear the mattress springs creak with his weight as he sat up.

"It's one of your record people. Cram? Ham?...oh. Cam. The boy says he just made a record for you."

"Oh, lord." Hank got to his feet and struggled into a robe. "Is he hurt?"

"Here." Liz surrendered the handset.

"Yes, this is Hank Howard...yes, sir, he is...oh no! Aw, gee. I'm sorry to..." Hank groaned out a sigh. "I don't have that kind of money on me...uh huh...no sir, that was a wrong thing to do...I agree...I...well, I can't do nothing right here...I can talk to the folks at Tupelo Amusement...I know 'em. I'm in the record business myself...hold the line."

Hank turned to his wife. "It's one of my new artists. He...he got into some trouble tonight and they'll let him go if I'll take custody of him. He got into some trouble."

"You said that already." Liz sighed. "What do they want?"

"They asked me, can I come pick him up and let him sleep it off here. They don't want to bother his parents."

"How old is this...person?"

"He's just a kid. Fresh out of high school. He can sleep on the couch. We'll get this straightened out in the morning." He looked at his wife; she said nothing. "I don't know what else we can do."

"You are on thin ice, Hank Howard." Liz went back to the bedroom and got under the covers.

"You still on the line, sir?"

"I...I'll be down there soon as I can...56th Street station...yes, sir..."

The only clothes Hank could find in the dark were those he'd worn at the office. They were still damp with sweat. He gathered them up and got dressed in the bathroom. He felt guilty and put-upon and almost in a self-pitying frame of mind. It was a long way down from the highs of the afternoon.

◊◊◊

"I'll be responsible for the damages. I know John Logan and his brother Bill. I sell 'em records all the time."

"He's still gonna have to come to court," the desk sergeant said. He looked at Hank, in his sloppy clothes, and expressed disdain with his eyes.

"I will try to settle this out of court. I'd call John right now if it wasn't so late. But I'll speak with him first thing on Monday. I'm a business man. They know me."

"You take this boy home and make sure he stays there. We've had him in here before. He's nothing but trouble."

"He is a good singer. I've got a record coming out on him. He and his group."

"I can't wait to hear that," the officer said. Irony corroded his speech.

Hank almost said something, but stopped himself. *Does no good,* he thought. *Mind's already made up; jury's already turned in the verdict.* "Do I need to sign anything? I can get him home right now."

"Yeah. Sign there and there." He pushed papers and a pen into Hank's hands.

"What'm I signing here?"

"First one says you're his guardian; you're responsible for him. Second one says you'll bring him to court when the date is set."

"I'm sure I can settle this out of court, sir."

"Fine. You still gotta sign."

Hank signed. With that, Cam was frog-marched out of the drunk tank. It reminded Hank of when Carl had his tonsils out; how wobbly and out-of-it he was. "Let's get you home, buddy."

"No home. Not there..."

With some effort, Hank got his new recording artist in the car. "All right, buddy. You just need to sleep this off."

"Not home. Old man'll kill me."

"Well..." Hank drove away from the police station. "I guess we can put you up. After all, I'm responsible for you..."

Cam belched and his head lowered to one side. He was asleep.

"These are the times that try a man's soul," Hank said to himself.

***Cam Cottner was still asleep*** when Hank woke up. He had to get up early, tired or rested, because of the children.

Hank peeked into the living room. His newest artist dozed on the sofa, curled with his back to the room. Liz had taken pity on the kid when Hank brought him home. Cam was too out of it to do much, but they got him cleaned off and put him in a pair of Hank's pajamas. He really looked like a kid in those; they had to roll up the pants cuffs and his hands were lost in the sleeves.

He collapsed on the sofa and Liz put a thin comforter over him. Her attitude had changed once she saw Cam. He must have had something that made women sympathetic; that was the only rationale he could summon over his first cup of coffee.

*What have I gotten myself into? Is it worth it?* Hank let himself wander into self-doubt. He didn't tarry there, but his concerns seemed sound. Putting out that record was a shot in the dark. It was so different it was bound to get some reaction, good or bad. He was certain of that. Beyond a moment's novelty, did it have legs? Was there any lasting value in what they'd recorded?

What would Carl and Kitty make of this stranger in their home? Kitty had come to, half-awake, and opened her door. "Go on back to bed, sweetie," Hank assured her. "We're okay. Go to sleep, sweetie." Kitty turned without a word and did as directed.

They'd be awake soon, both bouncing with excitement about going to the lake. It had to happen; Hank couldn't claim exhaustion, calamity or any adult reason for cancelling the trip. And it might be relaxing. *Be nice to just look out on the water and not think about anything.* He smiled at the idea, but knewhe wasn't that kind of guy. He didn't mind looking at television with Liz; some of the programs were good, and it was something he and his wife could share without a lot of demands.

*I'm going to try and relax. I can't keep it up all the time. A man's got to take his rest.*

Liz startled him. "How's the patient?"

"Dead to the world." Hank thumbed towards the living room. Liz looked in and gasped.

"He's awake. Part of him is, anyway..." She smiled and her expression bade Hank to see.

Cam Cottner had turned onto his back. He had a morning erection. He stirred and muttered; a part of him tried to come to consciousness. The way he looked when Hank fetched him from the police station, he thought the kid would end up in the hospital. He looked green around the gills; sickly and thin. He could barely put one foot in front of the other.

In the kitchen, Liz knocked over a container of oatmeal. It hit the counter, bounced, and landed in an open drawer of silverware. That got Cam's eyes open. "What? Who said that?" He sat up, as if suddenly ashamed of his erection. "Where am I?"

"You're okay, Cam." Hank eased around the doorway, in case the boy's biology still showed. Cam sat, draped in the comforter, his feet on the floor. He looked frazzled.

He squinted at Hank. "Mr. Howard. I know you." He looked at himself and then the room. "Why am I here?"

"You had yourself a night. I reckoned you'd sleep 'till noon."

"I could go for some of that, sir." He gestured with his sleeve to Hank's mug. "My head feels like it's got a big dent in it."

"Of course. Stay put." Hank walked around Liz, who had just swept up the spilled oatmeal. "Our guest is conscious."

"Oh." Hank poured a cup of black coffee and refreshed his mug.

"Here you are. That'll clear your head."

"Thank you, sir." Cam took a sip. "I'm so ashamed of myself, sir. Sometimes it feels like the devil gets into me. I don't mean to be that way, but sometimes it gets a hold of me."

Hank sat on the sofa. "Bud, when I was your age, I felt the devil inside

148

of me. I did some dumb things, I tell you what. Just bone dumb things."

"Did I hurt anybody?"

"You injured a jukebox. I'll take care of it. I know Sid over at Tupelo Amusements. But that's comin' out of your royalties."

Cam drank in silence. "From my record?"

"Yep. Have you listened to it yet?"

Cam squinted. "Has it come out?"

"I brought you some advance copies. Last night."

"Aw, shit. 'Scuse me, sir. I shouldn't talk like that, I know. It just slips out when I ain't thinking." He sighed. "I reckon I lost track of those records. I tried to play it for my old man last night. He said it sounded like trash. We got into it. You know, he ain't my real old man. He and I ain't relations, let's just say."

"Where's your father?"

"Buried in Priceville Cemetery. I never even saw him."

"What happened to him?"

Cam laughed. "Day I was born, he was so happy he forgot to look where he was goin'. Walked right into a streetcar. They found pieces of him all along State Street."

"I'm sorry to hear that. That must have been a shock to your mother."

"She kinda lost her marbles over that. They say she was never the same. She always acts...I don't know...distracted. Like she's not there."

"Did she ever talk to you about your father? What he was like?"

"They say I'm a lot like him. He had high spirits. Liked to kid around and have a good time. He was a singer too. Never did nothing with it, but he could play the ukulele an' sing pretty good. My aunt told me this. Momma, you don't mention him to her. She believes Jackson is my dad. They ain't even married. I don't like him and he don't like me. We get on one another's nerves, you could say."

"He doesn't seem to take much of an interest in anything."

"I ain't figured him out yet. Everything I like, he hates. Anything I'm happy about, he shoots it down. We'd be better off without him. But there ain't anything I can do about it."

"They say success is the best revenge. And let's see if your record doesn't bring you some success. Tomorrow morning I'm mailing out 300 copies of your record to radio stations and the music magazines. I feel it in here." Hank tapped his chest. "It's gonna go places. It has to. It's different. It's fresh. You have a terrific talent. It just needed someplace to, you know, focus it."

"Aw, thank you, sir. I reckon I can sing pretty good. I hope people will take to our record. I 'preciate your putting it out."

"Here's to success for us all." Hank offered his coffee mug for a toast. Cam got the drift and clinked his mug against Hank's. "So what are your plans for today?"

"I can't go home 'til Jackson goes to sleep, so Ida know. Guess I'll go to the movies, sit 'em til late."

"We're all going out to Tombigbee Lake. The kids have been wantin' to go since summer. Might as well get 'em out there while it's still warm. Me, I'm just gonna sleep under a shady tree. Have myself a beer and a couple of sandwiches." Hank swallowed the last of his coffee. "You're welcome to join us."

"I ain't been to a lake since I was a kid. Might be good to get outdoors for a change. Thank you, sir, I'd be happy to."

◊◊◊

Carl and Kitty were suspicious of the stranger in the living room. He joined them at the breakfast table. Liz made hash browns, bacon and scrambled eggs. Cam picked at his plate, but ate enough to get something solid in his stomach.

"Are you a big kid?" Kitty asked Cam.

Cam smiled. "I reckon you could say that. How old are you?"

"Six."

"I'm 19. I got a coupla years on you."

"19? I haven't never known nobody who was that old."

Hank chortled. He looked at Liz and she smiled. Kitty was so damned cute. Precocious. She had her mother's eyes and her forthright manner.

150

"Are you too old to go to Bom Bingbee Lake?"

Everyone laughed at Kitty's question. "I reckon I'm just the right age to go there."

"You can come swimmin' with us if you want."

"I'd be glad to. Thank you, ma'am."

"I ain't ole enough to be a mam."

"I ain't neither."

Finding clothes for Cam was the last challenge of the morning. Hank's shirts swam on him, but they had to make do. Cam's slacks were still wearable. His puke had aimed well at Claude Doakes' bar. The pink and black shirt went into the garbage can when they got Cam into pajamas.

Liz made sandwiches and put those, store-bought potato salad and a cherry pie into a wicker basket. "You fellas get this in the car; I'll round up the kidlets."

Cam carried the basket. Hank trailed him and unlocked the car trunk. "You know, Cam, it doesn't look like drinkin' is doing you any favors."

"I know it, sir. I wish I could stop."

"I ain't telling you how to live your life. That's up to you. But I think you'd be a hell of a lot happier if you didn't get in another scrape like last night. I would hate to have one of my recording artists in jail."

"I don't remember nothing that happened. It's like the lights went out." Cam smiled. "I know I'm trouble, sir. I try not to be but that's what I am."

"Well, I'm here to tell you it don't have to be like that. You got control of your life. You can maybe try harder. That's all I'm sayin'."

"I get lectures all the time at home."

"Maybe you should take 'em to heart. I just...I don't wanna see you get in trouble. You have a bright future, Cam. Or, you could have one. I'm not perfect. I make a mess of things. I try not to. I work hard at it. And I've gotten pretty good at tellin' when something isn't going right. I know when to stop. I hope you can learn that for yourself. I don't judge you. No sir. That's not for me to do. But I can see something's troubling you and I would hate to see you fail because of it."

151

"Well, I 'preciate that, sir. All's I can say is I'll try."

Hank nodded. Enough said.

The front door slammed. Carl and Kitty ran for the car, streaming towels and toys across the front yard. "Load up, gang!" Hank made sure everyone was seated before taking his place. He looked at Liz and smiled. "You know, maybe goin' all the way out there to the lake ain't such a good idea. We should stay home and...paint the house!"

"Daddy stop it!" Kitty cried. "We're going to Bom Bingbee Lake! Now!"

"Daddy's kidding," Liz said.

"The house *could* use a new coat of paint..."

"Daddy!" Kitty shrieked. "*Stop* it!"

Her parents shared a laugh. Hank backed out to the street, squinting in the sunlight.

◊◊◊

For a few hours, Hank Howard put all the pressures and concerns of his business out of the way. He hadn't been able to do that for a year—maybe two. He enjoyed chicken salad sandwiches and store-bought pie, waded in the lake to appease his kids and dozed under a tree.

It was warm but fall made its presence known. You could sense the season's quiet shift. The air had a certain smell, a different feeling.

Hank didn't talk much. He gave himself over to rest. If thoughts of business crept into his head, he swept them out. *Tomorrow; come back tomorrow.*

Cam, pale skinny body exposed to the sun, kept quiet. He seemed to follow Hank's lead; just lay back and soak it in. Don't think, don't worry, don't plan.

They stayed until 5, and Carl and Kitty complained when called out of the water. They were tired; Kitty was cranky. They slept beside Cam in the back seat of the car, towels beneath them to protect the upholstery from wet and grit.

They had warmed-over meat loaf and instant potatoes for dinner. The kids functioned enough to fork food into their mouths, then went to bed of their own volition by 8.

"I oughta be safe to go home in an hour. Jackson's asleep by 9 most nights." Cam joined Hank and Liz in TV time. Ed Sullivan offered a slate of approved entertainment, and then *Goodyear Playhouse* featured a serious gab-fest about an important issue.

"Let's run you home, buddy. I'm about to pass out." Hank got up and jingled his keys. Cam had dozed on the drama and awoke with a start. "Oh. Yeah. He's gotta be asleep by now." Cam stood up and turned to Liz. "Mrs. Howard, thank you for your kindness, ma'am. I apologize for the state I was in last night. I 'preciate your lookin' after me."

"You're welcome. You take care, now." Liz felt herself taken by this young man's charisma. He had been subdued, out of it, withdrawn, but he recovered, and he was grateful that someone had helped him out of a bad situation. She flashed back to forgotten high school crushes. This young man had that quality; she got caught up in it for a moment. As the car backed out into the road, she snapped back into the present. It was hard to put into words, or thought, that effect.

She looked in on her children. Carl in a huddle on his side, a Bugs Bunny comic book draped on the edge of the bed. Kitty, still as a photograph; the slight sound of her breath a reassurance that she was alive and well.

She went into the kitchen and surveyed the scene. The dinner dishes could sit until the morning. It'd be nice to have a dishwasher. She fought the urge to clean them. They stacked neat in the sink, ready for tomorrow.

A foul smell caught her attention. It wasn't from the sink; she looked in the cupboards and the refrigerator. Nothing seemed wrong. Then she caught a corner of pink fabric that hung over the edge of the garbage can. It was that boy's shirt; it smelled sour and foul, of sickness and worldliness.

She emptied the can into the larger one outside and made sure the lid was closed tight. Her stomach turned. It took her half an hour to get back her sense of calm and well-being.

## CAM & THE CATS
### (Hive 248-45 & 78 RPM)

**B+** "A FAMOUS IGNORAMUS" (2:32)

[Beehive BMI — Cecil Madison] A whole new kind of sound, halfway between r&b and hillbilly, is heard on this humorous high-speed ditty. Singer and ork are exciting and unusual. Could spin into a teen clamor item.

**B** "MIDNIGHT" (2:46) [Acuff-Rose — B. Bryant/C. Atkins] The Red Foley hit of years back, given a sultry socko treatment by this "cat music" combo. A moody stand that seems a natch for late-nite jocks. An artist to watch.

*Billboard*, November 13, 1954

## CAM AND THE CATS
### A Famous Ignoramus............................75

**HIVE 248**—Something new for the young crowd, in the vein of Bill Haley and His Comets but with a stronger rural feeling. Singer sells humorous lyric to great effect. Just different enough to go places for adventurous deejays. Could get action. **(Beehive, BMI)**

### Midnight...............................................73

Revival of the Red Foley oldie becomes a torch song with country rhythm. Decidedly different deck with striking atmosphere. Excellent piano/guitar work. **(Acuff-Rose, BMI)**

# 3

***The record took a few weeks to build,*** and then it broke like a storm cloud. Whenever a deejay played "Famous Ignoramus," he got cards, calls and telegrams asking to hear it again, condemning it as immoral trash or requesting the singer's photograph.

It entered the *Cash Box* charts at #55, and over three weeks, shoved aside the Lou Montes and Julius La Rosas into the #7 slot. *Billboard* saw it rise to #4 on the popular charts. In both magazines, "Famous Ignoramus" hit #3 on the country hit lists; *Billboard*'s rhythm and blues listings showed it at #9 by November's end.

Alongside the success of "Famous Ignoramus," Cross Records' release of "Hangman Blues" by The Lonesome Shadow was a record most disk jockeys were scared to play. Reports of radio stations being torched or vandalized after broadcasting it spread through the DJ community. Juke box companies were leery of the single after their leased machines suffered far worse damage than what Cam Cottner inflicted (and Hank Howard paid for). With all this against it, the single sold 400,000 copies across the nation and forced its way onto the charts to #11 in *Billboard*'s rhythm and blues tally.

The Lonesome Shadow's long-playing record, *The Real Blues!*, sold in such volume that it reached the lower berths of *Billboard*'s recently-instated Long Playing Records chart. Its brisk sales opened independent labels to the open season on rhythm and blues albums.

Hank Howard hopped on the LP train. He didn't have enough on any one artist for a full album, but he sequenced tracks by Rusty Gordon, Snake Eyes, The Four Fellers, Grover Epps and Buddy Riskin, a solo blues performer who Hank had cut one single on in 1953 to crickets and tumbleweeds. Hank wasn't sure where Riskin was, or if he still lived, but his three recordings, stark performances that harked back to Depression-era sounds, filled out an eclectic 14-track program that he and Cecil named *A Beehive of Rhythm and Blues*. Pressing albums wasn't possible to do in-house, and the project incurred some unwelcome expense.

Money from Cam's single and the Shadow's big sellers funded the debut Hive LP. It hit the stores in time for Christmas, 1954 and sold 30,000 copies by year's end.

"You know, it looks like we're successful," Cecil said, after he read an article about Hive's good fortunes in *Cash Box*.

"Hangman Blues" impacted Cecil's life in good and bad ways. Its notoriety made Cecil a hero to the black community in urban areas. At home, after the newspaper article on Hive, The Shadow and Cecil Madison ran in their Sunday magazine, it cost him his gig playing piano at The First Colored Church of Christ. Cecil was torn into by its pastor, Rev. Alvin Timmins, who said the finger-pointing of his interview (and the song) had set back race relations by 20 years and caused scandal and shame to his congregation.

Cecil no longer needed the gig. With Hive Records showing a profit for the first time, and songwriter royalties that amounted to more money than he'd ever had at one time, he took a good look at his life. He lived like a hermit in a—you couldn't call it a house. When it was new, and his parents' marriage was fresh, it might have been a home. Now it was just a place to live.

Its days were numbered. It leaned a bit further back every day. It was out in the woods, on a hill, away from the world. That had made it a haven to Cecil in leaner times. Now it was a hindrance. Cecil felt sad and isolated there. There'd once been a romance to reading by candlelight and cooking meals on a camp stove. That love affair was as dead as Cecil's parents.

With Hank as his liaison to the white world, Cecil opened a bank account. After his first deposits from royalty payments, he moved into town.

He toured some apartments that rented to black folks, but found them too full of noise and vulgarity. Cecil felt as ill-at-ease with black people as he did with most white folks. He was not much good with people and their crude, simple thoughts and delights.

He found a small house on one of the roads that edged the downtown business district. On a side street, with a vacant lot on either side, the little blue box, a bit larger than his shack, came with gas heat, electricity and hot and cold water. He paid an extra 10 dollars a month to have Coaxial as his house-mate. The cat made his displeasure well known when Cecil moved him, with Hank's help. Cecil tricked the cat by backing him into a cardboard box. Hank closed the lid, or tried to—he got a couple of bad scratches. But Coaxial stayed inside and they drove him into town.

Once they opened the box lid, the cat ran around the place, yowling and moaning. In his panic, he dashed under the bed. When Hank peeked down, Coaxial hissed and lobbed his claws. He just missed spearing Hank, who already had battle scars from this event.

Cecil had some bacon fat he'd saved in a jam jar. Once Hank left, he waited out the cat. The smell of the bacon fat was too much. Coaxial appeared and approached the jar with caution. Cecil daubed the cat's paws with the fat. Coaxial groomed himself as he took in this sinful luxury. His bath took over two hours. After that, he settled on a windowsill and purred himself asleep.

While Coaxial acclimated to city life, Cecil returned to his ancestral home. He took an axe to his front porch. He pulled up all the boards and poke the soil with a shovel until he heard the clink of glass. Then he dug up the money he'd buried. He knew there were six jars. He found five of them before it got dark. There was over four hundred dollars in curled-up bills and silver. He stuffed the money into his pockets.

Then he doused the place with kerosene and lit a match.

He didn't stay to watch the flames. He stumbled and skidded his way down the clay bank to the highway and walked, for the last time, his wooded route to town. When he unlocked the door to his home, Coaxial bounced to the floor and greeted him with miaows and leg weaves. He purred and Cecil felt at home. He picked up the cat and regarded him with a smile. Emotion overcame him as it seldom did. He let tears stream down his face. Coaxial looked concerned and tapped the tears with a paw. "It's fine," Cecil said. "We're good. We're just fine."

◊◊◊

"Famous Ignoramus" was sliding down the charts as Cecil and Hank arranged a new session for Cam and His Cats. Fame hadn't changed Cam so much as it gave him a green light to be himself. Skip Mosely did his best to collar the kid as TV hosts interviewed Cam and the band.

Cam presented well; he looked great on TV, and a viewer's first impression might be of a polite, gentle Southern boy.

Cam's interviewers wanted to get at the secret of his success. How was it that this petite young man could summon such sounds from his throat? Where did this come from? It had to be a gimmick; Steve Allen couldn't resist a condescending tone towards the boy. Cam laughed at the jibes, as if he were above them, and answered the questions.

When he was asked about the music he loved, Cam couldn't stop referring to rhythm and blues as "nigger music." He praised it to the skies, and said it was the best music he knew of, but that phrase dogged him.

No matter how many kicks Skip gave him, that word was hard-wired into the boy's vocabulary. "Oh, Lord," Hank exclaimed every time he watched his hot new artist talk on TV. Promises made over the phone to not say that word seemed forgotten on live television.

Hank and Cecil staged an intervention. With Skip's help, they got Cam into the Hive studio to preview some new material. Instead, Skip stood by the studio door. "Sit down, Cam," Hank said. He gestured to a stool. Cam sat. "You have a hit record. It's big all over the country. But...son, every time you open your mouth on TV, you're ruining it."

"We're losing sales in the rhythm and blues market," Cecil said. He showed Cam the new *Cash Box* charts. "Famous Ignoramus" was on the bottom rung at #20. "Black people like your music. Until they hear you say that word."

"What you talkin' about? I ain't done nothing wrong!"

"Cam," Hank sighed. "I don't know how else to say this." He put a hand to his forehead, as if the thought pained him. "We can't have you saying that word about black people. Not on TV, not to the press and not to your fans. That word will stop everything cold."

"What word?" A smile touched the corners of Cam's mouth.

"Nigger," Cecil said. "You do not say that word. Not to me, not to him...not to them." He gestured as if to include all of America. "That word is going to get you killed. Do you hear me?"

Cam turned to Hank. "How come he gets to lecture me?"

"Cecil owns one third of this company. He is responsible for a lot of

160

the success of Hive Records. He can speak with authority. Would it help if I said it?" Cam opened his mouth but no words came. "You do not say the word *nigger* in public. It is an ugly word. It hurts people. You are the biggest-selling act I've ever recorded, but I will drop you like a hot rock if you don't straighten up and fly right. Is that understood?" Cam sat silent, his gaze on the wall. "Is that understood?"

"Shit. Yes. All right. I won't say it no more."

"In my book, a man is as good as his word. I'm going to trust you to stand by what you've just said." Hank offered his hand. Cam hesitated, and then accepted it. They shook. Cecil held out his hand; they shook.

"We okay now?" Cam smiled.

"We're okay," Cecil replied. "And I'd like to run a couple of song ideas past you. They're not finished, but you helped out on that one line. Maybe we can sit down and finish these together."

"Really?" Cam looked at Hank, and then Skip. They nodded.

They worked for two hours at the studio piano, throwing lines around as Cecil hammered out and refined a melody. The result was "You're on The Wrong Train, Sweetheart." The lyrics used the analogy of a relationship as a train; the singer's girl was always on the wrong track, or arriving too late or not at all. Cam came up with a couple of stinging lines, and Cecil couched them in humorous asides.

Cecil came up with a loping, easygoing rhythm that suggested the sway of a train car without being too obvious. "I think we've got something here," Cecil said with a smile.

He asked Hank to come in and listen. Hank's face lit up as he listened. He liked the rhythm and laughed at some of the lines. He made a suggestion that the composers swap two stanzas. "You've got a little story going there, and that would give it a real ending." They agreed, and the new single was recorded the next afternoon in a three-hour session.

Hank brought Chili Burse in to play live with The Cats, and he seized on the song's skipping rhythm and brought it to life. He emphasized the off-beat. Skip contributed a rousing Atkins-style fingerpicking solo and some tasty licks. As Clue rumbled along on his bass, the strings created the clicking sound of railroad tracks.

161

Hank took acetates down to Dixie Doodle, but he had no doubts that this was another hit. He doubled his order at the pressing plants.

A year ago, Hank's MO was to press as few records as possible, so he could hope to pay for them. That worry was off the table. "Famous Ignoramus" would be re-pressed a dozen times by the end of 1955. It was bootlegged, like all big hits on small labels, but Hank could do nothing about that. What was that saying? *The cost of doing business.* Any success had strings attached, like barnacles suctioned to a ship at sea.

◊◊◊

Hank celebrated Hive Records' success by buying his wife an automatic dish-washer and a new clothes-washer and dryer. He also started a college fund for the children. He didn't want much for himself. Making himself successful was a boon to his home life, his relationship with Bets and the future of his kids.

He'd need to add an extension to the house. They had the space on their two acre lot. The kids would be teenagers before you could blink an eye. An older family needed more room. He had an architect out to survey the lot and he began designs on an extra bedroom and a larger living room.

Cam's court date came up, and Hank settled with the owners of Tu-pelo Amusements. For $300.00, they considered the matter settled, and Cam, Hank and Hive Records avoided bad publicity. *'Cat Music' Singer in Court Over Drunken Spree*: the headlines were easy to imagine. And that was as far as they went for the time being.

**"You're on the Wrong Train, Sweetheart"** was the second release by Cam and The Cats. Hive #252 was credited to Madison-Cottner-Howard. Backed with a country ballad Skip wrote, "Lonesome Moonlight," it equaled the success of the first single: #4 on the pop charts, #3 in rhythm and blues and both sides on the country chart. "Lonesome Moonlight" got to #2 there, with "Wrong Train" peaking at #5.

The group's appearances on *The Toast of the Town, Texaco Star Theater* and *The Colgate Comedy Hour* went over well. Hank grimaced at his TV set as Cam almost spoke the N-word, then caught himself: "The thing I love about ni...natural rhythm and blues...is the feeling. That's what we try to get into our performances." Cam charmed Ed Sullivan, who assured his audience of screaming teenage girls that "these fine boys will be back just as soon as we can work them into our busy schedule. We wish them all the success in the world."

On most of the shows, Cam and The Cats mimed to their recordings. On *Toast of the Town,* they had to play live, and cut loose. Cam mugged for the camera and did unexpected moves with his body and with the microphone stand. The audience reacted with laughter and shock at these antics. Most singers stood still, their arms awkward things as they snapped their fingers in time to the song, or made random gestures. Cam used his entire body to keep his audience guessing.

"The kid's humpin' the mike stand," the show's director noticed. "Cut to the guitarist!" When the lens again focused on Cam, it was from the midriff up. The expression in his eyes, which seemed to peer right into the soul of the camera, and the audience's reactions to things not seen in millions of American homes, garnered the group attention—good and bad.

Walter Winchell described Cam as "a lizard-bodied youth with menace in his stance and lust in his heart," and concluded that his antics were something Americans were best off without.

A reporter for Associated Press cornered Cam in a nightclub. "So, what gives with those moves?"

"Well, sir, when I get goin', I just feel the music. It just goes through me. You ever touched a live wire? 'Magine that feeling goin' on and on. That's what rhythm and blues does to me. How could you expect a man to stand still with all that juice runnin' through him? I sing what I feel, sir, an' my body feels it even more."

◊◊◊

Cam and his bandmates were invited to attend the Apollo Theatre in Harlem. A publicity agent slipped the offer under the door of the group's shared dressing room.

Coming back after a lip-synching segment, Clue noticed the blue envelope on the floor. "The Apple-O The-ater. Huh?"

"What's that?" Cam snatched the envelope from Clue's hands. "Holy shit!" He scanned the handwritten note that held three passes. "Oh, man. Y'all, we got us someplace to go!"

"What's the Apple-O Theater?"

"It's The Apollo, stupid. It's just the biggest thing in this town. This is where all the big ni—rhythm an' blues acts sing! Ruth Brown; The Dominoes; The Clovers. This is the real deal, man! We gotta go!"

"Harlem?" Skip frowned. "I don't think white folks are s'posed to set foot there."

"Hell, man, we got a record on the rhythm an' blues charts! We're fuckin' royalty. These people will welcome us in. An' we can all learn somethin' from 'em. Those black folks know how to put on a damn show!"

"I don't...we shouldn't..."

"Hell, man, it's free!"

Cam and Clue outvoted Skip, and they took a taxi to the theater. Cam wore his signature black and pink attire, with his bandmates looking meek and embarrassed. "Damn, man, looka there!" Cam beamed at the theatre's marquee.

"It's just a dang the-ater, man." Clue sniffled.

An astounded doorman admitted the group; an usher escorted them to a loge. Cam was aware that the eyes of the theater were on him, and he smiled and nodded to anyone who met his gaze. He felt nervous and excited and was relieved when the house lights went down.

The opening act was The El Dorados, who kicked things off with their big hit "At My Front Door." The mood of the theatre changed to one big party. Cam had witnessed this happen in some black churches where the singing had lured him into the back row. Below, people stood up, clapped their hands, stomped their feet, whistled, cat-called; some couples danced in the aisles.

The thing that got to Cam was this presentation of one great act after another. He thrilled at hearing some of his favorite records performed by the actual fucking people. Chuck Willis, man! There he was, singing "Feel So Bad." Cam couldn't restrain himself; he began to sing along with the songs he knew. Clue looked at him like he was nuts; Skip sat, arms folded across his torso, his brow set in disdain.

The second set opened with Rusty Gordon and his band. Cam stood up, excited. "Rusty! *Rusty!*" His shout carried across the theater in a moment of general murmur.

"Who dat?" Rusty mugged to the audience. The crowd roared with laughter. "Somebody turn on a flashlight so's I can see who out there yellin' for me!"

Cam leaned off the edge of the loge balcony and waved his hands. *He's a damn fool,* Skip thought. *Get us thrown out of here...*

A spotlight caught Cam; he squinted from the brightness and thought about animated cartoons where a character escaped from prison. He smiled and waved. "Does ah know you, white boy?"

"We're both on Hive Records, man!" Cam shouted.

"Well, damn, son, what you doin' way up hereabouts?"

"We was on Ed Sullivan." A rolling murmur ran through the Apollo.

Rusty squinted. He'd seen this kid around the Hive offices. *He's the guy stole my song, sumbitch.* He got an idea. "Y'all that new group. Cram an' His Spats, sumpin' like that." Everyone laughed, Cam loudest of all. "Well, why you jus' sittin' pretty up there? You come down an' do a song for the nice folks!

What y'all think?"

The crowd burst into applause. Cam was thrilled and scared. He looked at his band-mates. Clue shrugged: *why not?* Skip shrugged: *go make a fool out of yourself.*

"C'mon, guys! Let's do it!"

"I ain't got my guitar," Skip said. "And I ain't warmed up."

Clue looked bashful. "You get on down there. Do the hit."

Cam couldn't turn back. He left the loge and an usher guided him around the side of the stage and into the lights. The crowd laughed, applauded and booed in equal measure. Rusty looked at him with an exaggerated stage grin. His intention was to cut this little ofay asshole down a peg or two.

"Man, I gots to tell you. You stole my song!"

"Huh?" Cam's genuine shock amused the crowd.

"That funny song you been singin'. That one was writ for me!"

"I didn't know, Mister Gordon. They ast me to do it."

"They *ast* you to *do it.*" Rusty looked at the crowd. "*Mm* hm. They *ast* him to *do it!*" He shrugged; they laughed. "Well, I might fine it in my heart to *forgive* you. If you'll do *one thing* for me."

Cam's heart was in his throat. "Y-yes, sir?"

Rusty grinned. "Y'all gonna sing that song *right now*—with my boys!" He turned to the audience. "What y'all think about *that?*" Applause and laughter answered him. "Awright, then. You best step up to that there mica-phone right now!"

As the room applauded and laughed, Cam did as told. "B flat," he called to the band behind him. He remembered that was the key they cut the record in.

The band played in G. They'd been doing the number on the road in G; that's what they knew. It was a little too high and a little too low for Cam, but he found his note while the band played the opening vamp. *I'm a famous ignoramus...with the wisdom of a fool...* Cam looked up and saw smiles, hands clapping. He got a wave of confidence and sang on: *All the knowledge y'get in college never made you half as cool...*

166

It was a thrill to sing with a for-real rhythm and blues band. Cam made with the moves that got his lower half prohibited from TV. The audience egged him on; he swiveled his hips, fondled the mike stand and swung his head with abandon.

The sax man took two breaks and Cam clapped, hollered and danced in place. Sweat stung his eyes. He smiled at the crowd as if to say *ain't this great? Ain't I lucky as fuck?*

Cam wailed the last verse. His voice had found the sweet spot. Rusty stood to his side, making moves he'd seen Jack Benny do; exasperated mugs, shrugs and comical surprise. *Fuckin' kid is pretty damn good,* he thought. *He an ass, but he pretty good.*

Cam looked up to the loges. He caught Clue's wall-to-wall grin and he drove the song home to its conclusion. He felt deep relief when the band sounded the final chord. A wave of applause, like heat on an August afternoon, came over him. He bowed, smiled and waved. "Thank y'all so much. This means a whole lot to me. Thank you."

Cam turned towards backstage. Rusty caught his shoulder. "Whoa whoa *whoa!* Where *you* goin', man?"

"I'm goin' back to my seat so I can see the best show in the world! This is the best music there is, man!"

Rusty scowled skeptically. "Does that include *me?*"

"'Course it does, man. Y'all wanna hear Rusty sing?"

"*Yes!*" the audience shouted.

"Well, all right. Thank y'all again..."

"Y'all come backstage after the show. Okay?"

Cam nodded yes with a grin. He trotted backstage, aware of his perspiration, and an usher guided him up the ramp to the loge. He flopped into his seat, relieved but amazed at this turn of events. "How'd I do?"

"Oh, man! That was great!" Clue beamed.

"You did all right," Skip said. That was high praise; Cam accepted it.

"I think that was the best moment of my life," Cam said. He wished he had some whisky. Maybe later, backstage...

The show ended at midnight; they'd seen The Midnighters, Lavern Baker, and some smaller acts Cam didn't recognize. Skip and Clue enjoyed the show, but their minds were set on getting back to the hotel room they shared and hitting the sack.

"We gotta go backstage," Cam said. "Rusty said to come see him."

"Aw, man..."

"Aw, come on. You'll get to meet Lavern Baker!"

"Well..." Clue looked at Skip. Skip sighed.

"We'll go back to say hello. Then we all better get to sleep. We got to get checked out by 10 tomorrow."

"We'll just pay our respects," Cam said. "They was nice enough to let me sing here."

Cam stopped an usher. "Rusty said for me to come see him backstage." The kid squinted, unsure of this request, but he led the group through a rabbit's warren of narrow passageways to the green room. Most of the people they'd seen on-stage were there, smoking and drinking; a fug of haze hugged the ceiling.

Skip saw the booze bottles and groaned. "Don't make a damn fool of yourself," he hissed in Cam's ear.

"There he is!" Rusty called from across the room.

"Where's Lavern Baker? I got a friend wants to meet him."

"Oh!" Rusty laughed. "I can't say I blame him. She'll wander by."

"Man, I wanna thank you for askin' me to come on stage like that."

"Aw, man. I got to admit I been mad at you. 'Cos I know Cecil wrote that song for me."

"I didn't know. Honest. Hank asked me to do it." Cam knew this was a lie, but he didn't want to make an enemy out of this man and his friends. "I would of said no if I knew."

Rusty pshawed. "Hank gets excited. He forgets how things s'posta be."

"He is the talkin'est man I ever met." Cam looked at Rusty's glass. "Could I get somethin' to drink here?"

"You welcome to help yourselves there." Rusty pointed to a group of bottles and glasses. To their right was a portable record player with a stack of 45s on its automatic changer.

Cam poured himself a few fingers of whiskey. "Clue. Y'all want one?"

"Naw," Clue said. "I'm worn out."

"We've had a long day," Skip said to Rusty.

"The fun is just startin' right about now! Come on; make yourself comfortable."

Clue got to meet Lavern Baker. He could barely get a few stuttered words of praise out as he shook her hand. She was gracious about it; she laughed later as she told the story of the nine-foot-tall white boy she met.

Cam spotted Chuck Willis and shook his hand. "You write some damn fine songs, Mister Willis."

"Thank you. Maybe you can do one of my songs sometimes."

"I'd be honored to, Mister Willis."

Skip tolerated a half-hour of this meet-and-greet. He'd been up for 20 hours and he was done with consciousness. "Let's call it a night, Cam."

"Y'all go on if you wanna. I'm stayin' here."

"You remember where to go?"

Cam showed him his room key with the hotel tag. "I'll get a cab. Don't worry 'bout me!"

Skip sighed a deep rumble in his chest cavity. He had nothing else.

◊◊◊

The alarm clock went off to the right of Skip's head at 7 AM. He wanted another hour in bed, but they had to get on a plane at Idlewild at 10. That meant they had to be at the airport at 9—9:15 at the latest.

"Up," Skip said. He jostled Clue's shoulder. Clue's head was under a pillow. " I don't wanna."

"Up." Skip pulled the pillow back. Clue squinted in the thin morning light. "Aw, crap. I was sleepin' so good..."

"You can sleep on the plane. C'mon. You go get his majesty up."

Cam had his own hotel room—a small bone of resentment to his band-mates, but he was the star of the group, and he insisted upon it. Clue put on a robe and slippers and shuffled down the hall. The hallway felt weird to him; it was another world and it didn't sit right.

He found Cam's room and knocked on the door. He heard nothing. He knocked again, then pounded. "Cam! Get up!" Shouting did no good. He shuffled back to his room. "He ain't gettin' up."

"That son of a bitch..." Skip called to the desk clerk downstairs. "I'm travelling with a Cam Cottner, in 717. We got to get a flight at 10, and I can't get him up...you could? I 'preciate it, sir."

He turned to tell Clue they'd call Cam's room and keep calling until he answered. Clue was in the bathroom, running the shower and waiting for warm water.

Skip opened the door and walked down the hall. He heard the phone in Cam's room ring and ring and ring. It sounded hollow and lonesome in there. He counted 24 rings and realized something was wrong.

He called downstairs. "Yeah...I don't think Mister Cottner is in his room. I'm getting kinda worried. Could you check and see if he's in there?"

"Well...I guess I could send a boy up there...after all, he might be sick or something."

"Thank you." Skip waited in the hall for the elevator. It opened with a ping and a bellboy exited, concern on his face. "I'm the guy who called...I 'preciate your helpin' me out."

"I hope he's not dead or nothing." The kid had a ring of keys. He shook and jingled them and got the key to 717. "Here goes." He unlocked the door and opened it so quietly it startled Skip. "Mister Cottner?"

The room was vacant. Cam's suitcase—a chaos of clothes—sat open on its stand. A pink shirt hung off the side like a dog's tongue. The bed covers were tight. The bellboy patted the bed. "This ain't been touched, mister. Nobody's been in here since the cleanin' ladies come along yesterday."

Skip sighed. He sighed again. He gathered up Cam's suitcase and moved it to his room. Then he placed a collect call to Tupelo.

◊◊◊

It took the combined efforts of the police department and the fire department to track Cam down. A young man answering his description was found in the waiting room of the Port Authority bus terminal. His cat clothes were stained and torn and he lacked one shoe.

When asked his name, Cam replied, "Nope. I ain't nobody no more." His was a dead stare at the ground. He wouldn't acknowledge the police officers and had to be lifted to his feet.

They got him into a squad car and radioed ahead to their precinct. "He's alive, but he's a nut case," the patrolman reported.

He was seen by a police staff physician as Skip fretted in the hallway outside and Clue sat bored out of his gourd. He tried to sleep but who could nod off with all that *Dragnet* crap going on?

The staff doc ushered Skip in. Clue tried to follow, but a sharp look from Skip sent him back to his bench. "Your boy's been painting the town every color of the rainbow. Is he a narcotics user?"

"I don't know, sir. He likes his liquor. I try to ride herd on him."

"What, you're his manager?"

Skip explained. The doc finally got it. "Oh, yeah. I saw you guys on TV the other night. My kids are crazy about that music.

"This boy has heroin in his system. And alcohol. And some kind of barbituate. He's really weak. I hope you're not going anywhere soon."

"How come?"

"I'm sending this kid to Bellevue for observation. He shouldn't do anything until he gets that crap flushed out of his system. You have any idea where he got the stuff?"

"He was hanging out with some black guys in Harlem. I tried to get him to come back to his hotel, mister, but he wouldn't have it. You just can't talk sense to that boy. He does what he wants, when he wants."

The doctor sighed. "Well, we can't prefer charges. He might have been forced to take what he took. Or coerced."

"Cam is easily misled, sir." Skip sighed. "I'm about fed up with him."

"I could understand why."

◊◊◊

Skip called Tupelo. At the moment the phone rang at Hive, Hank was about to do something he'd been fighting off for months. He and Miss Bell were alone in the office, and there was something about her perfume, and the way she was dressed...

Since she walked through the door that morning, Hank's thoughts circled around her. He thought of his marriage; his children; of Liz, who stood by him and/or put up with him. None of that was fleeting. It couldn't be tossed aside for a whim.

He rose from his desk, tense and guilty, and walked towards her. His intention was to kiss her neck and ask her to get better acquainted. The *brrrack* of the phone upended him. "Hive Records...uh huh...oh, Lord. Hang on."

Miss Bell turned; Hank had frozen with his hands in mid-air. She put the phone in his right hand. "It's Skip Mosely. There's some trouble."

Hank's heart raced—from the diet pills and from the shock. "Skip. Hank here." The receiver buzzed with bad news from the Big Apple. "Lord God...I know...well, all's you can do is try...no, no. I wouldn't blame you for nothin'..."

Miss Bell looked at Hank for the forecast. He wrinkled his brow like a bassett hound and shook his head. "No, you do what the doctor says...I'll wire y'all some more money...hundred bucks do ya okay?...Fine. We can get the flight re-scheduled...Wednesday? Thursday?...awright, you lemme know. I'll have Miss Bell call the airline an' let 'em know...I'm sorry...I know...yeah...we're gonna sit him down an ' have a talk when you get him back here...all right... now, you call me...day or night, you hear?...Yep...uh huh...well, at least he's safe now...Lord God...all right. Bye for now."

Hank explained; the news upset Miss Bell. She'd never been up north, but she heard what a rough place New York City could be. "It swallowed him up and spit him out."

"Well, the difference is he *wanted* to be swallowed up. You got to *want*

172

that for it to happen." Hank exhaled and made a rubbery rattle with his lips. "Like I ain't got enough to worry about already."

Miss Bell called the Southern Airways booth at the Tupelo Airport and explained the situation. Once she mentioned that a passenger was in the hospital, she got leverage from the attendant. They put the three return tickets on standby. "They'll need to pay 15 dollars at the gate. Tell 'em to call American Airlines before they need to get a flight. That'll get 'em to Atlanta, and then Southern'll take care of the last leg."

Miss Bell asked for the phone number of the American Airlines booth at Idlewild Airport. She jotted it down and typed up a memo for Hank with the information. Miss Bell had three memo colors: pink for most urgent, goldenrod for medium-strength and green for not-really-that-big-a-deal. This rated a pink.

"Uh oh; the pink slip," Hank said as she thrust the paper on his desk. He said that every time, and Miss Bell was plenty tired of the routine. But she'd worked for some real jerks in her time, and Mr. Howard was much more of a gentleman. She could put up with a dumb gag.

◊◊◊

In his hospital bed in Bellevue, in a room he shared with a liver-spotted, wrinkled old man who only spoke Polish and coughed a lot, Cam came back into coherence and temporary sobriety. He was surprised to wake up and find himself in a hospital gown; *aw, shit* was his first thought.

Cam thought he was in jail for a few seconds. Then the old man hacked up half a lung and a nurse peered in the doorway. "You're awake, Mister...Crotter?"

"Cottner," Cam said. He wasn't sure he could speak; his voice was a croak. "Yes'm."

"How do you feel?"

"Like sumpin the cat dragged in, ma'am, to be honest." The nurse, a stoic black woman, felt Cam's forehead. She removed a thermometer from her blouse pocket, gave it three crisp shakes and inspected it.

"Open up; let's make sure you're normal." She planted the thermometer under Cam's tongue. 180 seconds later, she removed it. "97.9. That's good!"

"Ma'am, how come I to be in here?"

173

"They found you at the bus station. You were out of your head. Talking in circles. That must have been some wild party you went to!"

"Party..." Cam struggled to think. "I don't recall no party, ma'am. But it sure must of been something big."

"Dr. Presner will come by in an hour; then we'll get you some dinner."

"Where am I, ma'am?"

"Bellevue Hospital, in Manhattan."

"What?" Events that led up to the party at the Apollo came back to him. "Oh. That's right. I wadn't sure where I was."

"You get some rest, and the doctor should be here quarter of six."

The nurse reminded Cam of Cecil, that songwriter guy. Had the same deadpan ways. *The world must be full of niggers like that,* he thought. *Oh, I ain't s'pose to say that word.* Cam struggled to remember what had happened to get him from the Apollo Theater to a bed in Bellevue.

Flashes came to him—the stage lights at the Apollo (had he really sung a song there?); the dark backstage with the deep red curtains and the portable Victrola and the booze; some people he'd never seen before—not Rusty Gordon or Chuck Willis; a ride in a cramped cab forever and ever; the sense of being wedged in between two people with no room to move; the smell of... perfume? Naw, it was real musky, like logs in a fireplace. Then a flame, much smaller, heating up something in a spoon. The liquid was brown and it bubbled. Then a voice that said "We gonna play doctor, boy. You the patient." What the fuck could that mean?

Only garbled snatches of memory came, like flashbulbs at the moment they ignite...flares of brown skin and white teeth, candlelight and filmy curtains moving with the breeze...of pain and pleasure too abstract to grasp...

*My butt is sure sore,* he thought. He tried to move his gluteal muscles and they were tender. It took awhile for that to make sense to him. Ditto for the bruised area on the side of his upper left arm.

*This is like a movie, like an ama... am... when a guy loses his memory. Crazy, man.* Cam stared at the tile ceiling of the room, trying to grasp these slippery stray thoughts. Then it came together. *Holy shit, I been buggered by a nigger. Don't that beat all!*

He thought of that hair dresser in Tupelo. That boy was dying to slip his dick into Cam. Well, too bad; he wasn't no virgin no more. Not in that regard. *You just can't figure those people out, man. You try to be nice to 'em, an' look what happens. I don't get it.*

By the time Doctor Presner made his late afternoon rounds, Cam had remembered all he wanted to recall. *Fuck it*, he thought. *What's done is done. Long as it don't kill me, man.*

◊◊◊

Cam Cottner was judged an innocent victim of foul play. The narcotics flushed from his system, his bruises patched and healing, he was okayed for the trip home. The next morning, he was released from Bellevue. Skip and Clue met him. "What the hell happened?" Skip asked him.

"Y'all are better off not knowin'. That's all I got to say."

"How come you're walkin' funny, man?" Clue looked at him with amusement. "Walkin' like a duck."

"I twisted my ankle somewheres. Guess I fell." The truth, as Cam pieced together, would die with him. Nobody needed to know the real story.

"You are the luckiest son-of-a-bitch in the world," Skip said. They took a cab to Idlewild and made an afternoon flight to Tupelo via Atlanta. Clue passed out, his head propped against the passenger window of his seatrow. Skip sat beside him and read a Mickey Spillaine book.

Across the aisle, Cam sat in discomfort and humiliation. He welcomed this stretch of time where he didn't have to talk to anyone. He ate his meal and stared out the window at the sunset. The plane flew through the clouds and he could see night covering the Eastern seaboard. *All them lights,* he thought. *Wonder how many of them houses have my records?*

Once they boarded their connecting flight, Cam fell into a deep sleep. Images blew through his head, but he couldn't remember a one of them when Skip shook him awake. In a fog, he climbed down the little steps to the tarmac. Hank Howard awaited them, with Cecil at his side. They smiled and waved. Hank was a bit pale; he hadn't slept in two days. Part was from his diet pills; the other was his worry that his biggest artist, Cam Cottner, might go and die on him.

Skip's station wagon was parked in the airport's long-term lot. He and

175

Clue schlepped their instruments across the tarmac after a brief conversation with Hank. "Y'all drop by the office when you're feelin' up to it," Hank said. "Be interesting to hear about all that happened."

He turned to Cam. "You need a ride home?"

Cam shrugged. "Take me to the Mid-Town Hotel. I ain't ready to see nobody for awhile."

Cam sat in the back; Hank drove and Cecil sat in the front passenger seat. "Y'all were terrific in Ed Sullivan," Hank said. "Man, the audience about did backflips when y'all came on."

Hank waited from a reply of assent, a chuckle or another sign of life. Cam watched the night-time traffic stream past in the other lane and said nothing. The silence from the back seat curtailed any other talk. It felt to Hank like he was in a funeral procession.

They reached the Mid-Town Hotel. Hank paused the car. Without a word, Cam left the car and walked towards the check-in desk. No goodbye, no acknowledgment of Hank or Cecil. They watched him enter the building, and, via the lobby window, head to the front desk.

Hank looked at Cecil. "There's a whole world inside that kid's head. We'll never know."

"Nope," Cecil replied.

***Hank tried not to worry about his business*** at night, but a lot depended on Cam and His Cats staying successful. *I hate to even think this,* Hank told himself, wide-eyed in the dark bedroom. *Something bad's gonna happen. Don't know where, don't know when. I hope I'm wrong.*

Cam's hospital stay didn't get into the papers. Skip's stoic approach had saved the group and their label from sensational headlines. But the incident had to be addressed. Hank gave the guys two days to recover and called them into the Hive headquarters.

Cam looked a bit wan when he walked through the door. He was the last to show up. Skip and Clue were bored and tense waiting for him to arrive. "Well, there's the star," Clue said with a deadpan.

"Hooray for the star," Skip muttered.

"Am I late? I been feelin' under the weather. Mr. Howard," Cam said in deference to Hank.

"Have a seat, buddy." They gathered in the studio. Hank gave Chuck the afternoon off with pay. He wanted this conversation private. "So...seems like we oughta clear the air. If that's okay with you. 'Cos your personal business is your..."

"Personal business," Cam finished.

"Yes. I ain't nobody's schoolmarm. Y'all are adults, or damn close. We've all got to take responsibility for what we say and do. 'Specially y'all, 'cos you're in the public eye. People listen to what you say and keep an eye on what you do. So you have to exercise some...well, caution. Anything you do that another person sees...anything that is witnessed is fair game for newspapers an' such."

Clue and Skip grunted their assent. Cam's face reddened.

"What I'm tryin' to say here, buddy...this company has a lot invested in you. In your special talents. Cam, you're the most dynamic performer that ever came through my door. You're doin' great, an' I just want to keep it that way. I want all of y'all to be happy with your success. But you have a responsibility to this company, and to one another...to be careful as hell out there."

"So, y'all are gangin' up on me? 'Cos this is about me. I ain't no dummy."

Hank stood up. "I hate to see you take that attitude. This ain't a complaint. It ain't an indictment. It's just words of wisdom that young performers all need to hear. You don't want to get your face on the cover of *Confidential.* You don't want people talkin' about you—unless they're sayin' good things."

"Well, I can do whatever the hell I want. This is a free country, last time I checked. I can take care o' myself fine."

"The hell you can," Skip said. "I don't know what the fuck happened to you, an' I don't want to know. But I went through high holy hell tryin' to find you. I got the whole damn police force searchin' for you. And I kept that crap out of the papers. I saved your sorry ass. You're welcome." Cam opened his mouth, but nothing came out. "You could be lyin' dead in the damn snow, frozen stiff. You ain't smart enough to take care of yourself. And if I have to be your...your wet nurse, on top of everything else, then to hell with it! Get yourself another guitar."

"Hey, man, I'm sorry you feel that w—"

"You were full of heroin. Bombed out of your gourd when they found you. You didn't know your name, or where you was. You would have died! You're a good singer. You could become a great singer. You have that potential. But I can't run herd on you no more. If you wanna flush your life down the toilet, you're welcome to do it, but I am done keepin' tabs on you."

Cam tried to formulate a defense, but Cecil's face startled him. Cecil knocked on the studio door. Hank put on a smile and went to the door. "We're just havin' a meetin' here. Be just a second."

"We have a bunch of auditions. They're lined up." Cecil thumbed behind him to the front door.

Hank sighed. "Well, boys, that's all for now. Just..." Hank grasped for the right words. "Be careful. Think before you act. That should be everybody's golden rule from now on." He looked at Cam. "Does that sound good?"

"I'll try. That's all I can say. Awright?"

"I can't ask for nothin' more." Hank thought for a moment. "Y'all might wanna go out the back way."

Skip laughed. "No one knows me from Adam." He headed out to the front door, and nudged past hopefuls and their guitar cases. Hank guided Cam and Clue through Chuck's inner sanctum, which had a door that let out into an alley.

Hank watched them walk the alley and turn the corner. He locked the alley door and strode towards Cecil. "Let 'em in. And I hope there's somebody good out there."

Cecil sighed. "The law of averages says otherwise."

Hank had a mountain of dull work ahead. Public demand for Cam and The Cats meant that records had to be re-pressed, and new metal plates made as old ones wore out from constant use.

The record distributors had an automatic standing order for new copies, and much of Hank and Miss Bell's office time was spent keeping the records pumped out. He limited himself to overseeing one hour of audition time every afternoon from 3 to 4. He glanced at the clock. 1:20. *Damn, where does the day go?* He reached in his pocket for the tin of pills.

◊◊◊

Cecil and Miss Bell had a system. When Cecil gave her a hand signal, she allowed one performer or group to enter. She ushered them through the lobby and explained, in general terms, that a very nice black man would give them a listen. He was in charge of the new acts, and was a great judge of talent.

If a musician voiced any objection to Cecil, Miss Bell wished them well and sent them out the door. A few would-be Hive artists made such a fuss, but most were so thrilled to get an audition they'd sing to a gumball machine.

Cecil had developed a sense of what was commercial in the country and cat music market. The ideal artist had just enough backwoods to be convincing and just enough city to break out of his or her hometown. Cecil kept an account of each act in a ledger. Into the proper columns were performer name, address and telephone number (if available).

To the right was Cecil's assessment of their worth, if any. In a third column went three possible marks: √ for a performer likely to succeed, ⁄ for someone with potential but not possessed of the "it" quality and × for those who could not cut the mustard.

More ×s than √s lined that column. Cecil kept the book away from the hopefuls. The first auditioners were a quartet of chubby fellows with two fiddles, a mandolin and a banjo. They called themselves The Waveland Wonders. Their repertoire was mostly original, and sat somewhere between bluegrass and cat music. They had talent, but to a man their faces could stop every time-piece in the state. He taped two of their numbers and promised to let them know what Mr. Howard thought.

◊◊◊

The Waveland Wonders gathered themselves together, giddy and excited. Cecil knocked on Chuck's door. "Yeah?"

"Got that okay?" Chuck nodded. "Any good? What do you think?"

Chuck shrugged. "There's a whole lotta guys like 'em. They're good enough pickers, good enough singers..."

"But there's a whole lot of them. You know, I bet we could make money cutting acetates on these guys. I think a lot of 'em would be happy just to have a recording."

"Well, hell, Cecil, that's a good idea. Let's keep it 'tween us for now, awright?"

Cecil didn't know what the right reaction was; he said "sure."

"Got another pigeon out there?"

Cecil sighed. "Yep."

"Well, just for a 'speriment. Ask 'em do they want a record to take home. Five bucks." Chuck glanced at his work station. "I need some acetates. Some blanks. Would ya get some? Be good to have 'em on hand."

Cecil nodded. He'd have to run this by Hank, but it didn't hurt to try it out. He leaned outside the studio door and got Miss Bell's attention. "Next!"

◊◊◊

Inside his office, Hank's heart pounded. His blood felt hot in his temples. He hadn't had this sensation in a couple of years. He couldn't name it. He could associate it with feelings from his teens and 20s.

He left his office for a paper cup of cold water. He had three cups as he watched Miss Bell sweet-talking a pair of refugees from a coal mine. Her sweet laughter and pert body caused him to stare. *Lust! That's what it is! Just plain old tomcat lust.*

Hank had thought having two kids would take the wick off his candle. He and Liz hadn't made love in...he had to strain to think. Because they didn't feel privacy in their home. At any time, one of the offspring (or both) might barge in, needing a drink of water or feeling scared after a bad dream. Hank had been the mute witness to his parents' carousing and nothing else in life felt as bad or awkward. He hoped to spare Carl and Kitty that trauma and confusion. 'Cos, hell, life ahead of them was nothing but those things, mixed in with just enough joy and triumphs to keep a person going.

He had an itch that hadn't been scratched in a long time. He had a flash of the cartoon character Barney Bear, coming out of hibernation, hungry and yearning for action.

Hank hadn't gotten an erection in so long it shocked him when he felt the swelling. No eyes were upon him; he slunk back into his office and shut the door. He sat at his desk, hearing the hiss of silence and the muted sawing of a fiddle from the studio. *Lord, there ain't no market for that kinda music these days. Poor Cecil...*

*What do I do about this?* The presence of this animal inside him, roused from a long slumber, worried him. He sipped from a cold cup of coffee. *Hell, I'll go get a co-cola. Walk around the block. Get a hold of myself...*

The intercom's buzz jarred him hard. "Bigbee's on line one."

"Aw, crap." Bigbee was Judd Bigbee of Midwestern Distributors, and he was the biggest bore in the world. "Miss Bell, tell him I'm busy and to call back tomorrow..."

"He says it's urgent."

Hank sighed. "Well, have him tell you what he needs an' that I'll call him back in half an hour. Okay?"

Miss Bell sighed. "Here goes the next 10 minutes of my life."

Hank opened his office door without a sound and snuck past Miss Bell,

181

whose pencil danced on her notepad. He heard Bigbee's Iowa twang drone on her receiver. She said a litany of "uh huh"s as she wrote.

The fiddle sounded better in the lobby, and the vocalist had a nice burr to his singing. Two years ago, Hive could have done something with him. Now he was yesterday's news.

The afternoon was warm. It was hard to believe it was autumn. It'd be hotter if it wasn't, man. Hank walked to Jolly's and got a king-size Coke and a roll of peppermint Life Savers. He walked down two blocks, turned the corner to the left and walked another block. That feeling still gnawed on him. It was like anxiety; a sensation he didn't choose but was chosen for him. "Lord God," Hank said out loud. He startled an elderly woman and realized he'd spoken what he had been thinking. *Gotta watch that.*

He walked three blocks towards Hive's office, turned into the alley and let himself in through the back door. The pressing room was a mess. Discarded vinyl crackled under his shoes, and Hive company sleeves fluttered in the breeze as he opened the door. He heard something shift and fall. "Aw, heck!" Miss Bell said. She was in the supply closet.

Hank peeked in. "Can I help?"

Miss Bell was bent over picking up boxes of paper clips, rubber bands and #2 pencils. "Aw, I can't get the carbon paper. It's way on up there."

Hank admired her derierre. "Oh, uh, well heck, I can get it for ya."

"Oh, thank you," Miss Bell sighed. "You don't know what it's like, bein' so short."

Hank had to stand on his tiptoes and feel for the box of carbon paper. It took him three tries to touch it and drag it forward. Once the lip of the box was off the shelf, he seized it and brought it down. "We oughta have this someplace lower."

"My hero!" Miss Bell cried in mock-rapture. She laughed and smiled. Her smile was...well, it could light up the world. Hank laughed and watched his arm reach towards her. He watched his hand find the back of her head; felt the stiff crispness of her hairspray. And then he kissed her.

Miss Bell was shocked to her core. She resisted his second kiss and struggled out of his grasp. "Mister *Howard!*"

Hank felt numb. He had watched this happen like it was a movie. He didn't will it to be; it just was. He searched for words of apology. His throat was dry.

He thought he heard someone else in the room. He looked over his shoulder; no one there.

Cecil had come to the supply closet to get a pair of fresh acetates for Chuck. He witnessed the exchange between Hank and Miss Tinkle in silent shock. Cecil ducked behind a stack of wooden packing crates and held his breath. The shadows hid him.

"I, honestly, I don't know what came over me, Miss Bell. I apologize. I...I haven't been myself lately."

"It's all right," she said. Her tone of voice gave another message.

"Why don't you just take the rest of the day off...come back in the morning and we can talk about it. All's I can say is I'm sorry."

"You've always been a gentleman," she said, her tone a bit warmer.

Cecil made sure he couldn't be seen from the window in the door. Miss Bell got her purse and left. Hank went in his office and shut his door.

Cecil got the acetate blanks, plus half a dozen extra, and went into the studio via Chuck's door. "What took ya so long?"

"Couldn't lay hands on 'em. They were under something else. I brought some extras."

"Thanks. Give 'em the sales pitch."

Cecil sighed. Clayton Welly and Red Hosfield hesitated; they only had a dollar and 38 cents between them. "Gawly, Mawma would shore get a thrill outa hearin' us awna record," Welly sighed.

"A moment, gentlemen." Cecil knocked on Chuck's door. "They'd like the records." Cecil gave Chuck a five dollar bill from his own bankroll. He'd get half of it back later. The acetates made Clayton and Red giddy with joy and they left.

There was no Miss Bell to usher in the next hopefuls. Hank helped out and abided an out-of-tune solo artist who imagined himself the next Hank Williams. Hank allowed him two songs and then played the diplomat. "Y'know, the country music market is changing. Music with a beat is getting more popular. The traditional style, like you play, has kind of fallen out of favor. But things change faster'n you can blink an eye. Could be country music will come 'round to what you're doin'. Stay in touch, an' keep writin' songs."

Cecil failed to get the fellow's name; he was not given the acetate pitch. Hank saw the man out the door, then looked up and down the street. No one remained. He shook his head at Cecil.

"Thank goodness." Cecil attempted to capture the singer's unfortunate skill at just missing the notes he sang. That tickled Hank. "I'm no expert on country music, but..."

"That was more like hog-calling. So, anyone worth hearin' today?"

"A couple of guys. They call themselves The Waveland Wonders. They might amount to something. Chuck taped 'em."

◊◊◊

Cam Cottner had no intention of returning to the cottage apartment he'd grown up in. He was through with Jackson. The man could make a nun cry. He was just plain mean. Worthless.

At the Mid-Town Hotel, Cam could live like he wanted. Have friends over; have girls over; do things, all kind of things, safe from prying eyes and ears. Once the curtains were closed, the suite was his world.

His suite was apart from the other units. He could play records loud as he liked, any time he liked. And anytime he felt like having a party, all he had to do was pick up the phone and call around.

He invited Jimmy Lee from the record store over. Told him to bring his friends. They had to come in through the side door. The Mid-Town was segregated but, thanks to a slender alley way, potentially unwanted guests could come and go without notice.

"Why for you at a ho-tel, man?" Jimmy Lee asked.

"I'm lookin' for a house. Right now, this is good. I'm near everything. Hey, bring some new records. I'll buy 'em off you."

With misgivings, Jimmy Lee called some friends and told them about the white boy's party in the white folks' hotel. The general consensus was that Cam was an ass, but since he was all famous now, it couldn't hurt to hang out with him for an hour or two.

At 10 PM, the first guests slid through the alley and knocked on the door of Room 17. "C'mon in," Cam shouted. He'd been drinking and was of good cheer. Jimmy Lee brought his friends Tuck and Joe, a pile of new 45s and some cheap tequila.

"Damn, man," Cam said, weaving as he considered the records. "How much for all 'em?"

"Gimme 10 bucks, we be good." A portrait of nervous Alexander Hamilton was laid on Jimmy Lee's open palm. Cam stacked his automatic changer with the new records. His face twisted in concentration; his head felt muzzy.

"All She Wants to Do is Mambo" by Wynonie Harris was the first to take a spin. "Get Away Baby" by The Bees followed, and before the stack of records had finished, all parties present were pleasantly bombed.

Cam got a second wind and felt more stable. "I gotta ask y'all somethin'. It's real important to me. Am I stealin' y'all's music?"

This got a laugh from Joe, but Jimmy Lee thought about it. "That ain't easy to say. Some folks say so. But sinct you been makin' records, we got more white kids comin' in. They like rhythm and blues an' they hate what's on the radio. That Patti Page shit. Doris Day."

"I mean..." Cam struggled with words. "Somebody. Some boy like me had to come along an' put a stop to that shit. Push some real music into their faces. That's all I'm tryna do. Just say, 'there's more to this than Doris Day.' You know?" He belched; Joe laughed harder. "Naw, man, I ain't bein' funny. I'm ser'ous here. Dead seer'yus. I care about y'all's music. I really do."

"I can tell," Jimmy Lee said. "I 'member when you firs' come in the store. Your eyes was wide as saucers. Like you was Columbus discoverin' America." He laughed. "An' now America discoverin' you."

"Aw, man, I 'preshate that. I really do. I just...I worry about this all the time." Cam paused for a swig of bourbon. "Did I tell you I got to sing at the Apollo? The fuckin' Apollo Theater in Harlem! An' they liked me. I was about to shit my britches when Rusty ast me to sing. I think he wanted to make a fool outa me. But I showed him."

"Rusty, he a joker. He always tryna get a laugh. Outta everybody. An' you got to 'mit, you're quite a sight."

"Got hair like Billy Wright," Tuck said.

"Billy Wright a fairy," Joe said. "I don't hold it none against him, but

185

that's the word goin' 'round."

"*I* ain't no fairy," Cam snorted. The next wave of drunk splashed over him. "I ain't *nobody's* fairy."

"Nobody callin' you that," Jimmy Lee said. "But you do have the hair. How you keep that standin' up?"

"Hair spray, man." Cam had cans of the stuff all over the place. Joe found a can, shook it and spritzed some in the air. He sneezed from it. Everyone laughed.

As "Sittin' Here Drinkin' Again" by Christine Kittrell came on, someone knocked on the door. Five more guests arrived, including Darrell Penton, Cam's hairdresser. Darrell made Billy Wright look like a Sunday school teacher. He sat down next to Cam. "Well, hello. baby. You ain't come by to see me in so long..."

"I been out sellin' my records, man. I'll come by an' see you. I'm due for a new dye job."

"Honey, your roots showin'. Like a tree! You come in tomorrow an' I'll fix you up fine."

The last thing Cam remembered was the sound of Fats Domino. It was like he drifted off to sleep. He could hear talk around him, but he couldn't get his eyes open. And then the voices got dimmer and more distant...

"Our host done passed out on us," Jimmy Lee said. "See do we got a clean getaway." Tuck peered out the door and down the breezeway. He gave a c'mon sign and everyone but Darrell Penton departed Room 17.

This was an opportunity Darrell never, in his wildest dreams (and they were quite vivid) hoped to have. One-on-one time with this fine, beautiful white boy. He admired the sleeping, snoring Cam. His skin was like alabaster; so delicate, with the blue and red veins coloring that pale shell.

Those lips, so lush and red and full, were parted in an enticing way. Cam's breath stank of Old Crow, but Darrell could not resist touching them with his own; feeling their softness and warmth. It excited Darrell to have this adonis so available. All the hours he'd pined for this boy...

He felt Cam's face. His hands gentled the contours of his downy cheeks, fingered his chin and touched his ears. Cam murmured and stirred. "Wha the fuck, man..."

"It's just you an' me now, honey. I give you somethin' to wake you up." He slapped Cam's cheeks. The boy's eyes struggled open. "Where am I?"

"You in your hotel room, sweetie. Just you an' me."

Cam shook his head to try and clear the fuzz. "Where's Jimmy Lee an' them?"

Darrell laughed. "They all gone home. All's but me. An' I got somethin' you gonna like." He produced a tin canister the width of a pencil. "You ever had you some snow?"

"Snow?"

Darrell tapped out a small mound on the side of his hand. "You just sniff this up, honey. You gonna like it."

Cam inhaled the cocaine. It hit him like his veins were full of broken glass, fireflies and snowflakes. *No wonder they call it snow.* He sat up, feeling like 1,000 volts were in his system. "Aw, damn. I want some more o' that!"

"Now, now, honey. There's a thing called give an' take. I got what you want, an' you sure got what I want…"

Cam lost focus for a moment. He felt that wave of white energy fade. He wanted it back. And, one word at a time, Darrell's intentions dawned on him. Cam felt scared. He was not used to that feeling. "What do I got?"

"Oh, honey. You got everything. Everything Darrell wants in life."

Cam took another sniff; he felt like he had left his body. He was up on the ceiling, looking down on the scene below, a thousand miles on the ground. He watched the nigger boy take off his shirt, and kiss him all over. He felt his pants slide down his thighs, and then his underwear.

He took another long draw on the bottle of Old Crow…

◊◊◊

Rain pounded against the windows as Cam came back into what passed for consciousness. He was alone in his room; he was buck naked; his asshole hurt. Not the fiery pain he'd felt in New York, but the sensation was familar.

He strained to see the clock on the wall. It was 1:15 in the afternoon. He sat up slow; his head throbbed. The room was all ashtrays and empty bottles. The record player rasped in the runout groove of a single.

Cam got to his feet, winced at his rectal pain, and waddled to the record player. He shut it off. He felt cold, and got a terrycloth robe from the bathroom. It swam on him. He parted the curtains and saw a December rain. A million shades of gray; no hope for the sun.

Cam felt hungry and nauseous. The urge to puke rose up in him. He knelt over the commode and tried to heave. Nothing came up. He tried pushing his index finger down the back of his throat. He gagged to no avail.

*Fucked again*, he thought. *I guess I had it coming to me.*

Cam ran the bathtub water. He might be able to soak this feeling away. Then maybe he could eat something at the Rexall and go see a movie. Anything to kill this day. It hadn't killed him, although it tried.

◊◊◊

Miss Bell took the rest of that week off with pay. Hank made many drafts of a letter of apology; the crumpled papers littered his office floor. He sent a short message to her special delivery:

*Please forgive a man who did you wrong. I will live with this shame for the rest of my days. Please know that you are the heart and soul of this company, and that I value the good nature and expertise you bring to your job.*

*I hope that, when you return to work, we will be able to be friends and co-workers, and you have my assurance I shall never again act as I did. You are a fine person and I appreciate your opinion.*

Miss Bell returned to her job the following Monday. It was just another workday; she didn't mention the incident or Hank's letter. Hank stuttered out a weak greeting and retreated to his office.

An hour later, he opened the door. "Everything...okay?"

"Couldn't be better, Hank." Miss Bell ratcheted two invoice forms and a sheet of carbon paper into her electric typewriter. The keys thudded on paper and Hank returned to his desk.

*As 1954 ended, Hank's black artists* found themselves on the back burner. With Cam's records making such noise, Hank had to focus his attention on them. He hired PR men in major cities to push the single any way they could. Disc jockeys needed little persuastion to play the record; it made many regional #1 spots. Hank had custom picture sleeves made, based on the group's standard publicity photo, to encourage jocks to talk up the records. Some got onto the retail shelves, and prompted diehard fans to buy the singles a second time.

There was still demand for Hive's black artists; the coming of "cat music" hadn't changed musical taste of the black community. Hive's back catalog of rhythm and blues singles experienced an uptick in sales. Young white fans, having heard Cam name-check Hive's black performers, began to seek out the records.

Hive's other artists were left for Cecil to supervise. He felt himself spread thin. Snake Eyes needed a follow-up to "Slob With a Job." He wrote "Boppin' in the Shop," about a record-crazy guy who opens his own store and has some problems, but most of them are solved anytime he drops a needle on the latest slab of rhythm and blues. It was likable, but lacked the edge of the earlier song.

Snake Eyes liked it, to Cecil's surprise. But he had a ballad he wanted to try out. "Wasted Nights" was something Snake Eyes claimed he'd written, but had bought from a high school kid for 25 dollars.

"You sure about this, man?" Cecil asked as he ran down the song with Snake Eyes.

"What's the problem, Cecilio? Ain'it good?"

"It's fine. But this is a real change for you. I think it's a good flip-side, but I can't see it as the hit."

"So, Cecilio, you tellin' me it ain't a hit 'cos you didn't write it?"

"No, man. That has nothing to do with it. You just gotta think about the public. And what they expect out of you. Everything you've done has been, you know..."

"Sarcastico," Snake Eyes sighed. "I am tired of playing the role."

"I understand. Let's record both songs and we can decide after that. The important thing is to make a record. Dig?"

"Dug," Snake Eyes said.

He did a servicable job on "Boppin' in the Shop," and his tenor man blew an inspired 12-bar solo. They did two takes. Snake Eyes fluffed a line on the first take, but the band was hot. He got the words across on take two, but the sax let loose with a couple of clams. "I think we need to get one more," Cecil said. "If we can get the solid sound of take one with the solid singing of take two, we'll have a record."

"I am an eager beaver for the ballad," Snake Eyes sighed.

"But we might lose the mood if we do the slow song now."

"Can't you just..." Snake Eyes made a scissors move with his third and fourth fingers. Snake Eyes had fluffed the lyric right after the sax solo ended. There was a hairbreadth spot where a splice could be made.

"I suppose. I don't wanna make you do anything you don't wanna do."

"Groovio!" Snake Eyes brightened. "Let's get 'Wasted Nights,' amigo Cecilio!"

"Wasted Nights" was in a Billy Eckstine bag, and Snake Eyes sounded like he was spoofing that style of smooth singing. One take died when the bassist had a laughing fit. "What you laughin' at?" Snake Eyes demanded.

"It ain't nothin', man. You go about singin'."

They got it on the third take. The bass man was right. There was something comical about Snake Eyes' vibrato voice in balladeer mode. Cecil witnessed the performance with a mixture of fascination and horror. It wasn't bad; it wasn't good. What was the right word? *Morbid.* It sounded morbid.

Against his best judgment, Cecil indulged Snake Eyes and "Wasted Nights" went out as the A-side of Hive #258. *Cash Box*'s reviewer assessed the song thus: *Here's a potent take-off on the Eckstine-Prysock school of big blues ballads. Snake Eyes plays it straight, but his trademark comedy comes across strong.*

190

*Should lay 'em in the aisles—those who dig off-beat musical humor.*

Of the B-side, *Cash Box* was less enthused: *This apparent follow-up to artist's big hit is cute, but lacks the spark that made 'Slob with a Job' such a stellar stand. May get some plays.*

The awkward tape splice didn't help the record's cause. The band took a one-beat pause after the sax solo. Chuck tried for four hours to connect the two takes. A rhythmic lurch couldn't be overcome.

The single didn't chart, and it joined the Hive ranks of records that didn't get re-pressed. It was Cecil's first full-on flop, and he took the blame for letting an artist have their way in the face of common sense.

Cecil's new song for Rusty Gordon was weaker than "Decline and Fall." He knew it, and he hoped Rusty's over-the-top singing style might mitigate a flat number. Cecil had gotten the idea from hearing a couple of kids singing "Down in the Valley." He tried to imagine Rusty singing a country song like that, and his brainstorm seemed solid at first.

By the time he finished the song, he knew it was a bit strained. Taking pot-shots at an easy target was never that funny. Though Cecil didn't care for hillbilly music, his reasoning was that a black audience would appreciate Rusty poking fun at the scene.

Cecil prefaced "Down in What Alley?" with that idea—that Rusty might have fun razzing the tropes of country music.

Rusty's band couldn't get the right groove. Playing a forced rhythm, dead on the beat, wasn't their way. Rusty improvised an opening "Howdy, yew-awl!" and sang in a parody of a white Mississippian, but the band's hard time with the stiff musical style derailed six takes. Halfway through take seven, Rusty whistled and halted the band. "This one...I ain't feelin' it. You want my opinion? 'Cos I don't think it any good."

"I'm sorry you don't like it. Can you tell me what you don't like about it? Maybe we can fix it."

Rusty laughed. It was rueful. "Can't fix this thing, son. It broke."

"I'm sorry you feel that way, but I'm sure you and I can—"

"What you doin', givin' *my* songs to that little shit?" Cecil couldn't come up with an answer. "That 'Ignoramus,' man. I coulda had a hit with that thing. A big hit!"

191

"Well, why don't you record it for the rhythm and blues market? You do it in your act..."

"Naw, naw, man. You want me to look like I'm ridin' on his ofay tail? Naw, man. I don't do that."

"A hit record is good for all of us. And I'm writing more songs for everyone. Fast as I can."

"You write me somethin' better. And don't you go singin' it to that... boy."

"I've got another idea that is just right for you. I just need to finish the words."

"You *promise* me you ain't gonna show it around." Rusty's anger frightened Cecil, though his own face showed no reaction.

"You should be grateful you're getting songs from me. I write hit songs."

"You done got all dicty, man. We done for today."

"Wait!" Cecil stopped the sidemen from packing up their horns. "Why don't you all take an hour. Go have some supper. I'll have the song done when you come back."

Rusty relaxed. "You best not be snowin' me, man. I expect a good song. A funny song that people gonna like."

The sidemen left their instruments in the studio and drove off to get some barbecue. Cecil did have a notion for a song. He'd been reading about the plans to explore outer space. They were white people plans. Billions of dollars spent for white men to go float around in some space station. What if they sent *Rusty* into outer space? How would somebody like Rusty do on the planet Mars? The thought made Cecil chuckle.

He ran a 12-bar blues shuffle on the piano and words came to him. The sillier the better; he was writing about a clown, for a clown, to an audience of clowns.

Before Rusty and his crew returned, smelling of meat and smoke, Cecil had finished "Space Man Boogie," a humorous shuffle about a black astronaut who finds Mars a better place to live. Nobody to stop you from boppin' an' hoppin' or gettin' slick with a chick. The lyrics were close to being salacious. You never spelled it all out with Rusty, because he'd make it broader and wilder as he sang the words.

"This is more *like* it, man." Rusty's anger had been mellowed by ribs and whiskey. "Man, run that one down again so's the boys can get with it." The tenor sax man came up with a descending riff; the guy on alto harmonized to it and the bassist played an upward run. The sound was funny on its own.

With Rusty's slightly soused vocal on top of it, it was nonsense, a real throwback when you sized it up against "Hangman." But it sold records, gave Gordon a #3 rhythm and blues success, and picked up two competing versions—the first time one of Cecil's songs had attracted outside artists. A white harmony group The Carnivals, who presented a wholesome alternative to r&b vocal groups like The Spiders or The Eagles, took their version to #8 in pop. It was all money in the bank for Cecil, Hank and Hive.

◊◊◊

The success of Cam and His Cats continued to draw out musicians from little towns in Mississippi, Alabama, Arkansas and Louisiana. Some wrote to arrange an audition; their letters written in labored school-taught cursive, some close to illegible.

There was every reason to believe that the market for "cat music" was bigger than one act. Most of the auditioners were either too countryfied or too much alike. They'd heard Cam's two singles and decided they could do it themselves. It was a lightning-in-a-bottle problem. Everyone thought they had it, but 99% wound up empty-handed.

Hank Howard found one new singer, a 28 year-old, gaunt-cheeked blackland farmer named Cliff Roscoe, who wrote in the Hank Williams vein, but had a flair for clever lyrics and could sing well at a hot tempo. He had a four-piece band with a talented drummer. Having an artist who provided his own material was a gift; that the material was good and commercial put a bow on the package.

Cliff Roscoes were rare. The auditions were awkward, despite Cecil's pains to put the newcomers at ease. Most of these backwoods boys were put off by the presence of a black man—or to accept that he was passing judgment on them. The auditions wore on him. After a tough session with a white punk who took offense at Cecil's color, and couldn't sing his way out of a used condom, Cecil barged into Hank's office. "I can't do this anymore."

"Why, what's wrong?"

"I am. I'm the wrong person for these...I can do all right with Rusty, but these boys, they..."

"I get you. I wish these folks could see you the way I see you."

"Maybe you should take over. I don't like doing it. It wears me down."

"Well, shoot, I'm busy all day. I can't do it. Who else we got?"

"How about the Uranus guy?"

"Skinny?"

"He spotted Cam. He might be a better man for this job." Cecil paused for effect. "He's a paleface. He could get along better with them."

"Huh. Skinny might be a good supervisor for recording, too. Hell, it's easy to find out."

Hank called Skinny Griggs. He answered on the sixth ring. Hank got through the first sentence of his pitch. Skinny stopped the second one. "*Would I? Would I?*"

"You brought Cam our way, an' Cecil an' I figure you've got a pretty good ear for this kinda music..."

"When do I start?"

He started the next day. Cecil's relief was easy to see. His shoulders relaxed and he allowed himself to smile and joke with Hank. Cecil saw the future of Hive Records; rhythm and blues was riding in the back of the bus, which was driven by country boys who took their cues from those passengers.

Cliff Roscoe was Hive's second hit artist in the cat music division, which the trade magazines now called rock 'n' roll. He had a flair for writing about teenagers. Cecil felt a competitive envy of Roscoe's lyrics, but respected the man's skill with internal rhymes.

Cliff had the Hive artists' yen for liquor. He could handle his better than bantamweight Cam, but he seemed drunk most of the time. In the recording studio, his slurred diction had to be curbed with black coffee. Cliff sounded sloshed, which wasn't the right vibe for Hive's teen audience.

Cliff had a natural hit with his song "Black Pegged Pants," but his progressive drunk-ness ruined 30 takes. "What's the matter, buddy? You got a solid song here." Skinny beamed at Cliff. "Just sing it...have a ball with it. You got a hit here!"

"Wha'f I ain't good enough? Wha'f they don't like me?"

Skinny had no answer. He got Hank's attention through the studio window. Cliff was on the verge of tears. His drummer thought it was funny. His laughter released hostility from Cliff's altered state. "What the hell you think is so damn funny, Todd? What?"

*Oh, boy*, Hank thought. He entered the studio all smiles. "Hey hey hey! What's the matter in here?"

"Whadayou care?"

"I'm gonna put your record out. I been hearin' some good stuff but it keeps stoppin'. I'm dyin' to hear the whole song. How's about we take a break an'...why don't we go get some coffee? Down to Jolly's? Just get outta here for a minute."

Cliff looked up, his eyes red-lined with anguish. He nodded and set his guitar on the floor. "Get your coat, buddy."

"I don't need one."

Hank got his new artist outside. "Now tell me, buddy. What's on your mind? You seem upset."

"I ain't good enough, Miss'r Haard. I just ain't good enough..."

"Who says that?"

"Hell, man. Look at me. I'm losin' my hair. I ain't no kid. How you 'spect the kids to go for me?"

They made it to Jolly's. "How's about a couple of black coffees. Big ones." Hank got them and paid. "Let's walk around the block an' have us some coffee."

"You ain't answered me."

"Well..." Hank had no answer. He improvised. "You know, all it takes is a good song. And what young people like is a song that they can relate to. They hear so many phoney songs. They...they hear 'em an' they think, 'that ain't got anything I care about.' An' that's most songs out there.

"You might be older than them. But you think like they think. An' you say things they maybe think about, but things they'd never say out loud. 'Cos

195

some square out there would shoot 'em down. An' you come along sayin' these things. You make them feel like they have some purpose. You know what I mean?"

"I...I do?"

"Why, sure. Your song's all about a feller who's saved his allowance money for weeks to get this sharp new pair of slacks. He knows that his girl digs the latest fashions. And he's hopin' that this pair of pants will get his girl to like him more. An' he doesn't even realize that she already likes him 'cause of who he is. The pants are nice, an' all, but you don't get married to a pair of pants. See, there's a message in there."

Cliff looked up. "There is?"

"Yeah. An' I tell you, the minute kids hear this record, they're gonna get that message. An' it's gonna make 'em feel like somethin'. An' they'll buy your records. An' then you'll make more records. Now, you got a lot of good songs."

"I...I...yeah. I been workin' hard on 'em."

"See? You've done the hard work already! Now all you got to do is just stand there an' sing 'em. Sing 'em like you feel 'em. That's all you gotta do."

"Dang. You make it sound easy."

"I know it ain't, but I know you can do it. You have the voice and the songs and the message that is gonna reach out an' get to these kids. Startin' with this record. It's gonna go big." Hank sipped his coffee. "I can tell these things. I knew it the first time you walked through the door."

Hank had timed his speech to perfection. They'd rounded the block in the fall dusk and were in front of Hive's office. "Well, sir. How's about we get in there and make us a hit record?"

Cliff smiled. His eyes looked better. The flop-sweat was gone. After he threw up in the Hive studio can, and gargled with tap water, he got back under his guitar and Chuck cued up a new reel of tape. In 15 minutes, Roscoe and his band cut two useable takes of "Black Pegged Pants" and its ballad flipside "Always My Honey."

The single joined Cam and His Cats on the pop music Top 10 in February 1955. Cecil wished he'd had a cut on that record; it peaked at #2 by Valentine's Day, with the ballad getting up to #14.

Cecil's new song for Rusty. "What's He Got (That Makes Him So Hot)?" addressed the popularity of white rock 'n' rollers who Rusty felt were impinging on his turf. "What right's he got, stealin' my thunder? Where'd he get his ideas, I wonder?" resonated with Gordon, and he delivered the song like Louis Jordan, with a touch of gospel singing. He hit a falsetto note and held it for 6 bars at the finale of the record. His performance surprised everyone, including Rusty.

It was Rusty's first single to miss the charts. Hank loved the song, and figured it would be a big hit. He over-pressed the single and had to eat the loss. A year before, it might have killed the company. "C.D.B.," Hank said, and warehoused the unsold records.

Snake Eyes signed with *Pizzazz Records* in Hollywood and never set foot in Tupelo again. He didn't inform Hive Records of his move. He had one release left on his contract, which he didn't honor. Hank thought about suing him, but decided it wasn't worth the fuss and bother.

The Four Fellers broke up when their lead singer was sent to the state penitentiary for 99 years. He'd had an argument with the baritone and broken a bottle on the man's head. The baritone died in a pool of blood.

Rusty Gordon was the last man standing in the rhythm and blues department. He had four months to go on his two-year contract. Hank called him and asked him to come to the office and talk turkey.

"Rusty, you've had a pretty good run here. Some big records."

"Yes, sir, I have."

Hank fell silent as he groped for the right words. He looked into Rusty's eyes and asked: "Are you happy with this company?"

"Man, you askin' a hard question! I know my last record didn't go. But it was a good record!"

"This ain't anything against you, Rusty. That was a great record, an' I know sometimes the public...you got to catch 'em just right. I've been happy to have you on board. But..." Hank stood up and tried to pick his words with care. "Things are changing 'round here. This is turnin' into a whole 'nother kind of record label. This 'cat music' business. I mighta bit off more than I can chew."

"Hell, man, you gotta make money. It's a bidness. I understand."

"I would be happy for you to stay on here. I'd be honored. But I got to be honest. All my time is taken up with these new artists. I'm thinking that maybe Cecil could head up our rhythm and blues department. We need some new faces—'long with yours. But I can't put the time into it like I used to. I'm sorry as hell about that, but that's the situation."

"Me an' Cecil, we kyna butt heads. He ain't like you. Man, we use to have *fun* cuttin' a record! Didn't matter how long it took. Man, them some of the best times of my life."

"Thank you, Rusty. I always want the artist to be relaxed. Music should be made in a good mood. It comes across to the listener."

"Cecil, he like a school teacher. He don't smile without he has a reason. An' he don't always have a reason."

Hank laughed. "Yeah, he *is* like a teacher. No nonsense."

"And the man come up with such funny songs."

"Cecil's a mystery. Talented guy, a hard worker, and dependable as the sunrise. This label wouldn't be the same without him. But he's had his troubles. We all got 'em, but his are...well, I don't know *what* they are. But, you know, I can feel 'em. I don't think he'd ever talk about 'em. He's not that kind. Keeps it all bottled up."

"You see what I'm talkin' about. Goin' in there with him is like takin' a test. It's work."

"I could try to run your sessions. I'd be happy to make time for that. If you want to stay, I'll do everything I can to give you what you need. It's about time we bumped up your royalty rate. I been meaning to do that."

"A man from Decca Records called me." Hank turned to Rusty. His expression must have shown. He didn't respond. "He tole me they could put me on the Brunswick label. He say they lookin' for a top artist an' he been follorin' my records and all. I tole him I'd think about it."

Hank exhaled. "You know. I was expecting this would happen. You've been havin' hits and puttin' out fine records. A big label was bound to take notice. And I'll be honest. They can give you more money. Better distribution... promotion. I started this company so that black artists could be successful and make the kind of music they wanted to make. Now, you might not get that with one of those New York labels. They might push songs on you that you don't want to do, or ask you to cover another person's record.

"You are a great entertainer. You're a natural showman, and I think we've built up a good image for you. But maybe that's not enough."

"Man tole me I could be makin' a lotta money there."

"You'd prolly have to move up north."

"It's too cold up there for me. Well, I done said I'd think it over."

"I appreciate your tellin' me about it. A lot of guys would have kept it to themselves."

"Snake Eyes, man. He jus' up an' gone. Didn't say boo to me."

"I never could figure out what to do with him. Maybe he's better off in Hollywood."

Rusty laughed at the thought of Snake Eyes out with all those palm trees and swimming pools. Hank laughed out of nervous release. Rusty was going. *Once a fellow mentions a better deal, he's going to take it. No matter what he thinks.*

After the meeting ended, Miss Tinkle announced a new artist—or artists—that sought an audition. Ronald and Dwayne Moody had cut a couple of country singles for Bullet Records in Nashville. They heard the clarion call of cat music and found it easy to shift their style.

They had a habit of finishing each other's sentences, like Donald Duck's nephews. Hank took a liking to them, and signed them after they sang a harmonized version of "A Slob with a Job."

Hank got them together with Cecil; the song needed some changes to make it more pop-friendly. The boys were educated and easy to be around. Cecil didn't mind diluting his song, and did it with their advice. It didn't need much change; the sharp edges turned round and smooth.

The kids were songwriters, and for the flip-side they sang an eerie ballad from the deep woods. "The Longest Train" was their update of a classic folk song, with the story about a young man whose girl rides off to a new life that he won't share. To flesh out the record, Skinny Griggs brought in a trio he'd used on his garage sessions. They knew their stuff, and were a good fit for both sides.

Hive #257 went out as The Moody Twins with The Tupelo Three. The public liked them, and they presented well on TV. The single got to #8 on the national charts. Cecil appreciated getting a second revenue stream from his song; it balanced the Cliff Roscoe situation and reassured him that he was still of value to the label.

◊◊◊

In July 1955, Rusty Gordon signed with Brunswick Records. To be fair, he recorded a last Hive single three days before his contract took effect. The terms of his deal allowed Hive to release whatever remaining material they had on the artist within six months but forbade them from re-issuing older records after that date.

Cecil suggested the extended-play 45. "We can put this out now, and it will be on the market with his new record. If his next record goes over, we have two records out on him." *The Clown Prince of Rhythm and Blues* had an attractive honey-toned cover with a picture of Rusty mugging at the microphone.

It was snapped at Gordon's last session for Hive. The day before the date, Rusty and Cecil sat down at the piano and wrote a ballad—a departure from his carefree image. "Sunset" told the story of a man who had been waiting all day for the mailman to show. He awaited a letter from his girl, and just as the sun began to sink, it arrived. It said goodbye, and the singer looked upon the setting sun. The singer's last words were to that disc in the sky. "My heart's like you; it don't turn blue...it sinks into the night. But it'll rise another day; my sunset ain't gonna stay."

Coupled with "Batty Hattie," a silly novelty song written by the group's sax-man, "Sunset" regained Rusty's berth on the r&b charts at #6. His fans accepted him as a straight man. The EP sold well, and Cecil made sure that it had one of the group's originals, so it would generate income for them.

***Cam, Skip and Clue returned*** from a package tour on March 21, 1955. They'd been on the road for two months, and Hank got them into the studio on the 23nd to record their third single. Cam looked a little worse for the wear, with dark patches beneath his eyes and a pallor to his skin.

"When's the last time you had a check-up, Cam?" Hank inquired.

Cam shrugged. "Been awhile."

"You don't look so good. You should go see a doctor."

"I guess so. Hey, how's about some money?"

"You've all got some coming to you. Let's get a record, and then we'll settle up."

Cam had written a song with Clue's help. "Women Women Women (Be the Death of Me)" appeared to be a documentary of a randy young man's adventures on the road. "There's a door in every doorway, there's a ship in ev'ry dock; ev'ry place I go them girlies want to shiver, shake and rock," one line went. Cam sang it as a celebration and as the exhausted participant. "Gonna buy a desert island, gonna live there all alone; gonna stay there 'til the day comes I can't make it on my own," he croaked in the last verse; he was addicted to the pleasures of the flesh.

It was a 12-bar blues, set to a bump-and-grind, stop-and-start rhythm that Chili Burse hooked into with relish. Cecil pounded triplets and did arpeggios on the high keys. "Make it tinkly," Cam commanded him. "Whack on them things." Cecil whacked.

For the flip, Cecil had a ballad. "Sunset" had gotten him interested in writing slower material. "Deeds I've Done" was a meditative song about a person looking over his past affairs and seeing the good and the bad in his own actions. "There are times when I've been tender; there are times when I've been cruel. There are days when I've been righteous; there are days I've played the fool…"

Cecil had been inspired by the records of Charles Brown, and guided the sound of "Deeds I've Done" into that direction, with an after-hours sound of subdued drums, guitar and piano. Clue, whose modus operandi was to slap his bass strings, needed the most direction. "Just touch 'em enough to get a sound. Low and soft. I want it to sound like a musical instrument."

With some coaching, Clue got it, and Cecil added some of his best piano work. All it needed was Cam's voice, and the singer got the song. "God damn, man, this is poetry," he said, and his eyes were glossy as he sang the words; he sniffled in-between takes.

Hive Records could have released two blank sides with the name "Cam and The Cats" on the label and it would've sold. But Hive #260 was something special, precious and powerful. With a randy, rowdy blues on one side and a soul-searching ballad behind it, it screamed up the charts, vanquishing all opponents and hitting the #1 spot on "Cash Box." ("Billboard" had it at #3.)

Parent groups and churches complained about "Women Women Women." Calvin Boggs, mayor of Corinth, Mississippi, decried the record and demanded it not be played by radio stations. Many stations in smaller towns refused to play the record. Two organized record burnings were held in Flint, Michigan and Sheffield, Alabama. Reporters invaded Tupelo and interviewed Cam. "They're buyin' the records so's they can burn 'em, right? They can burn all they want, man. We'll just make some more!"

Hank took a more measured response. "The worst thing in the world is indifference. I'd rather have someone hate a record I put out than to yawn at it. Hate is a kind of love, if you stop and think about it."

"CAT MUSIC" SINGER: "THEY CAN BURN MY RECORD!" made better headlines than RECORD PRODUCER WEIGHS COSMIC SIGNIFICANCE OF HATRED. The wire services ate up Cam's comments. Hank's were left in only if a newspaper needed to fill up more space.

As "Women" approached the top of the pops, Cam was interviewed for the CBS nightly news in front of his apartment. With his momma in the background, dazed in her apron, Cam answered the reporter's questions about this new music: "It was bound to happen sometime. I mean, I myself have been hungry for a kind of music that said what I'm thinkin', an' had a rhythm to it… somethin' you can feel all over. Jazz music has it; country music has it. And the blues has it the best. Man, that there is soul music. It comes from the soul.

An' that's what I'm tryin' to do when I sing...people will knock it, y'know? It's somethin' they ain't used to. But they'll get used to it, all right. They're gonna have to."

◊◊◊

As the record crested, Cam collapsed on-stage in Atlanta. He was out cold; girls screamed and stormed the stage. Clue and Skip hauled him to safety backstage and then dashed out to grab their instruments. The screams of the teenage girls made Skip's ears ring. The tour was cancelled and The Cats returned to Tupelo.

"It's the same thing all over," Skip sighed. "He was up all night 'fore the show, carousin' with a bunch I didn't know."

"Couldn't you stop him?"

"Mr. Howard, short of cold-cockin' him...there ain't no stoppin' him. He's got his mind set on screwin' everything up."

"Yeah," Clue said. "He couldn't stand up straight 'fore the show. I had to help him onstage, like he had a leg broke."

Hank shook his head. "This cannot continue. He's not your responsibility. Ain't nothin' in your contract about babysitting." He bit his lower lip in thought. "We have a problem here. The kid could tear down everything we've built up. Well..." Hank shook his head again. "I'm gonna have to lay down the law on him. Before he can do any real damage."

Hank drew four hundred-dollar bills from his wallet. He gave two each to Skip and Clue. "This is my way of sayin' thank you for being professionals in the face of this..."

"Shit," Clue said as the green touched his palm. "Ain't no other word for it, Mr. Howard."

"I can think of a few." Hank smiled a hard smile. "Where's Cam at right now?"

"He's stayin' at the motel. He an' his stepdad don't get along no more."

"Gentlemen, I thank you for lettin' me know what's been going on. I'm gonna track him down right now. This cannot wait another day."

◊◊◊

Mister Cottner was in Room 17, in the bend of the ell of the Mid-Town Hotel.

203

The curtains were drawn and the room silent.

Hank knocked on the door to no response. He knocked harder; then he pounded. He heard the creak of mattress springs and muffled curses from within. Something metal bounced on the floor. Fingers fumbled with the lock on the door. Cam's ashen face appeared. "What is it?"

"Son, you are sick. You need help. I'm takin' you to the doctor."

"I ain't goin' to no doctor. I'll be all right." Hank leaned on the door to let in more light. Cam had no shirt on. His body was clammy-looking, puffy and sweaty, with a wine-colored bruise on his right deltoid. It matched the color that ringed his eyes.

"You look like you're enbalmed, son. There is something wrong with you. You're going to the doctor."

"No." Cam pushed the door closed, but Hank's shoe blocked the way.

"You put on some clothes. Right now. I am out of patience."

Hank pushed against Cam and got into the room. "Get dressed." He crossed his arms and tried to look stern. The scene brought to mind times when Carl had misbehaved. There wasn't much difference. Carl might be a little smarter than this mouthy, difficult kid.

Cam dressed in sullen silence. Hank herded him out the door and up the breezeway to his car. "You're gonna see my doctor. McFadden. He's a good guy. I just wanna make sure you're not gonna die on us."

The boy smelled of booze and body odor. He had trouble keeping his head up. The exertion of a few minutes ago had gone hard on him. His lips were chapped and he kept licking at them.

◊◊◊

Dr. McFadden was in the middle of a busy day. Hank was a friend, and the boy he had with him...death warmed over would sum him up. Something was wrong.

McFadden sweet-talked the mother of a kid with the sniffles into resscheduling their visit. He got Cam into an exam room. With his shirt off, he reminded him of the pictures that came out after the war of those poor souls in the concentration camps. He saw malnourishment, over-indulgence and...

"What's with this?" he asked. He pointed to the spreading bruise on

Cam's shoulder.

"Must of hit it on somethin'; Ida know."

The epicenter of the bruise was a scab-crusted pin-spot. A hypodermic had gone in there—one that hadn't been sanitized, and was likely already used by another party.

McFadden ordered a blood test. As he awaited the results, he took Hank aside. "This boy...there's something fishy here. I want to keep him under observation for a day or two. This *could* be the flu, or..." McFadden looked away. "I have my suspicions, and they're not pretty."

"It's for his own good. I'll pay for whatever they need to do."

An ambulance took Cam away. "I ain't sick. I don't know why you won't listen to me," he protested. His voice was weak.

◊◊◊

Hank had his business to run, and gave his work number to the head nurse. He and Miss Bell made sense out of the outstanding invoices. He flashed on the moment in the supply closet. His heart burned with shame. She had been such a professional about it all. *I wonder if she even thinks about that anymore...*

Hank haggled with distributors all afternoon. He got six commitments to send checks special delivery and picked up new orders for 5,000 records—all Cam and His Cats. The anger he felt towards Cam translated into hardball for those in his debt.

"Hank, it's a nurse on line one..." the intercom crackled.

Hank took the call. "Dr. McFadden wants to see you, soon's you can come by."

"Everything okay?" Miss Bell asked as Hank left.

"I sure hope so. I'm gone for the day." He meandered through late afternoon traffic to the hospital. He caught himself rocking back and forth in the driver's seat. *Nervous. I wonder if I do that all the time and don't notice it?*

The nurse paged Dr. McFadden and invited Hank to sit. Hank paced, He worried, convinced himself that worrying did no good and worried again. He was almost in a trance as Dr. McFadden's voice roused him. "Your boy does not have the flu. Please come with me."

They entered Cam's room. The boy was asleep. His brow shined with sweat. "Cam, you okay?"

"Don't try to wake him. He needs rest."

"Sorry."

"What's that? What's that?" Cam opened his eyes. "Mr. Howard." Cam eyed McFadden with suspicion. "Who's this? Who's this?"

"He's your doctor. It's okay."

"Gimme... gimme water." Hank poured a cup from a glass pitcher; he held the cup to Cam's lips and the boy gulped it down. "S'more, s'more." Hank refilled the cup. Cam grasped it with shaky hands. Water dribbled down his chin.

Dr. McFadden cleared his throat. "Can you understand me, Mister Cottner?"

Cam nodded.

"I'll be blunt. Mister Cottner, you have gonorrhea. A rather advanced case of it. I would assume you have been sexually active?"

"Yes, sir, I have." A weak smile edged his lips.

"This is nothing to smile about. And the blood test showed me some news I don't care for. There are traces of narcotics in your bloodstream. Opiates. Heroin is my guess. Would you agree?"

Cam said nothing, but his jaw fell slack.

"I thought so. The laws of my profession tell me that I must contact the police and report you as a user of narcotics. This is a federal offense, and I take these things seriously."

"Dr. McFadden, may I speak with you?"

They stepped into the tiny bathroom. "I am the manager of this young man. He is a musician with three hit records. It would be...it would be a huge blow to have him go to prison over this."

"I'm sorry that you have become involved with this young man. I understand it would cost you a lot of money to have him arrested. Bad publicity would be the least of your worries—and his."

"Yes. Whether he goes to jail or not, it would be a...a blemish. What can I do? He's just a kid. A dumb kid who's screwed up. I will see to it that he doesn't touch that stuff again."

Dr. McFadden sighed. "The law is the law, Mr. Howard. You're a family man, a businessman. You understand. I have no choice."

Hank thought. He questioned his own nerve; then he spoke. "How much is it worth to you, cash money, to let this one go? Right now; cash on the barrelhead."

The doctor quailed. "I've never...I couldn't do such a thing."

"A thousand dollars. I'll ride herd on this boy and keep him straight."

"You're kidding me. I—"

"Two thousand. All I have to do is walk two blocks to the savings and loan. $2,000 in five minutes. No taxes, no record. Just a donation for medical research."

McFadden regarded Hank with shock. His face kept blank. He shook his head. "I will accept it as a donation." He exhaled. "I can use it for some new instruments."

"I'm glad to help, sir."

"I would suggest you and your family find another physician. I can recommend Dr. Earl Gravers. He's a fine man and an excellent doctor."

"Can you wait here? Five minutes; ten if there's a line."

Outside the hospital, Hank congratulated himself. He'd seen things like this happen in the movies, but never figured they'd go over in real life. *We all have our price,* he thought. *And maybe that money will...it could cure polio. Or leukemia. It could end up doing some good.*

He was back in eight minutes. The teller balked at the large withdrawal, but Hank's business account was good for it. This money would have gone to Cam for royalties on units sold. It was a means to keep his career safe. He'd earn back that money on his next record. Assuming there would be one...

◇◇◇

Dr. McFadden took the money (20 100-dollar bills in a small manila envelope) and put it in his inner coat pocket. Nothing was said.

He entered Cam's room. Hank stood behind him, hands folded behind his back.

"Boy, you are *this* close"—the doctor gestured with his thumb and forefinger— "from a serious narcotics habit. It's only as a favor to this gentleman"—he gestured towards Hank, without changing his gaze— "that I am not preferring charges. You are getting away with a federal offense. Do you understand me?"

"Yes sir, I do, but—"

"There are no 'buts' anymore. If you turn up in this hospital again, or if any trace of narcotics is found in your system in the future, I will not and cannot extend this favor. You are on borrowed time. Gonorrhea and narcotics are a deadly combination. You will be coming in for regular check-ups and a blood draw will be taken and analyzed. Is that clear?"

"Yes sir."

Dr. McFadden left without another word. He brushed past Hank as though he wasn't there.

Hank walked to Cam's bedside. "You hear him? 'Cos that's the way it is from now on. You just paid for him to zip his lip. That was your royalty for the last record."

"What?" Cam sat up, angry. "That's *my* money!"

"And you're *my* investment. You got off scot free. You could be on your way to a big trial and prison time, son. What would your mother say?"

Cam laughed. "That ole biddy's tuned out, man. You could tell her straight to her face an' it wouldn't sink in."

Hank's face darkened. "This ain't anything to laugh about. You are a big deal. You have hit records. You've been on TV. You are the idol of young people all over the place. You...you owe it to 'em to be worthy of that praise."

"I don't owe no one nothin', man. I do what I wanna do. Is that clear?"

"You owe me your success. I think that gives me some say in what you do. Was this what happened to you in New York?"

Cam's face blanked. "I think so. I think someone shot me up while I was drunk. It might of been Rusty."

"Our Rusty? I've known him for three years. He's not that kind of man. He might know people like that; there are a lot of 'em in show biz. But I don't feature him using dope."

"Just like you to stick up for a n..." Cam bit his tongue.

"I am gonna forget you said that. And I am gonna stop you there."

"But..."

"No buts. If you want to flush your life down the toilet, then you and I are done. You ain't the only fish in the sea. Every day, bunches of young fellows come to audition for me. You're good. Maybe even great. But you're only good to me alive and well."

"I been told what to do all my life. I'm fed up with it."

Hank's face reddened. "That makes two of us. You know the game Monopoly? You used up your 'get out of jail free' card. There ain't another. That's all there is to it. I'm gonna leave before I hit you. I've never struck another man before, but I'm mad enough to do it now."

Dr. McFadden's zipped lip kept this news out of the papers. For Cam and the Cats' fan club, which, by the fall of 1955 had 26,000 members, the story was that he'd caught the flu and had to stay in the hospital for a couple of days. Publicity photos were taken of the singer in bed, smiling as he received a chocolate cake in the shape of a cat's head.

Cam's interview for CBS, days before his hospitalization, caught the interest of some of Hive's larger rivals. Steve Sholes of RCA Victor Records and Archie Bleyer of Cadence took note. Both had stables of staid mainstream pop artists and wanted an in on this new younger sound. RCA was quick to have its younger artists try out the "cat music" bit. The results were louder, brassier big-band pop with a leaden beat. Trombones and clarinets do not make rock 'n' roll music; nor do snow-white background singers.

Guy Mitchell's take on "You're on the Wrong Train, Sweetheart" for Columbia Records was passable. Producer Mitch Miller loathed the sound of the original, and had to be excused from the session. Session guitarist George

Barnes got a decent stab at the sounds Skip made, and the doo-wah chorus was mixed down. It made for a #2 pop record, and the royalty checks that came from that made up for the McFadden bribe.

◊◊◊

Hank Howard carried on with more releases in the new vein. The Moody Twins scored with their humorous accounts of teenage life. This suited Cecil's skill at writing funny songs. With details supplied by Ron and Dwayne, who kept tabs on what kids wore, ate and worshipped, Cecil wrote appealing, melodic songs. "Cheap Skate Date" told the story of a boy eager to impress the new girl in school with only $1.38 in his pocket.

"Calculus and Chemistry" expressed the singers' misery in learning such subjects until the narrator acquires a comely study partner. "My grades were a flop but my love life took off!" he cries with joy. Cecil brought in Rufe Cortland, a saxophone player he'd met who echoed the twins' phrases with a breathy, knowing tone.

Cortland took off on his own with "Squawky," an instrumental improvised in the studio with Cliff Roscoe sitting in on a twangy, slightly out-of-tune guitar. This led to Hive's second LP, *That Squawky Cortland Sound!* which included the hit, its B-side and 10 on-the-fly tunes, with a more reverent treatment of Duke Ellington's "Mood Indigo." That became Cortland's follow-up hit after DJs took to it. The single proclaimed "From the Hive Album 'That Squawky Cortland Sound!'"

◊◊◊

"We should cut an album on Cam," Cecil told Hank. "Strike while the iron is hot. I have some ideas..." Hank looked over the papers his partner had drawn up. He'd sketched a concept for the cover and thought about the approach.

"Huh," Hank said as he looked at the papers. The design, in pencil on typing paper, had a stick figure of Cam holding a guitar. The title, *Cam and The Cats!* stood above that image. A starburst to the left said:

SIDE ONE: THE HITS THAT MADE HIM FAMOUS!

SIDE TWO: SIX NEW HITS-TOMORROW'S FAVORITES!

Cecil's idea for the back cover was a group shot of the trio, with short biographies of them and a brief recap of their successes on radio, records and television. No copy was written, but headlines and notes made the intention clear.

"Well, where's your name in all this, Cec?" Hank looked concerned. "'Thout you, none of this woulda happened!"

"Aw, nobody cares about that. They just want the kid. Nobody going to put my face on a record cover."

"I insist there be something about you, and about Chili. That makes it clear that we've made a bridge. That's what I've wanted since I started this company. To bridge over the world of black music and white music. And you did that. Not me. I didn't write the songs. I produced the sessions, but I couldn't of done that without you. This kid wouldn't be where he is right now without the work you did. Hell, I'll write the copy!"

Cecil felt embarrassed. He shrugged. "It's your company."

"It's *our* company! When you gonna get that through your head? Whatever happens to us, you are one-third of Hive Records. And if Chuck hadn't put money into it, it'd be 50/50."

"Chuck earns his keep."

"He does. More than does. We couldn't get the sound we got without him. I hear Victor and Columbia are tryin' to copy our sound. And they can't do it!" He slapped his open hand on his desk. "They can't figure it out!"

"I heard the Guy Mitchell record."

"I double-dog-dare them to get the sound Chuck gets!"

Cecil knew it was time to end the sermon. "So you're on board with this album idea?"

"Of course. Of course. Let's get it going."

Cecil, Cliff Roscoe and the Moody Twins worked up songs as potential LP candidates. Hank called Cam and asked he and his bandmates to come by for a meeting. Cam seemed close-mouthed, if not contrite, and didn't make waves.

Hank had copies of the Hive LPs, plus copies of The Lonesome Shadow's *The Real Blues!* "This is where the market is headed, fellas. People aren't satisfied with five minutes' worth of music. They want half an hour."

Cecil had studied the LP market via the music magazines. "It's a bigger profit for everybody. You, me—anyone who has a part of the record album. It costs three times more than a single, but gives the buyer 200% more music. People take better care of them, and they'll play for years if they store them right."

"Am I on the front of this thing?" Cam asked.

"Of course. We were thinking you at the microphone, with the other fellows in the picture..."

"How 'bout it's just me on the front, an' everyone on the back?" Cam waited for protests; none came.

"We'll have some information about all of you on the back. There's room for about 3000 words and the song titles."

"What if we had an autographed picture on the inside? That'd make it special." Cam looked hopeful about his idea.

Hank laughed. "If this thing sells like I think it will, you'd be spendin' all your time signing pictures."

Cecil had a thought. "What if autographed pictures were put in some copies? Just one out of 100. It might get people to buy more than one album."

Clue scoffed. "Ain't nobody doin' that."

"Well, nobody's tried it before. What can pictures cost?"

Hank chimed in. "It's a good idea. We could run off 5" by 7" black-and-whites. Maybe 500; leave some white space for Cam to sign 'em. That's a pretty good gimmick, Cec! I say we try it."

The photog who'd done The Shadow's album cover could come by and get some in-studio shots of the guys. This led to a discussion on what the new songs might be.

"There's a couple of songs we do that everybody goes for," Cam said. "I think people would like to have a record of 'em."

Clue spoke up. "They like that 'Help Me Somebody.'"

"And that Ray Charles one," Skip said. "The one that goes 'I could cry, I could die.'"

"'Lonely Avenue,' man! If we could get a sax on that..."

"We've got a sax guy." Hank tapped the Squawky Cortland LP.

"How 'bout we do a gospel song? I love singin' those."

"We'd like to keep this as in-house as possible," Hank said. "A couple of songs like that are fine, but I want most of this thing to be our copyrights. We've got Cecil and some other boys workin' up new stuff for y'all."

"That 'Deeds I've Done' is almost a gospel song," Skip noted.

"Yeah, but it's a *dirty* gospel song," Clue joked.

Cecil cleared his throat. "It is not a 'dirty' song."

"I'm just joshin'."

"A gospel song might calm down some of those hotheads…those record-burners. Might get 'em to listen instead of reject us outright," Hank said.

"Some o' them church songs are like 100 years old," Cam said. His eyes were bright with excitement. "How 'bout 'Leaning on the Everlasting Arms?' We could do that one fast. Give you a good solo thing. Hey, maybe we could get a choir in on the backgrounds!"

"That's an old enough song, I'll bet you it's PD." Cam looked sideways at Cecil. "Public domain. Means anyone can record it for free."

"Well, hell! That does it." Cam stood up. "So when do we get started on this thing?"

***They got started two days later.*** Hank scrambled to book the photographer, Cortland, Chili and The Tupelo Three to join the sessions and had the songwriters check in with their progress. All stalled, including Cecil, so Hank went with "Lonely Avenue" and "Leaning" as the first new numbers.

With Cortland's tenor sax slithering around Cam's lead vocal, and The Tupelo Three providing a vocal chorus where needed, "Lonely Avenue" was done in two takes. Hank let Cortland blow two verses on the version they put on the album. It went a little over four minutes, but on an LP that was fine.

"Leaning" required Cecil's piano front and center. He'd played in church long enough to know what the song needed. The Cats took the song at a jubilee pace, and Chili gave it a train-track rhythm working the brushes on his snare. One of the Tupelo Three could sing bass, and he and Cam worked out interjections he could do on the song's chorus.

"We need us a lady's voice on this," Cam demanded. "We're goin' places but we need that high kinda voice."

Miss Tinkle was about to leave; Hank caught her in the lobby. "You ever do any singing?"

"I sing in church. I was in the choir for awhile."

"We're doin' an old-time hymn in there. Could you possibly..."

She could. "Lord, you boys are doin' this too fast!" she cried when a take fell to pieces.

"Yes, ma'am. I want it to feel like a revival meetin'."

"That ain't the way we done it."

"Aw, honey, give it a try. Can you sing high?"

"They said I was a second soprano."

Cecil ran scales with her to see how high she could go. She got above the soprano's high C on the piano. Cecil gave her wordless half notes to sing on top of the chorus. For such a small woman, she sang big. "Ma'am, you gotta back off that mike a bit. We're distortin' like mad in here," Chuck said.

Miss Tinkle couldn't back up without elbowing Clue, Skip or Chili, so Chuck rigged up a second mike and stood her in the far corner of the studio. She had two sets of *aah-aah-aah-aah*s plus a long *aaaaaaah*, and her corner of the room had a nice natural echo. It took six takes to get everything right.

Chuck played back the best take. Cam squinted. "It needs...like a what-you-call...the round thing you bang on..."

"Tambourine!" Clue said.

"Yeah yeah! Mr. Howard, you got one o' those handy?"

He did not, so a Coke bottle filled with screws, washers and pennies had to do. Chuck recorded an overdub with The Tupelo Three clapping their hands and Cam smacking the Coke bottle close to the mike. With reverb applied, it did sound like a tent meeting where everyone was getting salvation.

"Wow," Hank said when the results played back. "This is craziest thing we've ever done."

"You can cut a rug to it," one of The Tupelo Three said, his farmboy face broad with a smile.

"Leaning," with a songwriter credit to Cam Cottner, was the closing track on *Cam and The Cats!* The second side kicked off with "Lonely Avenue." In-between was a solid love ballad from Cliff Roscoe, "My Wildest Dream," two up-tempo boppers from the Moodys and Cecil's sequel to "Famous Igno-ramus," "I Ain't No Flash in the Pan." It expanded on the bragging rights of the first song as it pointed out the whirlwind success of Cam Cottner and his group. "You can burn my records all you please, but I'm still gonna bring the world to its knees...yeah, man! Say what you want, but I ain't no flash in the pan!"

Cortland and Skip worked out a duet solo, and Cecil hammered on the high keys and did glissandos with his index fingers.

"Man, that's gotta be the next single," Hank declared during playback. "What a plug for the album!"

Jerome Keating showed up for both sessions and got four rolls of action shots. The best one, everyone agreed, had Cam in the foreground, his brow sweaty, his face backlit from Keating's reflectors, singing his heart out, his left hand tilting the microphone down. In the background, Skip smiled—a rare sight—and The Tupelo Three crowded their own mike. A portion of Chili Burse's drumkit, and his left arm, made it into the scene.

For the back cover, Keating got a more formal shot of Cam, Clue and Skip. Cam changed his shirt for the picture; the one he'd worn to the session was soaked with sweat. Cam sat on a stool; Skip and Clue stood behind him, one hand each parked on Cam's shoulders. They smiled with a welcoming ease: they'd made it and they were happy to be there.

Hank penned the liner notes, after getting a little life story from Skip and Clue. He made sure his partner got due credit:

*What you hold in your hands is the result of months of hard work. The boys have played to big crowds all over the country, shown up on your TV sets and sold more records than any other act this year—or ten years from now.*

*Behind the scenes, talented musicians, songwriters and arrangers have helped this young man and his band achieve the live-wire music loved by 'cats' everywhere... but by 'squares' too! Cecil Madison, the composer of "Famous Ignoramus," "A Slob with a Job" and "Deeds I've Done," and who contributes a marvelous new number in "Ain't no Flash in the Pan," is in some ways the heart and soul of Hive Records. Cecil has arranged and produced most of the songs on this album. If you've enjoyed what you've heard, please give him a hand.*

The album hit the stores in August and sold, sold, sold. Monarch asked for replacement stampers three times before Christmas. The autographed picture gimmick worked well, though it was an added expense; an extra person inserted the pictures at the factory after the record had been sleeved and placed in its carboard jacket. A news report told of a teenage girl in Iowa who'd bought 20 copies of the album and gotten four autographed pics for her trouble. She papered her bedroom with the album covers, and a photo of her with the decorations made it into *Life* magazine.

Checks came in; big checks. Hank paid off all his debts, business and personal, and bought two 1956-model cars—one for Liz, so they wouldn't have to share one vehicle.

Cam and His Cats embarked on a tour of live appearances to promote their album. Hive had succeeded in getting the first LP of this still-new youth music, which the music press called rock 'n' roll. Why argue with them? With every square pop singer adding those words to a song ("Rock 'n' Roll Wedding," "Rock 'n' Roll Polka," "Rock 'n' Roll Inc.") the trend was hard-wired into American music.

Interviewed by Dick Clark about the album, Cam said: "Well, sir, we figured that if alla them jazz folks an' classical folks can have their albums, why not us young folks? We're sellin' more records than whatizname...Bach...an' we're proud of it."

"What's with the hymn, Cam? That seems different."

"Well, Mr. Clark, that's why we did it. To show that we love all kinds of music. You know, some of them old hymns are great songs. It don't matter what you believe in, you can still 'preciate the beauty of 'em."

"There's a girl's voice on that number. Is that your girlfriend?" Cam laughed out loud and his reaction made some girls scream.

"Naw, sir. That there's the sec'atary at Hive Records. She was there, an' I asked her did she sing. She sure could!"

"Well, I won't ask you to do that number here, but how's about treating us to something off this new album of yours?"

"Be glad to." The Cats did a scorching version of "I Ain't No Flash in the Pan," which was issued as a single to hawk the LP. It rushed up the charts to top pop, county and rhythm and blues in the same week.

After shows, Cam, in his own hotel room, invited interested fans to spend the lonely hours with him. It didn't matter to Cam whether things got intimate or not. Having someone there was what mattered. Solitude frightened him; he'd never admit that but he couldn't sleep without the breath of another person beside him, or a warm limb draped across him.

◊◊◊

"Could I have a word with you, Hank?" Cam looked contrite and calm.

"Always, buddy. What's up?"

"I was thinkin'... I got all this money rollin' in, an' I don't want to throw it away. I wanna do somethin' nice for my momma."

"What—get her flowers er somethin'?"

"Naw, sir. I intend to buy her a house. She's always wanted to have a place all her own, an' now that I have the money to do it...well, I'd be a jerk not to."

"That's mighty nice of you, Cam. That's damn thoughtful. How can I help?"

"Well, two things. One, maybe you could vouch for me. I mean, I got the money an' all, but I ain't an adult an' they might think I was funnin' 'em 'f I just went in and tried to do this. An' two: I don't know crap about buyin' a house. I know you bought one, an' maybe you could help me to find a nice place for her. She deserves it."

"You know, the folks we bought our place from still have some openings in our neighborhood. You've seen our place. It's quiet; gets good light and there's lotsa trees. Lotta nice folks; lotta kids."

"Yes, sir. That would be her idea of heaven. Bakin' cookies an' havin' the neighbor kids over. Bein' part of a neighborhood. She's been cooped up in our place for a long time. I'd really like to get this goin' soon. You know, in case I ain't popular no more."

Hank chuckled. "There ain't no worry in that department. Sure, I'll be glad to. When do we get this goin'?"

"When do you have time for it?"

Two days later, Hank drove Cam to the office of his realtor. Yes, there were lots available; most had new homes sitting vacant, taking up space. The man didn't flinch at the idea of paying for the place, in full, with cash. "Most folks like to take out a mortgage; pay it off a little each month."

"I'd rather put cash on the barrelhead. It's for my momma."

"Well, that's sure nice of you. Would you like to go see a couple of places?"

Clark Melson drove Cam and Hank across town to Silverbell Glen. Well-paved streets connected a neighborhood of 48 homes. Eighteen of them were sold, with four houses sitting empty. The rest were vacant lots that had been shaved of trees and underbrush.

The one Cam liked was on the far end of the layout. The house had two floors and a porch that ran the length of the front. It had a handsome green and white canvas awning. Cam could picture his momma sitting on that porch, visiting with her hens, being part of the block and enjoying her life.

It would be a life without Jackson. The endgame of this move was not to give Edda Cottner the good life, but to erase Jackson from the picture. Cam was wealthy now. He had clout enough to give the old man his walking papers. He would offer to pay rent on the apartment in town if Jackson wanted. He was welcome to it.

Cam intended to live in the new house—make the top floor his own, so Edda wouldn't have to go up and down the stairs all the time. Melson unlocked the front door and Cam admired the layout inside. It had a big, spacious kitchen with tons of room for Edda's kitchen clutter. There was an honest to God dining room—something they'd never had, a laundry room ready for a washer and dryer to be installed, an open living room area and a cozy bedroom for momma to sleep in peace.

Cam looked at two other places. They were nice, but the first one made the best impression. "How much would you take, cash, for it?"

"Well. This is a new one on me. What you're askin' would scare the pants off most people."

"I ain't most people."

Melson nodded. "Seven five. As it is now. You could move in tomorrow."

"Huh. Hey, let's see the back yard." They walked through high grass to a downward-sloping yard that was backed by pleasant-looking woods. Cam could hear the gurgle of a creek nearby. A big pine tree and a maple shaded the yard. He could see himself relaxing back there in a rope hammock, calling for momma to bring him some iced tea. "This is the place. When can I pay you?"

"We'll have to draw up the papers. Might take a couple of days."

"Clark, since he's paying in full, couldn't you cut him a deal? Maybe take 'er down to seven?" Hank winked at Cam.

"Well..." Melson inspected his shoes and kicked at the grass. "I can do seven. It's a good value for the money. And I believe it'll make your mother the happiest woman in Tupelo!"

"Shake on it?" Cam held out his hand.

Melson took it. "Done. Come in on Monday morning. Say, 11?"

"I'll be there."

"Congratulations, Mister Cottner. You got yourself a new house."

◊◊◊

Cam hadn't set foot at the Renaldo Apartments for a few weeks, except to get clothes and records. This morning he showed up with a smile and good news. He waited until 10, by which time Jackson was wrapping parcels downtown.

The screen door was unlocked, and Cam walked in shouting. "Momma. Momma! Drop what you're doin' an' sit down."

"I have cookies in the oven."

"Can they wait five minutes, Momma?"

Edda looked over her shoulder at the kitchen. "I...I guess so. What's the matter?"

"Ain't nothin' the matter. Unless you mean movin' into your own house, all paid for. If that's the matter, then yeah!"

Edda couldn't parse what her son said to her. Cam realized he'd garbled the message. She smiled and shrugged.

"Momma. I bought you a house. With a nice porch on a nice street with a lotta little kids. Nice neighbors. An' I'm gonna live there too."

"A...a house? For me?" Edda couldn't decide whether to smile or pout. "For me? Oh, Carmen. I can't believe it! Are you joking?"

"No ma'am. I been wantin' to do somethin' nice for you for so long. An' I have the money to do it. Bought the place in full. It's all yours. The deed's in your name. You can move in tomorrow."

"Oh, honey. I can't move tomorrow. I've got the warsh to do."

Cam laughed. "You're gonna have a warshing machine, Momma! An' a drier! No more hangin' wet warsh out on the line. You ain't never got another worry again!"

Edda smiled through her tears. "Oh Lord! I can't believe it. I just can't…"

Cam handed her the legal document; the deed to the house, paid for to the last penny. "Put this in a safe place. I got a copy of it too."

"Where is it?" She pointed to the deed. "Where will I live?"

"It's out a ways. Neighborhood called Silverbell Glen. We can drive out there right now."

"But my cookies…"

"Momma, turn the oven off. You can always make more damn cookies."

"Shouldn't we call your father?"

"Jackson ain't my father, Momma. You know that an' I know that."

"Oh…" Cam couldn't tell if Edda felt shame about this fact, or if she'd forgotten and needed a reminder.

"Get your hat an' come on."

Edda turned off the gas oven. The cookies were about done, anyway. She got her purse, her gloves and her sun hat. She looked back to be sure the oven was off. She opened the oven door to let out the heat and looked at the mess in the sink.

"Momma, get a move on!" Cam called from the front door.

◊◊◊

Edda Cottner was used to this feeling of flushed overwhelm; it was her standard mode in life. The sounds, lights, colors and shapes of the world outside her apartment baffled her. A trip to the grocery store left her dazed.

*It's such a pretty day,* she thought. She looked up at the deep blue sky and the vast scape of billowing clouds. The breeze felt pleasant on her face. She hadn't traveled farther than three blocks from her home in several years. The world beyond her street—beyond the Shop-Rite and the B & W Produce Market—had been forgotten.

"It's such a *big* world, isn't it?" she said in wonder.

"Sure is, Momma. Gettin' bigger every damn day."

The green of the world was vivid to Edda's eyes. "Don't drive so fast, dear. Jackson wouldn't like it—"

"I could care less 'bout what he likes or don't like. I'm gettin' us a nice new car soon's I can." Cam despised Jackson's 1949 Desoto Club Coupe. Its body was rusty in spots, and the damn thing was battered and bruised. Jackson could walk to his job at Gannser's. He only used it to buy beer or on one of his rare nights out to play cards. It rattled and creaked and the shocks were shot. .

"This is it." A handsome sign proclaimed *Welcome to Silverbell Glen—Your Neighborhood.* They drove down three blocks of neat new and new-ish homes, lawns well-kept, everything colorful and welcoming.

The Cottner home was in the back end of Silverbell Glen, at the ell where Holly Lane and Sweetgum Place connected. The home's address was 2 Sweetgum Place. Edda noticed the FOR SALE sign that had a new SOLD sticker placed on it. "Here it is, Momma."

Cam held the car door open for Edda and helped her disembark. "Oh my word! Carmen! I can't believe it..."

Cam kicked at the sign. "I believe we can pull this up now." He yanked up the sign and chucked it in the driveway. "How 'bout that porch?"

They walked up the short flight of stairs. "Oh my goodness!" Edda walked the length of the porch. "There's...there's so much of it!"

"There's a lot o' everything in here. Wanna go inside?"

"Oh. Can we?"

Cam laughed. "We got the keys." Cam unlocked the front door and pushed it open. "After you, ma'am."

Edda oohed and aahed at the kitchen space, the sweep of the living room, the glistening bathroom fixtures and the comfy shade-dappled back yard. "Oh, Carmen. I never in my life thought we'd...that I'd...that this would happen!"

"We could put in a dish warsher if you want. Save you a lotta time. You deserve to take it easy, Momma."

"And you got this from the man with the records?"

"I got this with the money I made from the records. Mr. Howard...he's the guy we should thank. He helped me to get where I am today."

"We'll have to have him over for supper some night."

"They live not three blocks away. They'll be over here all the time."

Edda eyed the slender staircase to the second floor. "Oh, Lord, I don't want to be climbin' those all day long."

"That's gonna be where I stay, Momma. You're gonna be on the ground floor where it's easy."

Edda hugged her son. All those bad things Jackson had said about him; they weren't true. He was tempermental and stubborn, but if he had it in his heart to do this for his own mother…

"Momma, you're about to bust a rib! Why don't we go to Hitcherson's Appliances an' pick you out a stove and warsher an' all that?"

"Today?"

"Sure. Sooner we get that stuff put in, sooner you an' me can start livin' here."

"What is Jackson going to do?"

"I can think of one thing real easy. We'll talk to him tonight."

◊◊◊

Cam had already consulted with the manager at Hitcherson's and picked out a stove, laundry machines and a new General Electric Mobile Maid dishwasher. They had them all on hold; he wanted to give Edda the idea she was picking them out.

Edda had no objections to whatever Cam showed her. "They're all so new and pretty!" Cam laid down cash for the appliances and paid an extra $25.00 to have them installed. The water and power would be turned on in the morning. Cam expected to have his mother ensconced there by the end of the coming week.

◊◊◊

"Where in hell you been?" Jackson was used to having his supper waiting when he walked home from Gannser's. "What, you take the day off?"

Cam followed Edda inside. He had a box of fried chicken and a plastic tub of sweet cole slaw. "Oh. Figured you'd show up again. Well, we been doin' just fine without you. It can stay that way."

223

"Sit down an' eat, old man." Cam got Edda to sit. "I'll get us plates."

"What in hell is this?"

"Things are gonna be different, old man. Sit down an' listen." He got plates and silverware from the kitchen. A pitcher of sweet tea from the fridge sweated on the lazy susan.

Jackson grabbed a chicken breast. He looked wary. He took a bite, as if to test it for poison. There was none; he dug in.

"Here's the way things are goin' to be. I bought a house for me an' momma. We're movin' there soon as we can."

"What? Where is it?"

"Out on the south end of town. In a place called Silverbell Glen." Cam spooned out some slaw for Edda, then for himself. "There's room enough for two there. You get the idea?"

"What the hell you sayin'?"

"I'm sayin' that we're done with you. You ain't my daddy. I knew that all the time. Hell, y'all ain't even married. Are you?"

"That ain't none o' your business."

"The hell it ain't. I don't owe you one damn thing. Neither does she. Do you?" he said to Edda.

"I...I don't know..."

"I do! You're welcome to stay here. Hell, I'll pay your damn rent every month. But you keep away from us. We'll be out o' here soon as we can, an' you can sit here an' drink yourself stupid for all I care?"

"Don't I got any say in this? I'm the head o' this household."

"That's a laugh. Momma, I'm havin' some people come over an' help you move. Pack things up an' truck 'em over to the house. I'll get 'em goin' tomorrow or the day after."

"What? You can't do this to me? What can I do about it?" Jackson's shock showed in his squinty eyes.

"For starters, you c'n drop dead. More slaw, Momma?"

***Now that he owned a house,*** Cam needed a car to go with it. Made no sense to be taking the bus or using Jackson's bucket of bolts, like he used to. Those days were gone.

Cam bought a Thunderbird, cash on the barrelhead. The salesman knew who he was and asked for an autograph. Cam had one of the promotional photos on hand, and personally inscribed it to his niece. "She'll go ape over this!" Cam talked the price down by $300.00. He spent what he'd saved at Gluck's Auto Detailing to get it painted pink with black accents. Interlocking Cs in black, with white trim, went on the doors and on the spare tire cover. The car became well-known to the highway patrol, sheriff and police prowl cars around the countryside and nearby towns.

It seemed designed to get attention, and Cam's lead foot on the gas pedal did him no favors. By October, he'd been in traffic court two times. Once was for zooming across railroad tracks just seconds before a fast freight roared past. A Highway Patrol car spotted this stunt and radioed ahead for the next available officers to stop the pink car.

"Some stunt you pulled there, pal."

"Did I hurt anybody?"

"No..." The officer paused in his ticket-writing.

"Did I hurt myself?"

"Not so's I can see."

"Then what's the big deal, man?" Cam smiled.

"$25.00 worth," the officer said. He tore the citation off his yellow pad. "See you in court."

◊◊◊

Cam Cottner rose early; the desk clerk rang him at 8. He showered, had break-fast in the cafe downstairs and returned to his room to make a series of phone calls. Lee County Utilities said they could start an account for him. Could he come by their offices now?

He brought his copy of the deed. The clerk pretended not to recognize him. "Is this your house, sir?"

"Yes'm. Just bought it for my momma."

"Well, ain't that a nice thing!"

Cam put down a 20 dollar deposit and was assured the gas, power, water and sewer services would be on by noon. "Where do I go t'get a phone?"

"Bell Telephone, over on South Spring an' Magazine."

The woman at the information desk did know Cam. "I have all y'all's records!" She used her clout to move Cam past the most tedious parts of get-ting an account registered. In 15 minutes, Cam had an appointment for 2:30 the next day. A man would bring a heavy black Bell telephone for the down-stairs and a seperate number (unlisted) for Cam's upstairs realm.

"Well, ma'am. You got my number now." He winked at her. She was cute. He smiled in the sunlight, outside, thinking of when she'd call and what would happen as a result.

◊◊◊

Life in the new house suited Cam fine. It was heaven for Edda. They had yet to move all her kitchen contraptions, which she still wanted despite her son's purchase of "every damn thing a lady could want" for cooking and food service. The saleswoman laughed at Cam's frankness, but put together close to $100 of dishes, bakeware, pots, pans and spatulas.

The delivery of this new materiel floored Edda. "What you think, Momma?"

Edda examined a cast-iron skillet. "It needs to be seasoned. That will take awhile. Oh, hon, can't we get my things from the apartment? That's all ready. That's what I'm used to." She saw the exasperation in her son's eyes. "These...these are lovely, but I hate to ruin them. I'd rather save them. They're

226

so pretty..."

She expected Carmen to be angry but he laughed. "Whatever you want, Momma. But let's hang onto these. You might bust a pan er somethin'."

He left Edda as she considered her new mixing bowls and whisks.

◊◊◊

Edda enjoyed the comings and goings of Cam's friends; always some new face to make a sandwich for, or to serve iced tea and cookies. Some of the people seemed to stay for days, and the upstairs was a din of music and muffled laughter through the night. A peculiar odor, as if a skunk had gotten inside, came through the walls. It didn't keep Edda up, but it concerned her.

Many of these visitors were high school girls, and Cam was careful to get them back home before their curfews. Much of this time was innocent enough; listening to records, cuddling, making small talk. The young man wasn't chaste. He had times where more innocent stuff suited him fine. But a couple of times a month, the desires of the flesh overcame him and made him a different person.

These changes coincided with the start and end of Cam's clean stretches. He reported for his monthly blood tests at Dr. McFadden's office. The doctor never appeared in person, but his presence was felt: the nurses treated him like a bum off the street, as though they couldn't get him out the door quick enough.

Cam stayed off the hard stuff. He felt himself starting to really like it, and that scared him. And though he felt that alcohol did him no favors, he partook daily. Booze in his system was never cause for alarm, but he made sure to lay off reefer and snow for two weeks before each blood test. He wished Dr. McFadden would drop dead.

◊◊◊

"Ain't No Flash in the Pan" got solid airplay, but its presence on the album confused sales. It was time to come up with a new single. Cam had heard a rhythm and blues single in a minor key that he liked. He played the record for Cecil Madison. "Reckon you could come up with somethin' like this?"

"I can write anything I set my mind to doing." Cam worked with him and "Been Gone So Long" resulted. It was a heart-wrenching story of a love-struck young man who kept trying to get back to his hometown and the girl who'd promised to be true. He's accused of murder and wrongfully sent to jail. By the time he gets out, and gets back home, he stands before that girl's tombstone. Its inscription reads: I WAITED FOR YOU.

Chuck recorded a demo of the tune, with Cam singing to Cecil's piano. They played the results, sweetened with Chuck's trademark reverb, to Hank. "Holy cow," he said several times as he listened. "That's damn different." Then he cocked his head and smiled. "You know what I hear? I hear strings." He mimicked playing the violin.

"That's for squares, man. That's Doris Day stuff." Cam sprung out of his seat. "I feature it startin' out with the bass. You know, that walkin' rhythm."

Cecil played a quarter-note figure that went down the E minor scale. "Yeah, man! Just that an' me singin'. Maybe some fingers snappin'."

"Then in the chorus, we open it up some," Cecil said. "Get Skip to come in. We could use Chili."

"Well, hell, let's get Cortland in on this too. I think I'm gettin' it now. Man, this would almost be a jazz record."

It almost was. Cortland downplayed his squawky side and summoned the buttery tones of a Lester Young. Cam wanted female voices singing behind him, and Miss Bell got four girls from her church to oooh and wahhh in harmony. The Hive studio was full of talent; Hank had to observe from Chuck's nook in the back. There, he had a brainstorm. He made his way through the crowd. "I got it! I've got it!"

Cam looked up at him, surprised. "Got what?"

"Suppose, now, that we go back to just you and the bass line at the end. At the moment the guy sees the gravestone. Your voice, maybe a brush on the snare drum and that bass. An' we fade out on that."

"But we've got an arrangement down. We've rehearsed it," Cecil complained. "That's a really different way for this record to go."

"How's about this? Let's do it like it's been arranged. Get that in the can, and then just for the hell of it, let's try the ending real quiet. We don't even have to do a whole take—just the last verse to the end. Okay?"

Murmurs of assent rose, and Hank went back to the booth. Chuck announced the new take, and it went without a hitch. Everyone knew their role and how to portray it. The song was a simple blues in E minor. Cecil dropped jazzy chords to give a familiar progression some flavor. He knew Cortland would key off that to good effect. The guy was a good jazz player when you took his gimmicks away.

Cecil and Skip hit and held the final E minor chord, which resonated and decayed in the room alongside the quartet's vocal. Cecil directed the girls to bring it down to zero. Hank looked at Chuck. "I think they got it."

"Should we do one more, just in case?"

"Naw. Unless they want to. You know, maybe that ending I thought up wouldn't work after all." Hank left the studio. "That was on the money! It sounds like a hit to me! Everybody happy with that take?"

"Wish I had more time to blow," Cortland said. "Eight bars, man. That's a short vacation!" The other musicians laughed.

"Well, hell. What if we did that for the flip-side? Cecil, what if we took the blues thing, like we have it here, and let Skip an' Cort go to town. Keep the girls in on it. Maybe you'd like to have a turn, Cec!"

"I'm good. But what would we call it?"

"Graveyard Blues," Clue said.

Hank snapped his fingers. "That's good! 'Graveyard Blues.' Man, Halloween's comin' up fast. If we get this to the jocks in time, they'll go for it. All right, fellows. Sort it out. I'm goin' an' get us a case of Co-colas."

"I'll come with you," Cam said. He realized how sweaty he was once they were outside the building. "Well, we got us somethin' different this time, ain't we?"

"We sure do. I used to worry that a record was too way-out. That doesn't seem to matter no more."

Hank and Cam hoisted a wooden case of cold sodas from Jolly's cooler. By the time they made it back to the studio, "Graveyard Blues" was underway. They uncapped two Cokes and waited outside the studio. Cortland blew blue and cool; through the window Hank could see Cecil conducting the quartet on when to come in. He used a pencil as his baton. He smiled and nodded as he guided their vocals.

Skip's solo overlapped the end of Cortland's. It sounded like one instrument evolved into another. He ended mid-phrase after Cecil waved both hands in the air. "We can go in now," Hank said.

"Refreshments, folks!" Cam called.

"How come y'all to stop?" Hank asked.

"We went over the line. I think we got close to four minutes." Cecil shook his head. "It was goin' so well."

"Well, let's hear it! Let's throw on both sides, Chuck!"

Cokes were consumed as "Been Gone So Long" played over the studio speakers. It wasn't cat music; it sounded big and brooding. The girls' voices were a good substitute for strings. Their voices had a haunted sound that violins couldn't summon. The song went a touch over three minutes, which was fine; it merited the length.

"Graveyard Blues" continued the mood of the A-side, and it was over-long for a side of a single record. "Why don't we just fade 'er out?" Cecil asked. "What's the longest we can go without pushing it?"

"Three and a half."

"We could do a real slow fade. Start it going down around 3:10; pull the volume down slow and steady to nothing."

"Can you do that, Chuck?"

"I can try." It took him four attempts, but he got the fade-out Cecil envisioned. It short-changed Skip's solo, but it was a dramatic way to end the recording.

"Hell, man, that's haunting," Hank said. "They ain't gonna know what to make of this one."

The public took to "Been Gone Too Long." *Cash Box* praised it, in their peerless lingo, as "a downbeat dramatic stand with loads of atmosphere. A different kind of record from Cam and His Cats, with femme thrush support and a real late-night feel. Adventurous jocks will like."

Cam's lack of presence on "Graveyard Blues," which was credited to "Squawky and The Cats" and labeled *INSTRUMENTAL*, caused some fans to grouse. It inspired a wave of B-side instrumentals; other producers realized this was a way to focus the attention on one vocal side and avoid two tracks undercutting each other on the charts. Both sides got plenty of radio action for Halloween.

*In Corinth, Mississippi, in the early hours* of August 29, 1955, a real-life horror story began. Cam got a 15 year-old girl pregnant—and gave her the clap. He'd met her at a hot dog stand on the highway. It was one of the only places open on a Sunday evening, and local teens hung out in the parking lot. Cam's Thunderbird got much attention as it pulled into the gravel lot.

Flora Boggs recognized him; she had all his records, including his album, which she had propped up on her night-stand. Her daddy, who was such a square, didn't like that; he'd railed against this new music and been among the chorus who wanted to burn records.

Flora was about to enter the 10th grade, and her father's square stance embarrassed her. He was so different since her mother passed on. He seemed to be in a permanent fog. Sometimes the fog would lift, and he'd show his old warmth. But the clouds would swallow him back up.

She had been at a church social when some friends invited her to get a hot dog and a root beer. Flora wanted to be popular, and she figured this would give the new school year a promising start.

She caught Cam's eye right away. Her honey-colored hair and those big blue eyes made him keep looking back at her. He knew she was younger than him. But it was 10:00 on a Sunday night, and she was out with a group of teenagers. She didn't seem to be any guy's girl. She looked like someone at a party who doesn't have a date.

They met at the mustard dispenser. He did the honors for her hot dog before he doused his own. They stood and talked; he invited her to sit in his car. It made quite a scene as they walked outside into the pink T-Bird.

Cam came on shy and polite, and told her about touring, singing on TV and making records. He had her from the first minute of conversation. It didn't take much for him to seduce her. She was hungry for such experiences,

231

and to have her first one with this enchanting, handsome boy with the twinkle in his eyes—it felt like she was in one of his songs!

"I know a nice quiet place where we can go," he said. "Might be a moon out tonight."

"I love nature. But I have to be home soon."

"It won't take long. What grade you in?"

"Tenth." Cam's heart sank for a moment, but Flora looked at him with those baby blues, and that adoring gaze, and he set aside his reservations.

No one else was parked at Corinth, and the trees were too full and thick to see much of the moon. Flora felt all alone with Cam; far away from anyone or anything and happy for the experience.

She responded to his kisses with a passion that surprised him. "Wow," he gasped. "You're good at this, honey!"

Bases were passed and Cam felt he was on third, with home plate in his sight. But shit, man, she was just a kid. He could get in hot water...

"We better stop 'fore we really get goin', honey," Cam whispered.

"No," she protested.

"I want you to know what you're gettin' into." Cam took off his shirt. Flora felt his bare chest. "Your turn, honey." He unbuttoned her blouse and removed it along with her thin sweater. Flora's young breasts bobbed in the darkness. "Aw, baby, you're beautiful," Cam sighed.

They made love in the back seat of his car with the radio on. As Cam climaxed, he heard himself singing "Deeds I've Done." He failed to note the poetic irony of the moment; he was consumed with the pleasures of the flesh.

The highway patrol always kept tabs on the pink T-bird. It was a way to make a dull night shift more exciting. You never knew where that damn car would show up. It was seen entering Corinth Park, and it had spent 45 minutes in a thicket of trees and brush.

A patrol car passed the T-Bird as it pulled out on the state road. The patrolman drove slow; the road had the double stripe and Cam couldn't pass it in return.

Cam took the first available exit and lost the patrol car. But another was waiting behind a billboard, and crept out behind the T-Bird. Cam was tracked to the residence of Corinth's mayor, Calvin Boggs.

As Cam and the girl shared a last kiss, Cam's radio blasted Dixie Doodle's all-night show; as she opened the front door of the house, Cam revved the engine to startle his one-time lover. She shrieked. Mayor Calvin Boggs looked out the window and saw the pink car, with its impressive CC logo.

He bounded downstairs before his daughter eased the front door shut. "It's 1 AM! You know you're s'pose to be in by 10:30! You better explain yourself, missy..."

"Daddy, you're always getting so upset. I'm sorry I'm late..."

"Three hours late!"

"I was out with a very nice young man. He had a flat tire out on the State Road. He didn't have the right tools, or something...I don't know about cars."

"Uh huh."

"A highway patrol car came by and helped him. They had the...that cross-shaped thing. Some kind of a wrench."

"What was the officer's name?"

"Nelson," she said—a made-up name. Since she was lying, she had to keep it up.

"Well, in the morning, maybe I'll call the Highway Patrol, see if they got a man name of Nelson. But right now, you march upstairs an' get in your bed. An' I don't want to have to guff from you when I get you up for school in the morning!"

"Yes, sir," she said, her voice iced with resentment.

Mayor Boggs forgot about the hypothetical Officer Nelson; he had a country budget meeting the next morning—a tedious affair that left him tired and cross by the evening. Flora Boggs went to school without protest. She wanted to tell the other girls about what had happened to her, but she knew word would get around and Corinth was a small town.

As autumn settled in on Mississippi, Flora wondered if she'd ever see Cam again. The Mayor kept her under watch but she found ways to leave the house after supper. The library stayed open until 9 on weeknights and it gave her an excuse to walk the five blocks to the main drag. She hoped that pink car would catch her eye, but it never showed.

Flora's grades improved, but her health began to falter. She began to feel flushed and nauseated—never to the point that she had to throw up, but she came close on a daily basis. She felt logy and exhausted by the last hour of school. She begged out of after-school activities. She needed to lie down for at least an hour before the mayor got home. Then she helped Jeanette the maid with dinner, or, on her nights off, did all the cooking.

"What's the matter with you, Flora?" Mayor Boggs ate his pork chops and dirty rice with a boar hog's zeal; Flora picked at her plate.

"I don't know, Daddy. I'm just not very hungry."

"Girl your age should eat. You're starting to grow up."

Mayor Boggs missed his wife Virginia. They'd been together 17 years and he felt he'd barely scratched the surface of a remarkable woman. She was the one who got him to campaign for office. He'd been happy as head clerk of the Land Records Library, where his days were pleasant, orderly and predictable.

Virginia was involved in all these civic groups for the betterment of the city. She had strong ideas about how Corinth (and Mississippi) needed to change. "It's been the 20th century for 50 years now and our state isn't living there."

The mayor agreed with her to an extent. He was all for better roads, buildings, police and fire departments, schools...his county, city and state were behind the curve. Virginia went too far, he felt, with her goings-on about the coloreds. There were some good ones, he agreed, some smart and ambitious ones who deserved to get ahead. He was all for helping them, but he couldn't fathom her championing of the ignorant, lazy and poor ones. They'd never amount to anything because they didn't want to succeed. They were happy with their lot. Some whites were like that too. You couldn't drum common sense and ambition into them. Any intelligent man could see that.

He abided her wishes to improve things for the lower-class people. He sometimes wondered what Virginia saw in him. She was college educated. She read books and magazines and all the things the mayor didn't have time or interest to pursue. How she ran a household, went to all those meetings and got so much read baffled him. He felt lucky if he got through the comics and the headlines of the daily paper.

Virginia got him his office. She built his platform, gave him the right mixture of progressive and conservative issues and came up with a clever campaign slogan: YOU WON'T GET BOGGED DOWN WITH BOGGS!

She'd been gone two years and he still talked with her. Not out loud; they'd put him in the nut house. He reviewed decisions with her in his head. *Would this levy be the best choice for the school board, dear?*

She always answered him. Her advice was unerring. The level-headedness she gave him won him a re-election. He could never convey this to his colleagues; nor could he explain it to himself. Calvin Boggs was admired for his sensible, clear thinking. He took credit for it, but gave nightly thanks to his Virginia, who seemed to live on beyond the grave.

*Are you in Heaven?* he asked her one night.

*There is no description for where I am now, dear. Know that I am safe and comfortable. I am being looked after, as you'll be when you join me. It's only a matter of time. You will like it here.*

Mayor Boggs never asked again. He intuited that such things were beyond the realm of reason, as he knew it. If it wasn't for Flora, he might have hurried to join Virginia. Instead, his daughter reminded him of how precious life was and could be. *I'm not ready yet,* he told Virginia. She had no reply.

◊◊◊

Flora Boggs' appetite faltered and flared up. She seemed to be gaining weight. Some mornings, across from her father at the kitchen table, she seemed so fragile and pale. "I do wish you'd see the doctor," the mayor said.

"I will, Daddy." She made an appointment to see their family physician the day after Thanksgiving—the first open slot they had on their schedule. Cold and flu season hit harder than usual; the waiting room was a litany of miserable sniffling kids.

She helped Jeanette with the preparation of Thanksgiving dinner. "Law, chile, you lookin' peekid," the maid noted. "Ain't no need for such a rush, hon."

"I'm seeing Dr. Drapner Friday. Don't worry about me. 'Sides, Daddy loves Thanksgiving." She made cranberry sauce and stuffing on her own—following her mother's recipes, which she'd written on index cards in blue ink.

Thursday morning Flora felt like hell warmed over, but she got herself out of bed and dressed, and fussed with Jeanette over getting the turkey in the oven. The mayor asked Judge Warvey and his wife to have dinner with them. They had a nephew in town who was invited to come along. This meant that the extra leaf had to be put in the dining-room table.

While struggling with the long clumsy slat of wood, Flora felt the floor crumple under her feet. She fainted and the leaf hit the floor beside her with a resounding whack. The mayor and Jeanette rushed into the dining room. They couldn't revive her. "Lawd, she's blue," Jeanette gasped.

"Call for an ambulance," the mayor hissed. "Flora...wake up, dear. Wake up!"

Flora came to in a hospital room 11 hours later. The mayor and Jeanette had a plate of Thanksgiving goodness for her. She smiled at it, but fell asleep before she could sit up to taste it.

The medics gave Flora a thorough exam the next morning, after she rested and was rehydrated. Within an hour, they determined the cause of her wan health. She was pregnant. She was approaching her second trimester.

Dr. Dravner struggled with how to break the news to her father. Mayor Boggs tended to react to things with hot blood. "Like for you to come by; I have some news about Flora."

"Is she going to get better?"

"Yes, but she's still got a ways to go. Please; come in so we can talk in person."

The news did not go over well with the Mayor. Dr. Dravner bore the man's raving and waited for him to cool a bit. He went over the calendar and determined that she was impregnated on or around the evening of August 28th. The night before her first day of school. The night she'd come in at 3 AM.

The clues he recalled added up: that pink car with the CC; the horrid jungle music he'd heard; the young, impudent boy behind the wheel.

He made some casual inquiries with cronies at the Highway Patrol office. "Oh, yeah," patrolman Lem Commons said. "We know this guy. He's one o' them rock 'n' roll singers. Lives in Tupelo..." Commons consulted with another patrolman. "Cottner's his name. We've stopped him 'least 20 times that I can think of. He thinks he's some hot-shot 'er somethin'."

A light went on in the mayor's head. *Now, Calvin, try to keep your calm. You know how you can fly off the handle. That never aids you...*

The mayor shushed Virginia's voice and drove home. He ran upstairs to his daughter's room. On her nightstand was one of the autographed pictures that had been run off for the album. Cam had a supply that he kept on hand to sign for fans.

Beneath his smirking smile and twinkling eyes, he'd signed **To Florra, a grate gal. Yours, Cam.**

Her phonograph, the one she'd begged him for on her 15th birthday, sat on her dresser. To its side was a metal rack filled with records. Among them were several by this horrid boy. 'Cat music,' they read. *He's no better than a common alley cat. He brags about it!*

He wanted to kill this careless, cruel young man. No, he wasn't a man. He had to be no better than a wild animal. He had known men like him on the battlefields of France in 1918. They'd haunted the Red Cross truck, desperate for morphine.

On a rainy night, he'd shot one of them, and felt nothing. It was how you would deal with a coyote or a buzzard. He rolled the dead man's body through the mud and left him in a trench. The death was caused by stray enemy fire, according to the official report. The young man, whose career in medical science was cut short by the war, was given a hero's burial.

The same would not happen for this degenerate. One of his recordings sat on the turntable. He dropped the needle on his daughter's copy of "Women Women Women." **Filth!** He yanked the tonearm off the record player and broke the disc on his knee.

He shuddered to think that this garbage had been under the roof of his home; that his daughter, not yet 16, had purchased it willingly! He pitched the records in the fireplace downstairs. He'd wanted to burn these records months ago. Now the truth was revealed. He was right. The worst nigger in his town wouldn't do such a horrible thing. Nor would he brag about it on phonograph records.

The records crackled and melted; unpleasant fumes roiled from the fireplace. Back upstairs, he broke the cheap glass on the picture frame and removed the signed image. It would help him when he made his search.

He ran a clean town. He'd drummed those abominable horror comic books out of town. Drugstore owners were afraid to stock those sordid paperback novels; if they had them at all, they hid them behind the counter. He'd do the same for this jungle music, once he took care of its brazen, diseased perpetrators.

Mayor Boggs had been air raid warden for his town during the second war. His service pistol from the first war was still oiled and maintained. He would hunt down this horror and rid the earth of him.

**Hank Howard rose at dawn,** excited for the new day. He bathed and shaved, his heart light and heavy all at once. *Something's in the air, he thought,* as he tasted Barbasol and spat it out. *I couldn't tell you what it is, but it's…it's big.*

He made a pot of coffee. As it burbled and sploofed, he prepared scrambled eggs, toast and sausages. Liz stirred as he emptied a slushy can of orange juice concentrate into a plastic pitcher. "What's all this?"

"Got up early. Thought you and the kidlets wouldn't mind if I made some grub. Get 'em up, wouldja hon?"

Sleepy-eyed, their hair in disarray, Carl and Kitty plodded into the kitchen. "Hamma neggs!" Kitty shouted. "Oh boy!"

"You're happy," Liz said to her husband. "We're happy."

"It's a nice feeling. And I'm grateful to God that things have taken such a turn for us." Liz held out plates as Hank meted out the eggs and links. "I know how hard you've worked, and I shouldn't have doubted you…"

"Hamma neeg splease!" Kitty bawled from the dining room table.

"Comin' right up!" Liz took plates in to their children. "You had every right to doubt me," Hank said to his wife. "'Til six months ago, I was barely making enough for us. Not even enough. I've had a streak of good luck. I was in on the ground floor of something new. You know, the big companies in New York and Hollywood are beating their brains out trying to figure out how to make records that sound like ours. Ain't it nice?"

◊◊◊

The telegram came before Hank's second cup of coffee. "Destiny calls!" Hank cried. He was kidding; it was probably a salesman, or one of those sad-eyed kids selling candy for their school gymnasium fund,

He swung the door open and startled a Western Union dispatcher. "Mister Hank Howard? Special delivery. Says I'm s'posed to take a reply. It's paid for."

Hank regarded the small beige envelope. "Come on in. Gimme a minute. How's about some coffee?"

"Sure; thanks!" The kid, fresh out of high school, had a bobbing Adam's apple and crooked teeth. Hank poured him a cup and ripped the top off the envelope.

It was a message from Steve Sholes with RCA Victor. It read:

CONGRATULATIONS ON THE CHART SUCCESS OF YOUR ACT CAM AND THE CATS. WOULD LIKE TO DISCUSS THE POTENTIAL OF THIS ACT ON RCA VICTOR. PLEASE REPLY WITH YOUR TELEPHONE NUMBER AT ONCE. CAN CALL TODAY.

"Holy Hannah!" At Liz's request, he handed the telegram to her. She read it and looked baffled. "This is good news. Isn't it?"

"It's very good news." He turned to the messenger. "I've got a reply. 'Am intrigued by your inquiry. Call anytime after 9 AM today at CL2-5363 here in Tupelo.'"

"Howja spell 'intrigued'?"

"Make it 'interested.' You can spell that one." The boy nodded and scratched in the new word.

"They'll have this in New York in 20 minutes." The kid gaped at the 20-dollar bill Hank placed atop his pad. His Adam's apple threatened to burst through his neck. He dashed to his motorbike and roared towards town.

Hank called Cecil. "I have big news. Can you be ready in 10 minutes? I'll swing by and get you."

"Of course. Are you all right?"

Hank chuckled. "You better believe it!"

He called Miss Bell. She had a country music station on in the background. "Can you get to the office ASAP? No time to explain, but this is big!"

"I reckon so..."

"If you get a call from New York before I get there, hold the line! It's a very imporant call." Miss Tinkle sounded amused; she'd been on the Hank Howard merry-go-round enough. *Probably some guy who owes him money...*

◊◊◊

Calvin Boggs visited Flora in the hospital. He had to see her, speak with her before he did what he'd planned. She was asleep and the ward nurse wouldn't let him in the room. "She was up all night with a bad fever. She's just gotten settled down. I don't want her bothered for 10 hours."

"But I have to see her!"

"Sir, you can't do her any good by waking her up. Rest is what she needs more than anything else right now. I can call you when she's up."

His protests ignored, he peered through the blinds that covered the small window to her room door. A lump moved, up and down, beeath the blankets on the bed. His Flora. The agonies she must have suffered in the arms of that soulless lecherer!

In the chapel on the hospital floor, Mayor Boggs sat in solitude and prayed. *Dear Lord, I have always felt your hand guide me. You know I place all my trust in you, and I know that I owe all that I am...all my achievements to you and your everlasting love. I'm asking you to guide me to do what is right. In the Heavenl;y scriptures it is written "an eye for an eye." Show me a sign, Dear Lord. Show me the way to do what is right for my Flora. She is the greatest gift of all the great gifts you have given me, and all that matters is what is right for her. I am yours. I am your agent, Lord. Guide my direction...*

The Mayor stood and glanced behind him at a small window. Outside, catacorner down the block, he saw a railroad crossing sign silhouetted by sunlight. He fixated on the X made by the two boards of the sign. An X meant a wrong done, a mistake made...something to be erased, removed, destroyed.

That was all he needed. He walked into the December cold, squinted against the sunlight, and got into his car. His pistol, wrapped in a shop towel, sat in the glove compartment. He removed it and put it in his coat pocket. It would bring heavenly vengeance down on a wicked sinner.

◊◊◊

"This could mean anything," Cecil said as he finished the telegram. "Maybe they want to pick up the records for national distribution."

"Wouldn't that be nice? No more worries about suppliers or shipping...

or bootleggers."

"It would take the pressure away from us. We could concentrate on making the records. As long as they don't try to give us a low percentage of the sales..."

"It's intriguing, ain't it? I'm damned curious to know what they want."

"We'll find out."

"Doggone it, Cecil! Aren't you excited? Don't you wanna kick up your heels?"

"I'll kick 'em up once I'm sure about it. I like your enthusiasm and I'm prepared to agree with it."

Hank laughed. What an odd bird! So careful and reserved. *Butter wouldn't melt in his mouth.* The rain promised by the weather man kicked in and they had to dash from Hank's car to the back entrance of the building.

Miss Tinkle was in the office when they arrived. "Nothin' yet. Now, what's this all about?"

She read the telegram. "You ask me, they wanna buy out the contract. Move them over to RCA."

"Naw. It couldn't be."

"What do you think I do all day, Hank?"

"You're always busy. I don't know."

"One thing I do is I read 'Cash Box' an' them other magazines. I've read about this before. You got somethin' they want. They can't stand to see a little company doin' well. You got the goose with the golden egg. They want that goose. All there is to it!"

"Aw, this Sholes character maybe just wants some advice from a what-you-call. A peer."

She laughed. "We ain't their peer. We're their competition! Don't you know nothin' about business?"

"I like to think I do."

Miss Bell started to say something she might regret. The phone's ring saved her. "Hive Records; home of the hits...yes...I'll see if he's available..." She gestured with her head to Hank's office. "It's New York. Mr. Sholes for you on line one."

***Calvin Boggs was out of his jurisdiction*** by 50 miles. The car trip, made less pleasant by heavy rain and washed-down clay mud from the hills, gave him time to think. His anger hadn't ebbed, but doubt colored it. A passage from the Book of Matthew came into his thoughts:

*For if you forgive others their trespasses, your heavenly Father will also forgive you, but if you do not forgive others their trespasses, neither will your Father forgive your trespasses.*

As he drove into town, he passed the headquarters of Hive Records. He hadn't made note of the name of the outfit behind the degenerate's recordings. He realized he hadn't slept, or eaten since last night's dinner. He'd barely touched that. He parked at a metered spot in front of a cafe. He paused at the meter and fed it a nickel. As a representative of Corinth, he had to respect the laws of neighoring towns.

He had coffee, grits and toast. As he ate, he prayed again: *Lord, grant me the gift of forgiveness. Help me to not act in anger, nor with violence. I pray to you for the reason and calm I need to best deal with an unpleasant situation. Perhaps the boy will turn out to not be as bad as I think. As you say in Luke: 'Judge not, and you will not be judged; condemn not, and you will not be condemned; forgive, and you will be forgiven.' But my girl; my dear Flora. You took her mother from me, Lord. Isn't that enough? Have I not served you well? Can I find peace in my heart? I pray that you will grant me a level head and a reasonable heart in this matter. Perhaps an agreement can be reached...*

Then the thought of his daughter, pursued and deflowered in the night...she was still a child. Still a child! She had struggled with her mother's death alongside the Mayor. The loss of Virginia had brought father and child closer. He began to see what a delightful, smart and promising young lady Flora had become.

She worked hard at school, and was well-liked by faculty and students. She had won first prize in an essay contest on the topic "What Mississippi Means to Me." She was a shining example of the promise to today's youth. And that promise was ruptured...defiled...ravaged by this worldly heathen. He'd seduced her with his so-called music, not knowing her name, but certain that he would meet her, or someone like her, and have his wicked way with her.

*Calvin, there is a thing called murder,* he heard Virginia say. *There is a thing called murder, and even a crime of passion is a ticket to the gas chamber.*

*Yes, my dear, but what jury would convict me? Who would not see the story from my side?*

"Yes, sir?" The waitress behind the counter stared at him.

"Did I speak?"

"Yes, sir. I thought you mighta wanted some more coffee."

"Y-yes, that's what I wanted. Thank you."

*Calvin Boggs, you are out of your mind. I know you better than anyone else. You are not fit to carry out this deed.* Virginia's voice took on a scolding tone when she spoke to him.

"I'll talk to the boy's parents. They will understand. They'll want to make things right." The Mayor jarred as he realized he'd spoken those words.

"Ready for the bill?" the waitress said. She smiled.

The Mayor finished his coffee and left two dollars, although the check was 35 cents. By the front door was a telephone. A Tupelo directory hung from a string. He flipped through the residential listings. *Cottner, Edda.* It was the only listing for that name. A residential address; a street name he didn't know.

He wrote it down and walked across the street to a Sinclair gas station. A colored boy ran the gas pumps. "Son, do you know this address?"

The clerk read the address aloud. "28 Silverbell Court." He shook his head. "It ain't around here." He turned to the manager, a stout white man. "Mister Hill, you know where Silverbell Court is?"

Mister Hill thought. "Hey, it's that new place out about...I reckon four, five miles from town. 'F it's where I think...let's look at the map."

He had a four month old map of Tupelo. Mayor Boggs fidgeted as the man took time out of his busy day to squint at the two-point type of the road-map. It had no index, so it was a long process to find Silverbell Court.

*You are a fool. I'm ashamed of you, Calvin Boggs. I want you to know that. Ashamed.*

"I don't blame you," he said out loud. "I'm not happy about it."

"Huh?" The non sequitur jogged Hill's attention to a new corner of the map. "Here she is. Take you 15, 20 minutes to get there. You drivin'?"

"Yes, sir."

"'Cos that'd be a mighty long walk! I'll show ya..."

Mister Hill sold Mayor Boggs a Tupelo map for 50 cents and took a red pencil to it. He drew the route for the old man to follow. It looped around a bit, but he went over it twice and Boggs understood it.

"I thank you, sir, for your time and trouble."

"Glad to do it." The maps were free to cash customers. Mister Hill figured the old coot could spare a Ben Franklin. He flipped the half-dollar and it pinged on the ground. Mister Hill cursed and picked it up from the gravel.

◊◊◊

"Honey, we never did get my things from the old place. I still would like them."

Cam hadn't been to sleep yet, and Momma made a mighty fine breakfast. He was tired, but in a good mood. "Well, hell, let's go get 'em. Jackson oughta be gone by 10. You got your key?"

"Oh, Lord, I hope so..." Edda left a crackling skillet of bacon.

"Momma, you can check after we eat." Grease spattered from the pan.

"Oh, Lord." She returned to breakfast, finished it, and set a plate before her son. Three fried eggs surrounded by curls of blackened bacon; it looked fine to Cam.

After they ate, Cam reminded Edda to check for the key. It was still on her key ring alongside the new ones for the house. "I'm glad I didn't throw it out."

"We gonna need some boxes, I reckon. You mean to take everything? You don't need it."

246

"Well, I'd like to just look at it. See if there's anything special. You know my good graters are over there."

"Momma, I bought you a new set of those damn things. You don't need two!"

"I still want to go and look. If you don't mind."

Cam laughed. "Hold your horses. I'll take you there. I still got some o' my records I wanted to get."

"You and your records."

◊◊◊

"I am the manager of Cam Cottner and his group, yes." Hank's hand trembled as it held the receiver. "I'm also one of the owners of Hive Records here."

"Your label has been doing very well across the board. Especially with Cam and His Cats. We feel that they're the future of popular music. We're going to see the day when your Frankie Laine and Perry Como are no longer on the hit parade, I'm sad to say."

"Yes, Mr. Sholes, I agree. Public tastes are changing."

"I don't believe in wasting time, Mr. Howard. I would like to buy your contract in Cam Cottner and his group. I might also be interested in some of your other artists."

Miss Bell listened in from her phone extension. She glanced at Hank with a *tolja so* look. "Pardon me a moment, sir." Hank cupped the phone. "They want to buy Cam and The Cats! Buy 'em outright!"

Cecil smiled. "Can't hurt to see how bad they want 'em. This could be good for publicity."

Hank nodded. "Mr. Sholes, I'm certainly willing to hear your proposition."

"I appreciate a man who can make fast decisions. RCA Victor is prepared to offer you the sum of $50,000.00 for the release of Cam and His Cats from Hive Records."

"Would that include all existing masters?"

"Of course. Any unreleased material would also become the property of our firm. If the artist has recorded his shopping list in your studio, Victor will assert their ownership of it."

"Well, now, I doubt that would make the hit parade!" Hank laughed and Steve Sholes gave a polite chuckle. "You're asking an awful lot for the price, sir. We've put in a lot of hard work to get this act where it is today..."

"We can go as high as $75,000." Hank looked at Miss Bell. Her wide eyes told the story.

"I appreciate your taking that into consideration, sir. But you see, if I lose this artist on my roster, I'm going to need to sink some capital into finding and promoting new artists. Our capital has been exclusively focused on this new music, and our present facilities need some improvements—"

Sholes sighed. "Our final offer to you is $100,000.00. We can't go higher."

"You'll make that back in the first six months, sir. This boy is going places." Hank looked at Cecil with a grin. This was fun.

"$100,000.00. Take it or leave it."

"Pardon me a moment." Cecil cupped the phone. "Lord, that's close to a quarter of a million dollars. What should I do?"

"Take the money and run. We can find other white boys who sing the blues."

"Lord, I'd be set for life. *We'd* be set for life."

"Ask him to send a contract," Miss Bell said. "Tell him you need your lawyer to look it over. Tell him you need to discuss it with the artists."

Hank nodded. "Before I make this decision, I really need to discuss this matter with Mister Cottner and his bandmates. After all, they're not livestock. They have a say in this too. If you'll send me a contract detailing your offer, I'll have my lawyer look it over and I'll see what the boys think is best for their career."

Miss Bell nodded. Hank had said the right words.

"Well, then. We'll get a copy of the contract out air mail today. It should reach you by Wednesday. We'd like an answer by Friday. And if any other firm approaches you about this act, we ask that you not speak with them."

"That's fine. I'll have my secretary give you our mailing address."

Sholes thanked Hank for his time and finished his business with Miss Bell. Hank slumped into his office chair. "Lord God. You know, it might be best for those boys. They're bigger than we are. It's going to run us ragged trying to keep up with them. I never thought I'd see the day when this would happen."

Cecil shrugged; he didn't know what to say.

◊◊◊

Mayor Boggs found Silverbell Glen after an hour's confused search. In his exhausted state of body and mind, simple tasks became taxing. It didn't help that Virginia kept haranguing him. She was like that. She could be the soul of kindness, but when her husband was in the wrong, she wouldn't let him off easy.

"I understand you, dear, and I agree with you," he spoke to the empty street. "I am willing to forgive, but they have to meet me halfway."

*You had no business to take that pistol with you. How can they be reasonable when you wave that at them?*

"I have no intention of using it, Ginny. I intend to solve this in a civil way."

*I know you, Calvin Boggs. You're hot-headed. You're stubborn. You let your impulses get the better of you.*

"I have in the past; I admit it. I'm the first to admit it. But our daughter...she's all I have..."

*You still have me, dear. If not in body, in your thoughts. I won't leave you.*

Mayor Boggs turned onto Magnolia Way, the entrance to Silverbell Glen. He saw the new, handsome homes in their picturesque lots, their lawns tidy and crisp, and he forgot why he had come to this place. He stalled at the intersection of Magnolia and Osage until it came back to him.

Virginia had to mention the pistol. He opened the glove box and saw its dull blue-black metal. He debated, and touched it with his right index finger, when a voice startled him: "Lookin' for someone?"

"Oh...y...yes, yes I am. I'm trying to find..." He looked on the map and realized the address was on the slip of paper in his coat pocket. He fished it out.

249

"Here...I'm trying to find 28 Silverbell Court. Would you know..."

The man smiled. He was crisp and clean, like the lawns. "If I was you, I'd take a right here, and go two blocks. Then I'd take a left and get onto Redbud Road. You wanna ride that around—it'll start to curve. An' it turns into Silverbell Court."

"Red...bud...road."

"That's it! Welcome to our little slice of heaven, mister!"

"Thank you..." Mayor Boggs just missed running over the man's feet as he took the right turn. He missed the turn on Redbud Road and got stuck in the cul de sac of River Birch Place. "There's something wrong..."

*Yes, there is, Calvin, and it's with you. If you have any sense left, you will turn around and go home. Let the law take care of this, Calvin.*

"But Ginny. There's no going back. If you were here beside me, you'd see it my way."

The Mayor struggled to tune Virginia out as he backed out of the cul de sac. He drove in reverse to Redbud Road and turned left. He felt better now that he was on the right street.

The man hadn't lied. The street curved; at the curve, it became Silverbell Court. He realized he was at the wrong end of the street. The first address he saw was 64. 28 would be on the same side of the street. The lots were larger on this street. Their lawns were dappled with broad oak trees, and their grass was deep green, cool and inviting.

*Cottner.* It was the green house set back in its lot. That pink car! He remembered it from that night when this began. He had bearded the lion in his den. This was no lion; this was a coyote, a vicious heartless beast...

*You can turn back, Calvin. You can still turn back.*

"No, dear. I cannot." He willed himself to leave the pistol in the glove box. His body rebelled. He watched his right hand open the box and then grasp the oiled metal and wood. He pushed the gun into his right coat pocket and opened the car door.

◊◊◊

"Where are my gloves?" Edda had her sun hat and purse. The gloves completed her personal holy trinity.

"You don't need 'em. It's hot out!" Cam felt keyed up. He wanted to lay down and sleep for 10 hours. But he'd never get any peace until she went back there. *She'll see what a shit-hole it was. It'll make her glad she's gone from there. It'll be worth it just to hush her up...*

"I found them! I found them!" Edda smiled. "They were in my purse."

"The whole damn world's in that purse."

Edda stopped cold before the screen door. "Who's that coming?"

◊◊◊

His throat was dry and his head buzzed. He paused at the start of the flagstone walkway. The pleasant variety of colors beneath his feet soothed him. He walked up the path and climbed the wooden stairs. The green and white of the shade fluttered above him.

A woman of about Virginia's age, though much pudgier, stood on the other side of the screen door. Her eyes showed nothing; they met his without emotion or reaction. The mayor stood for what might have been three hours, uncertain what to say, his brow damp with sweat.

"I..." The hoarseness of his voice startled him.

The woman's face assumed a bland, sweet smile. "Yes?"

"G-good morning. Missus... Missus Cottner?"

The gun. Its weight shifted as he moved.

*Don't you take it from your pocket, Calvin Boggs. I'll never forgive you if you do.*

"We're about to leave the  house, sir. Are you selling something?"

"No ma'am. I am wondering if I could discuss something with you. It's quite important."

She paused on the other side of the screen door. "My son doesn't like me to buy from peddlers. He gets so mad at me—"

"I am no peddler, ma'am. Are you the mother of a Cam Cottner?"

"Yes..." She peered. "You're not the man from that record company."

"Thank the good Lord, ma'am, I am not. May I please speak with you?

251

This concerns your son."

"We've had so many young girls come by for him. They all want his autograph." She shook her head and chuckled.

"Your son is quite popular with girls."

"He certainly is. Especially since he made those records. He really is a good boy. He used to come to church with me. How that boy can sing a hymn!"

"Please, ma'am, allow me to come in. I won't take up much of your time..."

"I don't know...we need to get going..."

Boggs pulled on the screen door. It opened. Edda stood as if in a frieze; he edged inside and stood beside her.

"Momma, I'mo buy you all new..."

*There he is! The despoiler of my dear child. How haughty his bearing. Arrogant youth. He disgusts me...*

Cam looked ascance at the quivering, sweaty man inside the door. "Whattaya you want, mister?"

"A-are you...Cam Cottner?"

Cam nodded.

"The young man who makes the records?"

"Yes, sir. Mr. Howard handles my business affairs."

"Th-this is not about business. Is this person your mother?" He gestured to Edda.

"Yeah. Why?"

"Mrs. Cottner, this is a...a very personal matter...it isn't anything you would want for your neighbors to hear. I'm quite sure it would embarrass you."

"Oh?" She hesitated and looked at her son. He smiled and shrugged. He thought to make the circular motion at his temples, but wasn't sure Edda would understand. "Well, if it's serious..."

He stepped towards her. His eyes were red. He frightened her. She backed from him, unsure what he might do. "I am sorry for the intrusion, Mrs. Cottner. But once I say what I have to say I know you'll understand." The mayor felt in his right-hand coat pocket without thinking. The oiled, heavy metal felt cool to the touch.

"Well..." She looked at the living room and gestured towards the couch. "Sit down, sir. Would you—"

Then the telephone rang.

◊◊◊

"We should call him first," Hank said to Cecil. "Sort of warm him up to the idea."

Hank dialed the new number for Cottner, Edda. It rang eight times.

◊◊◊

Edda Cottner froze. First a strange man, an angry man, barges into her home, and now the telephone. She knew she had to stop the phone ringing, but how could she do that and attend to this man?

The man pushed past her to the telephone in the hallway. "The line is out of order," he said. He listened; a voice buzzed in his ear. "I'm...I'm with the phone c-company. W-working on...on the line. Try your call again shortly."

"Mister, what the hell you tryin'—"

Cam's tone of voice alarmed the old man. He felt inside his coat pocket. Cam's eyes widened; his mouth fell open.

He cradled the telephone and adjusted his crooked glasses. "And now, Mrs. Cottner, Mister Cottner, will you sit with me? We have a grave matter to discuss. A young girl's life is at stake."

"What the *fuck,* man!" Cam saw the pistol in the mayor's right hand.

He had pulle it from his pocket without thinking. He raised the gun in the air, his intention to calm them both down. Edda Cottner gasped at its sight. "Please don't pay this any mind, ma'am. I...I'll put it away. I didn't mean to scare you."

"What do you want?" Edda's voice took a high, panicked tone. "What do you *want?*" Her volume doubled.

*You blamed fool,* Virginia said. *See what you've done! I told you this would go wrong, Calvin...*

"Not now, Virginia! Leave me alone!"

"You don't leave, I'm callin' the cops. Get the hell out!" Cam shouted.

"Please, please. Don't mind me. If we can just sit and talk..." He could not seem to get his right arm down. The one thing he wanted was to put the pistol away. Out of sight, as a show of good faith.

Cam walked toward the hall. The man's eyes, and his gun, tracked him. Cam reached for the telephone. He dialed 0.

"Please...son..." He stood up. *If they would just listen to me...* "No, no, no..."

A flash of hellfire filled the room. With a deafening din, holy terror broke loose. The phone nook in the hallway was now a jagged wound of plaster, wood and asbestos. "Holy shit! Are you fucking *crazy?*" Cam cried out.

Edda stood frozen, afraid to breathe. An awful silence became a ringing in the mayor's ears. His heartbeat pounded in his temples.

"No no no no." The hellfire went off again. In his fear and confusion, the Mayor couldn't relax his grip on the trigger of the pistol. Another section of the hallway shattered into raw fragments.

Tears blurred his vision. He struggled to unlock his grip, to calm his muscles, to relax and put the firearm away.

Then Cam charged him. "Go next door! Call the police!" The mayor lost sight of the woman. This young man was wiry but strong. Stronger than him. He grabbed the Mayor's am with one firm hand, and smacked at the pistol with the other. From his mouth spewed vile, brutal words. Was this a beast? A vision from hell?

The voice was so loud, strident. So full of hatred and anger. This anger had thrust itself deep into the virgin body of his daughter. This anger had to be stopped.

The Mayor wrenched his right hand free and emptied his pistol into the form of this demon, this illusion. He squeezed until no bullets remained. Red spattered; flesh and bone ruptured as the wall had done. This damage could not be rebuilt. It was final.

254

The Mayor heard wailing and weeping. He fell to his knees where he stood. Prayer was his last solace. "Oh, Heavenly Father, please forgive me. I did not want to do this. I did not wish this to happen. Perhaps this is a dream; a vision put forth to test my faith. If I have failed, please show me your tender mercy..."

◊◊◊

"Look at all the cop cars," Cecil said. He'd never seen a crowd in Silverbell Glen. Neighbors visited; couples played cards or had cookouts on fair nights. Police cars were new to this street. Hank pulled onto someone's lawn and ran for the house. Cecil sprinted in his wake.

"Sir, what's happened?" Hank crawled through the crowd of neighbors and passers-by. He got the attention of an officer. "Sir, can you tell me what..."

"Some nut-case walked into the house and started firing a gun. Killed this kid. Couldn't have been 20. Blew him to bits."

"Oh, Lord."

A gap in the crowd confirmed Hank's suspicion. The door was flung open; police officers stood, stunned and silent. Cam's mother sat on the ground beside the lifeless shell of her son. A policewoman talked with her. Hank couldn't hear the conversation; both spoke in a near-whisper.

"I'm sorry, ma'am," one of the medics said. "We'd better..." He and his partner walked in a stretcher. The medics lifted the dead body of Camren Cottner onto the stretcher and covered it with green blankets. The ambulance door sat open for its deposit.

"Good God." Hank stood in front of the ambulance, unaware that he was in the vehicle's way.

"Out of the way, mac!" the driver shouted. "C'mon!" Hank scuttled off the street. The ambulance didn't need to run its siren. It drove off. With that, the crowd dispersed. Some of Edda Cottner's neighbors lingered. Hank heard snippets of their voices...small pieces of the story that had just ended.

"He's gone, Cecil. He's gone." Cecil considered asking an officer for more information, but knew better. He wouldn't get answers.

"I was right. I knew something was wrong." Hank seemed stunned. He'd never seen anything this bad. He'd led a different life. Cecil had been around death enough to be used to it. Never death by violence, but a succession of relatives, neighbors and friends who'd passed away. Death was something that happened to everyone, regardless of who they were or where they lived. You couldn't undo it. So you had to accept it, and keep moving forward until your turn came.

He couldn't express these thoughts to Hank. There weren't easy words. "Let's get back to the office," he said in a calm tone. He put his hand on Hank's shoulder and guided him to the car.

Hank sat behind the wheel and gathered himself together. He shook his head side to side in a series of dimishing arcs. "I'm sorry this happened," Cecil said. "The boy had troubles but he was talented."

"Did you ever see $100,000 blow up right in front of you?" Hank attempted to smile. "Just gone. Blink and it's gone."

"We should get back. They'll be calling you. Once this gets out, it'll be in every front page in the country."

"Lord." Hank started the car and wheeled out onto Silverbell Court.

There was more to say, but no one could say it yet.

# 4

***Cam's service made national news.*** Adults who'd rolled their eyes at their children's fascination with this flashy, sassy baboon sobered as their sons and daughters sat in depressed heaps or sobbed in their bedrooms.

Hank, Skip and Clue were among the pallbearers. By all rights, Cecil should have been with them; he watched the event from a safe distance. He felt a mixture of relief and remorse as he saw the coffin lowered into earth.

As Hank expected, he was called upon to speak about Cam Cottner and his passing. He spoke off the cuff and thus rambled. "The heating fuel shortage is over," one wire-service reporter quipped to another. "Just hook a hose up to this guy and let him roll."

In a much-quoted passage, Hank summarized the events of Cam's career: "Chance brought me in contact with this remarkable young man. I was the shepherd of a failing flock until Cam Cottner showed me that my dreams could come true. He understood black music in his heart and soul, and transmitted that feeling to a white audience. This to me is a remarkable feat. I am honored to have been the conduit of his voice and his music. Though he made only 14 recordings, maybe 40 minutes of music, his work will live on and continue to reach new audiences. Mark my words, his influence will last for many years."

◊◊◊

Mayor Calvin Boggs suffered a brain embolism while in custody for the shooting of Camren Cottner. He was found in a coma in his cell. Transferred to the city hospital, he died within 36 hours.

An autopsy revealed the cerebral embolism had been present for about 18 months. His general physician hadn't thought to check for warning signs that, after the fact, seemed obvious. "Patient shows signs of confusion, often has to have instructions repeated orally," his physician's chart notes read.

Flora Boggs was treated for gonorrhea in a private hospital. Megadoses of penicillin helped curtail the disease. The Mayor's younger sister Imogene became the girl's legal guardian. Flora had her 16th birthday while still carrying Cam Cottner's child. Flora's physicians advised against an abortion; she was too far along in the pregnancy.

Charlton Boggs was born on June 3, 1956. The boy was raised with the help of Imogene, who doted on the toddler. (Flora named her son after her favorite film actor, Charlton Heston.)

◊◊◊

After Cam's service, Edda Cottner returned home and felt alone. The house was paid for, and in her name. The shock of her son's death had done something to her. Things seemed clearer now. She took up new interests, including bird-watching and ceramics. In the afternoons, she began to research her family's history. She started with her own.

As her son said, she and Jackson were never married. In the fog that overtook her after the birth of Carmen, she thought they were, but there was nothing in the Lee County Bureau of Records aside from her brief union with Oscar Cottner. She couldn't recall how she met Jackson, or how he came to live with she and her boy. But that was not relevant anymore. She could sweep it away like the dust and pollen on her front porch.

Oscar's will left Edda with sufficient house money. The addition of her son's record royalties made the pittance Jackson contributed to the pot superfluous. That doubled for him.

Edda worked up the courage to go to The Renaldo Apartments and look after her kitchen things. She waited until mid-morning, when traffic was light, and lurched Cam's Thunderbird towards town.

She hoped to make a quick and quiet visit, but her presence was noticed by her old neighbors. "Why, Edda! I thought you had moved out to the country? What brings you back to the slums?" Miss Holland laughed. She took a drag on a Kool menthol cigarette.

258

"I left some things behind. My son did, too. I thought they might still be there..."

"Oh, hon, that stuff was out on the curb last month. What's-his-name left. Went away. Left all his things in there. Crosby was furious." Miss Holland cackled and showed yellowed teeth. Crosby was the hot-tempered manager and she lived to rile him.

"All gone? Everything?"

Miss Holland shrugged. "The kids had a ball with them records your boy used to have. They were sailin' 'em all over the place." A broken sliver of black vinyl caught her eye. She pointed. "There's a piece. They were all over christendom. Crosby about busted a brisket when he saw that!"

"Oh." Edda looked up at her old place. "Oh. Well. There's on point then, is there?" She turned and walked down the courtyard to the street, where the poorly parked T-Bird awaited its next series of stop-and-go movements. Miss Holland watched her ex-neighbor trod off.

"Well, I never," she said to herself. An ash from her Kool drifted into her eye. The pink car was gone once she'd picked it out.

◊◊◊

Deceased, Cam Cottner was the perfect recording artist. No worries about what he might say or do; no burden to Skip Mosely on the road. No road to go on; Skip returned to his job at the post office and did the odd session for Hank Howard. Edda Cottner grieved the loss of her son—the idea of her son. She did not understand the person he'd grown up to be. It was all a blur. As her view of the world came into sharper focus, the people of her past misted into oblivion. She thought of Carmen every day, many times a day. But he wasn't clear to her any longer.

Miss Bell had good marketing ideas. The LP was reissued as *Cam Cottner Memorial Album* with "Been Gone Too Long" added as the final track. The singles were re-pressed on gold-colored vinyl as commemorative keepsakes. Extended-play discs with colorful covers shuffled the 14 tracks, including "Graveyard Blues." (No mention was made that Cam had left the building while this number recorded.) In time, the three solo recordings Cam made for Skinny Griggs were added to his legacy. Skip, Clue and Chili did tasteful overdubs to complement the boy's raw performances. Hank brought The Tupelo Three in to do vocal backgrounds, but never issued those versions.

Those performances, alongside an alternate take of "Leaning," were issued as *His First Recordings*. The EP topped country and pop charts in 1957. All releases had liner notes by Hank Howard (often ghost-written by Cecil Madison) that recapped what he'd said at bygone press conferences.

"Y'know, we don't really need to put out new records," Hank said to Cecil. "Watch that tree. It's comin' up on your left."

Hank taught Cecil how to drive. Cecil never had the opportunity to learn; hadn't really considered it. But with money rolling in, so often and in such abundance, he felt a need to spend some of it. He bought a 1957 model Chrysler Saratoga. He liked the look of it and found it in sky blue, his favorite color.

Hank, a patient coach, eased Cecil into the driver's seat by trial and error. He got his license and felt a new freedom. To his delight, Coaxial enjoyed riding with him. He'd sit curled up in the front passenger seat; sometimes he'd stretch up, lean against the passenger door and watch the world whiz by. He commented on the view. "Oh Lord, he's yellin'," Cecil said many times as an amused mantra.

◊◊◊

Would-be Cams still made their visit to Mecca, where Hank dropped whatever he was doing to hear them. He picked up a few white rock 'n' rollers, two gifted country singers with pop crossover success and a white girl whose idols were Sarah Vaughn, Billie Holiday and Ella Fitzgerald. Corrine Staph did an album of jazz standards, backed by various cats around town, including Chili Burse. *You and The Night* got onto the album charts and Miss Staph's contract was purchased by Verve Records for $25,000. "One-fourth of a Cam," Cecil joked.

With no black artists on the Hive roster, Cecil began to write for other labels. He placed a string of humorous songs with The Cruisers, an r&b quintet whose forte were what they called "crazy operas." Cecil wrote these songs on his own time, and would have pitched them to Hive artists if they were a good fit.

Artists came and went. Cliff Roscoe's hits dried up and he called it quits. He went to work on an oil rig and played his guitar for fun, when he felt like it. The Moody Twins left for college and found their calling. Ronald majored in classical literature and became a professor at Tulane; Dwayne got into the NASA program with a degree in physics. (A 1990s CD collection of their recorded work was called *Smart Guys*.)

◊◊◊

Cecil took his first plane trip in March 1958. Deft Records, the label that carried The Cruisers and other r&b stars, invited him to supervise a recording session for the group in New York.

He enjoyed the experience. In their Manhattan studio, under a cloud of second-hand smoke, black and white musicians, songwriters and producers were on equal ground. Race wasn't mentioned. A person's worth was paramount.

Cecil's laid-back, dry humor went over well; he said little, but what he did speak tended to have everyone bent over with laughter. Arnold Hoffman, the head A&R man at Deft, was impressed that Cecil could coach the singers without offending them. He had a good ear, knew his way around the keyboard, and projected skill and confidence.

"Cecil, this is where you oughta be," Hoffman said, over dinner at Sardi's. "I could use a good producer. Someone who can really work with the talent. I think you're the guy for the job. You'll get a salary and Hill and Range will sign you as a songwriter. You can write all you want. There's money to be made, my friend. Money and good times."

"I like it here. Let me think it over, Arnold." They shook hands. Cecil had one day on his own before his flight back to Tupelo. He walked through Washington Square, explored the Village, was impressed by the temple of books that was The Strand, caught a French movie with subtitles called *Le Craneur* in a small theater where viewers sipped espresso coffee and sat in reverent silence.

It was the kung pao shrimp that did it. He'd never heard of it, and its heat and piquancy caressed his palate. He thought of being able to have this dish whenever he felt like it, in a world that seemed bigger and smarter than he'd ever known...

He walked the theater district at sunset, and, in the alcove of an office building, admired the coming and going of what seemed like a million people. When he was a boy, he was afraid of Tupelo's downtown. He could recall that terror. Whatever was behind that was gone. Long gone.

This was a city he would never exhaust and that would not fail him. *There's good and bad everywhere you go,* he thought. *Feels like there's too much good to fall short.*

# *Cecil broke the news to Hank on April Fool's Day.*

"I feel like New York is the place. It's hard to explain. You'd have to be there to understand. But it's the place I need to be."

"I've never been there, but I've always wanted to see it." Hank swigged his Coke. "Deft is a big label. They could really get you to hit your stride. I hate to lose you...but I get it."

"I was afraid you'd be offended. I worried all the way home."

Hank was sad and excited in equal measure. "You'd just be spinnin' your wheels here, Cec. But, you know, I've been thinkin' about getting back into recording the blues...the real blues, like The Shadow. The down-home, backwater stuff...no polish to it. Just...raw feeling."

"Arnold told me there's a market for folk music and blues in colleges. He goes to the folk and jazz festivals. I could introduce you."

"I like Arnold's work. I'd be happy to meet him."

Cecil called Hoffman and said yes to his offer. A contract came special delivery; he signed it and returned it. He was to start at Deft on June 1st. His salary was $300.00 a week, not counting his songwriting income. Arnold would introduce him to Jules Aberbach after the move. Hill & Range had indicated their pleasure at signing him as a writer.

Cecil's copyrights with Beehive Music would remain, and he elected to retain his one-third ownership of Hive. "Hard to say no to free money."

"You earned it in advance, Cec." Hank paused; he had something to say but wasn't sure of it.

Cecil knew something had to come out of those pipes. "What's up?"

"Cec...I got a crazy idea. How about we cut an album on you. Your versions of all the songs you wrote for Hive artists? Just you and the piano. Maybe get Chili to sit in on drums."

"Who on earth would want to hear that?"

"Hey, brother. Don't knock yourself! Those songs sold a lotta records. I'm sure there's someone out there who'd wanna hear the composer singin' 'em."

"Well, you can press 100 copies and maybe you'll sell 10."

◊◊◊

*He Writes 'em—He Sings 'em!*, recorded in three sessions in April and May, comprised what Cecil felt were his better songs for the record label. He skipped over some of the fluffier novelty songs, and with Hank's encouragement, included "Hangman" as the closing track.

The sessions were loose, open affairs. Musicians heard about them and dropped in to play. Some of Rusty Gordon's old sidemen blew in, and the longer track time of the LP gave them room to stretch out. Skip and Clue showed up for three songs they'd recorded with Cam, and The Tupelo Three provided backup vocals on half the album.

It felt like a jam session. Hank left mistakes in and included chatter in-between tracks. He pressed it with a full-color cover—a great studio shot from the session with Rusty's boys—and wrote the liner notes that praised Cecil's achievements and wished him the best of luck in his new life.

Cecil's sales predictions were close: it didn't sell in great numbers, but it sold small and steady over time. *Billboard* gave it a starred review that said:

*Cleffer Gordon, whose name is a mainstay on the Mississippi label, bids farewell to his musical alma mater with this swinging, easygoing revue of blues, rhythm and rock 'n' roll tunes he helmed. Madison is in the league of Lincoln Chase and Otis Blackwell as a rhythm scribe. Solid support from the waxery's sidemen makes this session a casual delight. Could break out.*

◊◊◊

Cecil hadn't much house to put in order. Among the things he kept were his satchel of song lyrics, a few changes of clothing and one box he sealed with tape and string and marked FRAGILE.

Coaxial knew something was up but trusted his human friend that all this disarray would end well.

263

His final days in Tupelo had a bittersweet cast. He walked streets he knew like his skin with the knowledge he'd never see them again. He dropped by his few haunts; they now seemed ragged and paltry. The sun-bleached, paint-peeling storefronts, the bus stops, the whites-only cafes and movie theaters he'd never entered; all felt lost and unreal to him. He couldn't believe he'd lived with them so long, gotten so accustomed to them.

He produced his last session at Hive Records on May 26th. Hank had made the acquaintance of a young man who sang on a streetcorner downtown. He watched the singer for half an hour and didn't recognize any of his songs. Hank introduced himself and invited the singer to audition for his company.

Rufe Waland was a disciple of B. B. King and T-Bone Walker and sang country blues with a city beat. Alone with an electric guitar, he sang through a damaged amplifier that gave him a distinct sound. In the Hive Studios, over their maintained equipment, the magic was gone. "Gee, where's that frazzle sound?" Hank asked Rufe.

"My ole amplifier make that sound. It ain't no good."

"Hey, man, you had a great sound out on the street. Where's that amp?"

Hank drove Rufe to his boarding house to fetch the amplifier. The singer seemed embarrassed about it. "It don't work no good. I was gonna thow it away..."

He plugged it in; sparks popped from the back of its casing. But his guitar, once plugged into it, sounded like a wailing, fuzzy spirit. The effect was mesmerizing.

Chuck left his lair to inspect the amp. He opened up the back and chuckled. "Got you a loose tube. I can fix this thing quick."

"No no!" Hank insisted it be left as it stood. Cecil sat at the piano only to help Rufe tune his strings. The singer recorded two original songs, "It's Bound to Get Better" and "Bend in the Road." Cecil recognized snatches of old blues lyrics, but the songs were something new. Chuck grumbled about the distortion and static interference; a faint voice from a radio station could be heard through the amp. Hank countered that this sound had a new feeling, and could be a sensation. "What do you think, Cec?"

"Well. It's a raw sound, kind of lonesome, but it's got feeling. A lot of deep feeling. It's what we kind of got away from, last couple of years."

Hive #286 gave the label a new hitmaker. "Cash Box" awarded it a B+ and noted:

*Eerie low-down blues enchanter from new artist. Topside is a hymn-like uplifting deck. Flip should appeal to afficionados. Could get heavy juke play. Ought to eye it.*

A request came from Victor Cross for more material from The Lonesome Shadow. The album had moved 100,000 copies with little promotion. Cross, according to *Cash Box*, had long-players in the works for all his artists.

◊◊◊

The last time Cecil saw Hank, he was heading out to find The Shadow. He had three copies of *The Real Blues!* under his arm and a royalty check in his coat pocket.

"I do wish he'd get a phone put in. I've offered to pay for one. He just don't want it." Hank gestured with the album; Cecil got it.

"I'm leaving in the morning. I just wanted to say goodbye. Glad I caught you."

"Cec, I am too. I got to admit, man, this is hard for me."

"I know."

"Really hate to see you go. It won't be the same 'round here."

"I'll miss this place." Cecil gestured to the Hive building. "I was thinking I might send some acts here to record. Get that Tupelo sound."

"Anybody you send me I'd be happy to record. Just let me know. Keep in touch. Call me once you're settled."

"I will. I'll write you soon's I get there."

Hank's eyes got this serious cast, like he was on the edge of tears. He cleared his throat. "You know, one thing I regret." Hank looked down for a moment. "I kept meaning to do it. We never had you out to the house. I would have liked for you to meet my wife and kids. Have one of Liz's fine dinners." He looked up with remorse. "Why didn't I do that? What was wrong with me?"

"It's okay, man, it's okay." Cecil leaned against a parking meter. "You were trying to keep this place going. You had a lot on your mind."

"Don't make excuses for me. It's a civil thing to do, an act of friendship.

265

And I didn't ever think of it 'til now. It makes me feel rotten inside. I'm no better than…them." He gestured to the random people passing by—white folks, rich and poor, with the world on their side.

"You did something better, man. You invited me into your world. Your real world. I will miss being a part of this. Probably all I'll miss about this town. But it's a big thing. And I won't ever forget it. I couldn't if I tried."

"I 'preciate your sayin' that. I hope I've been helpful to you, Cec."

"And I hope I've been helpful to you." Cecil extended his hand. Hank took it and they shaked.

"Well," they said over each other. "I better get goin'. I should get a phone put in at his place." He gestured with the album cover. "Be a hell of a lot easier than playin' detective."

"Could you please tell him how grateful I am? I never had a chance to say anything. Too much hubbub."

"I'd be glad to. I imagine he knows. That song is…boy, if anyone ever comes up with something to top that…wow."

"It'll happen. Might not be while we're still alive, but…"

Hank nodded. "Well, take care, my friend, and if you're ever in town again, we'll have you out to the house. I'm thinkin' about buyin' a new place. A little bigger. Two kids take up a lot of space. An' they're just gonna get bigger."

It was a difficult farewell. Cecil broke it with a final wave and he walked away from Hank's car; away from Hive Records. Hank took off in the other direction. Cecil's Saratoga was parked around the corner.

He unlocked the door and sat in the car. He didn't feel like going to the house. Nowhere appealed to him. He was in-between lives for the moment.

He clicked on the radio and ran up and down the dial. Snips of commercials, news, weather and talk; it took some time to find music. What he found was the last 30 seconds of "Women Women Women." As it ended, a disc jockey spoke:

*That goes out to Carol and Linda in Muscle Shoals. Boy, it's funny to think how upset people got over this record! We'll miss Cam and The Cats, that's for sure. Now here's a big platter by… The Platters!*

It was "My Dream," which was a bald rewrite of "My Prayer." Cecil scoffed at the chutzpah of Buck Ram, the song's so-called composer. The effrontery of it all made him laugh, and he shook that far-away feeling.

◊◊◊

By 10 am, Cecil's worldly goods were in the trunk and back seat of the Saratoga. His clothes and a few dishes were boxed in the trunk. The satchel of song lyrics were tucked on the floor behind the driver's seat.

On the right side of the back seat was the sealed box. It had three copies of every record he'd written or produced. Some were great, some were dumb, but they were his. He wadded newspaper around them so they wouldn't get broken; some of them were on 10-inch shellac discs.

Cecil held the passenger door open for Coaxial, who sniffed and then hopped in. "Got somethin' for you, bud." Cecil had half a can of tuna fish chopped up, with newspaper underneath it to catch stray chunks.

Cecil took a last look inside the house. It was empty; every trace of his time there swept out and waiting for the junk man on the curb. An empty house feels lonesome and small. Cecil stood for a couple of minutes and watched dust motes play in the sunlight. "Thank you," he said to the house. He locked the door and put the keys in the mailbox, as the landlord had asked.

Coaxial had noshed. He groomed and settled in for a nap. Cecil imagined the cat sitting in some Village windowsill, soaking up the winter sun. He'd grow old and fat on that sill, in that city light.

On the outskirts of Atlanta, Cecil stopped at an Esso station to fill his gas tank. The Saratoga rocked to a stop and woke the cat. He stretched, yawned, and asked "Rr-nak?"

"Rr-nak," Cecil replied. He topped off the tank, bought a Coke and returned to the driver's seat.

Coaxial sighed and blinked at Cecil. Cecil blinked back. The sky-blue Saratoga, a brighter hue than the cloudless expanse above it, faded to a pinpoint down the highway.

# *Epilogue*

**Hank Howard continued Hive Records,** with its focus on black music, and did well during the early 1960s roots music fad. A series of informal blues sessions, recorded with a live ambience, led to successful albums in what Hank called *The Blue and Gold*, the latter word referring to Tupelo's world-famous honey.

With the profits from these albums, Hank built a larger, more modern studio across town. It was opening in time for the musical upheaval of 1964. To Hank's bemusement, rock 'n' roll musicians showed up again. They had shaggy hair and sullen demeanors, but weren't otherwise different from the rockers of the last decade. Hank put a few singles out, but none of them did well. He tried to push Hive rhythm and blues material on them, and got an excellent garage-rock revamp of "A Slob with A Job" on a Jackson group called The London Rogues. It bubbled under the *Billboard* Hot 100 at #119 for one week.

Its release inspired a telegram from Cecil Madison, now an established producer for Deft Records. Valued for his cool head under pressure, and an unerring sense of new trends and staying ahead of them, Cecil produced and wrote a large string of hits and promising near-misses for Deft.

Cecil kept his promise to Hank, and sent a steady flow of artists to Tupelo to record at Hive. Though he'd happily record anyone who came through the door, Hank Howard continued Hive Records as a primarily blues label until 1972. He hadn't issued a record by a white performer since 1967, when local garage band releases came to a halt. By then, the musicians he heard were gone to places he didn't care for—or Vietnam called and they went to face hell.

Hank switched to real estate in 1972. Two decades of navigating the perilous waters of the music biz had jaded his enthusiasm. Real estate had its sharks and crooks, but they seemed feeble after dealing with Victor Cross and assorted scumbag distributors. Hank's pleasant, welcoming personality was ideal for smooth-talking potential developers and luring new home-owners to sign on the dotted line and join the world of eternal debt.

Carl became caught up in rock 'n' roll music after The Beatles crashed America, and showed interest in his father's work. He learned quickly and had a good mind for the intricacies of the recording booth. Chuck Honeycutt became a Methodist minister in 1971 and Carl slid into his job without a seam showing.

The Hive studio was too well-oiled to shut down, and with his father's blessings Carl continued the studio, which was home to many classic 1970s sessions for a wide swath of artists. He renamed the place Tupelo Honey Soundworks in 1976. Famous performers were seen around Tupelo; most of them unknowns to the locals, who didn't keep up with popular music.

◊◊◊

Charlton Boggs grew up in Tupelo in a house not far from the original Hive headquarters. Flora Boggs waited until the boy was two years old and introduced him to Edda Cottner. She informed the surprised woman that she was a grandmother. Edda's shock turned to joy when she saw the well-behaved, rosy-cheeked toddler—the spitting image of her departed son.

"We'd better not tell him the truth," Edda decided. Camren Cottner joined the skeletons in her family closet. Edda doted on Charlton and was a warm substitute for a daycare facility. Charlton spent as much time with Edda as with Flora or Imogene. They all encouraged his talent as it developed.

Edda saw it first. Charlton was fascinated by her old out-of-tune piano, which was just a piece of dusty furniture; she didn't play. He plinked on its keys, wide-eyed at the sounds it made. By accident, he discovered that two or more keys, played at once, produced chords. He didn't know what they were called, but understood that the keys worked together.

Charlton quailed at piano lessons, but learned his chords and became a decent if rudimentary keyboardist. Charlton was an instant fan of The Beatles in 1964. Like his father, he amassed a large collection of records—anything

English, or that sounded like the British groups, was exciting to him. Charton stole deposit bottles from neighbors' carports and back porches to finance his record habit.

In the 10th grade, he joined a rock band called The Obvious Mystery IV. His vocal style was imitative of Mick Jagger, as were hundreds of garage band frontmen, but he had a natural knack of how to work a crowd.

By this time he'd heard his father's musical legacy, which he thought was corny and old-fashioned. He'd found his mother playing the singles. "Man, that's outta date, Mom!"

"Guess it is. But this is what I grew up with." Her smile spooked Charlton; her eyes told a different story.

Charlton just missed serving in Vietnam. Bored with junior college, he dropped out in 1977 and formed a rock group called The Battle of Malvern Hill. He picked that name out of a book on the Civil War. A couple of ex-Obvious Mystery IV guys, still in town, joined up. Chaz, as he called himself, wrote a batch of songs, all trying to get at the spookiness he saw around the cracks of life in Mississippi. "Man, these are fuck'n downers," Scott Yon, the lead guitarist said. "Sum'pn cool about 'em though."

The songs, which gave Yon considerable room for long solos, took shape. With their minor keys and ponderous tempos, they were heavy going, and Yon wrote some uptempo stuff to balance Chaz' dark epics.

"We got 'nuff for a album," Chaz noted. The songs, honed by live performances, where they went down well, seemed ready for the big time. Granma Cottner gave the group money to record demos at Tupelo Honey Soundworks.

Malvern Hill, as they were renamed, were signed to MCA in 1978 on the strength of their Soundworks demos. Carl Howard knew a guy at MCA who owed him a favor, and got the Malvern demos under his nose. "This could go big," Carl told him.

During the album sessions at the Soundworks, Johnny Quillan, the group's drummer, saw a blown-up photo of Cam and His Cats on the studio wall. He squinted at Chaz Boggs. Through a bourbon filter, he realized something, and spoke it out loud. "Y'look jus' like that guy in the pisher, man." Quillan pointed his drumstick at the image. Chaz laughed at the idea, but recognized a resemblance.

Mention Malvern Hill to anyone who was in high school from 1979-

1983 and they'll have memories. They might mention the group's biggest hit, "Drunk as Hell (High as a Kite)," Scott Yon's clarion call to teen substance abuse that outraged parents but made its accompanying album go gold. They closed countless proms with the recording of their 11-minute slow-burner "Strange Lorraine," one downer of a Southern gothic death story. Chaz had read some Poe and Lovecraft and tried to put that vibe into a rock song.

*Rolling Stone* said, in its review of a Malvern Hill album: *Imagine being up all night, still drunk, standing outside and watching the sun rise. It's the creepiest time of day or night. You're not asleep but you're not awake. You're somewhere heavy and thick and deep. That's what this record feels like. There's mildew, death and decay in these grooves, for sure. But there's also a kind of life. Something intangible, but it's there.*

Malvern Hill's members joined the rock 'n' roll death list when a chartered prop plane went down while flying through a South Florida thunderstorm in August 1986. The whole band perished; their bodies were burned beyond recognition when the wreckage could be approached.

◊◊◊

Charlton's death undid Edda Cottner. Those who hadn't known her in the 1950s were shocked to see her vitality dim, and her eyes go gray. She suffered from heart murmurs and the strain of her son and grandson dying in their prime pushed her back to when she was with Jackson. Thoughts of that dark, bitter man haunted her. How had she withstood him for so long? Why had she withstood him at all?

None of this inner turmoil surfaced on her flat, bland appearance. Flora and Imogene did their best to cheer her, but Edda had lost the will to live. She succumbed to a small heart attack in 1989. Her fortunes were willed to Flora, who funneled much of this windfall into her work for children's rights. She became well-known as an advocate for children forced into labor in distant countries, and those who suffered from abuse or neglect in her own country.

◊◊◊

Hive Records' master tapes were thought to be lost. They'd been safe all along in the bank's safe deposit chamber. Over time, it filled four large drawers. As interest in early rock music grew in the 1970s, European collectors and historians interviewed Hank Howard about his legacy. "It's all gone. Hell, tape was expensive back then. I guess we just recorded over 'em. Couldn't see any use in saving 'em." Roots music fans had to make do with reissues culled from the best surviving examples of the shellac and vinyl records.

After quadruple-bypass heart surgery in 1989, Hank was an invalid; Liz cared for him until his passing in 1991. His will bequeathed the entirety of Hive to Carl. His son learned of the master tapes when the bank called. They were moving to a new location, and needed permission to move the contents of those four file drawers. The only other person who knew of them was Cecil Madison, who died in 1990 from the AIDS virus.

Carl Howard felt overwhelmed by this find. His father had worked the lost tapes angle into a legend; like most legends, it was bullshit. Carl began an immediate program to transfer the original reels to digital audio tape. The tapes had been stored in ideal archival conditions, and with a few exceptions they played as well as the day they were first used.

The tapes' discovery made international news, and three die-hard music collectors came over from England to catalogue the tapes. They attempted to decipher the scrawls of Hank Howard and Chuck Honeycutt, transcribed the writing to computer documents, listened to the DATs and logged their contents properly. They discovered multiple versions of some of the label's hits and classics. This material has since been reissued and restored with a level of obsession and care that might have baffled the men and women who recorded them.

A couple of sessions didn't survive, among them the ill-fated recordings of Maggie Woodburn. Hank *had* recorded over those tapes, ashamed at how wrong he'd been with her. The search continues for Hive 211, the final single of Maggie Woodburn. Though "My Heart's Fire" and "Search for Love' were reviewed in *Cash Box* (they rated a C+), no copies are known to survive. No one has yet thought to track down the singer's grand-daughter, Dorothy Woodburn McTew, who has one unplayed copy in an old hat box, passed down from Grandma and stuffed into a cluttered hall closet.

Carl Howard donated the Hive/Tupelo Honey archives to the Country Music Foundation before his passing from cancer in 2016. The master tapes, housed in climate-controlled cabinets, no longer needed but too important to throw away, quietly disintegrate in their final resting place.

If you liked this book, you might enjoy
these other novels by Frank M. Young:

*Fools Like Me*
*An American Failure*
*Never Odd or Even*

Available from Tref Books

RedwingBlackbird

Made in the USA
Middletown, DE
25 March 2021